TRUSTING LOVE

WELCOME TO HARDY FALLS

BETSY HORVATH

VARIOUS MINDED BOOKS

Copyright © 2017 by Betsy Horvath.

All rights reserved. No part of this publication may be reproduced, distributed or transmitted in any form or by any means, including photocopying, recording, or other electronic or mechanical methods, without the prior written permission of the publisher, except in the case of brief quotations embodied in critical reviews and certain other noncommercial uses permitted by copyright law. For permission requests, write to the publisher, addressed "Attention: Permissions Coordinator," at the address below.

Various Minded Books
PO Box 792
Quakertown, PA 18951
Email: admin@variousmindedbooks.com
www.variousmindedbooks.com

Publisher's Note: This is a work of fiction. Names, characters, places, and incidents are a product of the author's imagination. Locales and public names are sometimes used for atmospheric purposes. Any resemblance to actual people, living or dead, or to businesses, companies, events, institutions, or locales is entirely coincidental.

Edited by: Kendra L. Clayton

Trusting Love / Betsy Horvath. -- 1st ed.
ISBN 978-1-943725-06-9

ACKNOWLEDGMENTS

Many thanks to all of the wonderful people who have believed in me through the years. I'm sure I didn't make it easy for them! And I'm grateful most of them still talk to me.

Special thanks to my wonderful, hard-working, editor, Kendra Clayton. I tried to be good and do what she told me to do, but, well, sometimes I rebelled. I take full responsibility for any inappropriate grammar, comma usage, or sentence structure. Typos are the computer's fault.

And–last but definitely not least–huge, big, heaping helpings of thanks to everyone who reads this book!

1
———

"Oh, crap!" Josie Kline tightened her mittened hands convulsively on the steering wheel of her aging sedan as it started to slide off the snow-packed highway—again. "Salt, people!" she yelled at the absent road crews, who apparently thought a late-October surprise blizzard wasn't worth the effort. "Salt is our friend! And some freaking snowplows might be nice, too."

Shoulders tight with tension, she guided the car back onto the road. Well, where she thought the road should be. It was kind of hard to tell exactly where the hell you were driving when all you could see was snow whipping into your windshield by a gale force wind. Heck, in this ocean of white, the only reason she was pretty sure she was still on the highway in the first place were the occasional mile markers.

"I mean, I get that it's not even freaking Halloween yet, but this is the freaking Pocono Mountains, you jerks! Pennsylvania! We get freaking snow, for Christ's sake."

Yelling at the nonexistent road crews didn't help much. She felt like a rubber band wound too tight and ready to snap.

And yes, yes, yes, she shouldn't have been driving in these

conditions in the first place. She'd meant to get an earlier start, but it had taken her longer than she'd expected to pack up her things, get the car out of the garage where it was stored, and leave New York City. Even so, the stupid weather forecasters she'd listened to before heading out had all insisted the storm would only drop a couple of inches of snow, even in the Poconos. Josie had grown up in this part of Pennsylvania. Driving in snow and avoiding deer were two of her best life skills. She could make her car dance through a couple of inches of snow without even breaking a sweat.

Too bad this was not a couple inches of snow.

Once she'd realized the storm was going to be a lot worse than anticipated, she should have stopped and found somewhere to spend the night. Even the truck drivers seemed to be giving up. But it hadn't gotten really, *really* bad until she was about ten miles away from Hardy Falls. And since Hardy Falls, Pennsylvania, was her ultimate destination, she'd kept going. Ten miles, she'd reasoned, would be nothing at this point.

Wrong!

She tapped the brakes gently as the car rocked in an especially strong gust of wind. All this wind was bad because the trees still had most of their leaves, and the wet, heavy snow was weighing them down. Broken branches and falling trees would take down wires and block roads, just a few of the many reasons why storms like this could be deadly in the mountains. Her mother was the chief of police in Hardy Falls, so Josie had heard lots of stories about what could happen.

She shouldn't have trusted the forecast. She should have stayed in New York. But who knew they'd be *this* wrong?

"Not like I had an apartment to stay in, anyway," she muttered, hands gripping the wheel, giving the car more gas so it could get up an incline, and praying when she felt the tires spin, the tail shimmy. "Or a job. Or anything except this stupid car." She breathed again when the road leveled out.

"Kicked to the curb, remember?" The sound of her own voice was soothing, even if what she was saying sucked. "Laid off and thrown out of the apartment. Way to go, Josie."

In fairness, she knew that if she'd asked, her former roommates would have let her stay another night. The girl they were replacing her with wasn't due to move in for a couple of days, anyway. But Josie had just wanted to get home. After the blows of the past week or so, she needed to reinvent her life—needed to see where she was going and where she wanted to go. She needed to *think*, goddamnit, and home was a good place to do that. A safe place to start over.

Assuming she could get there.

Drawing in another deep breath, she put her car in the lowest gear possible and crept down a hill that felt like a ski slope. She wished she could see landmarks so she'd be able to tell how much further she had to go. On this wooded, lonely stretch of highway, everything looked the same in the unending, swirling whiteness.

This was not a snowstorm. This was a snowpocalypse. *Beware, the end of the world is nigh for it is covered with frozen precipitation.*

Giggling a little hysterically, Josie struggled to keep the sedan under control.

Maybe she should stop. Pull over and wait it out. As much as she hated to give them any credit, the crews would be through sooner or later. This was a major road, so they'd be out tending it when they could. But she couldn't be that far away from Hardy Falls, and if she stopped, she'd never get started again. Besides, she might get hit by someone else stupid enough to be out driving in this insanity.

It would have been nice if she could have called her mother to get some advice. Jacqueline Kline would at least know what the road conditions were like ahead. But cell service, which was never great, had already been knocked out.

Well, it was probably for the best. She'd wanted to make her explanations in person, so nobody knew she was on her way. If her mother found out how idiotic she'd been, she'd come riding to the rescue and then they'd both probably get stuck.

Josie suddenly noticed a different quality to the snow and stared in amazement as a squat, square building sitting at the side of the road came into view. It was a bar, with lights glowing in the windows and neon beer signs flashing red, blue, and yellow out front.

What the hell? They were *open*?

Most importantly, she recognized the place. This was the Country Time Bar and Grill, a tavern on the outskirts of Hardy Falls, owned by her best friend in the whole wide world, Hannah Frederickson.

Josie was home.

Home.

She blinked hard to keep from breaking down in tears of relief and gratitude and, distracted for one crucial moment, stepped on the brakes way too hard.

"Oh, God. Oh, crap. Oh, shit."

Hands clenched on the wheel, her stomach knotted as she felt the tires slide into a slow motion turn. The brakes did nothing to halt her forward momentum, as the car did a graceful, inevitable 400-degree spin and came to a stop in the middle of the highway pointing directly at the Country Time.

So, *that* was a sign. *Stop, you moron.*

Wheezing a little from the adrenaline, Josie decided that she wasn't going to argue with the universe any longer. She was done. There was determined, there was stubborn, and there was bone-deep stupid. No way in hell was she going to make it, regardless of how few miles it was across town to her mother's house. For whatever unknown, harebrained reason, someone was obviously inside the Country Time, and she had a hunch that someone was Hannah. More than likely, Deacon Black,

Hannah's bartender-boyfriend, was there too, and that was fine. Heck, they could be having sex on top of the bar for all Josie cared. She was getting off this hell-road and waiting out the rest of the storm with her friends.

Sadly, the universe did not appear to be impressed with her decision because when she hit the gas, the wheels of the car spun uselessly. For a few moments it slid back and forth, but it never actually went anywhere.

Great. Now she was going to have to slog her way through the snow and get Hannah to help push her off the road.

Not willing to face the cold just yet, she put the car in reverse, then in drive, repeatedly rocking it back and forth. A thrill of triumph washed through her when she felt the wheels finally gain traction and the vehicle lurched forward. Weaving like a snake, she slid into the Country Time's parking lot.

Then she tried to stop again.

"No!"

For one breathless moment, she was sure she would crash into the brick building. The irony of totaling her car in the parking lot of her best friend's business flashed through her mind, along with most of her life. In the end, it was close, but the old sedan finally came to a stop with its bumper kissing the wall.

"God."

Panting, Josie let herself slump over the wheel before raising her head to look around. Murphy Lanes, the bowling alley next door to the Country Time, was dark, as was the gas station across the street. Why in the *hell* was Hannah open? Surely she wasn't expecting any customers.

On the other hand, what did it matter? Someone was in there.

Suddenly and irrationally terrified that her friend would leave before she got inside—where the heck would she go?—Josie braced herself, grabbed her purse and a duffel bag from the backseat that contained more of her clothes, and opened the driver's door.

The cold slap of wind knocked the breath right out of her body, but she managed to stand and muscle the car door shut behind her. Forcing her way through the wall of the storm to the front entrance, she pushed open one of the wooden double doors, stumbled inside in a whirlwind of snow, and wrestled it closed again.

Then she was inside the Country Time's taproom.

And it was warm.

And bright.

And not snowing.

Josie felt weak from the sudden release of tension she'd been carrying for miles—days, weeks—and for a moment she was a little afraid she'd faint. She shook her head to get her brain working again and immediately regretted it when ice rained down from her knit cap.

"Are you nuts, lady? Why are you out in this?"

2

Jumping at the sound of the unexpected male voice, Josie dropped her purse and duffel bag with "splats" on the floor and spun around, trying to blink the snow off her eyelashes so she could see better.

A man she didn't recognize was standing behind the large bar that dominated the room, watching her curiously. Who the heck was he?

Josie blinked more rapidly, frowning. She might be living in New York City now—or she had been—but she knew everyone who worked at the Country Time.

Disoriented, she glanced around to make sure she was really in the right place.

Yup, there was the familiar wood paneling gleaming golden brown, the stained glass lanterns that threw splashes of color onto scattered small tables, the neon beer signs, the country music playing softly in the background. And, the biggest clue— the painted sign over the door reading "Welcome to The Country Time Bar and Grill." This was definitely the right place.

So who was this guy?

Josie turned her attention back to the man standing behind the bar, and saw that he was leaning forward, strong arms braced on the polished bar top, big hands clasped in front of him. He had brown, almost black, hair framing a square-jawed face, and he was watching her with a definite gleam of amusement in thickly lashed, dark eyes.

Oh, great. He was hotter than hell, and she looked, she was sure, like the abominable snowman.

Er...woman.

Not that she cared.

Much.

"Who are you?" she demanded.

He raised his eyebrows.

"Who are you?" he countered, his voice deep with a slight Western drawl. Definitely not from around here.

"I asked you first."

Not the cleverest comeback in the world, but it had been a rough day.

The man smiled broadly, a white slash of teeth gleaming against his dusky skin.

"Normally I'm the dishwasher."

The dishwasher? No way. And wasn't he going to ask her if she needed help or something since Snowmageddon was obviously raging outside? He was pretty darned calm about a woman staggering in out of a raging blizzard.

"But today," he continued, "I'm the guy who'll get you a drink if you want one."

"Um, thanks," she said, feeling like she'd tumbled into an alternate universe. Realizing she was freezing, she took off her sodden coat and hung it on a peg at the door, stuffing her hat and mittens into the pockets. Even though she'd only been out in the storm for a few minutes, melting snow dripped off it, while rivers of the stuff seemed to run down the back of her neck under the collar of her sweatshirt. Her jeans were cold and sodden against her thighs and calves from slogging through the snow in the parking lot. Shivering, she picked up her purse, walked to the bar, and perched on one of the barstools, looking around at the empty space.

"Is Hannah here?" she asked. Maybe her friend was back in her office.

"You know Hannah? She and Deacon were going to try to make it in, but they live on the other side of town, and the storm got bad fast." The man shrugged. "I told them not to bother trying. I live a lot closer so it was easier for me to get here, and I don't mind spending the night."

"Oh." Although it was reassuring to know that, whoever he was, Hannah trusted him with her business, Josie wasn't sure she wanted to be all alone and isolated with a strange man in the middle of a blizzard. She did have some sense of self-preservation, although it may not have been evident the last few hours.

Not sure what to do, she chewed on her lip.

"I'm assuming you're stuck," he said after a moment. "Nobody's out in this."

"You are," she pointed out.

"I'm just here to run the generator. Power's bound to go out and we can't risk losing all the food. Figured I'd open since I was here anyway, lucky for you."

No, Hannah couldn't afford to lose the food. A month or two ago, her Uncle George, who had been working as her accountant, had embezzled all of the Country Time's money and taken off for Las Vegas, leaving Hannah in a fight for her business life. Any more setbacks would put her under.

"I'm Josie Kline," she told him, deciding to let him know she was related to the police chief. If he worked here, he should know Chief Kline.

His eyes snapped up to meet hers. "Kline?"

She nodded. "I'm sure you've met my mother."

"I have. I was pretty impressed when I found out the town not only had its own police chief, but a female one at that. Progressive."

Oh, good. It sounded like he hadn't met her mother in an official capacity.

"I should call her," Josie said. Jackie was probably running around like an idiot, but she'd want to know Josie was in town. She'd also be able to tell her what she thought of this man. If her mother didn't think it was safe for Josie to stay here, she'd find a way to come get her.

She pulled out her cell phone, but still didn't have any bars. Not a surprise.

"Can I use the bar phone?" she asked the man.

He shrugged and pointed to an old touch-tone phone hanging on the wall behind him.

"I think we still have service."

"Lucky. It's a miracle you still have electricity," she said, pushing off the stool to join him on the other side of the bar. It felt crowded back there, especially since the man was big—tall and broad shouldered. His shirt was pushed up to his elbows, and she could see the olive skin of his forearms sprinkled liberally with dark hair.

Forcing herself to focus on the task at hand, she lifted the receiver and punched in the number for the police station.

"Chief Kline," her mother's voice barked into the phone. Apparently, she was manning the desk while her troops were in the field.

"Hi, Mom," she said. "It's me."

"Josie?" Jackie's voice softened a little but retained the edge it normally held when she was in full "cop mode." "I can't—"

"I'm here in town," Josie interrupted. "I'm kind of stuck."

"Where are you?" her mother snapped after a surprised pause. "I didn't look at the caller ID."

"I'm at the Country Time, and—"

"What? Hannah's there?"

"No, she's not here. Some guy is tending the bar." She shot the man a look. "He's not Deacon."

"And proud of it," he said, turning away to stack glasses.

"Let me talk to him," her mother demanded.

"Here." Josie held out the receiver. "She wants to talk to you."

The man rolled his eyes but was smart enough to take the phone.

"Chief," he said. "Yes...yes...I'm here to run the genera...yes."

He was silent as her mother spoke, then shrugged. "Fine with me. If she tries to empty the cash drawer, I'm pretty sure I can defend myself."

Jackie must have replied, because he grinned.

"Right," he said, and turning, held the receiver back out to Josie. "She wants to talk to you again."

"Okay," her mother said when she was back on the phone. "That's Mateo Guerrero. He works for Hannah, and I've already checked him out. He appears to be a good man in a crisis."

"Checked him out" meant that her mother had run background checks on him. It made sense. Jackie considered Hannah to be one of her own, and after what had happened with George embezzling Hannah's money, she was probably on high alert.

"Okay," Josie said. It was nice to know Mateo Guerrero wasn't on the police radar. Her mother was very thorough.

"Look, since you're safe and inside, just stay put. Do *not* try to get through. Morton Shaller, the asshole, wasn't stocked up on materials to treat the roads in town because he thought it was too early." Her mom's voice dripped with sarcasm. "Apparently God disagrees. The roads are practically impassable, and we have trees down all over the place. It's a goddamned mess."

"Don't worry," Josie said. "I'll stay here until the storm's over."

"Honey, I don't care when the storm's over, just sit tight and I'll come get you as soon as I can. Roads are going to be shit for a while. Mort's an idiot, but God!" Jackie's voice rose in frustration. "Who knew we'd have a blizzard in October? We're in Pennsylvania, for Christ's sake—not flipping Canada!"

"Go back to work, Mom," Josie soothed. She knew that tone. Her mother was stretched to the limit. "I'm fine, and I'll stay put."

"Good. I'll call when I can come get you."

"Just be careful. Even super cops can slide on the ice." Sometimes Jackie was so worried about taking care of everyone else that she forgot to watch out for herself.

"Will do. Try to get some rest." Her mother sighed. "You picked a hell of a time to visit."

"Didn't I just," Josie muttered as she disconnected the call.

"Sounds like you're staying, huh?" The man— Mateo—said.

She put her hands on her hips and turned to face him.

"What do you think?"

Before he could respond, the phone rang and scared the ever living crap out of her, since she was standing right next to it. Mateo raised his eyebrows, obviously telling her to answer, and after a loud exhalation, she did.

"Hel—"

"God, Mat, it's horrible outside." Hannah Frederickson's warm voice sounded more than a little panicked. "Please, please, *please* say you'll stay and run the generator, because there's no way I'm going to make it through to relieve you tonight."

"Yeah," Josie said, "it's not Mat. And trust me, it's a lot worse out there than it looks."

There was a pause before Hannah spoke again. "Josie? Is that you?"

"Yup," Josie confirmed. "It's me."

"Wait." Hannah sounded confused. "But...didn't I call the Country Time? Did I call your phone by mistake?"

"No," Josie said. "I'm like...here."

"Here?"

"At the Country Time."

"At the...Josie!" Hannah practically shrieked her name. "What the hell? Have you even seen what the roads are like?"

"Yes, Hannah. I saw them. I drove here," Josie said dryly.

"But how? Deacon and I tried to make it through, and we had to turn back even in his SUV."

"Stupidity, fear, and determination," Josie told her friend. "I'm not going any further. Looks like I'll be bunking here tonight."

"We can try ag—"

"No," Josie said firmly.

"If you made it from New York—"

"No," Josie repeated. The last thing she wanted was for her friends to be out for no good reason. "Everything is a lot worse around here, and Mom said the roads in town are terrible."

"We could try a different—"

"Hannah, no! You and Deacon are not going anywhere. I am perfectly fine."

"Well, if you're sure..." Hannah said reluctantly.

"I am *so* sure. Mom knows where I am, and she told me not to move. You know she wouldn't say that if she didn't mean it. Besides, the electricity's still on here."

"That's amazing. Sure hope it stays that way."

"Me too," Josie agreed fervently.

"If it doesn't, the generator is only big enough to run the refrigerator and freezer. Mat's still there to run things, right?" Hannah sounded worried. "I can't lose all of the food. I just can't."

"Don't worry, he's here," Josie soothed, refraining from

pointing out that she was perfectly capable of taking care of a generator, too. Mat walked past her at that moment, and she thrust the phone at him. "Talk to your boss," she ordered.

He scowled at her but took the receiver. "Yeah?"

There was silence as Hannah spoke on the other end.

"Of course, I'm staying. I told you I would."

More silence, and his frown deepened as he turned to look at Josie.

"Sure. I already told her mother I'd watch out for her."

Josie folded her arms. Who said she needed anyone to "watch out" for her?

Hannah talked again, Mat reassured her again, and then he passed the receiver back to Josie.

"Here," he said gruffly and walked away.

"Such a charmer," Josie said into the phone.

Hannah laughed in her ear. "I just wanted to let you know that Mat's a good guy and you can trust him."

"Okay."

"I don't want you to be stressed because you're there alone with him," Hannah continued earnestly. "He's a friend of Deacon's. They worked together on an oil rig off the shore of Texas or somewhere, so Mat looked Deacon up when he needed a change of pace."

"Okay." Josie had to admit, the fact that Mat was friends with Deacon settled her even more than hearing her mother say he checked out. She'd learned to trust Deacon's judgment when they'd been friends in high school, before he'd left town to join the army.

"So, look," Hannah said, "there are clean blankets in a box in my office. I think they're clean, anyway. And there are air mattresses, too. There've been a couple of times when weather caught me by surprise and I couldn't get home, so I decided to prepare for the worst."

"That's great." At least Josie wouldn't have to curl up on empty cardboard boxes tonight.

"Just rummage around. I have no secrets."

"Right." Josie laughed because it was such a lie. "Like that time when we were juniors and I found your diary, and you said you didn't care if I read it because you didn't have any secrets, and I saw that stuff about Sam and how he—"

"Shut up!" Hannah yelped. Josie could practically hear her blush. "You're lucky I don't tell Mat to just kick you out, you witch."

"What did she say?" A deep, muffled voice spoke on the other end of the line, which meant Deacon was right there with Hannah. They were probably sprawled together on the sofa or in bed.

"Nothing, buttercup."

Josie gagged at Hannah's saccharine sweet tone and the sound of kissing that followed. When they'd been in high school, Hannah had been all about Deacon's older brother Sam, back when she, Josie, and Deacon were juniors and Sam was a senior. Hannah hadn't paid any attention to Deacon, even though it had been perfectly obvious he'd had a crush on her. Josie had never understood it, because it had always seemed clear to her which one she should pick.

Hannah's high school fling with the elder Black brother hadn't lasted long, but a few years later Sam had breezed back into her life. Josie hadn't liked that at all, but there wasn't much she could do about it. Especially since she'd been in New York by then and hadn't even known Sam and Hannah were back together until it had been going on for weeks.

It did not surprise her when she'd found out the relationship had imploded again, although she'd been a little shocked to find out why. Apparently, Sam had been caught screwing Louise Weber —one of Hannah's friends, who also happened to be working for her at the time—in the backseat of Louise's car in the parking lot of the Country Time. Josie's mother had cited them for indecent exposure, and gossip had spread like wildfire through town.

Louise had run off, Sam had gone about his life as an attorney for a high-end law firm, and Hannah had been left to pick up the pieces. At least Deacon had been back in town by then, working as a bartender at the Country Time. It took another year or two, but *finally* Hannah noticed the other Black.

And Deacon wasn't a kid anymore.

When Hannah found out about George running off with all her money, Josie had been afraid she would let Sam into her life for a third time. Apparently he was being extremely helpful, which was highly suspicious in itself. Josie's mother had told her during one of their phone conversations that he was looking over legal paperwork for Hannah and had helped her hire a private investigator to try and track down her wayward uncle.

But Hannah seemed to have finally learned her lesson, because she was living with Deacon, and Sam was the one hovering in the background.

"You are lucky I love you," Hannah's voice sounded in her ear again.

"Love you too, babe," Josie replied.

"When the power goes out, you can use the candles and flashlights. They should be in the boxes with the air mattresses."

"All right."

"Make sure Mat locks the door."

"I will," Josie promised.

"And either you or Mat call me if anything happens. I mean *anything*. We'll get there, even if we have to walk."

"What's going on?" Deacon's voice asked in the background

before there was a large, violent-sounding sneeze. Hannah shushed him.

"I mean it, Josie," she said.

She knew it was true. Hannah wouldn't care that she lived miles away from the Country Time. Wouldn't care if she had to walk through streets Josie's mother said were practically impassable. She would find a way to get there.

Josie felt herself breathe deeply for the first time since she left the city. She was in a place where she was no longer alone.

She was home.

"We'll be fine," she said, smiling into the receiver. "Stay there and snuggle with Deacon. My mother will come as soon as she can."

"I'm serious. You call me. The advantage to an old-fashioned landline is that it should stay up longer than cell service, and it doesn't need electricity. That's why I never converted at the Country Time or at home."

"Yes, dear," Josie said placating her friend because she was just babbling now. "Thanks for letting me stay, Hannah."

"Pfffft. I'll see you as soon as I can."

Josie hung up and sniffled, just a little.

"Sounds like you and Hannah are pretty tight, huh?"

She jumped because she'd sort of forgotten Mat was there. He was standing at the end of the bar watching her.

"We're best friends," she told him.

She'd met Hannah Frederickson in third grade, and they'd been inseparable through most of their school years. Things had changed when she'd gone off to college, and then to work in Manhattan, but as far as Josie was concerned, they were besties forever. Hannah might be with Deacon now, but Josie didn't think things had changed all that much. She sure hoped not.

Mat nodded. "Too bad she's not here, then."

As he spoke, the wind howled outside and Josie knew if the

old building hadn't been made of solid brick it would have shuddered under the impact. The lights flickered but, amazingly, stayed on.

She had a feeling she wouldn't be seeing Hannah for quite some time.

3

___

Really wanting to get out of her wet clothes, Josie got a penlight from her purse in case the power went out, grabbed her duffel bag, and headed to the ladies room to change. After drying her hair with a bar rag and draping her sodden jeans across the top of one of the stall doors, she went back to the taproom to find that Mat had made her a sandwich. It was enough to make her to feel downright charitable towards the man.

While she inhaled the food, he wandered around making sure everything was closed down for the night . Then, to her surprise, he came back from the kitchen wearing a big, down parka.

"What are you doing?" she asked, confused.

He zipped the coat up to his chin. "I'm heading out to see if I can find an open gas station. You can take care of the generator if we lose the electric while I'm gone, right? I shouldn't be too long."

"Yes, of course I..." She shook her head. "Wait. What? You're going out in this? Are you insane?"

"Depends on who you ask." He jammed a striped knit hat

down over his dark hair. "We had no idea the storm would be this bad, so we're a little low on fuel. Probably have enough to make it through, but I thought I should take advantage of you being here and fill up the empty cans before the electric's out everywhere and none of the pumps work."

Josie gaped at him. Couldn't he hear the wind? "You're nuts," she told him. "You'll end up headfirst in a ditch."

He shrugged as he wrapped a thick scarf around the bottom half of his face and tucked it into his coat, then grunted out some unintelligible noises.

"I didn't understand a word you just said."

He pulled the scarf under his chin. "I said, I'll be fine. I may be from Texas, but I've lived a lot of places. Ain't no weather I haven't seen or driven in, including snow." His slight drawl thickened as he fell into a cowboy persona. If he'd been wearing a Stetson, he probably would have tipped it at her. "Besides, my pickup has four-wheel drive and a lot of ground clearance. I didn't have much trouble getting in when Hannah called me at noon, and I figure if you could make it here from wherever, I can surely go a mile or two."

"Uh-huh. You know the storm is worse now than it was earlier?" As if in agreement, the lights flickered dangerously, but stayed on.

"I expect it is," he said placidly while he pulled on gloves, fished keys out of his pocket, and jingled them around until he had the right one.

"It was just dumb luck I got through at all." Josie wasn't sure why she was bothering to argue, because it was clear he wasn't paying the slightest bit of attention.

He shrugged again.

Men. Always thinking they know best. She doubted she could get him to listen to reason, but it really was dangerous for him to be on the road. Now that she was safe, she realized how truly stupid it had been to keep driving in these horrible conditions. And the storm had done nothing but intensify since she'd been inside the Country Time.

"Even if you find an open gas station, which will be a miracle, you're going to have a hell of a time getting back," she pointed out.

"I'll make it. Hold down the fort." Before she could move, he pushed open the kitchen door and walked out.

"Crap!" Quickly jumping off the barstool, she hurried after him, but shoved into the kitchen just in time to see the back door slam shut on a howl of wind and his muffled voice cursing.

"Wonderful." She ran to grab her coat with some half-assed notion of chasing him, although she had no idea what she'd do if she caught him. Grab his ankles? Strangle him? Both were viable options.

Pulling on her still-wet parka, she raced back to the kitchen, all the while knowing she was wasting her time. He had too much of a head start on her. Damn her mother for teaching her to care about other people. She wrenched open the back door, then let out a piercing scream at the sight of a dark, hulking, snow-encrusted figure standing right on the other side.

The figure started, then pushed past her into the kitchen and slammed the door shut before unwinding its scarf and glaring at her.

"Jesus Christ, that was loud," Mat said.

Josie put a hand to her breast, hoping her heart wouldn't jump out and start dancing around the room.

"You scared me!" she yelled at him.

"Well, you didn't do much for me either. Where the hell were you going?"

"I was chasing after you, you moron!"

"Why?"

"Because I was trying to save you!"

"Great. Thanks. I need a drink." He turned on his heel and went into the taproom, shedding ice as he went.

Josie was about to march after him, but her wet coat was making her cold again, so she took it off and hung it on a hook near the supply room. By the time she got out to the bar, he was already opening a bottle, melting snow and ice glistening on the parka stretched across his broad shoulders and the hat he was still wearing. He glared at her.

"What the hell is that shit?" he snapped.

She frowned. "It looks like whiskey."

"No!" he barked. "Not this shit. *That* shit." He gestured. "Outside." The cowboy was gone, replaced by one pissed off man.

Josie relaxed and bit back a laugh.

"I thought you said you knew all about snow."

"Yeah! Snow! That crap is not snow. It's like trying to walk on a slushy."

She spread her hands.

"Welcome to Pennsylvania?"

"My ass." He grabbed a glass. "Want some?"

Well, why not?

"Sure." She perched on a barstool as he got another glass and filled them both, sliding one across to her before coming around to sit next to her.

Josie drank and felt the warmth of the alcohol hit her system.

"Went for the good stuff, huh?" she said, taking another sip. "Hannah will not approve."

"Hannah will be fine with it," he muttered.

"I guess you decided not to power through and drive off in search of your mythical open gas station?"

"Obviously." He took a long drink before putting down the glass and filling it again from the bottle. "I changed my mind when I fell on my ass in a snowbank three feet from the back door and slid under the dumpster."

Josie choked back a laugh. Well, that explained how he'd gotten so snow-covered so quickly.

Mat shot her a glance. "I can't believe you drove in that."

"You were going to drive in it."

"I was smart enough to change my mind."

"Yeah, well I would have changed my mind, too, if I'd known how bad it was going to be. It wasn't even snowing in the city."

"Which city?" he asked, sipping.

"New York."

He coughed on the whiskey, then stared at her. "Jesus, lady. You drove from New York City in this? And you called me crazy."

"It was fine when I left," she insisted. He was looking at her like she was an absolute idiot which, in fairness, she was. "New York's not even going to get hit. The roads didn't get really, *really* bad until I got close to Hardy Falls. And I stopped, didn't I?" She glared at him. "I didn't even try to make it through town."

"I guess." He drank some more.

"I told you not to go."

"Yeah, yeah, yeah." He sounded even more annoyed.

The wind howled and the lights flickered again, then abruptly they went out, plunging the room into darkness. It wasn't yet five o'clock in the evening, but even on a good day the sun went down early at this time of year. With the storm raging outside, it was already a deep pewter gray on the other side of the leaded glass windows.

"Oh, now that's just perfect," Mat growled beside her.

She could hear him breathing, even though she couldn't exactly see him.

"Do you, um, have a flashlight?" she asked.

"Somewhere."

Before she could offer him the penlight she'd shoved into the front pocket of her jeans, a bright beam pierced the dark. Once her eyes adjusted, she realized it came from his cell phone. Grunting with apparent satisfaction, Mat pushed himself to his feet and went around the bar to a shelf on the back wall. He rooted around and then flipped on what appeared to be a powerful torch.

"Hannah said there were more flashlights and candles back in her office," she told him as he pocketed his phone.

"Good. Sorry, I have to go start the generator."

Before she realized what he was doing, he strode through the swinging door to the kitchen taking the light with him, which plunged the taproom back into darkness.

Jerk! He could have at least waited for her to come with him. Fumbling in the pocket of her jeans, she pulled out the penlight. Luckily, it actually worked. Then she set off in search of her annoying companion.

When she pushed into the kitchen it was empty, but she heard a throaty roar outside indicating the generator had just come to life. A moment later, the back door opened and Mat lumbered in, then shoved the door closed against the angry wind and snow that tried to follow him. To her surprise, he locked it, pulled off his hat and gloves, and threw them on a nearby counter.

"You're just going to have to go outside again to plug things into the generator," she pointed out, reasonably.

He growled something she couldn't make out, since he'd wrapped the scarf around his face again.

"What?"

Obviously irritated beyond measure, he yanked off the scarf. "I said give me a damned minute."

She blinked. "Okay. What are you going to do? Wave a magic fairy wand over the refrigerator to get it going?"

"No. I'm going to shoot rainbows out of my butt," he snarled and stalked over to an electric panel on the wall. When he opened it and flipped some switches, the refrigerator and freezer both whirred to life.

"That *is* magic," Josie said.

"It's a transfer switch. Thank God Hannah had the wiring done, so we don't have to run extension cords."

"Oh."

"But the generator she's got is pretty small, so we can't run anything else or we'll risk overloading it."

"That's what she told me when I talked to her."

Mat stomped the remaining snow off of his boots before pulling off his extremely wet coat. He gathered up everything, including the flashlight, hat, gloves, and scarf, and headed back to the taproom. "I need another drink."

Rolling her eyes, Josie followed him. He threw his things on a high stool set up behind the bar for the bartender and, putting down the light, grabbed the bottle and the glass he'd been using earlier.

After he poured himself a shot and downed it, he held up the bottle.

"More?"

"I'm good." She didn't think more whiskey would be the best idea, especially since she could feel the effects of her incredibly stressful day catching up with her. Turning off the little penlight so she wouldn't waste the battery, she perched on a barstool.

Mat poured himself another drink and sat beside her again.

Josie couldn't help but study him as he sipped from the glass, although she tried not to be obvious about it.

Who was this guy? What was he doing working at the Country Time? Hannah had said he'd needed a change of pace, but from what?

"Too bad you don't have dry clothes, too," she said after a moment, wanting to break the silence. His jeans had to be as wet and uncomfortable as hers had been earlier, especially after his slide under the dumpster.

"I do." He drank. "Came prepared."

"Oh. Good."

It seemed closer in the room than it had before, the shadows pooling around the single flashlight making everything more intimate.

"I guess we're both stuck here for the night," she said, then winced because that almost sounded like a come-on, which wasn't what she'd intended.

No, it wasn't.

He swiveled on the barstool to face her fully, his expression hidden in the shadows.

"I guess we are," he said.

Oh boy.

Josie cleared her throat. "Uh, Hannah said there are a couple of air mattresses and some blankets in her office, along with flashlights and candles." She could feel his body heat radiating through the sweatshirt he was wearing, smell his soap and the slight tang of sweat. His hair was just long enough to curl.

"Good to know."

"So there should be an air mattress for each of us," she hurried on. "I'll set up in Hannah's office, if that's okay, and I'll bring you some blankets. I'm guessing it's going to get pretty cold in here now that the power's out."

He smiled slightly and turned back to his drink. "Thanks. I'll bunk down in the taproom. It's closer to the generator, anyway. And the bar."

"Okay." Josie told herself she was glad that he wasn't even trying to make a move on her.

"You're right about it getting cold," he said. "I checked the heater earlier. It's gas, but it's older than dirt and doesn't have a battery ignition, so we're screwed there."

Even with the wind, Josie could hear the roar of the generator outside. The room already seemed to be getting colder, but that could have been her imagination.

"I hope Hannah can afford to keep the generator working for a while," she said. It was a real concern. With this bad of a storm, they might not get electricity back for days. Gasoline could get expensive.

"Yeah, she can't afford anything." Mat looked at her. "I'm assuming you know what happened, right?"

She nodded. "Her Uncle George ran off with all of her money."

"Right. And this little storm is going to hurt. She really is at the end of her funds."

Josie frowned. "I know."

When Hannah found out that George had stolen her money, she'd had a decision to make. Go bankrupt or try to keep the business going with absolutely no capital. Things became even more dire when the bank she'd been using for years turned down her request for a loan for operating expenses.

Hannah, being Hannah, refused to give up. She'd held a fund-raising carnival and fortunately, the community had turned out. Josie hadn't talked to her since the event—unless you counted today—so she didn't know how much money had been raised. It couldn't have been enough to keep the business going forever.

It suddenly seemed very bad that she hadn't called Hannah to find out. She could have taken five minutes when she'd been forced to leave her desk to run to the bathroom. She'd just kind of...forgotten.

That seemed bad, too.

"She's got a real fight on her hands," Mat said. "She probably told you that Pat Murphy finished his renovations on the bar at the bowling alley next door. Hell, he was supposed to have a grand reopening event thing tomorrow. Guess it's canceled now because of the storm, but still. It will be open soon."

Josie hadn't known things were that far along, which made her feel even worse.

For years—no, generations—the men and women who bowled at Murphy Lanes had come across the parking lot to do their eating and drinking at the Country Time. Pat hated it, as had his father before him, but until now neither had bothered to put money into the food service part of the bowling alley to try and compete. Now Pat was going for it, apparently wanting to take advantage of Hannah's money problems to steal her customers and put her out of business. He might very well succeed.

"I just don't get why he's trying so hard," she said. "I mean, yes, fix up the restaurant if you want to, but focus on the families and build on the fact that you already offer pretty good pizza."

"Do they? I've never actually been in the place."

"Oh, yeah. It's the one thing they do reasonably well. When I was a kid and my mom was busy, we always tried to talk the babysitters into taking us there for a game and a slice."

"You grew up here?" he asked, watching her curiously.

"I did. Left for college and ended up in New York City." She shrugged. "I just wanted something different, you know?"

"I do. I joined the army right after high school." He shot her a small smile. "Texas might be big, but I still needed some space."

Josie nodded. She understood that very well. Her mother was so competent, her older brother, Jordan, so smart, and her sister, Jenny, so creative, that she'd just felt like she needed to get away. Go someplace where people didn't know who she was, didn't have set expectations because her father had run out on them and her mother was the chief of police. Go some-place where everybody didn't know her name.

"With the number of people in Manhattan, it's amazing how invisible you can be," she said.

He smiled. "Not like here, that's for damned sure."

It made her laugh because it was true. "Figured that out already, have you?"

"You know the librarian, Ms. Gregory? I took over the room above the bookstore that Deacon was renting from her, and I've never been through a more thorough interrogation in my life. The army could learn something from her."

Josie smiled affectionately. Mathilda Gregory, who had been the librarian in the town for as long as she could remember—probably as long as anyone could remember—ran a successful real estate empire. She gave Deacon's father, Dr. Trevor Black, steep competition when it came to buying up local properties. The difference was, Ms. Gregory thought of herself as the unofficial owner of Hardy Falls and, as such, cared about the people who lived there.

"You're lucky you didn't end up in an article in *The Hardy Falls Gazette*," she said. Ms. Gregory ran an online newspaper and worked with the journalism department at the local university to cover what passed for news in Hardy Falls.

"I've shown up a couple of times." He shrugged. "But it's okay. The guys I used to work with in the army and on the rig gossiped just as much, and they were all up in my business, too. I guess I'm sort of used to it."

"Why did you come here, anyway?" she asked, tiredness and alcohol making her even less tactful than normal.

He didn't answer for a long moment.

"I needed a change," he said finally, echoing what Hannah had said. "How long are you in town?"

It was Josie's turn to think about what she wanted to say.

"A while. Probably a few weeks." Maybe the rest of her life if she couldn't find another job.

He seemed to sense that she wasn't telling him the whole truth.

"Something wrong?"

Well, she might as well come clean. It wasn't like she was trying to hide it. Or could hide it, for that matter.

"I lost my job in Manhattan and got kicked out of my apartment."

Mat shook his head. "Man. That sucks."

"Yeah."

"Were you working there long?"

"Longer than I should have. I guess this is a good thing. Forcing me to explore other options and all that."

That was how she was trying to spin it in her head, anyway. But the fact was, she didn't really know what she was going to do now, hence her trip home to rethink her life. She'd been working for Milhouse Advertising ever since she'd graduated. Heck, she'd done all of her internships at the company, so the transition to employee had been fairly seamless. It had taken a couple of years, but she'd finally worked her way up to the top creative team—the one that handled the account for the biggest client the firm had.

Not that it had done her much good.

Mat was watching her, eyes very dark in the dim light, and it dawned on her again how isolated they were, alone in the taproom with the wind howling and the snow falling outside. She should have been nervous; after all, she didn't know him. But she really wasn't, and that *did* make her nervous.

She drew in a deep breath, taking in the scent of him, the strength of him, and watched him watching her. She could see him take a breath of his own and go still like a predator. And she knew without a doubt that if she just said the word, made one move to show she was willing, they would probably end up back in Hannah's office wrapped up in blankets together. Wrapped up in each other. Maybe they wouldn't even make it to the office.

It was tempting. But it wasn't what she wanted. It might take her mind off her problems for the night, but everything had consequences.

Instead of moving forward, she pushed away from the bar. "I'd better go find those air mattresses and blankets." Her voice sounded husky even to her own ears.

He watched her silently for a moment, then nodded. "Probably a good idea."

Josie turned on her little flashlight and walked quickly to Hannah's office. After some searching, she found the promised supplies, including some battery operated camp lanterns. She grabbed one for Mat, then hauled it, one of the air mattresses, and two random blankets out to the taproom.

"Thanks," he said from his position at the bar.

"I think I'll get settled," she said. "I know it's really early but I'm exhausted from the drive." It wasn't a lie, she realized. Now that the adrenaline from the drive and everything that had happened since was leaving her system, she felt like she could sleep for a week.

"Want another sandwich in case you get hungry?"

"I'm good." She had a granola bar or two. Getting her purse and the duffel bag from the floor where she'd dropped it after changing clothes, she turned back to the man at the bar.

"So, um, I'll see you in the morning."

Mat didn't look at her, just picked up the bottle and refilled his glass.

"Goodnight, Josie Kline," he said.

She beat a very hasty retreat.

4

———

Mat sat at the bar studying the short hallway leading to Hannah's office. The intriguing Josie Kline had firmly closed the door between them, but if he knocked, there was a good chance she'd open it for him. He wasn't stupid. He knew when a woman was interested.

But he could already tell that anything he started with Josie would not be a quick hookup. She'd be way more complicated than that, and he wasn't in the market for complications. Not anymore.

Finishing the whiskey in his glass, he debated on another but ruled against it. He'd already had more than was probably wise, and if he didn't watch himself he might be tempted to go knock on that door to see what happened. Instead, he got up and took the used glasses with him behind the bar, dumping them into the bus tub before putting the whiskey bottle back on its shelf and digging out his duffel bag.

Since he was alone, he stripped out of his wet, clinging clothes and quickly pulled on dry ones from the bag. Then he visited the john and threw his wet pants and socks over the sink before heading back to the empty taproom and rolling out the air mattress on the floor between some tables.

Truth be told, he wasn't even looking for a quick hookup at the moment. In fact, Josie was the first woman to tempt him in months. There was just something about her that appealed to him; something to do with her big blue eyes and sassy attitude.

He'd always been a sucker for sass.

Whatever the reason, it was kind of reassuring to know his drives weren't dead, although they sure as hell picked an inconvenient time to resurrect themselves.

The air mattress was pretty crappy, but at least it had a foot pump, which was handy for inflating the thing. Once it seemed to be solid enough, he stretched out with the blankets and flipped off his flashlight to save the juice. He clasped his hands behind his head and stared into the shadows, listening to the wind blow with wild intensity outside. He'd check the generator in a couple of hours to see how it was doing on fuel. Fortunately, he'd always been a light sleeper.

Hell, he might not be able to get to sleep at all tonight anyway. These days he usually distracted himself with the television, drifting off to some talking head or other. Now, in this muffled, dark space, there wasn't a lot to do besides think. Thinking usually meant dwelling on Gail—what she'd done, what he'd missed—and that was *not* relaxing. Still, although he'd brought a book and even had a battery operated radio, he made no move to get either from his duffel.

Strangely enough, his ex-fiancée wasn't the only female occupying his thoughts. The woman currently sleeping in Hannah's office was there, too.

Josie Kline.

She was kind of a puzzle. It was a little surprising she'd come all the way home to Hardy Falls instead of staying in New York to look for her next job, especially when there was bad weather in the forecast. The meteorologists had blown the call, but you never knew.

Of course, then he remembered she said she'd gotten kicked out of her apartment, too. The city was expensive, especially when you weren't working. Or maybe she'd just needed a break before getting on with her search.

Maybe she was running away. Sounded to him like life had kicked her in the teeth.

He knew exactly how that felt. Sometimes you didn't see it coming and you got slammed. Then all you wanted to do was escape. Josie was fortunate she had family she could run to, at least for a little while.

Mat shifted. He really didn't want to think about family. He hadn't spoken to his since he'd walked out of his wedding three hours before the ceremony eight—wait, nine—months ago. Although his mother had been calling lately, leaving messages demanding he get back to her, he hadn't bothered to comply. If it had been an emergency, she would have said so in her voice-mail. Besides, neither of his sisters or his father had tried to get in contact with him, so it couldn't be anything too important. He had precious little desire to be berated—again—for something they didn't understand.

No, he didn't want to think about family.

He shook himself and tried to settle the way the army had taught him, but his mind refused to stop churning.

If taken feature by feature, Gail would be considered more attractive than Josie. At a distance, anyway. He'd always been surprised that a woman who probably could have made a career as an actress had chosen to be an elementary school teacher instead.

When he'd met her, he'd believed that fact showed depth of character. It was just one of the many reasons why he'd thought he loved her, why he'd asked her to marry him and change her name from Gail Thomas to Gail Guerrero.

Josie had a clear, open face. He bet that she'd have a hard time sneaking around behind a guy's back.

But he'd been wrong before.

Mat sat up and dropped his face in his hands, rubbing briskly.

Jesus, he was an idiot. Why the fuck was he even thinking about this? Josie was definitely not what he was looking for.

Then he remembered her long, long legs and the sweet little butt he'd noticed when the sweatshirt she was wearing had ridden up.

Restless, he grabbed his flashlight and stood. He desperately wanted more whiskey but forced himself to get a bottle of water from the bar's mini fridge instead, downing it in a couple of swallows. That reminded him the mini wasn't running on the generator, so he grabbed the milk and cream stored there and carried them out to the main refrigerator in the kitchen.

He wished he could take a walk but listening to the storm told him it wouldn't be a good idea, so he made his way back to the taproom. Restless, he paced over to a window and tried to see outside, but the old leaded glass just reflected back the light of his flashlight. It shook when the wind roared.

If he really wanted a woman, it wouldn't be that hard to find one who'd be willing to take what he had to give with no strings attached. Hell, even the other Kline sister, Jenny, had given signals she might be open to his advances, although he suspected she'd be as complicated as Josie.

He got the book and the radio from his bag and stretched out on his makeshift bed. The radio brought in nothing but static, and he stared at the same page of the book for five minutes before giving up and turning off the flashlight.

It was going to be a very long night.

5

Tired as she was, Josie assumed she'd go right to sleep, despite the fact that it was early and there was a major distraction bunking down in the taproom.

She was wrong.

Although she rolled herself up tightly in the blankets to try to stay warm and closed her eyes, the air mattress was too soft, and the room was too cold. On top of that, her thoughts were whirling around like a tornado on steroids, veering haphazardly from her lack of a job to her lack of an apartment to what she was going to say to her mother to the contemplation of said distraction in the other room.

Finally conceding defeat, she sat up in the nest of blankets and leaned against a handy file cabinet, wishing she could surf the net or check email on her phone.

"So what?" she muttered to herself. "I should just sit here in the dark and sing show tunes?"

Well, she could always go out to the taproom, and—

"No." That was a nonstarter.

Okay. What else?

She needed a resume, right? Hers was in pretty good shape,

but it required some updating. And she would have to reinvent her life, which was bound to take a little time.

Josie turned on her flashlight and got up. She found a notebook and pen on Hannah's desk, settled back in her nest, held the pen over the paper, and considered. First, she should make a list of everything she had to do to move into her next phase of life.

The list turned out to be depressingly long, and she was sure she'd forgotten some things.

"Alright, resume first, then," she decided. "I can work on everything else later."

She stopped after her summary statement began with, "I don't want to work like a dog."

Perhaps she should be in a slightly better frame of mind before she tried to start out on her new path. Besides, there was no reason she couldn't work on all of this after the storm. It wasn't like it was going anywhere.

Curling up in the blankets again, she resisted the urge to suck her thumb.

She just needed to feel useful. To get moving. To remind herself that she was actually employable and capable and a worthwhile person. To silence the voice in her head screaming that she would never, ever, ever, *ever* find another job. She'd been working since high school. Suddenly *not* working was...disorienting.

If she had a short-term goal, a task she could focus on, she'd feel better. Something she could do and be useful, but not one that required too much of a commitment, so she could leave when it was time. With the severance from Milhouse, she wouldn't even need to be paid, at least for now. Just something to get her out there and underway.

Wait.

Josie straightened from her fetal position as a thought occurred to her. Wasn't she smack-dab in the middle of a situation that fit the bill? *Hannah* needed help. She had to keep the Country Time open, and she couldn't do it alone.

Yes, yes, yes, she thought, starting to get excited. It was so obvious. She would help Hannah. She would work for free, of course, and that would save her friend money. All right, maybe she'd never worked in a restaurant or bar or anything like that before, but she was an extremely competent person, and she could learn. Surely there must be plenty of stuff she could do around here, even without experience. And then she'd have a purpose again.

The relief of actually coming up with some sort of a plan settled her enough that she was finally able to drift off to sleep. She woke hours later, feeling barely rested, to early morning sun streaming in through the office's single tiny window and the sound of Mat's voice rumbling out in the taproom.

Was someone else here?

Josie hoisted herself to her feet and groaned as every muscle protested, her breath a cloud in the cold air. Pulling her hands through her hair to put it in some kind of order, she wrapped herself up in one of the blankets before opening the office door and trotting down the hallway.

She heard Mat say, "Sure, Chief," and realized he must be on the phone. Talking to her mother, one would assume. He hung up just as she stumbled into the room.

Mat turned to face her, and she saw that he was wrapped in a big, pink blanket. His beard was heavy and his dark eyes were shadowed, as if he hadn't slept well either. But he smiled when he saw her, almost as if she amused him.

"Good morning?" he asked with a quirk of his eyebrows.

Josie yawned, covering her mouth with her hand. She felt like she was about five hundred years old. It was amazing what a few months of stress followed by a frigid night on the floor did to a person. She probably needed to sleep for a week. In a bed, not on an air mattress.

"Whatever. Was that my mother?"

"It was." He lounged back against the wall and crossed his arms over his broad chest, drawing her eyes to the width of his shoulders draped in the incongruous blanket. "She said state crews were working on the highway, but the main road through town is still blocked because a big tree came down right in front of city hall. So it will be a little while before she can come through and pick you up."

"I can get home myself," Josie muttered.

He snorted. "Sure you can."

He was probably right to be skeptical. Even if the town's crews were out working on the roads—and she was sure they were—things were bound to be a mess for a while.

"I told her not to take the time to come pick you up, because either Deacon or I can get you home. But she insisted, so she'll be by eventually."

Josie frowned at him, not pleased he was making decisions for her. Then she realized what he'd said.

"Deacon? Are he and Hannah coming in?"

"Yup. He called to say they were on their way." Mat shook his head. "The idiot was sneezing his fool head off, but he won't let Hannah drive alone. And he'll probably want to help shovel snow."

"I can help, too," Josie said, squaring her shoulders, ignoring the pull of her muscles.

He didn't look like he believed her, but he was smart enough not to argue.

"Want some coffee?" he asked instead.

Josie felt her eyes grow damp with gratitude. "Yes."

"We can't start the coffee maker, but the stove is gas. I figured I'd just light a burner and make it on top."

"I'll do it," she said, knowing the drill after having lived through many snowstorms. She might be paranoid about lighting a gas burner with a match, but she could do it if she had to. Especially when coffee was on the other end.

"Nah. I got it."

Josie had trust issues, so she was a little worried he'd blow them both up. But she really wanted the coffee, so she kept her mouth shut. Fortunately, Mat got a burner lit without incident and, working quickly, put water and coffee into a saucepan. Once it came to a boil, he poured the mixture through a filter he'd stuffed into a handy funnel, dividing it between two mugs. The result wasn't gourmet by any stretch of the imagination, but it was hot and it contained caffeine, which could not be overrated.

"Thanks," she said, feeling almost reverent as she cupped the warm mug filled with steaming liquid between her cold hands.

Mmmm...coffee...or a reasonable facsimile thereof.

Since the Country Time was on public water and sewer, they could still use the toilet and, with baking soda, sort of brush their teeth. They even shared Josie's granola bars for breakfast, because neither of them wanted cold cuts at that time of day.

And if the way Mat's mouth moved or how his dark eyes glinted when he smiled made her stomach quiver now and then—well, that was just her little secret, wasn't it?

The loud crunch of tires on what had been a silent road outside made Mat look out the front door. He was grinning when he turned around.

"Here comes the boss lady."

Hannah!

Josie hurried to stand next to him and peer out into the cold, white world. In the seemingly endless sea of snow, a big, black SUV turned cautiously into what should have been the Country Time parking lot, pushing its way to the building. She could see Deacon driving, with Hannah riding shotgun and waving at them wildly. Josie waved back, smiling until she thought her face would split. It had been such a long, long time since she'd actually seen her friend. Yes, they talked on the phone and exchanged emails, but even keeping up with that had been difficult over the last couple of months.

The SUV pulled to a stop near the door and Hannah, dressed in a bright red parka, jumped out, leaping through snow drifts to get to them. Inside the entrance, she knocked the snow off her boots and then pulled Josie into a hard, tight hug, dislodging the blanket she was still wrapped up in.

Josie held on to her friend for dear life and tried hard not to cry. This was homecoming. Why had she ever thought that she needed to go to the city? Why hadn't she realized what she'd be leaving behind when she left Hardy Falls?

"God, it's good to see you," Hannah exclaimed, her face flushed under her bright hood. "Why are you here? Why didn't you tell me you were coming? Why did you believe the weather reports?"

"Maybe you should let her go so she can breathe," a male voice said, sounding affectionate and amused.

Josie looked over Hannah's shoulder into Deacon Black's twinkling blue eyes and grinned at him. He was bundled up in a black anorak and looked happier and more relaxed than she'd ever seen him, despite the fact that his nose was almost as red as Hannah's coat. As she watched, he turned away to sneeze violently.

In spite of the germs, she let go of Hannah to launch herself at him.

"Good to see you, kid," Deacon said, kissing her forehead.

He had always called her "kid," like she was his little sister, when in fact she was a few months older than him.

"It's nice to see you, too, big guy." She leaned back in his embrace, and he returned her smile, deep brackets carving around his hard mouth.

Hannah was a lucky girl.

Then he sneezed violently, and Josie had to duck to avoid flying snot.

"Sorry," he snuffled.

A throat clearing behind her made her pull away and turn to face Mat. He had his arms crossed and was scowling for some reason.

"We need to get shoveling," he said to Deacon. "That snow's really drifted, so it's going to take a while to open the paths."

"Fine. Calvin and June will be here soon. Calvin's going to plow the lot."

"Still a lot to do," Mat grumbled. He stomped off to the kitchen and returned a few minutes later wearing his parka and carrying two snow shovels he'd gotten from somewhere. He tossed one to Deacon.

Deacon caught it and, shrugging, followed him outside.

Hannah shook her head as she closed the door behind the men and took Josie's hand.

"Come on," she said.

Josie only had a second to wrap herself up in her blanket again before she found herself being dragged through the taproom towards the office.

"What are you doing?" She tried to resist, but Hannah was strong. "I'm going to get my coat and help shovel."

"No you're not," Hannah said. "You're going to tell me just what in the hell is going on."

6

Josie pouted as she was shoved into the office, but was too tired to try and resist. After she helped Hannah make some space in the little room by bundling up the blankets of her makeshift bed and standing the air mattress up in a corner out of the way, she dropped heavily into the visitor's chair.

Hannah walked around the old metal desk, and sat down. "Did you get any sleep?"

"Not much." Josie yawned hugely. "But at least I'll be sleeping in a bed tonight and you'll probably be stuck on the floor."

"My glamorous life." Hannah settled back in her chair. "Soooo…" she said, dragging out the word. "Did you need the second air mattress?"

Josie scowled at her, because it was perfectly obvious what her friend was really asking.

"Yes," she snapped. "I slept here. Mat was in the taproom, not that it's any of your business."

Hannah shrugged but looked unrepentant. "Everything you do is my business."

"Oh, that is such a bunch of bullshit."

"It is not!"

"It is. Almost as much bullshit as Mat pretending to be the dishwasher."

Now Hannah frowned. "Of course he's the dishwasher. He took over after Billy left to join the carnival."

Billy, Hannah's last dishwasher, had quit in the middle of the fundraising carnival to pursue a new career path emptying trash cans on the road. Josie's mother said he was currently in Florida, wintering with the rest of the crew. It was not a huge loss. Still…

"Mat seems a little…overqualified."

"He's been a freaking godsend. Especially after Jason, my second bartender, quit to focus on medical school and Mat took over that, too. The man can never leave. I'll follow him and drag him back." Hannah leaned forward, her frown deepening. "So you slept the sleep of the virtuous. Great. Then tell me what's wrong."

Josie shifted uncomfortably.

"What makes you think something's wrong?" she hedged. She'd been planning on telling Hannah everything, of course, but that didn't mean she liked having to do it. Talking to Mat had been easier because he was a stranger so she didn't care as much what he thought of her.

"Well, duh! Because you're here, and you should be in New York working on some big-ass project." Hannah tilted her head and a long brown curl fell across her striking face. "Come on. Spill. What's going on? The last time I talked to you, you were practically working twenty-four/seven, and that was only a couple of weeks ago. Now you suddenly show up here."

Restless, Josie pushed out of her chair and walked around the desk to get to the office's single, stingy window. She looked out on the white expanse of the parking lot.

"This window leaks like hell," she said absently.

"Tell me something I don't know. Like why you're here."

Josie glanced back at her friend and saw she was lounging in her desk chair, arms crossed, face determined.

"Why? Because you're going to beat me up if I don't?" she teased.

"Maybe."

A noise outside drew Josie's attention back to the window. A big red truck suddenly came into view, the plow attached to the front breaking through drifts of snow like the prow of a boat breaking through water. It drove past, then backed up and made another pass.

"Who's...oh." Hannah had come to stand next to her. "June and Calvin are here."

June Esperanza had been working as a server at the Country Time since Hannah and Josie were thirteen. Hannah's mother had died in a car accident when she was eleven, so when June had landed in town, she'd fallen into the role of mentor to the young girl. Heck, she bossed Josie around, too, and she *had* a mother.

Josie often wondered what Hannah would have done if June had not been a constant in her life, especially considering that her father, Fred Frederickson, tended to forget she existed unless he needed her. When Fred died of aggressive lung cancer a few years ago, June had been the one to help Hannah pick up the pieces.

Josie hadn't been there, or she hadn't been there long, anyway.

The thought made her feel even guiltier.

"I guess Calvin owns the big red truck?" she asked.

"Yeah. He's wonderful. I don't know what I would have done if he hadn't promised to come plow the parking lot today. Thank God he'll do practically anything June asks."

Josie knew that June had met Calvin Hardy almost as soon as she'd blown into town, a little more than fifteen years ago.

According to the stories she'd heard, the cocky waitress from the wrong side of the tracks and the young prince of Hardy Falls, home for a summer break after finishing college, had taken one look at each other and fallen hard.

Well, June had fallen hard. Calvin hadn't clued in right away. Once the summer was over, he dumped June and left town to work at a big architectural firm in Philadelphia, returning only for brief visits with his parents. Then a few months ago, he'd moved back to Hardy Falls, divorced and wanting to help his father care for his mother, who had early onset Alzheimer's. He also took over the family hardware and building supply store.

Knowing June as they did, everyone in town had been shocked that she'd eventually forgiven Calvin for ditching her. The two had somehow resolved their differences and were pretty much inseparable now—even stronger than they'd been before.

It was enough to make a girl jealous.

The big truck had stopped and was idling further down the side of the building, probably at the back door.

"Good. June'll be here soon." Hannah sounded satisfied as she returned to her seat at the desk. "Might as well wait to tell me what's going on until she gets here. Then you won't have to repeat yourself."

Great.

Sure enough, a minute later June Esperanza strode into the tiny office looking like she was ready to kick some ass and take some names.

Josie suspected the ass highest on the list to be kicked was hers.

"Josephine Kline, what the hell are you doing here?"

In spite of everything, Josie smiled. "Hi, June."

The other woman held out her arms and Josie walked into

them, hugging her tightly until June set her back and glared at her, hands tight on her shoulders.

Josie felt herself hunch reflexively.

"Well?" June demanded. "Why aren't you in New York working your ass off? And why the hell did you drive in a storm like that?"

"Yeah. Tell us already," Hannah said from her seat at the desk. "We'll just bug you until you do."

Josie sighed, knowing it was true. These two would hound her relentlessly until she caved and spilled her story.

Drawing in a deep breath, she pulled away from June. "So, um, I maybe ran into some issues in New York," she admitted, wishing she didn't care that they were going to think she was a dumbass.

"What kind of issues?" June's sharp, dark eyes snapped with challenge as she seated herself in the visitor's chair.

"I kind of got...laid off."

Both women blinked at her.

"Excuse me?" Hannah asked.

"Downsized. Made redundant. Whatever." Josie ran her chilled hands through her hair and wrapped the blanket more tightly around her body. She should check to see if her coat was dry.

"The hell you say!" June thundered. "Are those people fucking idiots? I don't know what you did, but I know it was a lot."

Josie shrugged. "Apparently that didn't matter."

"But you said you were working on the team handling the biggest client." Hannah frowned at her in obvious confusion. "Right?"

"Yeah." Josie plucked at a thread on the blanket.

"And you were at the office every time I talked to you these last couple of months, so you must have been busy."

"I sure was," Josie confirmed. "Busy" was an under-statement.

June waved a hand. "So how the hell could they let you go?"

Josie sighed. She knew she hadn't done anything wrong, but it was still humiliating. "I think Don, the leader of the team I was on, told them my work wasn't good and he didn't need me."

Hannah's sudden scowl was intense. "That asshole? You said he was trying to push you out almost as soon as you started."

"Yes." After she'd moved to her new position earlier in the year, she'd found out that the team lead, Don Corso, hadn't wanted her—he'd wanted to hire a friend of his but had been forced to take her because she was internal and the company was in the middle of a hiring freeze. He'd immediately punished her by piling on extra work and giving her all of the least interesting assignments.

"So he said he didn't need you and the people in charge actually *believed* him?" Hannah sounded incredulous.

"Management didn't really know what I was doing, because they only ever talked to Don. He made sure he put himself in the middle of everything."

"Christ on a cracker, Josie!" Hannah yelled, leaning towards her as if she wanted to strangle her. "You knew there were problems. Why the hell weren't you already looking for another job? Or at least trying to make sure people knew what you did?"

"Because I was too busy working!" she defended herself. "The big client we were supporting hadn't been happy with the results, and they'd threatened to pull all of their business. We had to do a complete makeover of all of their campaigns—a total rebranding. There's going to be a big presentation to the client right before Thanksgiving, so everyone was working twenty-four/seven."

Even so, Hannah was right. The situation she was in now was at least partially her own damned fault. She'd seen how

Don was shoving her aside and marginalizing her contributions, but she'd let it pass because she hadn't wanted to get into it with him. Fat lot of good that had done. She should have confronted him or found another job.

"Thanksgiving's still a few weeks away." Hannah waved her arms. "Why the hell did they lay you off *before* this big hoohah?"

Josie could only shrug, because she didn't understand it either. It was one of the reasons she'd been so blindsided when she'd gotten the call from HR.

"I don't know. The gossip is that the company's in a lot of debt and the banks are pressuring them to cut costs before the end of the year. I guess since Don told them I was useless, there was no reason for them to keep me."

"I'll bet that asshole's looking to move up the corporate ladder, isn't he?" June said darkly.

"Probably," Josie agreed. "So?"

"So he wants to be a frigging hero." June got up to pace in front of the desk. Because the space was so small with three of them in there, it meant she was basically walking in place. "Get credit for cutting costs by sacrificing someone he didn't want, anyway. Pretend he cares about the company when he just wants to get rid of you."

Josie couldn't argue with that because it was probably true.

"Slimy son of a bitch." June shot her a look. "You got a severance package, right?"

"Yes." And it was a nice one. She'd been there long enough to be grandfathered into some benefits that new hires didn't get.

"Good." Hannah settled back in her chair. "Can you keep up your apartment in the meantime?"

Josie shifted because this was another thing she hadn't wanted to admit. "Sure," she said, then winced when Hannah narrowed her eyes at her.

"What?" her friend demanded.

"What, what?" she countered, trying to look innocent.

"Don't be an ass," June snapped. "What's wrong with your damned apartment?"

Josie sighed and gave up.

"Okay, look. I had this sweet studio apartment in Manhattan, right?"

Hannah's frown deepened. "Right."

"It was really tiny, but it was in a terrific location. What I didn't tell you or Mom was that it was a sublet. The guy who owned it worked on my old team at the company, but then he got caught boning one of the building maintenance men on the back stairs. He got fired, his wife kicked him out, and he needed a place..." she trailed off when she saw Hannah's expression. "What?"

Hannah exchanged a look with June. "She worked in a soap opera."

"I thought Hardy Falls was full of melodrama," June agreed.

Josie rolled her eyes. "Anyway, Gerald needed his place and I didn't have a formal lease with him—it was more like a handshake agreement—so he told me to move out."

"When was this?"

"Um, four months ago." Josie winced.

"And you didn't tell us?" June thundered.

"Why should I?" she protested. "I had a place to go. Three women I worked with had a four-bedroom apartment in Queens. Their fourth roommate had moved out, so they said I could live there."

Hannah's brow creased. "Isn't Queens far away from Manhattan?"

"Yes." Queens might be considered part of New York City, but her commute had been over an hour each way. Which was why she hadn't bothered going home much the last couple of weeks.

"Okay," Hannah said. "So you're renting with these three other women, and they'll be looking for you to—"

"No," Josie interrupted, just wanting to get the story told at this point. "They won't. After I got downsized, they asked me to move out. Apparently one of them has a friend with a great job as a supermodel or something, and they'd been wanting her to move in so they'd get invited to parties."

"Jesus Christ." Hannah looked drained. Well, she should try living through it. "You've lost your job and your apartment within a couple of days?"

"Pretty much."

"And I thought my life was crap." Hannah shook her head. "What now?"

That was the million dollar question, wasn't it?

"Now I'll get another job," Josie sighed. "What else?"

"But, you're here for a while?" her friend prodded.

"A few weeks," she said. "I'm going to take a little while to figure out what I'm going to do."

"You realize you have to tell your mother all of this," June said.

Josie felt her shoulders slump. "Yeah." If she thought telling all of this to Hannah and June was bad, telling her mother would take it to a whole new level. Jackie would look at her with those sharp cop's eyes and see right through her.

Hannah smiled unexpectedly, and it lit up the tiny office.

"I know this makes me sound like a total jackass considering all the crap you're going through, but I'm glad you're home, Josie."

Josie returned the smile and felt something relax inside. "I guess I am, too."

7

"Hey, pudding pop."

Josie turned to see Deacon was standing in the office door. He appeared to be covered in snow.

Hannah raised her eyebrows. "Pudding pop?" she asked.

Deacon shrugged. "Snow angel?"

"Speaking of which," Hannah gestured at him, "have you been making them?"

"Mat's an aggressive shoveler." Deacon grinned. "Don't worry. I am, too."

Hannah rolled her eyes.

"Anyway, Calvin was wondering when you were coming out, because he has a present for you."

Hannah's smile was sly. "And you don't mind?"

"Not this present," Deacon said cryptically.

"Even I don't mind him giving you this present," June said, then grinned sharply. "But keep your hands where I can see them."

Deacon sneezed into his shoulder and waved a hand. "Come on."

He turned and walked away. Cackling, June followed him.

Hannah shrugged. "Guess we'd better go."

Glad they'd finally stopped talking about her problems, Josie made a quick detour to trade the blanket for her coat and mittens before trailing Hannah through the kitchen and out the back door.

She was momentarily blinded when she stepped from the dim interior of the building into the winter world with the snow reflecting a brilliant white in the morning sun. Everything probably would have been hushed and silent, too, except the generator near the door was roaring for all it was worth.

Walking away from it, Josie went to stand with June next to the muscular, red pickup parked nearby. Calvin Hardy, looking big and capable in his winter gear, was at the tailgate of the truck waiting for Hannah. Since he didn't have on a hat, the sun picked out the streaks of silver in his dark hair, and when he saw her, he smiled. It was charming and just a little rakish.

June was a lucky woman, too.

A plume of snow at the bowling alley next door caught her eye, and she thought she heard the whine of a snowblower over the generator. Pat Murphy must have people there cleaning off the parking lot already. She wondered if he'd been able to save his food—surely he'd stocked up if he'd been expecting to hold his grand reopening today. Maybe they'd catch a break and everything had been ruined, which would set Pat's plans back. Not that Josie wished something that bad on anybody, but Pat could cover losses a lot easier than Hannah.

"Calvin!" Hannah's squeal brought Josie's focus back to her friend—just in time to see her throw herself at Calvin and cling to the older man like a monkey.

"I should probably be pissed off," June said dryly when Calvin wrapped his arms around Hannah. "He really seems to be enjoying this."

Hannah kissed Calvin firmly on the mouth and June frowned.

"Hey!"

Calvin looked over at them and grinned, his dark eyes twinkling.

"I didn't feel a thing," he assured June.

She marched over to him and tugged Hannah away.

"Hands off my man, you hussy."

"Yeah," Deacon said from where he and Mat stood on the other side of the truck, each holding a snow-covered shovel. "Keep your hands on your own man."

Hannah turned big, limpid eyes on him.

"But Deacon, I had to kiss him," she protested. "Did you see what he brought me?" She waved towards the truck. The tail-gate was down and Josie saw there was a large box in the truck bed. "I might have to kiss him again."

Calvin laughed at June's expression and bent down to peck her cheek. She grabbed his hair and pulled him into a kiss that wasn't nearly so innocent. When they broke apart, they were both panting and Calvin's eyes looked distinctly glazed.

"I feel left out," Deacon groused.

"Like I'd kiss you when you're dripping with snot," Hannah wrinkled her nose, although she sounded a little worried. "You've been sneezing all morning. Maybe you should stop shoveling and take something."

Deacon waved that away. "Nah. I'm fine." He sneezed again.

Josie ignored them all and walked around to the back of the pickup to see if she could figure out what was inside the mystery box.

"It's another generator," she said, turning her head sideways to read the description.

"Yes!" Hannah beamed at the box like a proud mother, hands clasped at her breast. "And Calvin is my new boyfriend." She shot Deacon a look. "*He's* not dripping with snot."

"It's a nice powerful one, too. A lot bigger than what you have," Mat said. Josie started and turned to see he'd come up behind her without her realizing it. "If we plug the bigger generator into the system, we should be able to run more than just the refrigerator and freezer. Maybe the water heater so we can do dishes, but for sure the heating system and the stove. They're not huge draws, since they're natural gas. And we can use the second generator with an extension cord. The townspeople are going to want to get out of their houses—you might as well give them someplace to go."

"And we found an open gas station two towns over, so we bought more fuel," June added, pointing to gas cans lined up in front of a big toolbox bolted to the truck cab.

Hannah sniffled, blinking rapidly. "Thank you." Her words sounded wet. Then, suddenly, she started to cry.

"Hey! Hey, now," Calvin looked alarmed and actually took a step back. "Why are you crying?"

June elbowed him in the stomach. "Because she's happy, you moron." She wrapped the younger woman in a warm embrace while Deacon, looking as uncomfortable as Calvin, stroked Hannah's hair.

"It's okay, kid," June told her. "There are some perks to being friends with the guy who is now the sole owner of Hardy Hardware. You know we've got your back."

Hannah sobbed louder.

"Christ." Mat leaned his shovel on the side of the truck and pushed Hannah and June aside to jump up into the bed. "Help me with this," he ordered Deacon. "Just having the damned thing here won't mean anything if we don't get it hooked up."

Deacon looked torn, his face drawn with concern.

"She never cries," he said. "Never."

"So?" Mat said unsympathetically. "Everyone needs to cry sometimes."

"Even you?" Josie demanded, because the man was a total ass.

Mat grinned at her. "Wouldn't you like to know?" He jerked his head at Deacon. "Let your lady be and get it in gear, Black."

Still looking troubled, Deacon propped his shovel next to Mat's, then got into the bed of the truck. Calvin stepped up and nudged June, Hannah, and Josie further away so he could help them lower the big box to the ground.

"After we get this done, I'll finish plowing the parking lot," he told Hannah as Mat jumped out of the truck and Deacon went to get the gas cans.

"You will?" Hannah burst into tears again.

"Hannah?" Deacon straightened. "What's wrong now?"

"Oh, for Christ's sake, get her out of his line of sight or we'll never get any work out of him," Mat groused, working with Calvin to pull the generator out of the box. "You," he pointed at Deacon. "Shovel a path to the door so we don't drop this damned thing getting it where it needs to be."

Deacon tore his eyes off Hannah.

"But—"

"She's fine. Go!"

Deacon snapped off a salute.

"Sir, yes sir." He jumped out of the truck and, after another massive sneeze, grabbed his shovel and began tossing snow.

"Come on," June said, wrapping her arm around Hannah's shoulders and turning her towards the Country Time. "Let them do their thing. We need to check out the food situation." She glanced at Josie. "You, too."

"Okay."

Mat wasn't the only person who could command obedience.

As they passed Deacon, Hannah pulled away from June so she could reach up and kiss him on the cheek.

"I'm fine. I love you."

He loved her back. It was written all over his face. Josie was surprised his pupils weren't shaped like little hearts.

"Black!" Mateo barked.

Deacon kissed Hannah a little more forcefully than was necessary and started shoveling again.

"Make sure he doesn't get too wet," June called to Calvin.

He saluted her, just as Deacon had saluted Mat earlier.

"Yes, ma'am."

June rolled her eyes. "Ass."

"Yours," he called after her.

June chuckled.

"Yes it is," she called back to Calvin as she held open the back door for them. "Wait until you see what I do with it tonight."

His jaw dropped and she laughed harder, pushing Hannah and Josie inside.

"Ew! TMI!" Hannah put her gloved hands over her ears. "Make the pictures stop!"

"Oh, like I needed to know what you and Deacon were doing in the supply closet on Thursday night."

"You're the one who peeked," Hannah protested, drilling a finger into June's shoulder. "Pervert."

"I needed paper towels and a bartender," June retorted, flicking Hannah's ear, "not an anatomy lesson."

"Ow!" Hannah clapped her hand over her ear. "Goddamnit, I hate it when you flick."

June laughed at her.

"I think you're both perverts," Josie said, stripping off her mittens and laying them on a nearby prep counter. She was trying not to feel jealous, but it was hard. She'd never had a relationship like what Hannah had with Deacon or June had with Calvin. There'd been a few boyfriends, but things always fizzled.

Hannah smirked at her, then pulled a clipboard off a hook on the wall near the supply room and brought it back to June. Soon, both women were muttering about temperatures and food safety procedures while Josie stood around feeling utterly useless. She'd be better off shoveling snow in the parking lot.

The back door opened and Mat strode in. He went to the circuit breaker box, flipped a few switches, and went back out.

"What's he doing?" Josie asked. "He turned off the refrigerator."

"Hooking up the new generator, I guess." But Hannah frowned worriedly.

A few minutes later, Mat came into the kitchen again.

"We have the generator Calvin brought plugged into the system," he told them, going to the electric box. "This one's the size you need, Hannah. The other's way too small."

Hannah paled and spun to face June. "I'm not supposed to be buying this thing, am I?"

June propped her hands on her hips and glared at her. "I'm pretty sure Calvin knows you don't have any money. I doubt he'd just hook something up and expect you to pay for it."

"Technically, I'm the one hooking it up," Mat pointed out mildly as he worked. After a moment, the refrigerator and freezer whirred back to life, then Josie heard the heater come on.

"Heat," Hannah said prayerfully. "It's heat." She looked for all the world like she was going to cry again.

Mat grinned at her, which made his brown eyes twinkle. "I know how to make a woman happy."

Josie bet he did.

He closed the box and went back outside. Warm air started to take some of the chill out of the room.

"Feel that heat," Hannah said, throwing her hands up in the air. "I swear, June, I'm seriously thinking about stealing Calvin."

"Try it and see what happens, chickie," June invited.

"Try what?" Deacon asked as he shoved open the back door and walked into the kitchen.

"Try seeing how much I wuv woo," Hannah cooed,

throwing herself at him, and kissing his bristly chin. Deacon smiled down at her with a dopey expression on his lean face.

"God, you are so whipped," Josie told him. She was delighted to see her friends snuggling together, but *Jesus*. This was getting to be a bit much.

"I sure am." Deacon grinned and gave Hannah a kiss on the cheek that was somehow more intimate than watching them neck. "And she can whip me some more after I'm finished shoveling out front."

"I wish you'd just stop." Hannah frowned up at him. "Calvin and Mat can get the rest done."

"After this." He kissed her again, this time on the mouth, then headed to the taproom and, presumably, outside.

"He's so stubborn, but he's such a good man," Hannah sighed. "How could I have missed it for so long?"

"I feel the same way about mine," June said.

Both women stood for a moment with equally sappy expressions on their faces.

Disgusted, Josie got her mittens and pulled them back on.

"I'm going to help shovel," she announced. The work would keep her mind off of her own inadequacies when it came to the dating scene.

"Don't be pissy because you're jealous," Hannah called after her, as she shoved out the back door into the blinding light.

"I'm not jealous," Josie muttered. She marched up to Mat, who was doing absolutely nothing productive, just standing and watching Calvin use his pickup truck to push a massive mound of snow across the parking lot and into the field on the other side.

"Give me your shovel," she demanded.

He looked down at her, eyebrows raised and face flushed from the cold.

"Excuse me?"

"You're not using it," she pointed out. "Give it to me. I want it."

"Sounds familiar," he said.

"You are a pig," she informed him and grabbed the shovel. Since he was leaning some of his weight on it, he stumbled before he got his footing again. Josie grinned viciously, stuck her nose in the air, and strode back into the building.

"There's no snow in there," he called after her. She ignored him.

Hannah and June had their heads together, going over the list on the clipboard. They looked up in surprise when she came back in.

"I thought you were going to shovel," Hannah said.

Josie held up the shovel, but she didn't slow her pace. "I'm going to help Deacon," she said.

"Don't you be chasing after my man," Hannah yelled, as Josie pushed through the kitchen door into the empty taproom.

"As if he'd even notice me."

She opened one of the old, wooden double doors at the front entrance and stepped outside, only to get a face full of snow.

"Crap!"

"Oh, man. Sorry!" Deacon snorted, obviously trying not to laugh. "The wind picked up just as I tried to throw it. What are you doing here?"

She held up the shovel. "I'm helping."

"Okay?" He shrugged and sneezed, then wiped his nose on his sleeve.

"That's disgusting," she told him.

"Sue me. I ran out of tissues."

"Oh, for God's sake." She propped the shovel up against the building and went back inside. Pushing into the kitchen again, she ignored Hannah and June who were now over at the refrigerator, grabbed a handful of paper towels, went back outside, and shoved them at Deacon.

"Blow," she instructed.

He looked at the wad of paper towels. "They're not soft. They'll hurt."

"I'll hurt you. Blow."

He took off his gloves and jammed them in his pocket, then ripped off a paper towel and blew his nose.

"Ouch," he said, and held out the used paper towel to her.

"If you think I'm going to touch that, you are sadly mistaken," she told him.

"Well, what am I supposed to do with it?"

"How the hell should I know?" She flung her hands wide. "Throw it somewhere."

"It will kill whatever it touches," he muttered, but did as she suggested. "Thanks," he added, as he pulled his gloves back on.

"No problem." She picked up her shovel. "Where should I start?"

"I don't know. We just need this whole front area clear." He paused as Calvin's truck came around the building, pushing a wave of snow. The truck paused, backed up, and switched direction to pile it off to the side. "I really need to get a plow for my SUV," Deacon said. Josie could hear the longing in his voice. "That way we won't have to count on Calvin to come and bail us out every time it snows."

"And you don't want Hannah depending on anyone but you," Josie added. She decided she might as well shovel out her car, since Calvin wouldn't be able to plow that close to the vehicle.

"I'm not like that," Deacon groused.

"Right." She judged the quickest path to the car and applied herself to the shovel. The snow was wet and heavy, and she couldn't hold back a grunt as she lifted.

"Lightweight," Deacon called.

She curled her lip at him and tossed the shovelful of snow his way.

"Hey! I'm sick!" Deacon yelped when the snow hit him in the face.

She laughed at him, then danced away when he threatened her, his shovel brimming with more snow than she could lift.

"No fair! No fair!" She giggled, ducked, and spun.

"Having fun?" Mat's droll voice said from behind her.

She whirled to face him, then gasped when snow hit her in the back of the head.

"You shit!" she yelled at Deacon. "That is so cold!"

He laughed.

Mat smiled, although his eyes moved between the two of them.

"Just give me the shovel," he said to her. "I'll do it."

"No." She started shoveling in earnest, ignoring him when he tried to take it from her. "I've got this. Go help someone else."

He opened his mouth to argue, then shut it again when they heard the sound of a vehicle coming down the highway. Usually there were tons of cars whizzing past the Country Time at every hour of the day or night, but today the road had been empty. Josie shielded her eyes from the sun and saw a large, dark blue SUV pull into the parking lot. It rumbled across the space Calvin had cleared, circled, and came to a stop next to her. The driver's side window slid down.

Josie smiled.

"Hi, Mom," she said.

8

"Hi, honey." Jackie Kline's eyes were bleary and red-rimmed, but her smile was bright.

Josie reached through the open window to hug her mother around the neck, settling deeper into the feeling of *home*. "I missed you."

"Missed you too, baby." Her mother set her back, and her smile faded a little. "Something's wrong."

The "mom radar" was always on target.

Josie sighed and rubbed her mittened hand over her face. "There's been a lot going on," she said.

Jackie's eyes narrowed. "And you're going to tell me all about it."

It wasn't a question, it was a statement.

"Sure." Because of course she'd spill the whole sad tale to her mother. Jackie would know if she tried to hide something. Besides, she'd eventually figure it out when Josie didn't leave.

"Good," her mom nodded. "Are you ready to go? I'm heading home to catch a nap while Harry mans the shop. Never could sleep on that stupid cot the town council gave us for the break room."

Josie looked at the huge snowdrift that was her car, catching Mat's eye where he stood, watching her.

"What about my car?" she asked, turning back to her mother.

Jackie's eyes slid between her and Mat, and she shrugged.

"Roads around town are still for shit now anyway," she said. "Especially if you don't have four-wheel drive. Just leave it for now. Mort had an emergency load of road salt delivered, and the guys are getting out to treat everything. I can bring you back to get your car after we both get some sleep. You look almost as wiped out as I feel."

"I am kind of tired," Josie admitted, yawning before she could stop herself. "I should probably stay and help Hannah get set up, but I think I do need some rest first." And a bed. A bed would be a very good thing.

Her mom's dark eyebrows raised. "She's going to open? Can she? Legally?"

Josie shrugged. "I guess."

Jackie's face snapped into a frown. "Hmmm."

"Hey, Chief Kline." Josie turned to see Hannah coming towards them, a broad smile on her face. Deacon and Mat followed, and soon they were all clustered around the SUV.

"Did you keep everyone safe last night?" Hannah asked.

"We did," Josie's mother smiled before she frowned again. "You're opening?"

Hannah held up her hands. "Don't worry. June's going through the stock now to make sure nothing's past the temperature limit, but it should be fine since the generator ran the refrigerator and freezer all night. We'll make sure everything's okay before we serve food. Promise."

Jackie nodded. "Make sure you do. People aren't supposed to be out driving around unless it's necessary, but you know they'll get bored." She frowned. "Come to think of it, I'm not sure you people were supposed to be out driving yet, either."

"It was sort of necessary," Hannah argued.

"Maybe." Jackie didn't sound convinced.

"I'm going to head home unless you need me," Josie told Hannah. "I'm going to help you, but after the drive and sleeping on the floor all night—"

"Yeah, it's not the most comfortable air mattress in the world," Mat said to Hannah. "You need to upgrade."

"And were you and Josie sharing that air mattress last night?" Josie's mother asked mildly.

"Mom!" Josie felt her face flush with heat.

Mat grinned. "Don't worry, Chief. Your girl was safe and alone in the office."

"It's fine. Go," Hannah said, and Josie could hear the chuckle in her voice. "We're okay. I'll see you later when we have more time to talk."

"I want to help," Josie repeated, not sure her friend understood that she was serious.

"Sure, sure. There's tons of stuff you can do," Hannah said patronizingly

Josie wanted to argue, but another yawn overtook her. She really was beat. And now she was going to have to tell her mother about New York, which would drain her even more.

"I'll be right back," she told her mom, suddenly remembering her purse and the duffel bag. "I just have to get my stuff."

"Take your time," her mother said, waving a hand. "These guys will keep me company."

Wonderful.

Josie pushed the shovel at Mat, then trotted into the Country Time. After collecting her duffel bag and the clothes from yesterday, she grabbed her purse and hurried back outside. Calvin had stopped plowing, and now he and June were standing with the others at the SUV. Hopefully they weren't all chatting about her.

"Okay, Mom," she said, breathless as she jogged around the vehicle to climb into the passenger seat. "I'm ready."

Her mother quirked an eyebrow at her. "Sure you don't need anything from your car?"

"No, I'm good until I come back to clean it all off."

"Suit yourself." Jackie smiled at the others. "We'll see you all later."

"See you." Deacon turned, let out a huge sneeze and wiped his nose with one of the paper towels Josie had brought him earlier.

"For God's sake, take something for that damned cold," Jackie snapped.

"Yes, ma'am," Deacon said insincerely.

All of the women rolled their eyes.

"See you later, Josie," Mat called, just as her mother started to put up her window. "And don't worry—your snoring wasn't that bad."

"Jerk," she yelled at him.

He laughed, and everyone stepped back as Jackie put the SUV in gear and pulled away.

Once they turned onto the highway, Josie could see that her mother had been right about road conditions. Although plows had obviously been through, the wet snow had turned into a slimy coating that was incredibly slippery where it was untreated.

"I hope everyone stays inside until the road crews come through," she said.

"Me, too." Her mother shrugged. "But they won't."

"No. They won't," Josie agreed. "People are stupid."

"Sometimes," Jackie shot her a look. "So, why don't you tell me all about it, baby girl?"

"All about what?" Josie hedged.

This time the look her mother gave her was bland.

"Josie."

Josie felt her shoulders hunch.

"I just don't want you to think I'm stupid," she said.

"What's making me think you're stupid is that you don't want to tell me the truth."

Josie sighed. Well, there was no point in hiding it, was there? Clutching her damp jeans to her chest, she started to talk.

As her mother carefully made her way through the snowbound streets of Hardy Falls, Josie told her everything that had happened in New York. Don. The job. The apartment. All of it. Her mother didn't comment. She just listened as she drove, holding up a finger now and then for Josie to pause the narrative while the police chief waved at someone shoveling, stopped to offer assistance, and checked on her town as they headed home.

It was a relief, in a way, to be able to tell her mom exactly what was going on. To not have to try and hide it or make it sound better than it was.

When she finished, she stared out the side window and watched the streets flow by. Hardy Falls was such a pretty, little town in the snow, she thought. It covered up all of the imperfections.

Jackie was silent for a long time, carefully maneuvering through the snow-packed streets.

"So, it sounds like you're moving home," she said at last.

Josie swallowed. "Just for a few weeks. If it's okay with you."

Jackie snorted. "Please. If it had been up to me, none of you would have left. I haven't even done anything with your old bedrooms yet."

"Oh." Josie fidgeted. "So, um, is that all you have to say about what I told you?"

"I'm trying not to head this car to New York to take out that dick you were working for or those moronic girls you were living with."

"Really?" Josie was a little surprised by the anger in her mother's tone. Jackie Kline might carry a gun, but she never threatened anyone.

Her mother looked at her. "What do you mean, 'Really'? What did you think I would say?"

"I thought you were going to tell me I was a moron for not doing something sooner," Josie confessed. "Or maybe yell at me because I didn't tell you what was really happening."

Jackie was silent as she turned the police SUV into the shoveled driveway of the familiar, brick-front, two-story house where Josie had grown up.

"For the record," she said finally, "yes, I'm a little upset that you didn't tell me all of this shit was going on. I wish you hadn't been afraid to come to me."

Crap.

"I wasn't afraid," Josie hastened to assure her. "I was...ashamed."

"Now that," her mother said, parking in front of the attached garage, next to a little pickup truck, "*is* stupid." She turned off the engine and got out. Taking a deep breath, Josie followed.

The sidewalk leading to the front door was cleared, and even the evergreen bushes lining it had been brushed off. On the generous covered porch, her mother pulled the house key out of her shirt pocket, but before she could unlock the door, it opened. Jenny Kline, Josie's older sister and the middle Kline kid, grinned at them from the foyer. She was looking cheerful in an old striped hoodie, a hat with tassels that dangled past her shoulders, and sweatpants she'd owned since she'd was sixteen.

Josie tried not to resent the fact that her sister still fit into those pants.

She failed.

She also tried not to be instantly annoyed by Jenny's bright, laughing blue eyes or the way her smile wrinkled her adorably freckled nose.

Her sister had been having a rough time of it, too, she reminded herself. She'd moved back home a couple of months ago when she and her boyfriend, Stefan—an avant-garde sculptor—had finally split up after Jenny had caught him screwing one of his interns.

"Josie!" Jenny hugged her and rocked her side to side before stepping back. "Mom said you were in town. Picked a hell of a time to visit."

Josie muttered something, because it dawned on her that she was going to have to tell her whole story again. Thank God her brother, Jordan, wasn't around.

"You shoveled," Jackie said as they all trooped into the house. Jenny quickly closed the front door to shut out the cold air. "I thought you and Missy were working today."

The comment was mild and, as far as Josie could tell, without judgment. But the smile slipped off Jenny's face and she looked a little wary.

"Mrs. Black called to cancel," she said. "Their electric's on, but their driveway hasn't been plowed yet, so she had to reschedule her charity reception. Missy and I don't have to go today." She laughed a little. "Good thing, huh? Considering the roads and all."

Melissa Leon and Jenny were best friends and partners in a house cleaning business. It seemed to work out pretty well for both of them.

"It *is* good," Jackie confirmed, as Josie and Jenny followed her through the living room. In the kitchen, a round kerosene heater sat off to one side of the large space. Josie put her jeans on the kitchen table, dropped her purse and duffel on the floor, and walked towards it, holding out her hands to the warmth.

"Mrs. Black must be pissed about the driveway," Jackie said, taking off her hat and gloves.

"You can say that again." Jenny smiled slightly, moving to stand next to Josie. "I don't want to be Richie Dunlop when she gets ahold of him."

"Couldn't happen to a nicer guy." Their mother started to unwind her scarf, then paused. "Better not," she decided. "The bedroom is going to be pretty cold."

"Too bad we're not as important as the Blacks. The electric wouldn't dare go off for them. When did you start working for Deacon's parents?" Josie asked her sister.

Jenny shrugged and leaned against a kitchen cabinet, toying with one of the hat's long tassels.

"A few weeks ago. Missy and I were looking for another house because we lost Mrs. Webster. She went into a nursing home."

"Oh, I didn't know that." Josie felt a pang of sadness at the thought of the smiling woman who had always handed out fruit on Halloween because she figured the kids got enough candy. "I'll have to go visit her when the roads are better," she said, thinking about all of the changes that had happened in town since she'd been gone.

Jenny looked at her a little oddly. "So, you're staying, then?" she asked.

"For a while." Josie hesitated, then shrugged. "I kind of lost my job," she admitted.

"Oh, gosh. I'm sorry." Jenny reached out and squeezed her arm.

"She'll tell you all about it, I'm sure." Jackie rolled her shoulders tiredly. "I'm heading to bed so I can get some sleep before I have to get back to the station to relieve Harry. Jenny, since you're here, would you be able to take Josie to the Country Time to get her car later?"

"Sure."

"Great." She patted Jenny on the shoulder and yawned

widely. "You'd better get some sleep, too, Josie, before you fall down."

"Yes ma'am," Josie said.

"I'll wake you up in a couple of hours, Mom," Jenny put in.

Jackie smiled. "Thanks." Turning, she headed down the dark, cold hallway.

"I appreciate you taking me to get my car," Josie told her sister after their mother's bedroom door closed behind her.

"No problem," Jenny said, studying her. "Mom's right. You look beat. You should go set up in your old bedroom."

"I will." She wished people would stop telling her she looked like hell. "Just wanted to warm up first."

"Good thing we have the heater." Jenny tugged on her hat tassels. "I'm sorry you lost your job."

"Thanks," Josie sighed. "I'm sorry about Stefan."

Jenny shrugged. "I should have known he was sleeping around." The words sounded unconcerned, but Josie knew her sister. She saw the hurt in her eyes. Their circumstances might be different, but life had smacked both of them right upside the head.

"I'm still sorry."

"It's okay. I'm dealing with it." Jenny shook herself. "So, you were at the Country Time last night, huh? When Mom called, she said Mat Guerrero was there to run the generator."

Josie gathered up her damp pants from the table. She'd hang them in the guest bath for now.

"Yeah. Do you know Mat?"

"Sure." Jenny smiled. "All the girls in town know Mat. I mean, did you even look at him? He's gorgeous."

"He's okay." Josie realized she was frowning. Just how well did her sister know Mat, anyway?

"*Okay*? Please. Next you'll be telling me Deacon's just marginal."

"I always thought Deacon was cute, not that anybody ever

listened to me." There might even have been a time, a long time ago, when Josie had wondered if Deacon would maybe ask her out. But those days were gone, and she was really happy with the way things had worked out.

"So," Jenny said with a studied casualness. "You were at the Country Time with Mat all night, huh? That must have been...interesting."

"It wasn't interesting," Josie protested.

Jenny grinned. "Not at all?"

"No. I slept in Hannah's office. He was in the taproom."

Jenny's eyes widened. "Well, good, but I wasn't thinking things would have gotten quite that far."

"Oh." Oops.

"Mat's actually a really great guy." Jenny turned and walked over to get a mug off the shelf. "I'm going to make some tea. Want some?"

"No thanks."

"Then you'd better go get settled in." Her sister shot her one of her normal happy smiles. "We can get your car later this afternoon. Not like I have any other plans."

"Okay. Thanks." Josie smiled at her, gathered the rest of her things, and headed up the stairs to her old bedroom.

Seriously, how well did Jenny know Mat?

9

After Mat helped Deacon and Calvin clear the Country Time parking lot and walkways, he got in his truck and followed them across town to Hardy Hardware, where they did the same for Calvin's business. Once everything had been plowed, shoveled, and salted within an inch of its life, Mat felt like it was okay to admit that he was tired as all hell.

He wished he could chalk up his exhaustion to back-breaking work after a night spent on the floor on a cheap-ass air mattress. But sadly, part of the reason he was tired was because he'd lain awake a lot longer than he should have thinking about Josie Kline's big blue eyes.

Which meant he was stupid.

"Looks like we're finished, so I'm ready to head out if Deacon is," he said when he joined the other men at the hardware store's front door. Deacon had left his SUV behind in case Hannah and June needed it, so Mat was giving him a ride back to the Country Time before heading home.

"I'm ready," Deacon said. They shook hands with Calvin and climbed into Mat's truck. As soon as Mat pulled out onto the highway, Deacon dropped his head back against the headrest.

"I feel like shit," he moaned.

Mat shrugged. "Tell your lady, and I'll take you home."

"Can't do that. She's going to be working like an idiot to make sure she can open, and we have to figure out what we're going to be cooking and how, and then she'll want to stay overnight to handle the generators."

Yeah, his friend was stuck on Hannah big time.

"She'll understand," Mat said. "You think she wants you sneezing on everything?"

"I just need some aspirin." Deacon groaned a little as they bounced over a ridge in the road.

He was being a moron, but it was pointless to argue, so Mat just kept driving. A few minutes later, he pulled up in front of the Country Time and threw the truck into park before turning to Deacon.

"Tell Hannah to call me if she needs me," he said.

"We'll be fine." Deacon said it almost like a mantra as he opened his door. He paused to let loose a massive sneeze. "*Jesus.*"

"Right. See you later." Mat shook his head as he watched Deacon stagger to the building. Oh, *sure* he was fine. Mat would be getting a call to come back in a couple of hours, so he'd better try to get some sleep.

He frowned at the drifted mound of snow that was Josie's car parked nearby.

What the hell had that fool woman been thinking, driving in a flipping blizzard, anyway? Too stubborn to stop, that's what she was.

Jerking his pickup into gear, Mat pulled out of the parking lot, going a lot slower than usual. Chief Kline was right—the roads were for shit.

He frowned again. And Chief Kline's damned daughter had driven here from New York City, for Christ's sake.

There were a few vehicles out on the highway now—mostly SUVs or trucks—but it still felt almost deserted as he turned into Hardy Falls.

It was a good place, he mused. It looked a lot different than the relatively flat plains of southeastern Texas, that was for damned sure. You didn't have the tall mountains there, like the ones that stood out beyond the outskirts of the town here. Just waving oceans of grass, or in the case of Galveston, sand.

As he drove past the cottages and tall, skinny townhouses that made up this part of town, he saw that people were out and busy. Snowblowers shot plumes of snow into the crisp air as driveways and sidewalks were cleared. Children ran around in yards, building forts and throwing snowballs. People shoveled, cleaned off cars, and basically dug themselves out so they could get back to the business of living.

A guy so bundled up and covered with snow that he looked like a moving snowman paused in his work to wave when Mat drove past. Mat waved back, although he doubted the other man could see him.

They were a friendly lot here in Hardy Falls. Maybe a little too interested in what other folks were doing, but Mat was used to that. It didn't matter where you lived; people always wanted to know everyone else's business.

He pulled over when he saw Old Albert Cromwell out shoveling the sidewalk in front of his neat, little bungalow. Leaning over, he lowered the passenger window of his truck.

"Hey, there," he called to the old man. "Need some help?"

Albert, who had to be at least eighty, straightened and smiled, showing that he'd neglected to put in his teeth again today.

Mat understood that the guy didn't like his dentures because they apparently hurt sometimes. What he didn't get was how he never seemed to have trouble finding companionship among the elderly female population of Hardy Falls. In fact, he'd just broken up with Ms. Gregory, Mat's landlady, and there were rumors he was already hooked up with someone else. Continence must be its own reward.

"Hey, Mat," Albert yelled back. "Kinda got a lot, didn't we?"

Mat grinned at him. "A lot for me."

"Oh, yeah, that's right. You're one of them southern boys, ain't you?" Albert moved closer to the truck.

"Pretty much," Mat admitted. "But I can still sling some snow if you need a break."

"Nah." Albert shrugged. "Nice to be out in the fresh air."

Mat was freezing his balls off, even in the heated cab, but he didn't argue.

"I've shoveled a lot of this stuff in my day," Albert said. "Even when I owned my farm. I had a plow then, but there was always shoveling to be done, and my Mabel insisted the walkways be neat as a pin." Mabel was Albert's late wife and, according to Calvin, she had been the love of his life.

"Well, you had to keep your lady happy," Mat said. He knew how it went.

"I sure did."

Mat tried to think of a way he could convince Albert to let him help without dinging the old man's pride. No matter how much snow Albert had shoveled over the years, it just didn't seem right to leave him alone to deal with this batch.

As he was considering his options, a pickup pulled up behind him and a kid, probably in his early twenties, hopped out of the cab.

"Hey, Pops!" The newcomer waved. "Mom sent me to give you a hand."

Albert smiled and returned the salute, but he looked a little peeved.

"My daughter," he grumbled to Mat, "thinks I can't do a

damned thing for myself. They live twenty miles away. She oughtn't to have sent the boy out when the roads were still chancy."

"I guess she worries," Mat said.

"That girl." Albert shook his head. "I might be a little slow, but I can still get the job done."

"Bet you can." Mat shifted back into his seat and yawned widely. "Well, I'm going to head home."

Albert waved him off and stepped back to join his grandson as Mat carefully pulled out onto the road.

After he'd gone through the one traffic light in town—which was currently blinking yellow—he pulled up alongside the Best Pages Bookstore. Locking the truck, he let himself in the tenant entrance, trotted up to the second floor, hit the head in the shared bathroom—thank God for city water so he could flush—and finally unlocked the door to his own little room at the far end of the hallway.

Slipping inside, he closed and locked the door behind him, then leaned back against it with a sigh that sent a fog of breath into the chilly air.

Bright, mid-morning sun streamed in through the single, large window, lighting up the small space and highlighting the shabby charm of ancient crown molding and built-in shelves on either side of his big bed. It really wasn't a bad room, he thought. It actually had been a bedroom back in the day, as opposed to a converted closet or enclosed porch. But what had no doubt been considered a relatively generous space in the late 1800s was a little cramped when you shoved a modern king-size bed into it.

On the other hand, he didn't have much else. Not anymore.

He pushed away from the door and walked around the bed to the tiny kitchenette. When he'd talked to Ms. Gregory about taking over Deacon's lease, she'd explained that she couldn't give everyone private bathrooms, but she'd made sure each person at least had his own sink and stove top. Mat kind of wished there was an oven, too, because he liked to cook. But it didn't matter. If he felt the urge, he'd see if Hannah would let him help out in the kitchen at the Country Time.

He grabbed a glass from the lone wall cabinet over the sink and filled it with water, pleased that the pipes weren't frozen. As he drank, he looked out the window at the bright blue sky, the snow-covered mountains, and the main street of Hardy Falls.

Back in Galveston, he'd had a big, modern condo, which he had hardly ever used and sold for a song when he'd moved in with Gail. In a lot of ways, this was better.

Turning, he considered the room again.

This wouldn't be the best place to bring a woman for the night, though. Just the lack of a bathroom would be a deal-breaker.

Mat shook his head, put the glass in the sink.

Obviously, he needed to get some sleep. Sooner or later—probably sooner—he'd hook up with a willing lady for a quickie. But if he was even considering bringing her home with him, he was more tired than he'd thought.

Working quickly, because it was goddamned cold, he toed off his boots and stripped out of his damp clothes before pulling on some sweats and crawling into bed. He turned on his side, nestled under the thick blankets and chilly sheets.

And thought about Josie Kline.

10

When Josie had gotten Jenny to take her back to the Country Time to pick up her car, she'd discovered that Mat had been right—the prospect of food and companionship had brought the townspeople out in droves.

She'd tried to offer to help, but Hannah had been too busy to even talk to her and had basically thrown her out.

Josie guessed she understood. Sometimes when you're frantic, dealing with someone who doesn't know what they're doing is far more trouble than it's worth. She certainly didn't want to increase Hannah's stress level, and most of the regular staff was there, anyway. Even Mat. So she'd let herself get kicked out, worked with Jenny to clean the snow off her car, and gone back home to bed.

That was Saturday. Tuesday night the power had come back on, which was a bit of a minor miracle. Apparently, there'd been upgrades to the grid and blah, blah, blah, or something. Josie wasn't exactly sure, because she'd tuned her mother out when she had tried to explain. But the important thing was that the electric was on, the roads were salted, and Josie was ready to fully implement her plan to help Hannah—whether her friend wanted it or not.

So Wednesday afternoon, rested and energized, she headed out to the Country Time.

It was nice to see activity in town, she thought as she drove through. It was nice to see people walking around, even if they were still bundled up to their eyeballs; nice to see stores open and cars on the road. The kids were disappointed because the official weekend Halloween activities had been canceled, but it was still reassuring to see things returning to normal. She felt closer to everyone somehow, as if they'd all survived a crisis, even though power outages were a common occurrence in these parts.

They'd probably have a few newborns show up next June or July, too. Josie smiled at the thought. She figured you could track storms in Hardy Falls by looking at the jumps in birth rates. After all, what else was there to do in the cold and dark except get particularly friendly with your loved one?

Her smile faded.

She didn't have a loved one. She'd had boyfriends, of course, but they'd never gotten to that level. She'd never been swept away, like Hannah was with Deacon. She'd never fallen so deeply in love that she hadn't been able to climb back out, like June and Calvin.

Maybe it was a Kline family trait. Her father had apparently found it easy to walk away from his family. He sure hadn't looked back when he'd run from his pregnant wife and two small children for the surfing life in California.

Her brother Jordan, who kept track of things, had sent an email to her and Jenny a couple of years ago telling them that Jimmy Kline had been arrested for cooking meth in his basement. Since it was his third strike, he wasn't going to get out of prison for a long time, if ever.

Josie had tried to feel the loss, but he'd taken off before she was even born, so she couldn't quite do it. She didn't know him, and he sure as hell had never tried to get to know her.

She shook her head to dispel the dark thoughts as she pulled into the Country Time parking lot, driving around back to park with the employees' cars. Since she recognized one of the cars as Hannah's, she knew her friend would be inside getting ready to open, just as expected.

It was blessedly quiet when Josie climbed out of the car, the big generator idle. That was a good sign. She glanced at Murphy Lanes and frowned at the sign shaped like a bowling pin, flickering with neon out at the road. There were bright lights in the building and a few cars in the parking lot. Pat was obviously up and running.

Well, hopefully Hannah had gained some traction over the past couple of days.

The Country Time's back door wasn't locked, so Josie walked into the kitchen, then paused to grin at the big man scrubbing the cook top and cursing in Creole.

"Kevin!" she yelled, delighted because she hadn't seen him when she'd stopped in on Saturday night.

Kevin Barbet turned around, a wide grin splitting a round face the color of coffee and wet from the sweat of his efforts.

"Hey, girl." He threw down the scouring pad, stripped off his rubber gloves, and opened his arms for a hug. "I have not cleaned that bitch of a fryer yet, so you can give me a hug, no?"

"Yes!" She landed against his massive chest and wrapped her arms around him as he gave her a big, comforting bear hug. "I'm so glad to see you."

"They tell me you were here." He set her back and frowned at her. "You drive from New York in this storm? That's crazy."

She hunched her shoulders. "It wasn't supposed to be bad."

"Eh." He waved that away. "You know better than to believe the forecasts. When I was a boy, my father was better at guessing the weather than these people now with their fancy computers."

"How are your wife and kids?" Kevin was working three jobs so he could send money to his wife and children in Haiti.

"Fine, fine." He looked wistful for a moment. "We are waiting to get the approval for them to come here. Then maybe we can all be Americans." He shook his head and shot her a grin. "I am hopeful, no?"

Josie squeezed his hand. "Always."

The kitchen door opened and Josie was a little surprised to see Mat stride in. Didn't the man ever go home?

He handed Kevin a knife. "Thanks. The plastic strapping on those crates was a bitch."

Kevin waved it away and pocketed the weapon.

"You carry a knife around with you?" Josie asked. She wasn't sure how she felt about knowing the big, genial man was armed.

"You think I'm gonna hurt my kitchen knives?" He flicked her nose with a finger the size of a sausage. "Always something needs opening or cutting in a kitchen." He went back to the stove and pulled on the thick, yellow rubber gloves he'd been wearing when she'd first come in.

"Hmmm." Josie studied him, then turned to head into the taproom, only to pull up short when she realized Mat was standing in front of her, arms crossed. The position showed off his very well developed biceps and pulled the dark blue Country Time polo shirt he was wearing tight across his shoulders.

"What?" she demanded when he didn't move.

"I'm just wondering why you're here, is all."

Josie crossed her own arms and stuck out her chin.

"I'm here to see my friend, not that it's any of your business."

Kevin made a noise that might have been a chuckle, but

when she turned to glare at him, he was industriously scrubbing the stove top.

Mat didn't seem impressed by her sarcasm.

"She's busy."

"I realize that. I'm not here to chitchat. I'm here to help."

That did elicit a response. He laughed.

"Yeah? Ever work in a restaurant before?"

"No," she said defiantly, "but there are plenty of things I can do."

Mat raised his eyebrows. "Like what?"

"I have absolutely no idea. Now, get out of my way." She shoved him aside, but she knew the only reason he moved was because he wanted to.

As she stomped out of the kitchen, she heard Kevin whistle.

"She told you, no?"

Mat laughed again, and she let the kitchen door slap shut behind her. She wished she could slam it in his face.

She could damn well do *something*. She wasn't useless.

Josie marched past the bar, waved at June, who was doing table setups, and strode down the short hallway to Hannah's office. The door was open, so she walked right in.

Her friend was sitting behind her desk frowning at her clunky, old computer.

"I'm here to help," Josie said abruptly. "Tell me what to do."

Hannah looked up, blinking. "Huh?"

"I told you that I want to help. So I'm here to do it. And don't say no, because you need me."

Hannah settled back and studied her, swiveling her chair a little bit from side to side, which made it squeak ominously.

"What do you want to do?" she asked at last.

Josie dragged her hands through her hair with frustration. "Well, I don't know. Whatever you need. Maybe I can wait tables or work with Kevin in the kitchen."

Hannah quirked her eyebrows. "You've never waited tables in your life."

"No," she admitted. She'd worked her way through college in offices, not restaurants. "But I can do it." She tried to sound more confident than she felt. How did June and the other servers remember who'd ordered what and where they were sitting? Well, she guessed she'd learn.

Hannah sat forward. "How about running the dishwasher? Think you can handle that?"

Josie tried not to pout. After all, she'd just said she'd do whatever it took.

"I can wash dishes," she said reluctantly. She might not like washing them, but she *could* wash them.

"Great!" Hannah clapped her hands together and stood. "Mat needs to be bartender tonight because Deacon's finally down for the count."

"Really?" Josie was instantly concerned. "He hasn't gotten any better?"

"No." Hannah sighed, but she looked worried. "I think he let that goddamned cold get so bad that he got worn down and picked up the stomach bug that's been going around town. I had to make him stay home this morning because he was, um, in the bathroom all night."

"Oh. That's too bad." Josie felt sorry for the big guy.

"And then Grace called to say that she was sick, too. So we're really short staffed today."

"She got it? Poor Gracie." Josie thought of the cheerful young waitress and winced.

"Sounds like it. That crap—oops, sorry—strikes hard and fast. A lot of businesses have been hit in the past couple of weeks, but we'd been lucky. Guess that ran out. At least Mary Alice said she could come in to help June tonight, so we'll have two servers. With Mat handling the bar, we should be okay. If you take care of the dishwasher, I'll be able to help Kevin with food prep or whatever."

Josie frowned at her. "I hope you don't get sick, too."

"Yeah, you and me both. I could feel Deacon's germs crawling over me all night."

Josie took a step back.

"Keep them to yourself."

A sudden pounding on the office door made them both jerk in surprise. Josie spun around and saw Mat standing on the threshold, looking impatient.

"You about finished in here?" he asked abruptly.

Hannah raised her eyebrows at him. "Why?"

"Because nobody locks the freaking doors in this town, and Deacon's brother just came wandering in saying he had to talk to you."

"Sam's here?" Hannah got up and rounded the desk. "What does he want?"

"Like I'd know," Mat grumbled. Then he smirked. "June's trying to find out."

"Oh, God." Hannah shoved him out of her way and hurried out to the taproom.

Mat grinned and went after her.

Josie drew in a deep breath before she followed them. Man, that smile was lethal.

11

Josie walked into the taproom and saw that Mat was behind the bar pouring himself some coffee. Deacon's older brother, Samuel Black, was sitting on a barstool facing Hannah and June, who were both standing with their arms crossed, glaring at him. Sam appeared unfazed.

He glanced her way, and Josie found herself momentarily distracted by his dark blue eyes. Well, Sam had always been considered the pretty brother, with his athletic build and dark, curly hair. But she knew him too well to be fooled.

"Sam," she said.

He nodded. "Josie."

"Why are you here?" Hannah demanded, returning his attention to her.

"Adam was in town to see me about something else, and he wanted me to give you some info he picked up in Las Vegas."

Hannah's eyes widened.

"Who's Adam?" Josie wanted to know, settling down at the end of the bar.

"Did he find George?" Hannah asked at the same time.

Sam shot Josie a look. "Adam Kouris is a private investigator who works with my law firm quite a bit. I put him in touch with Hannah when her money was stolen." He turned back to Hannah. "No, he didn't find George," he said. Josie watched her friend deflate. "He wanted me to tell you that he doesn't think George is in Las Vegas, anymore. Adam was there on other business, but he's still keeping an eye out for him."

"Because he can't believe George got away." Hannah nodded. "I'm so grateful Adam is doing that even though I can't pay him."

"It bugs the ever-living shit out of him that an elderly accountant gave him the slip," Sam said. "But none of his contacts have heard anything, and they've been listening."

"Lot of people in Vegas," Mat pointed out. He was leaning on the bar top, coffee mug cupped in his hands. "And even the grocery stores have slot machines."

"True." Sam shrugged. "And maybe the old guy's lying low. But Adam thinks that if George was still winning, he would have gotten a lead by now—even if he was paying cash for everything."

Hannah slumped onto a barstool. "If he's not in Las Vegas, he could be anywhere."

Josie was surprised when Sam actually looked sympathetic. That was new.

"Maybe," he said. "We think he might be running out of money."

"It wouldn't surprise me." Hannah sounded glum because, of course, most of the money the man would be running out of had been hers.

"Adam wanted me to let you know, in case George doubles back and heads home."

Hannah's spine snapped straight. "He wouldn't dare!"

"He'd better not try," June growled.

"Why would he come back here?" Josie asked.

"It's familiar," Mat said. "Sometimes people want to be

some place familiar, even when it's not the smartest thing to do."

There was a strange note in his voice that she couldn't quite interpret.

Sam shrugged. "It's just a thought. You might want to stay alert in case he tries to contact your aunt."

"Oh, I'll damn well stay alert," June said icily. "And if that bastard comes around Hannah again, he'll find himself missing a few pieces."

"Don't do anything you'll regret," Sam warned, looking a little alarmed.

"I'm pretty sure whatever she does, she won't regret it," Mat told him.

June's grin was all teeth.

Without warning, the kitchen door pushed open and Jenny walked in.

"Hey," she said, strolling over to the bar.

Mat scowled at Hannah. "Seriously. Can anyone in town walk through this place whenever they want?"

Hannah shrugged.

Josie stared at her older sister. "Since when do you have blue streaks in your hair? They weren't there this morning."

"I was bored." Jenny hoisted herself up onto a barstool. She was the shortest of the Kline kids, always calling herself the hobbit in the middle. "Hey, Sam," she greeted Deacon's brother, then turned her attention to Hannah. "I swung by here between houses because I have some news for you."

Hannah threw up her hands. "Jesus Christ, more news? What now?"

Jenny looked surprised.

"Sorry, sorry." Hannah waved it away. "A lot going on."

"Maybe it's good news," Josie pointed out, although she was afraid it wasn't.

"Let's just say it's something she probably needs to know."

Jenny leaned her elbow on the bar and smiled at Mat when he pushed a bottle of water at her. "Did you hear that Missy and I work at Dr. and Mrs. Black's mansion now?" she asked Hannah.

"You do?" Sam frowned. "Since when? I thought they had a service."

Jenny smirked. "They did. Then they didn't."

"Ah." Sam sighed. "Mother."

"You betcha. And since your mom's already been through all the other cleaning services in town, she was desperate enough to pay our asking price. It was either that or vacuum the house herself."

"Yeah, *that's* not going to happen," Sam said with confidence.

"No kidding." Jenny focused on Hannah. "So, Mrs. Black is having a reception for one of her charities tonight, and Missy and I were there this morning doing a final pass through."

"Fascinating," Hannah said dryly.

"You'd be surprised," Jenny said. "Especially since there were lots of extra staff around getting set up—caterers and servers and like that. They were talking, so I listened. "

"Okay," Hannah said slowly, obviously not sure where this was going.

Josie was wondering the same thing.

Jenny leaned forward, eyes intent. "Pat Murphy's grand reopening for the bowling alley restaurant got delayed by a week because of the storm, so he's going to have it Saturday. He's out advertising the new date."

"So?" Josie demanded, wanting to strangle her sister.

"We knew it would be this weekend," June said. "That was his backup date."

Jenny ignored them and remained fixed on Hannah. "Did you hear that he hired a manager for the new restaurant and food service?"

Hannah frowned. "I heard he was going to hire someone. It makes sense."

It did. Based on how he'd been handling the restaurant, Pat needed all the help he could get.

"We haven't seen anyone around," June said. "I figured he hadn't been able to find someone willing to work with him and was too stubborn to postpone his damned reopening."

"He found someone." Jenny reached out to grip Hannah's forearm. "It's Louise."

Sam straightened abruptly on the barstool. "Louise?"

"What?" Hannah barked.

"Louise? He hired our Louise?" Josie tried not to shout, but what the hell? "Our Louise who slept with Sam?"

"They weren't sleeping," June pointed out.

Sam scowled at all of them, his face rigid. Surprisingly, he didn't try to defend himself.

"Why would Louise come back?" Hannah asked hotly. "She left town two years ago."

Jenny shrugged and shook her head. "I guess since Pat's her godfather, she—"

What?

"What?" Hannah screeched the question before Josie could. "Since when is Pat her godfather?"

Jenny looked at her with some confusion. "I guess since she was born?"

"Why the hell didn't I know that?" Hannah yelled.

"Why would you?" Jenny still looked confused. "It's not something that comes up a lot. I didn't even know until the person I was talking to told me." She frowned. "And I'm not sure how she knew."

"We were friends!"

"Louise is going to run Pat's restaurant?" Sam interrupted to ask. His voice sounded strained, as if he was speaking through clenched teeth. "She's staying in town?"

Jenny looked at him.

"Yes," she said carefully. "She's staying. Apparently, the only reason she isn't here now is because she couldn't leave her other job as soon as she wanted to. She's been helping Pat prepare for this reopening thing long distance, then she got delayed by the weather. But she'll be here sometime today to take over operations. One of the servers I met at the Black's is going to be working in the new restaurant, so she was chattering on about all of the plans."

"Excuse me." Sam got up and walked out.

"Should we go after him?" Josie asked. Sam's expression had been strange—flat and tight at the same time.

"He'll be fine," Hannah said absently, not taking her eyes off Jenny. "Louise is really coming back?"

"That's what I heard." Jenny frowned. "Actually, I'm surprised I didn't hear about it before now. Pat's been working on updating the restaurant for weeks, and it sounds like Louise has been involved almost from the beginning, but nobody knew. They really must have wanted to keep it under the radar."

"But why?" Hannah exclaimed in frustration. She got up and walked away, pulling her hands through her hair before turning back. "Why go to the trouble of trying to keep this a secret? It's crazy. You can't keep a secret in freaking Hardy Falls, and everyone's going to find out she's back when the restaurant opens, anyway."

"Pat's playing with you," June said shortly. "He's good at that." She went behind the bar and got a clean shot glass, then poured herself a drink from one of the bottles.

June used to date Pat, but she'd broken up with him before Calvin moved home. Pat had never forgiven her, and he seemed to think that she'd humiliated him in front of the whole town. Maybe she had.

"Did you know that Pat was Louise's godfather?" Josie asked her.

June shrugged. "He never mentioned her."

"What does it matter why they're keeping things secret?" Mat asked practically. "It doesn't change the fact that Pat is competing for business." He was still leaning against the bar near Jenny, close enough that she could reach over and touch him if she wanted to. Josie tried not to be aggravated by that. After all, Mat didn't mean anything to her.

Hannah came striding back, and the expression on her face was as tight as Sam's had been.

"Thanks for coming to tell me all this," she said to Jenny.

"I didn't want you to be blindsided." Jenny shifted. "I wish I'd known about it sooner." She looked at the time on her phone and cursed as she jumped to her feet. "Damnit, I'm late. Sorry."

"Thank you!" Hannah called again, as Jenny hurried out. When the kitchen door slapped shut behind her, Hannah looked at Josie. "I can't believe Louise came back. I can't believe she didn't tell me she was going to."

Josie didn't know why she would expect Louise to confide in her, but she got up and hugged her friend around the shoulders. "How about I go talk to her and find out what's going on?"

"I should—"

"No." Josie squeezed her again. "She won't talk to you. She's probably still pissed off."

"Why should she be angry?" June demanded hotly. "She's the one who slutted around with Hannah's boyfriend in her own damned parking lot."

Josie shook her head, because she didn't have an answer to that. "I'll talk to her," she repeated.

"Okay." Hannah's smile wavered. "Thanks."

June poured another shot and tossed it back.

"Easy there, slugger." Mat tugged the bottle away. "We need you fully functional tonight. Back away from the alcohol."

June snarled at him.

Hannah pointed at the other woman. "Coffee," she said, then turned to Josie. "I can't worry about this now. We have to open, and I have to show you the dishwasher."

"Yay?"

Josie docilely followed Hannah into the kitchen, where she was suited up in an apron and rubber gloves, much to Kevin's obvious amusement.

When Hannah showed her how to run the dishwasher, Josie was relieved to find that, although the thing stood about six feet tall and looked like it would eat her if given the opportunity, it didn't seem to be that hard to work. You just opened the door on one side, pushed in the special dish racks, closed it, pressed a button, and *voila*! She only wished everything in her life was this easy.

Hannah instructed her to thoroughly scrape the dishware, showed her where the chemicals were kept, explained about cleaning the sprayer jets and the drain, then fell silent. She looked nervous.

"What?" Josie demanded, yellow rubber-gloved hands on hips. "I can do this, Hannah."

"I know, but—"

"Besides, Kevin will be here if I have a problem, right?" she asked him as he worked through his checklist. He waved, smile bright.

"I will be here, boss lady," he assured Hannah. "I'll make sure everything is okay, yes?"

Hannah chewed her bottom lip. "Okay. Um, I really could run the dish—"

"Eh!" Josie drew her finger over her throat. "You know as well as I do that you're going to have to be running around tonight. Let me help, Hannah," she said seriously. Having a purpose, any purpose, was already making her feel more like herself.

Besides, it was a *dishwasher*, for Pete's sake. She could run a freaking dishwasher.

Hannah smiled and patted her shoulder. "Sure. You've got this. I'm just being stupid."

Out in the taproom, the music volume went up and they heard the voices of the first customers. Hannah really should open earlier, Josie thought absently. Then she could get the lunch crowd, too.

"Looks like we're starting," Hannah said. "There won't be many dishes for a while. Maybe you can help Kevin for a bit? I have to place a couple of orders, and Sam's visit put me behind."

Josie nodded firmly. "No problem."

"Great." Hannah shot Kevin a look and left the room.

When Josie turned to Kevin, she saw he was studying her like she was a bug under a microscope.

"What should I do first?" she asked, trying to sound confident and in control.

"I thin' you will cut the onions," he said, then grinned widely. "Then maybe I show you how to clean the bitch of a fryer."

Josie nodded with determination.

She could do this.

12

Josie had never realized that a restaurant kitchen was both regimented and completely insane at the same time. She guessed it made sense. If the army, er, kitchen didn't have standard operating procedures, it wouldn't win the war. On the other hand, there was no way of knowing what the enemy, er, customers would throw at you.

Hannah didn't start table service until later in the evening, but food orders started to come in from patrons at the bar almost immediately. While Kevin danced between the grill, the hotdog roller, and the big refrigerator, Josie chopped and cut and sliced and delivered completed orders out to the bar when Mat couldn't come get them.

Once Kevin was satisfied that she wasn't going to kill herself, he gave her a quick lesson on how to run the fryer, and soon she was dunking baskets of sliced potatoes for fries, sending the thick smell of grease and oil billowing into the air to be sucked out by the exhaust fan. As things got busier, he even let her put sandwiches together or help him make different side dishes according to recipes that Hannah had tacked to the workstation.

Dirty dishes were starting to pile up at the dishwasher, but it seemed more important to keep the kitchen running. Where the heck was Hannah? Shouldn't she be here by now? Surely she didn't expect Kevin to handle all of this alone.

The back door opened and Mary Alice Norton walked in, looking like a cheerful dandelion with her flyaway hair tied up in a bright yellow ribbon.

"Oh, hi Josie," she said, a smile lighting up her plain face. Her rather protuberant blue eyes practically beamed with good will. Since Mary Alice had only been there a couple of years—she'd replaced Louise—Josie didn't know her all that well. But she couldn't remember ever seeing the other woman get angry. Anxious, yes. Overwhelmed, certainly. But not angry. Josie had always thought that hiring her had been one of Hannah's better decisions.

"Hi, Mary Alice." She returned the smile. "It's wonderful that you could come in."

"Oh, of course." Mary Alice looked concerned. "I hope Deacon and Grace are okay. I keep telling Gracie that she needs to eat better and take care of herself, but she said that she doesn't have time to eat good food."

"I'm sure she does her best," Josie said diplomatically. On one visit home, she'd gotten into a discussion with Mary Alice about what she considered to be a good diet. Brussels sprouts and broccoli featured prominently.

"I just hope she's getting enough vitamin C." Mary Alice took her purse and her coat to the supply room to hang them up, then hurried out to the taproom.

She was back a few minutes later, tearing a page off an order pad and putting it on the counter.

"We're already starting to get busy," she told them. "I hope it gets even busier. Then tips will be good. Hannah started table service because I'm already here."

"We be ready," Kevin assured her.

"I'd better get back. Old Albert just came in with his friends. They'll want beer." With a swirl of her yellow ribbon, Mary Alice was gone.

"They'll also want burgers," Kevin said and threw a few patties on the grill.

"Don't you have to wait for their orders?" Josie asked.

"*Non*. I know." Kevin picked up the paper Mary Alice had left, read it, and handed it to her. "This one's easy. You can do it."

Josie took the slip from him. Two chicken salad sandwiches. Okay. She went to the refrigerator, pulled out the appropriate plastic container, and took it back to the counter. She read the recipe card carefully, got the appropriate bread, added the appropriate toppings, and scooped out the appropriate amount of chicken salad. Mary Alice came back.

"Is the order up?" she asked.

"Yes." Rushing, Josie dumped on more chicken salad, plated the sandwiches, added the sides, and handed them over.

"These look good." Mary Alice smiled at her and rushed out again.

"I'm thinking you go a little overboard there," Kevin told her.

Josie frowned. "No, I didn't." Hmmm. Well, the contents of the tub did look a lot lower than before. But the amount of chicken salad on the recipe card seemed kind of stingy.

The big man shrugged and flipped the hamburgers, plating them just as Mary Alice came in with some more orders.

"Albert and his friends want their usual," she said to Kevin.

Kevin handed over the burgers. Mary Alice's big eyes got even rounder.

"How do you always know?"

Kevin tapped his temple. "I see things."

Mary Alice shook her head in awe and rushed out of the

kitchen. The door slapped shut behind her, then opened again as Hannah walked in.

"About time," Josie told her.

"I didn't want to interrupt your fun," Hannah said, going to a closet and grabbing one of the chef aprons stacked there.

"Who said it's fun?" Josie argued as she added sides to an order.

"Hah!" Kevin snorted. "Of course it's fun working with me, eh?"

"Well, that part is fun," Josie assured him. She finished what she was doing and put the plate where he could easily add the meat. Hannah, wrapped in the apron, her hair pulled back, stepped up beside her and took the next order away from her.

"I'll handle these. You get with the washing, lackey."

Josie snapped off a salute and marched off to the dishwasher.

Yikes. There sure were a lot of dirty dishes piled up already.

Eying the full bus tubs with some trepidation, she pulled off the thin latex gloves she'd been wearing for food prep, and donned the thick, yellow rubber ones she was supposed to use for this.

"Huh, that's weird," Hannah said behind her.

"What?" she asked, turning.

Hannah held up the plastic container of chicken salad. "We're way down," she said, and shrugged. "Strange. Guess I'll have to make more before we get really busy."

"Yeah," Josie smiled weakly. "Strange." She exchanged a look with Kevin. The big man rolled his eyes before he went back to the grill.

Josie frowned at him. Was it a crime to try to make the customers happy?

Then the second part of Hannah's statement struck her. Wait—*get* really busy? Weren't they already really busy?

She soon discovered that the answer to that question wasn't just no, it was *hell* no.

Things started out well enough. She carefully scraped each plate the way she'd been instructed, went through the pre-rinse process, loaded them into the racks, and pushed the racks into the big stainless steel dishwasher. That was easy enough; she just had to keep an eye on the chemicals. Soon, she felt like she was getting into the groove of the work. Heck, Hannah was even beaming at her like a proud parent.

Then things started picking up. Mary Alice and June twirled in and out through the swinging kitchen door, picking up orders and bringing back empty plates. Hannah and Kevin mamboed around each other in an almost synchronized routine. And Josie just tried to stay ahead of the mountain of used plates, flatware, and glasses.

How did Hannah do this every night? And just how many dishes did the Country Time have, anyway? Would they run out? Would it make the customers angry if the food didn't come on a plate?

Josie started working faster, afraid that if something went wrong, it would be her fault. She still scraped the dishes, just maybe not as well as she had in the beginning. Hey, at home there were nights when they just shoved them in the dishwasher and didn't scrape them at all. This machine was a thousand times bigger, so it had to be a lot more powerful, right?

Okay, maybe she had to put some of the plates through a second time because they came out a little crusty, but it was still faster than taking the time to scrape everything. And *fast* was the word of the evening, she thought, as the dirty plates and glasses kept coming in.

Then she opened the dishwasher door to pull out the latest rack of clean plates, and saw that there was a lot of water in the bottom of the machine. Strange, but maybe in her panic she hadn't noticed before.

Shoving in a new rack, she closed the door, and pushed the button to start it up.

There was some noise, and water sloshed out under the sides.

"Hannah!" she called. Or screamed. Whatever. Hannah jumped to her side, saw the situation, and hit the emergency stop button—which Josie totally could have done if she'd thought of it.

"Crap," Hannah muttered. "Crap, crap, crap." She looked at Josie. "Have you been scraping the food off the dishes?"

"Yes?" Josie chewed on her bottom lip. "Mostly?"

Hannah sighed, long and loud. "You have to get it all off," she said, and Josie could tell she was trying not to lose her temper. "There aren't any magic elves in the machine to do it."

"No." Josie put her hands on her hips and tried to look competent. "But at home it doesn't seem to matter."

"Your home dishwasher runs for forty-five minutes because they know damned right well you won't scrape the plates even though you're supposed to. These restaurant machines are basically just sanitizers."

Josie felt her shoulders slump. "Oh."

"It's okay." Hannah's voice was gentler now. "The drain is clogged. Happens to all of the newbies. We've been busy, so I haven't been paying as much attention to you as I should have."

Because she'd thought she could trust her. Josie slumped further.

"Why don't you take a break?" Hannah said, her attention back on the dishwasher. "I'll get this fixed up and you can start again."

"But you're busy. I can work on the food for a while—" Josie protested.

"Nah. It's under control." Hannah waved her away, already stripping off her latex gloves. "We're in a lull now until the late bowling leagues are finished. Take advantage of it."

Josie pulled off her rubber gloves. "But—"

"Go." Hannah pushed her towards the kitchen door. "If it was warmer, you could get some fresh air, but since it's freaking cold, you'd be better off going to the taproom."

"Okay." Despondent, Josie did what she was told.

In the taproom, most of the tables were full of people wearing bowling shirts, so apparently Pat Murphy hadn't managed to lure the leagues away yet, which was good. She spotted Calvin at the crowded bar watching June, just like he always did. Albert Cromwell and his friends, Harry Newman, Joe Horton, and Martin Scanner, were sitting at a table across the room and laughing, probably at each other.

She managed to find an empty table off to the side and sank down into a chair with her back against the paneled wall. Clasping her hands on the scarred wooden tabletop, she stared down at her fingers, white and wrinkled from the water that had seeped around the cuffs of the gloves, and tried not to feel worthless.

Despite the effort, her thoughts spun rapidly out of control.

You can't even run a stupid dishwasher. How are you ever going to find another real job? You'll never be employed again. They were right to lay you off. Your ideas sucked and this dream of reinventing your life is a joke. You're just fooling—

"Brought you some water." Mat's deep voice interrupted her thoughts. A plastic bottle appeared at her elbow.

God. She was *not* in the mood to deal with attractive, surly bartenders at the moment.

"You should drink it," he said when she didn't move. "It gets hot in the kitchen, and you're probably dehydrated."

Since he was right—damn him—she picked up the bottle, unscrewed the cap, and took a long, long drink of water. It tasted wonderful.

Mat surprised her into looking directly at him when he

pulled out the chair opposite her and sat down, his legs bumping hers under the tiny table.

"What are you doing?" she demanded.

"Sitting, praise baby Jesus." He took a sip from his own water bottle, and she saw a drop of liquid escape to roll down his cheek and throat, slipping under the collar of his polo shirt.

"Aren't you supposed to be tending the bar?" she asked, desperate not to think about the disappearing water droplet and where it might be going because, seriously, she had enough problems.

"June's got it covered."

Beyond him, Josie saw that June was indeed behind the bar. As she watched, the other woman shot Calvin a million watt smile before handing him a glass mug filled with beer from one of the taps.

"Sure hope she pays attention to all the customers, not just her boyfriend," she grumbled.

"Yeah." Mat considered her. "So, what's wrong?"

Josie looked away and toyed with the plastic bottle. "Nothing."

"Bullshit. You're sitting here looking like somebody ran over your puppy."

"I'm on a break." A forced break, but a break nonetheless.

"Right." He didn't sound like he believed her. "You might as well just tell me."

She was quiet for another moment, then sighed. He'd find out, anyway.

"I sort of broke the dishwasher," she admitted as she met his eyes again.

He looked surprised. "Already? That was fast. What did you do? Does it still run?"

"Hey! What do you mean, 'already'?" she snapped. "For your information, it still runs but there's water all over the place."

"Oh." He relaxed back into his chair. "Okay. For a minute I thought it was something serious."

Josie scowled at him. "Didn't you hear me say there was water everywhere?"

"You probably just clogged the drain. Didn't scrape the dishes, did you?"

"I scraped them!" she defended herself.

"Obviously not well enough." He shrugged. "It's no big deal. Once the drain gets cleaned out, you'll be good to go."

"Still." She felt her scowl morph into a pout and hunched her shoulders. "I should be able to do the damned dishes without making more work for Hannah. I feel like a moron."

Mat cocked his head. "Then why stay?" he asked curiously.

"Huh?" Josie blinked at him, honestly confused.

"I mean, this isn't your job, so why not leave it to the people who actually work here?"

She straightened. "You think I'd cut and run out on Hannah like that?"

"Why not? You could. There's nothing keeping you here." Mat, apparently oblivious to the dangerous ground he was treading, waved a hand. "Hannah would understand."

"She needs help," Josie argued.

"That's why she pays the rest of us the big money." He grinned. "And we won't blow anything up."

Oh really?

Josie knew she was being a little over-sensitive, but that smile, charming as it was, just pissed her the hell off. So she'd never worked in a kitchen before. Sue her.

As exhaustion gave way to bubbling temper, she pushed to her feet.

"Hannah's been my friend since forever and I'm going to help her," she informed him haughtily. "I might not do everything right, but I'll do what I can."

He had the nerve to laugh. "Like what? Break something else?"

Asshole!

"You know what? Go to hell," Josie invited, then skirted around the table and stomped back to the kitchen and the goddamned dishwasher.

She would do the hell out of those dishes. She would do the dishes better than anybody had done dishes in the history of the world. She would scrape the plates so clean they sparkled *before* they were washed. She would be helpful if it freaking killed her.

And Mat Guerrero could suck it.

What had just happened?

Frowning, Mat watched Josie march over to the kitchen door and shove it open with such force that it slapped back and forth a few times after she went through.

Still puzzled, he drained his bottle of water, then took it and the one Josie had abandoned to the bar and tossed them into the recycling bin.

"What was that about?" June asked, moving past him with some mugs of beer.

"I have no idea."

He'd only been trying to be friendly, for Christ's sake. Maybe make Josie feel a little better, since she'd looked upset. He had no idea what he'd done to make her so angry.

Besides, what he'd said was true. Josie didn't work here, and if running the damned dishwasher was going to be this fucking traumatic for her, then she shouldn't bother. If she is making more work and breaking stuff, she should leave. Hannah sure didn't need the extra stress and he, personally, didn't need Josie Kline invading his personal space.

Thinking about the woman getting pissed off for no reason was pissing *him* off, so he told June he had the bar again and threw himself into the work. Unfortunately, it didn't help his mood much.

"Where's your ID?" he snarled at a kid who sat down on a barstool across from him.

The kid raised his hands and slid back off the barstool.

Mat drew in a deep breath and tried to pull himself together. Scaring off the customers was bad.

Forcing a smile, he drew a beer from the tap and pushed it to another guy he recognized as a regular.

The guy raised his eyebrows, took his beer, and headed to a table, even though he usually stayed at the bar. Mat had a feeling his smile wasn't much better than his snarl.

Why had he bothered to talk to Josie, anyway? Hadn't he decided to stay away from her as much as possible? She was tempting, that was for sure, but she definitely wasn't for him.

Complications.

Except, he thought as he frowned at the drink he was mixing, she'd looked so sad as she sat alone at that little table.

No, he corrected himself, she'd looked defeated.

He didn't know her very well, but he would have thought nothing could defeat her. Confuse her, yes. Defeat her, no.

Mat handed Ms. Gregory the White Russian he'd prepared and ignored her interested stare.

And yet, even though Josie didn't have to, she was staying. She was determined to help her friend.

Thoughtful now, he got together some drink orders for Mary Alice.

Josie wasn't running away.

There was a lot to be said for that.

13

They lost Hannah around ten o'clock.

Josie was at the dishwasher, pushing in and pulling out racks of dishes and glassware without incident—thank you very much—when she heard her friend groan. She turned to see Hannah, hands clasped on her stomach, rush out of the room. Concerned, she ran after her. Hannah rushed into the ladies' room and practically launched herself into one of the stalls.

It was not...pleasant.

Josie told June what was going on, and June called Deacon. He was there fifteen minutes later, pale and wild-eyed. Five minutes after that, he escorted a shivering, weak, yet still protesting Hannah out to his SUV.

Josie was glad to see them go. They could keep that stomach bug to themselves.

Unfortunately, just around eleven, she realized they hadn't. Mary Alice came into the kitchen, threw down some food orders, and raced for the bathroom. Thank God Mary Alice's boyfriend, Johnny, had been at the bar and was able to take her home.

And then there were four.

Yikes.

Suddenly, Josie didn't have to worry about fighting for the opportunity to help out.

Somehow they made it through the rest of the shift and, although Josie couldn't do much, she did feel like she made a contribution. June must have agreed, because her lean face brightened when Josie told her she'd be in the next day. Of course, since Deacon was taking care of Hannah, Mary Alice was out, Grace probably couldn't work a whole shift, Kevin had to be at one of his other jobs, and there wasn't any money to hire temporary staff, June would have been relieved if a hedgehog had agreed to show up.

Josie was finally able to go home around one in the morning, and, after crawling upstairs on feet that felt like they were screaming, slept the sleep of the dead until noon the next day.

When she finally woke, she blinked at the ceiling for a moment then, groaning, pushed herself up into a sitting position.

"Ow."

Every muscle in her body ached. How in the *hell* did Hannah do this every day?

Hauling herself out of bed, she shuffled to the bathroom, drew a tub of hot water, and soaked until it got cold. She felt better when she got out. That was encouraging. Maybe she wasn't old after all.

In a cheerier frame of mind, she got dressed and headed down to the kitchen for some coffee and maybe something to eat.

Would she get shredded with muscle if she kept going to help at the Country Time? Maybe develop abs?

Josie patted her stomach. She had abs. They were just politely hiding from prying eyes.

When she walked into the kitchen, she saw Jenny had

made a pot of coffee and was sitting at the table drinking
deeply from a thick mug. Jenny's presence was a little surprising, but her sister didn't clean houses every day. Most likely she
was taking time to work in her tiny art studio/shed in the
backyard.

"Hey," Josie called as she went to grab a mug for herself.

"Hey," Jenny responded, grinning at her. "How are you
today?"

Josie turned. "What do you mean?"

"I mean you haven't exactly done this kind of work before,
so you're probably sore."

"Nope," Josie lied and flexed her biceps at her sister. "Grrr. I
am mighty and powerful."

"Yeah right, nerd-girl."

"Nerds can be fit," Josie protested, and poured herself some
coffee. "I used to walk on a treadmill desk all the time."

"Sure." Jenny snorted. "Treadmill."

Josie frowned as she put creamer in the coffee and stirred.
"Everybody thinks I'm a wimp." She glared at her sister. "I'm
not even thirty, for heaven's sake."

Jenny shrugged. "Standing on your feet all night working in
a restaurant is hard. You're not used to it."

Josie scowled. "And you are?"

"Well, duh." Jenny looked at her like she was crazy. "I
worked at the diner, remember? And now I clean houses for a
living."

Oh. Right.

"Trust me, sometimes cleaning can put kitchen work to
shame." Jenny sighed and drank her coffee. "Especially when
you work for Mrs. Black. That woman had us running around
like nuts yesterday, and we were just supposed to be doing a
quick walk-through before her party."

Josie took her mug over to the kitchen table and sat down
across from her sister.

"Why do you do it?" she asked, genuinely interested. "You don't have to keep cleaning houses. You could do anything."

"Yeah? Like what? Work at the Wal-Mart?" Jenny snorted.

"But you've taken a lot of courses."

"At the art studio in town, sure. They qualify me for a job exactly like what I'm doing." Jenny shrugged. "This is a decision I made, Josie, and I'm happy. Having this job lets me set my own hours and do my own work. If Stefan had stuck, then…" She trailed off and looked away for a moment. "Well, maybe my life isn't exactly perfect, but it's my life, isn't it?"

Josie knew her sister wanted to be an artist. *Was* an artist. Some of her pieces, especially her oil paintings, were almost magical. She definitely had a gift. Still…

"Is it worth it?" Josie asked. "You're still young. You could go to school, get a degree, and get a different job. Is it worth it to keep trying to do the whole art thing when it never seems to get you anywhere?"

Jenny didn't answer. Instead, she took her mug to the sink, rinsed it out, and put it in the dishwasher. Then she turned and faced her.

"Yes," she said simply, and left the room.

"Great." Josie sighed because she could tell her sister had been hurt by the question. But Josie honestly didn't understand why Jenny kept pushing. She was, what, thirty-two? She wasn't getting any younger and she was smart. Did she want to clean houses her whole life?

Was it any of Josie's business if she did?

Man, families were hard sometimes.

"Might as well go on in to the Country Time," she muttered. "Maybe I can screw up there, too."

After grabbing something to eat, Josie drove back across town. When she got to the Country Time, she was relieved to see June's car already sitting behind the building. June would tell her what to do.

She parked and went inside, finding June in the kitchen, her long dark hair pulled into a tight ponytail. The thick, yellow rubber gloves she wore were a striking contrast to her bright blue cowboy boots.

How the hell did the woman wear cowboy boots while working in the kitchen? Josie had been seriously considering bringing in a pair of fuzzy slippers.

"I'm here," she called, as she shut the door against the cold wind.

June spun around, then let out a breath.

"Holy shit, you scared the crap out of me!"

Confused, Josie frowned and pointed at the door. "Didn't you hear me?"

"I was thinking."

Based on her expression, the thoughts were not good.

Josie spread her arms. "Well, I'm ready to help," she said. "What do you want me to do?"

Now June scowled at her. "I have no freaking idea."

So much for direction.

"Okay...what are *you* doing then?" she asked. Maybe she could help with that.

"Everything!" June waved her hands around. "I'm trying to get the kitchen clean and food prep started, then I have to go out and get things set up in the taproom. Mat will be in soon to take care of the bar, thank Christ, but I'm not sure Grace will make it in at all. If she doesn't, there won't be anybody to wait tables, and then—"

"Hey, hey." Alarmed, Josie stepped up to the older woman and grabbed her shoulder. "Calm down. I've never seen you like this before."

It was true. The unflappable June was seriously flapped. In fact, Josie was horrified to see tears swimming in the other woman's big dark eyes.

"What the hell's wrong?" She was seriously freaked out now.

"Nothing, nothing. Shit." June pulled away and yanked off the rubber gloves. She got a tissue from the box on the shelf behind her and blew her nose before turning back. "Deacon had to take Hannah to the emergency room this morning."

"He did?" Josie grabbed both of June's arms. "What happened? How is she? Why didn't anyone call me?"

"She's fine." June reached up and squeezed one of Josie's hands. "The bug slammed her hard—way worse than Deacon—and the doctor thinks she was really dehydrated. They pumped her full of fluids and gave her some mega-strength medicine to hopefully settle her stomach. She's still there, but he said she's going to be released soon."

"Thank God!" Josie's head was spinning. She let go of June to rake her hands through her hair. "Why didn't they call me?"

"They didn't call me either." June's smile was sharp " I let Deacon know I was less than pleased with that decision. Apparently, the stupid twits didn't want to worry us." Another hard grin. "As if we wouldn't worry anyway."

"We need to go to the hospital."

"No." June grabbed her. "Hannah will be fine. She just needs some rest. And we need to keep her business open tonight because she can't afford to let freaking Pat Murphy get the upper hand."

"But—"

"Do you think I wouldn't close this dump in a heartbeat if she was in bad shape? Trust me, it's under control."

"Okay," Josie said reluctantly. She didn't like it, but June had a point.

"Okay." June dropped her hands and turned away, toying with the rubber gloves lying on the sink counter. "And...Calvin was throwing up this morning, too. He had to stay home from work."

"Oh, geez." The hellacious stomach virus had claimed another victim. "I hope he's okay."

June jerked her shoulder. "He's strong." She bent her head. "He's strong," she repeated, more quietly.

"He'll be fine. It just has to run its course." Wanting to offer comfort, Josie stepped up behind her and patted her on the back. "Sounds like it's working its way through everyone in town. Hannah was run down, so it hit her harder."

"I guess." June didn't look entirely comforted, but she did manage a real smile. "And the good news is Calvin will be staying with me until it blows through. He can't risk passing it to his mother."

Josie wasn't sure why June seemed happy about sharing her space with a man who was bound to require the bathroom, um, frequently over the next day or two. On the other hand, she reflected, it must be hard to be as in love as June and Calvin obviously were, and not be able to spend every spare minute together.

"Can I help you clean in here?" she asked.

June shook herself and looked around the kitchen. "I think I'm finished. I was going to start on the food prep for tonight."

"I can chop stuff up," Josie insisted. "Kevin said I did a good job. Tell me what to do."

"Hmmm." June eyed her, then shrugged. "Okay, well, we need more of some of the salads for the sides and sandwiches, so maybe you can start on them while I go deal with a few other things."

Josie was beginning to have second thoughts. After all, last night she'd been working under Kevin's supervision. "Um, is that anything I could do instead?"

"I can do it a lot faster than I can explain it to you, and there are instructions for all the food prep. I'll only be gone a couple of minutes." But June looked uncertain.

"Okay." Josie said, careful to keep her voice confident. If this was what June needed, she'd handle it.

June got her set up with an apron and the instructions for the items they needed to make before they opened. Chicken salad, tuna salad, coleslaw, and pasta salad. Okay. Easy.

"Just follow the directions," June said, still looking a little worried. "Don't try anything freestyle. And call me if you run into trouble. I'll be around."

"I have cooked before," Josie told her, a little offended by the lack of faith.

"We don't have time to chuck a batch of chicken salad and remake it if you put in too much salt," the other woman retorted. "Just...come get me if you need help."

"I'll be fine," Josie insisted.

June hesitated, then nodded and left.

After she'd gone, Josie drew in a deep breath and let it out slowly.

"I'm such a liar," she told the room, then pulled out one of the instruction cards.

She wanted to call Hannah to see how she was doing, but didn't want to bother her if she was getting some rest. Taking out her phone, she texted Deacon instead, telling him that she was thinking about them and warning him that they'd better never keep this kind of thing from her again.

Almost immediately, she got a response.

H is resting, he wrote. *All is well. June already handed me my butt.*

Josie smirked, because she could just imagine.

June knows best, she replied, then sent him a heart emoji. *Get rest. Under control here.*

He sent back one word: *Shudder.* Then followed it with a smiley face.

Josie smiled when she saw it. She really wanted to go to the hospital to be with them, but Hannah and Deacon needed her here more.

So for now, she'd concentrate on keeping Hannah's business alive.

With a renewed sense of purpose, she picked up one of the index cards June had left for her and, working carefully, started chopping and mixing and stirring. Eventually she ended up with a large bowl of something she dearly hoped at least resembled chicken salad. Hesitantly, she tasted the mixture, then let out a sigh of relief when it seemed okay.

After offloading the chicken salad into sealed containers June had pointed out earlier and storing them in the refrigerator, she started on the macaroni salad. The macaroni had to cook and cool before she could go further, so Josie figured she'd get that part started, and then work on the tuna salad or coleslaw while she waited.

Although taking this step into multitasking made her a little nervous, she found the pan for the pasta and filled it with water. While it was heating, she started gathering the ingredients for the coleslaw.

It became quickly apparent that Hannah's industrial stove heated up a lot more quickly than the one they had at home, and the water was boiling before she'd had a chance to do more than track down the cabbage. Well, that was good. It meant she'd be done sooner than she thought. And wouldn't June be happy to have a few things off her plate? So to speak.

Humming, because she was feeling kind of pleased with herself, Josie dumped the box of macaroni into the boiling water, waited for it boil again, and turned down the heat before returning to the coleslaw prep. She was contemplating the ingredients list when she heard a loud sizzling noise. Whirling around, she found a torrent of yeasty-smelling foam boiling over the top of the macaroni pan and pouring straight into

June's clean burner. She must not have turned the heat down far enough.

"Oh, crap, crap, crap." Springing for the pan, she grabbed the handle to pull it off the burner, just as the back door banged open.

Yelping, Josie whirled again and before she could stop, basically threw a pot of macaroni and very hot, if not boiling, water at Mat as he walked into the kitchen. Fortunately for him, he was far enough away that he didn't get caught by the brunt of it.

"Shit!" he yelled, jumping backwards.

"Oh, God!" Josie cried, horrified, and leapt towards him. She slipped, almost went down, then managed to right herself as she reached him. But because she was still holding the pan, she hit him on the arm with it.

"Ow! Christ!" he bellowed, getting out of her way.

The man could move, that was for sure.

Josie had enough time for that thought before her feet went out from under her. She landed on her ass, managing to twist at the last minute so she sat on the linoleum and not in the middle of a pile of very hot, partially cooked macaroni.

14

"**G**oddamnit, woman!" Mat yelled. "What the hell!"

"What's going on in here?" June shouted, barreling through the kitchen door. She skidded to a stop when she saw Josie on the floor. "Are you okay? What happened?"

Josie ignored her. "Are you burned?" she demanded of Mat, tossing the pan aside and getting to her knees. "Did I hurt you?"

"Not for lack of trying," he growled, turning to close the door, then pulling off his gloves and helping haul her to her feet. "At least you weren't aiming at my face." He looked down at his jacket and plucked off some soggy macaroni before unzipping it.

"You startled me," Josie said, defensive now that she knew he was okay. She folded her arms over her chest, wincing when one of her hands rubbed against the fabric of the apron. It hurt like a son of a bitch, but she'd deal with that in a minute.

"I was coming in to work," Mat pointed out. "Because *I* actually work here. How the hell was I supposed to know I'd get attacked as soon as I walked in the door?" He took off his wet coat and hung it over a kitchen stool.

"It was an accident!" Josie shouted at him.

He shrugged.

"It might have been an accident," June said, interrupting Josie before she could say anything else, "but it sure made a mess."

"I know! I know! I'll clean it up!" Josie gestured wildly and her sore hand bumped against a counter top. "Ouch! Shit!" Crap, that hurt.

June's face snapped into a scowl. "What is it?"

Mat got to Josie before June could, and took her hand in both of his to look at it. He frowned.

"You didn't burn me, you burned yourself," he accused.

"Because that's the way my freaking luck works," Josie grumbled, trying without success to pull away. "I throw a pot of hot water at you, and I'm the one who gets hurt." Although, honestly, she was glad her stupidity hadn't injured someone else.

"It looks like it's only first degree." Mat transferred his glare to her face. "Did you burn yourself anywhere else?" He grabbed her other hand to study it. "How about your legs when you fell?"

"I'm fine. I'm wearing jeans and I missed most of the water." She tried to move away again, but he tugged her over to the sink and ran the water.

"What are you doing?" she demanded. "It's nothing. Ow!" she squeaked when he put her burned hand under the cold water.

"It's not too bad," June said, pulling her hand out of the water so she could see it before putting it back. Between the two of them, Josie was beginning to feel like a puppet. Or a family pet.

"I told you," she said to Mat.

He scowled at her, his eyes dark brown under the slash of his brows.

"Just keep it under the water," he told her.

"Sit. Stay. Good dog," Josie muttered, but she kept her hand where it was because the icy water was indeed helping.

"We have some cream for minor burns," June told her. "But it's still going to hurt like hell. You might not be able to run the dishwasher tonight."

"No, I can do it," Josie insisted. "I'll be wearing gloves."

"Chemicals are not your friends at the moment."

"Maybe I can make sandwiches or something, then." She had to do something.

"We'll work it out." June looked around the kitchen. "First, I'd better clean up this mess."

Josie started to move, but Mat shoved her hand under the water again.

"Not long enough," he snarled. "Would you just keep the damn thing there?"

"I'm fine!" she snapped back. "I've hurt myself way worse than this before."

"If you don't stay there, I'll hurt you way worse right now," June told her.

Because she was afraid she meant it, Josie stayed put while June skirted the puddle of steaming macaroni and headed for the cleaning supply closet. Josie winced as she watched her pull out a mop and a rolling bucket.

"June, this is my fault. I'll just—"

"I said I'd do it." June dragged the rolling bucket closer to the spill. "Just get out of my way and go sit down or something. Mat can bring you a wet rag and that cream we use for burns."

"But—"

"Go."

Josie saw the determination in her face and knew she was wasting her time.

"Fine." She turned off the water and pushed through the door into the taproom.

Mat followed a moment later, carrying a tube of something and a bottle of pain relievers. He put the tube on the bar, then handed her some water and a few of the pills.

"Ibuprofen," he said. "You'd better take some."

She'd never admit it, but her hand really did hurt where the red burn had spread across the back of it. Ibuprofen seemed like a good idea, so she complied. After she'd taken the medicine, he handed her a clean bar rag that he'd run under cold water.

"Wrap your hand in this for a while."

Reluctantly, Josie took it from him and did as instructed.

"I need to help June clean," she protested. "I know you think I'm an idiot, but I'm not going to stick her with all that extra work."

He looked gratifyingly surprised. "What the hell are you talking about? I don't think you're an idiot."

"But yesterday—"

"For God's sake, woman. I was just trying to help. You didn't have to stay yesterday." He smiled a little. "Today you do. We need all the help we can get."

Josie frowned, trying to see if there was a dig buried somewhere in that comment. Mat ignored her and pulled a laminated piece of paper out from under the bar.

"Just let June do her thing, and don't argue," he said as he glanced over it.

"I don't argue," Josie muttered.

Mat laughed as he put the paper away. "Right."

For a moment, Josie watched him move around behind the bar, going from task to task with assurance.

"What are you doing?" she asked finally.

"Opening checklist." He didn't even look at her.

"Oh." Josie ran her finger over the bar top. "Hannah's really organized."

"Yeah," he said absently as he bent down, presumably to

check supplies. "It's like I'm back in the army with all the SOPs."

"I thought the kitchen was like the army, too," Josie said, delighted to be right about something.

"Yup. There are standard operating procedures for everything." Mat stood from his crouched position and grinned. "Well, not for when a woman throws boiling water on you, of course."

Josie felt her face flush.

"Sorry."

"Not the worst thing that's ever happened to me," he said casually, and continued what he was doing.

She wondered about that. "You were in the army?" she asked. "Did you serve with Deacon?"

"No." He pulled out a pocket knife, slit open a box he'd gotten out of the cabinet, and started stacking paper napkins under the bar. "I didn't meet Deacon until we were working together on the oil rigs in the Gulf."

"Oh." She thought about everything she knew about oil rigs in the Gulf of Mexico and realized it wasn't much. Well, except for that horrible oil spill they'd had a couple of years ago. "Where were you? Off the coast of Louisiana?" She thought that sounded pretty smart, but honestly she only knew it because of all the news coverage of the spill.

"Texas," he said shortly, still not looking at her. "Off the shore of Galveston."

"What did you do?" she asked, and leaned on the bar as he straightened.

"I'd been working there a while, so I was Engine Responsible," he said. "Deacon came on as a Motorman."

"That means nothing to me," she assured him.

He finally glanced at her and grinned, moving to the cash drawer. "Basically, we just watched the engines with various degrees of intensity."

Josie thought about it. "It must be hard to get a job on the Gulf of Mexico," she said. "There must be a lot of people who want to work there."

He shrugged. "Yeah, but not as many as you might think. It's tough. You're on the rig for weeks at a time, so you're isolated. You lose touch with people back on the mainland. Then there's the weather..." His hands stilled from sorting money, and he looked off into the distance. "You haven't done anything until you've made it through a tropical storm out on an oil rig." He looked at her, shrugged, and went back to counting. "A lot of guys can't take it."

"I guess." She cocked her head. He was holding something back, but she couldn't imagine why. "Did you start working there after you left the army?"

He nodded abruptly. "I was in for a while. When I decided to leave, I just couldn't stand the sand anymore. I wanted something with water." His grin was ironic. "I got my wish."

"And they hired you because of your military experience?"

Mat was silent for a long moment. "And my family knew people," he said finally.

The kitchen door pushed open and June strode into the room.

"Enough chit-chat," she said to Josie. "We need to get moving. How's the hand?"

"Okay." Josie peeled back the bar rag. The skin on her hand was pink and tender, but at least it was the back of her hand and not her palm. She wiggled her fingers experimentally. "I'm fine."

"Hmmm." June looked doubtful. "Well, I just spoke to Grace. She's definitely coming in, but it won't be until a little later because she has to make up a test. I sent Jenny a text to see if she could help out, but she and Missy are working at another party the Blacks are giving. God knows why." June shook her head. "I don't think we'll be able to have table service."

Josie stiffened. "I can—"

"You've never waited tables and it's going to be busy tonight, hope to God. You'll need help."

"Then I'll work in the kitchen and you can handle the tables."

"You'll be too slow." June drew her hands down her face. "I don't know what to do," she admitted. "And my mind is fucked because I keep thinking about Hannah and Calvin."

Such vulnerability was so rare for the other woman that Josie couldn't think of anything to say.

"I've got an idea," Mat said. "You know Old Albert's friend, Martin Scanner, used to be a bartender, right?"

June scowled. "No."

"Well he was, and he still is sometimes over at the VFW."

"Are you suggesting he come in and bartend? He can't handle a busy bar by himself."

"Why not?" Mat asked. "It won't matter anyway, because you know Albert, Joe, and Harry will all be right back here helping him. They'll love playing bartender for the night."

"Hannah can't afford to pay them."

"She can't afford to lose business either. If they're willing, you can handle table service and be out here in case they run into problems. I'll take over the kitchen."

June's eyebrows raised. "You cook?"

"I've done my share. I actually like being in the kitchen, and Josie can help me unless it's too painful." He shrugged. "That way, we can keep it going until Grace comes in."

June frowned thoughtfully. "Okay," she said at last. "I'll call Martin, and we'll see how it goes. But," she added looking at Josie, "you don't do anything that will make your hand worse."

Josie rolled her eyes. "You know, it's just burned, not falling off. It's not even blistering."

"First, you may think that burn isn't anything, but it's going to hurt like hell in latex gloves and water. You can trust me on that. I'm just trying to spare you. Second, you don't have blisters now but you might develop them, and I don't want them popping or anything.

"But—"

"Put the cream on it. Then I need you to run an inventory of the nonperishable supplies." June went around the bar and got a clipboard from underneath. "Here's the list."

Josie stuck out her bottom lip.

"Inventory?"

"It needs to be done, too. Nobody's had time to run one for over a week and we'll be in trouble if we run out of something," June pointed out. "We have to place orders with enough lead time to actually get the crap. There are a ton of things you can do to help that don't involve the kitchen."

"Oh."

"After that, you can start putting together the table setups. Come get me when you're finished with the inventory." June frowned. "I was going to have you clean the bathrooms, goddamnit, but not with a burned hand."

Josie batted her eyes. "Shucks."

"Bitch."

"Since Josie's doing the inventory, I can do the bathrooms after I finish my list," Mat volunteered.

Josie gawked at him. "You clean bathrooms?" Big, sexy, Mat Guerrero cleaning a toilet was hard to imagine.

"Of course I clean the bathrooms." He frowned at her. "We all take turns."

June cackled. "Yeah, and it's my week, so I lucked out." Her grin morphed into a scowl. "Or maybe not because I'll have to do all the food prep."

"I really will be able to help with that," Josie assured her. "My hand hardly hurts at all."

"You might get the opportunity." June sighed. "Come get me if you need me." She turned and walked back into the kitchen.

"Okay," Josie said. She grabbed the tube of cream Mat had brought out earlier. Fumbling, she tried to pop the cap, but the tube was new, so it stuck.

"Let me help." Mat took the tube from her, popped the cap, and squeezed some of the cream onto his fingers. "Give me your hand," he said.

Josie complied, and he enveloped her burned hand in the warmth of his for a second before smearing the cream onto the pink skin.

"We need to rub it in," he said, his voice low and gruff as he massaged the back of her hand.

The soothing motion of his fingers was intimate, and Josie's mouth went dry. His hand was so much bigger than hers, hardened by years of hard work. They were skin to skin, and she couldn't think of a single thing to say. Mat frowned down at her hand with fierce concentration, his dark hair falling over his forehead in a way that made her want to brush it back.

Finally he straightened and dropped her hand like he was the one who'd been burned.

"Okay," he said.

She blinked at him, not entirely sure what he was talking about for a second. Then she realized she was staring at him like an idiot and felt her face flush.

"Gotta go," she croaked. Grabbing the clipboard June had left, she made a beeline for the supply room.

Once inside, she closed the door behind her and leaned back against it, resting her head on the cool wood.

"God, you're a moron." She rubbed her hands over her face, feeling the slickness of the cream soothing the bite of the burn.

First, she'd hurt herself so she couldn't do as much as she'd wanted to, and then she'd mooned over Mat like she was a silly schoolgirl. He was probably behind the bar laughing at her right now.

"Grow up." She smacked herself on the face with her burned hand. "Ouch. Crap."

Taking the clipboard, she walked to the back of the closet and began counting boxes of napkins. She stopped when she realized she'd counted the same boxes twice.

Sighing, she started again.

15

———

It was a crazy night. Martin, Albert, and the rest of the crew showed up around four in the afternoon, eager to lend a hand at the bar. Once they were set up, June stayed in the taproom and Mat moved to the kitchen.

Josie's burned hand was sore, but at least it hadn't blistered. Even so, the gloves were painful. So instead of doing dishes or helping with food prep, she made herself useful by carrying orders out to the taproom, bussing the dirty dishes, and basically being a lackey.

Once Grace came in, June taught Albert how to use the dishwasher. The old man seemed to have a ball running the big machine, working his way through the plates and glassware that had been piling up. Josie couldn't help but notice that the water did not overflow.

June sprang her around midnight. Unable to think of a good reason to stay, Josie headed home, churning with a strange combination of adrenaline, exhaustion, and depression.

She pulled her car into the driveway and parked next to the town-issued SUV her mother drove. There was no sign of

Jenny's little truck, so she assumed her sister was still working at the Blacks. She bet Jenny hadn't burned *her* hand on partially cooked macaroni

Sighing, she got out of the car.

Josie had expected her mother to be asleep, so she was surprised to see a light in the kitchen when she let herself into the house. Walking to it, she found Jackie sitting at the table drinking something she was pretty sure wasn't soda.

"Hi, Mom," she said, going over to kiss her on the cheek. "Busy day?"

"You have no idea." Jackie arched her eyebrows. "You look a little...frazzled."

"Everybody at the Country Time is sick with a stomach bug, so tonight was interesting. Thank God June is still okay." And Mat, but she didn't add that.

"I heard Deacon had to take Hannah to the hospital," her mother said, sipping.

"Yeah." Josie wasn't surprised Jackie already knew what was going on. The police chief of Hardy Falls kept up with her community.

Realizing she was thirsty, she went to the refrigerator and grabbed a bottle of water. "So Jenny's not home?" she asked, twisting off the cap and taking a long drink.

"Not yet." Despite the alcohol, Jackie's eyes were sharp. "What's wrong with your hand?"

"What?" Josie looked down and realized she was cradling her hurt hand against her chest. "Oh, nothing. I just burned it."

Jackie gestured. "Let's see."

Rolling her eyes, Josie went to the table and let her mother examine the burn.

"It looks like it's not too bad, but put some antiseptic cream on it before you go to bed."

"Yes ma'am." Josie pulled her hand back and took another

drink of water, pausing when she saw her mother was still watching her.

Uh-oh.

"I wanted to talk to you," Jackie said.

Uh-oh.

Josie took her time lowering the bottle. "Okay," she said cautiously.

"Oh, don't give me that look. We haven't had a chance to talk too much, and I was wondering if you've been thinking about what you're going to do next."

Josie hunched her shoulders. "It's only been a couple of days," she muttered.

"I know, but you can't wait too long before you start looking for another job. I don't want you to get so sidetracked with Hannah's problems that you forget about your own."

"I won't. I know I need to work," Josie said. Maybe the Country Time, with all of its issues—not to mention its very attractive dishwasher/bartender/cook—was a distraction, but she certainly had not forgotten that she was unemployed. "I'm going to start next week, after Hannah's back on her feet."

Just saying it made her tired. She hated looking for a job, which was one reason why she'd kept the last one so long.

"All right." Jackie pushed herself to her feet and took her empty glass to the sink, then turned and ran her fingers through her short cap of still-black hair. "I know you love Hannah. So do I. I know you want to help her. And maybe you just want to be doing something to take your mind off your situation."

Her mother knew her very well.

"But I worry." Jackie walked over and kissed her forehead. "That's kind of *my* job."

Oh, geez.

"I'll find something," Josie promised. "And I have savings and severance, you know. I'll be fine." *For now.*

"I know you will." Jackie sighed. "I wish I could have afforded to send you all to college, then you and Jordan wouldn't be saddled with student loan debt. I don't always agree with Jenny's choices, but at least she didn't have to deal with that."

Despite the fact that Josie and Jordan had worked the whole way through college, they'd both still ended up with sizable loans. Josie suspected Jordan had paid his off early, but he was an investment banker and making a heck of a lot more money than she ever would.

"Mom, it will be fine." She tried to sound positive, even though the reminder of her student loans, for which her mother had co-signed, made her slightly queasy. "There are tons of jobs out there. I'll find one."

"I don't want you to think I'm pushing you to leave. I'm not. You can stay here forever if you want to." Her mother's mouth twisted. "I'll hate it if you end up back in Manhattan."

"I know." But Josie also knew that's probably what would happen. All of her contacts were in the city.

For some reason, she found the thought of leaving the mountains to go back to the hustle of urban life very depressing. Maybe she could find something closer to home, like in Scranton or Allentown.

Jackie sighed. "I just want you to be happy and healthy and successful."

"Is that all?" Josie teased. "How about rich?"

"I guess rich is nice, but I sure don't have any personal experience with it, so I'll settle for the rest." Jackie yawned widely.

Josie laughed. "I think it's time you said good night."

"I suppose." Her mother yawned again. "Will you be going in to the Country Time again tomorrow?"

Josie nodded.

"Then we'll probably miss each other. I hope Hannah feels better."

"Me too," Josie agreed fervently.

"Sleep tight. Try to relax. And take care of that burn." Her mother smiled, and headed down the hall to her bedroom.

Josie finished the water and put the empty bottle in the recycling bin, then went to her room.

She wasn't quite sure how she felt about her mom's little heart-to-heart talk. She knew Jackie had only said something because she was worried about Josie's future. Honestly, Josie was a little concerned herself.

Actually, she was freaking terrified, which was probably one reason she hadn't been looking for another job. It was easier to pretend she wouldn't need one.

Which was stupid.

In her bedroom, she closed the door and sat on her bed.

No, this wasn't her bedroom anymore, she reminded herself. This was the room she was borrowing for the moment. It would be good to remember that.

Sighing, she stretched out, head on the pillows, hands folded on her stomach, and closed her eyes. Immediately, she became aware of how much she smelled like grease and fried food, and pushed herself up again. She got up and stripped off her clothes, threw them on a chair, and pulled on her pajamas.

When she laid back down, she realized she still smelled, but it wasn't quite as bad. Probably her hair, but she couldn't do much about it unless she took a shower, and that was just too much effort at the moment.

She watched the light from the bedside lamp create shadows on the ceiling.

This room had always been a haven. Her own little piece of the house, where she could be who she was and not who everyone expected her to be.

In the city, she'd become who everyone expected her to be. The good little soldier. Look where it had gotten her.

But there was all that debt.

Restless again, she got out of bed and went over to her laptop, which was set up on her old school desk, and turned it on.

The truth was, savings or no savings, severance or no severance, she would need money soon.

When her computer had booted up, she took it with her back to the bed and surfed the net a little. The hatred and anger she found spewing there didn't do much to calm her down. Looking for a distraction, she pulled up the bowling alley website to read about the reopening event rescheduled for Saturday.

Pat's web page was actually better designed than she'd expected, with embedded videos showing him giving a tour of the new bar and restaurant, and links to the news coverage it had received.

He shouldn't have given the tour himself, though, because he was nervous on camera, so he was stiff when he talked, and a little awkward. Besides, his massive body made him look intimidating rather than welcoming.

Josie shook her head as she watched the videos, seeing missed opportunities. Really, the bowling alley could so easily be an amusement venue, appealing to kids and adults. There wasn't anything like it for miles. If they beefed up the arcade, made the new restaurant more family-friendly, had some community events...

She frowned and got up to get a notepad, then settled back on the bed and jotted down some ideas.

Not that she wanted to help Pat, but why couldn't he see that his business had awesome, untapped potential? You'd have to go to Scranton or East Stroudsburg to find a place like what she was envisioning. That wouldn't be the case for long. Between the nearby university and the casinos popping up every damned where, the region was growing. Soon, someone else would open a "fun center" and Pat would have missed his chance.

She scribbled for a bit, then, out of curiosity, opened the Country Time's website. One look had her groaning and settling back against her pillows.

Dear God in heaven, what in the world had Hannah been thinking? Did she want everyone to party like it was 1996? Josie shuddered. Great googly moogly.

The photos were dark and drab. The write-up was boring. The fonts were big and clunky. Pat might be misbranding his business, but his web page was kicking Hannah's page's butt. She didn't even have a menu or a list of the beers on tap, for God's sake!

Social media was even worse. When she checked, Josie saw Murphy Lanes had a presence on most of the major platforms. It wasn't terribly active, but at least it was there. The Country Time was conspicuously absent. There were some Yelp reviews, but otherwise, nothing. *Nada.*

"Oh, we are so having a come-to-Jesus talk about this," Josie muttered to herself.

Here was something she could do to help. She could redesign Hannah's website and social media presence. She could come up with a plan to show the Country Time as the great place it was. Then, when she was gone, Hannah would have something to take to a web designer.

Rebrand.

Reimagine.

Change.

As if a genie had been uncorked and was rushing to leave its bottle, Josie's mind flooded with ideas. She felt the familiar increase in heart rate, the itching in her fingers to get the thoughts down before she lost them.

Knowing she wouldn't be able to sleep while her head was buzzing, she crossed her legs, pulled her computer into her lap, brought up her web design program and some favorite stock photo sites, and got to it.

As she worked, Josie felt herself starting to settle for the first time in days, maybe weeks.

She knew this.

She could do this.

At some point in the night she fell asleep, curled up next to her laptop.

16

When Josie woke up, it was early afternoon and she was alone in the house.

Standing under the hot water in the shower, she thought about the work she'd done planning out Hannah's website and social media presence. It had been fun. More, it had reminded her of what she really liked to do—coming up with ways to help businesses reach their potential.

At the advertising agency, she always seemed to be implementing other people's ideas. Maybe her vision had been different a time or two, but she'd never had the standing to move forward with it.

Hannah obviously didn't have a clue, so Josie would have a lot of input into whatever direction they went. Assuming she could convince the woman to do anything at all which, knowing how stubborn her friend was, might be kind of iffy. She'd definitely have to spin it right so Hannah would understand why she needed to care.

But that was a problem for another day.

Josie finished her shower, dressed, ate, and then headed back to the Country Time. As she drove through the chilly

Hardy Falls afternoon, her thoughts switched from Hannah's pitiful website to concerns about the night to come. The Country Time was never dull, that was for damn sure. At least her burn felt and looked a lot better, so she was pretty sure she'd be able to wear gloves and run the dishwasher.

And if it started hurting again, maybe Mat would rub more cream on it.

His hands were so big and strong, they'd seemed to swallow hers. His touch had been slightly rough against her skin.

She couldn't help but wonder what it would feel like to have those hands on other parts of her body.

Drawing in a deep breath, she tried to push the thought away.

"Consequences," she muttered to herself. "Complications."

But, as her mother had pointed out the night before, she wouldn't be in town forever. Couldn't she have a fling with a hot guy while she was here, assuming the hot guy was willing?

Josie was pretty sure he was. Willing, that is. She might not have had much luck with men, but she could recognize interest when she saw it.

Was she running away from something that might be complicated, but nice?

What if it ended up being more than nice?

Maybe...

Driving past the bowling alley, she turned into the Country Time's parking lot and pulled around the building. There were already a couple of cars there, and to her surprise, Deacon's SUV was one of them.

That was a relief. If Deacon was back, it meant Hannah was better.

There was a car and a pickup truck next to it. June. And Mat.

Josie drew in a deep breath.

She parked and slogged through the brisk air to the back

door, then, thanks to an unexpected gust of wind, pushed it open with way more force than was necessary. As it crashed against the wall with a loud bang, the group of people gathered in the kitchen turned to stare at her.

"Hi." Who said she didn't know how to make an entrance?

"Close the damned door," Mat barked, recovering from his surprise. "It's freaking freezing out there." He sounded grumpy and annoyed and sexy as hell.

"Lightweight," she said and complied.

The fact that she found him insanely attractive even when he was basically snapping at her was a very bad sign.

He and Deacon were leaning against the prep counter, and June was perched on a stool near the dishwasher. What had Josie rushing forward, though, was the sight of Hannah flopped in her desk chair, which someone must have brought in for her.

"What the hell are you doing here?" she demanded as she glared down at her friend. "You should be out at least another day."

"Nice to see you, too," Hannah said, looking pale and tired.

"We were just discussing why Hannah is here," Deacon informed her. "And it's because she's being a stubborn idiot."

When Josie turned to him, she could see his blue eyes weren't as bright as normal. "You both should have stayed home today," she told him.

Deacon grinned. "She wouldn't," he said and jerked a thumb towards Hannah.

"She couldn't," Hannah corrected.

"She could have, but she refused," June said.

"I'm fine," Hannah insisted, waving her hand. "I'm just going to do the books, place orders, pay the bills, and that sort of thing. If I feel bad, I'll pull out the air mattress and sleep."

"You're a control freak," Josie told her.

Hannah crossed her arms and pouted. "Isn't anybody happy

that I'm here to do the paperwork and make sure we stay in business?"

"Whatever." June shrugged. "We kept the place running last night without you, didn't we?"

Josie winced and shifted on her feet.

"Yeah, sorry about burning myself and being of no help whatsoever."

"You were a big help," June protested, although Josie was certain she was lying.

"Speaking of which, let's see the burn." Mat held out his hand and without thinking she put hers into it, barely controlling a shudder at the warmth of his fingers closing gently around her chilled flesh.

Oh, boy.

He looked up at her through his too-long hair, and she saw that his dark eyes were even darker than before, his nostrils slightly flared.

"Well?" June demanded, breaking the mood.

"Looks good," Mat said and let her go.

"Great!" Hannah smiled weakly. "Mary Alice is still out, and Grace really shouldn't work two nights in a row. I can't be around food—"

"I'll do it." Josie straightened her shoulders, trying to ignore Mat. "I'll wait on tables with June. I saw what she was doing last night and—"

"—so I called Jenny and she's coming in to help out," Hannah finished.

"—she'll be able to..." Josie trailed off and blinked at her friend. "What?" Since Jenny had already been gone when she'd gotten up, she hadn't talked to her sister today.

"I called Jenny, and she's coming in to work as a server." Hannah looked worried.

"Oh."

"Don't be mad," Hannah said quickly. "June's going to be working the floor, too, but Kevin finally got this crap."

"That's too bad." Josie felt sorry for the big man.

"Mat's going to have to cook again. And Deacon's probably going to need help at the bar because he's still sick."

"I feel fine!" Deacon protested.

"With Jenny here, June will be able to jump in wherever she's needed. There still won't be enough people working on a Friday night, especially since I can't really do anything, but it will be better." Hannah plowed on.

Josie crossed her arms.

"I appreciate your help, Josie. You know I do," Hannah persisted. "This isn't about that. This is about making things work tonight."

Josie sighed and let her arms drop again. Hannah was right and she was being childish. After all, this wasn't about her; this was about what Hannah needed for the Country Time. Jenny had lots of experience in restaurants. If her sister had been able to help out last night, things would have gone a lot smoother.

It was just that Jenny always seemed able to handle everything. She wouldn't have burned herself throwing macaroni on a man. She would have just been Jenny and done whatever needed doing.

"It's a good idea," she said, and forced a smile. "Jenny will be a lot of help."

Hannah visibly relaxed.

"So...the dishwasher?" Josie made sure she was still smiling.

"And helping Mat with food prep."

Mat?

Oh wait.

Josie's mind, which she could admit was a little sluggish sometimes, kicked into high gear.

Hannah was proposing that she and Mat work together all night again. Closely together.

She looked at him and found him watching her, eyes hooded and intense.

That could be...interesting.

"Don't even think about throwing hot water on me," he said in his deep voice.

Oh, yes, this situation was definitely looking up.

"You'd better be nice to me then," she said. Her voice came out a little husky.

His mouth kicked up on one side. "I can be nice."

"I'll bet you can."

When she realized she'd said that out loud, Josie winced and just barely resisted the urge to cover her face with her hands. *God.*

Mat laughed and June got to her feet.

"On that note, I'm off to get the taproom ready." She looked at Hannah. "You go collapse in your office like the idiot you are. When's Jenny showing up, anyway?"

Hannah, who had been watching Mat and Josie with an interested gleam in her eye, carefully got to her feet.

"Around five."

June shrugged. "Fine."

Deacon moved to support Hannah. "Let's get you to the office, honey," he said and winked at Josie before herding his woman out of the kitchen.

Geez.

"Prep cards are on the counter," June told them. "You two okay for now?"

"We're fine," Mat told her. "I know what's up."

June shot them both one more look, nodded, and left.

Which left Josie alone with Mat.

And she'd be alone with him most of the night.

Again.

Yikes.

She took off her jacket and carefully hung it on a hook.

Then, because she wasn't a coward, she met his eyes. When he smiled, she swallowed. Hard.

"Um, where do you want me?"

His smile widened.

"I mean, what do you want me to do?"

Now he was grinning, his teeth white and his expression wicked.

"Okay, I'm going to shut up now."

He laughed at her and walked over to the locker to get an apron, tossing her one over his shoulder.

Fortunately, she caught it. "Thanks." She wasn't quite sure she could handle much more of him smiling at her. The man was hot when he was frowning, but when he smiled it was nuclear.

And why was he smiling at her anyway? Could he read her mind? Did he know that now that she'd let herself acknowledge the possibility of a fling, all she could focus on was the way he moved?

Those broad shoulders...that tight butt...

He sure had a body on him.

She drew in a deep breath.

Easy there, girl. This still isn't a good idea.

Mat tied on his apron and went over to the food prep counter. He grabbed some of the menu cards and rifled through them.

"I think we need chicken salad again. Can you check?"

"What? Oh, sure." A little dazed, Josie pulled on her apron and got the plastic tub out of the refrigerator. "Looks like it's pretty empty."

"Okay. We need more potato salad, too. I'll get potatoes cooking so they have time to cool." He grabbed a pan and put it in the sink, then bent to get potatoes out of the big bag under the counter. "It's good that Hannah still makes these salads here and doesn't buy them premade."

"Like I said, she wants to be in control." Josie shook herself when she realized she'd been admiring him as he bent over.

"It's still good. We're opening soon." He straightened and glanced at the clock. "I could get the first round of hotdogs going. Can you grab me a pack out of the freezer? Then, assuming the gloves don't hurt your hand, you can help me chop things."

"You actually trust me with a knife?"

"Maybe." He looked at her and grinned again. "But I'm definitely keeping you away from the boiling water."

"Fine," she grumbled because she knew she'd never live that down. Of all the pans of boiling water in all the world, she had to throw hers at him.

She got the hotdogs, he handed her a knife, and then they didn't talk much—just moved from task to task. Her burned hand was a little sore, but she could ignore it and thought she did pretty well.

Josie was surprised when orders started coming in from customers at the bar. She hadn't realized what time it was. Everything was ready, so they shifted modes from prep to deployment, as Mat called it.

All she knew was it was a hell of a lot less stressful handling things with him in charge than it had been when she'd been trying to do everything herself.

"You must have worked in kitchens a lot," she said as she finished a sandwich and added the chips.

"Off and on." He smiled a little. "It's okay. I like it." He went to the refrigerator to get some chicken wings, walked to the fryer and adjusted the temperature, then put the wings in a basket and dunked them into the hot oil. They went under with a "hiss." With no hesitation, Mat moved on to the grill, flipping the burgers sizzling there.

"Did you work in the kitchen when you were on the oil rig?" Josie asked, going to the warming tray for another order of fries. French fries were apparently a staple food in Hardy Falls.

"Everyone pitched in on the rig. We got supplies in, of course, but it wasn't like it was catered or anything. You wanted to eat, you figured out how to make something." He frowned at the warmer. "We're going to need more fries soon, but I don't want to cook them with the wings. It's great Hannah has that drawer warmer, but she really should invest in a second fryer so we can keep things separate and not have to juggle so much."

All of that apparently meant something to him.

Josie was about to comment, when the back door opened and Jenny walked in.

Her sister waved at her and smiled at Mat. "Hey."

"Hey yourself," he rumbled in return.

Josie wasn't entirely sure she liked that rumble.

"It was great that you could come in tonight," she said to Jenny.

Her sister shrugged. "I wish I could have been here last night. Sounds like June could have used the help."

Josie stiffened because *she* had been there. *She'd* helped. Some, anyway.

"With you here, Josie will be able to stay with me in the kitchen tonight," Mat said. "I'll be glad not to have to do everything myself."

That was nice of him to say because they both knew he'd basically be doing everything anyway.

Jenny smiled at him, eyes dancing. She was wearing a tank top that showed off tanned, toned arms and crept up to reveal a flat stomach. Say what you will about cleaning houses, Josie thought, it certainly kept you in better shape than sitting at a computer for twelve hours a day.

She resented that.

"I haven't seen a situation you couldn't take care of," Jenny said.

Mat returned her smile. "Better go get changed into your Country Time gear."

"June said she'd have a polo shirt for me in the office. The blue will match my look." Josie's sister swung back her hair, drawing attention to its vibrant blue streaks. Smiling at Mat again, she left. Mat watched her go.

Josie wanted to smack him on the head with a frying pan.

"I'll get started on the dishes," she said because she didn't want to be standing next to him right at that moment.

Mat turned to frown at her. "There aren't that many."

"I don't want to get behind."

Josie went over to the counter where they'd been piling dirty dishes and glasses, and pulled on the thick, yellow rubber gloves she was coming to hate.

For the next hour or so, she watched Jenny whirl in and out of the kitchen, handing in orders and picking them up, laughing about something Albert or one of his cronies had said, bitching about one of the college students who hadn't wanted to show ID, and generally having the time of her life. She even got a bunch of tips, which she stuffed in the communal jar to be split later.

June came in, too, looking a lot less stressed than she had the night before. When asked, she said that things were going so well she was going to give Deacon a break to let him rest.

"We've got it under control in here." Mat waved her away.

It was nice of Mat to use "we," but Josie knew perfectly well that he would have been fine without her.

They all would have been fine without her.

And yes, she was being melodramatic and angsty, but it was how she felt.

What was she, thirteen? All she needed were the braces.

"I'm going to take a break," she said after June left. She just wanted a few minutes where she didn't have to watch everyone else be competent.

Mat turned from the grill, looking concerned.

"You okay?"

"Sure. Just need some fresh air and a chair for a minute."

He studied her a moment longer, then nodded. "No problem. The dishes are caught up anyway."

Well, that was something. After the initial bobble with the whole scraping thing, she'd actually gotten the hang of the dishwasher.

A new career is born.

The thought depressed her, so she stripped off the gloves and the apron and placed them carefully at her station.

God. She had a station.

Josie grabbed her coat and walked out the back door into the cold, clear night. At least the wind had died down, so it wouldn't be slicing through her as she sulked.

She headed for the little employee break area, then hesitated when she saw Deacon was already sitting there. So much for sulking. It was probably just as well.

"Hi," she said as she walked over to him.

He grinned at her. "Hi, yourself."

Using her coat sleeve, she cleaned the remnants of snow off the unoccupied plastic chair and sat across from him, trying to see his face in the flickering parking lot light.

"What are you doing out here?" she asked. "I thought you'd be with Hannah if you weren't working."

Deacon shrugged. "She's sleeping. I didn't want to bother her." He ran his hand over his brutally short hair. "She shouldn't have come in tonight. The stomach bug hit her a lot harder than it hit me, and she's wiped out. But she insisted."

"That's Hannah." Josie settled in her chair. "How are you feeling?"

"I'm okay." He made a face, then grinned again, teeth slashing across his shadowed features. "Like I'd admit it to you if I wasn't."

She snorted. "Remember how I found you limping in the library that day in high school? You told me you'd stubbed your toe."

"I had stubbed my toe!" he protested.

"Yeah, you'd broken your toe, asshole. You couldn't even admit that."

He laughed. "I'm stubborn."

"Tell me about it." She considered him. "You're happy, right?"

It was a stupid question. Anybody could tell he was happy.

"Ecstatic." Deacon's smile lit the darkness. "Never thought Hannah Frederickson would give me a second look. Now she gives me three or four. And that's before I get dressed." He leered good-naturedly.

"TMI!" Josie put her hands over her eyes, then lowered them to return his smile. It was nice to see him so happy.

"What about you?" he asked, leaning forward suddenly, as if he was reading her mind. "Are you happy?"

Josie felt her smile fade at the direct question.

"Well, I did just lose my job and my apartment," she pointed out. She couldn't remember if she'd actually told him about it, but if she hadn't, Hannah had.

"Yeah, but even before then. Were you happy with how things were going?"

"Sure," she said automatically. "Don't worry. I'll get back on track. Just had my legs knocked out from under me."

He looked unconvinced.

"Josie!"

They both turned at the sound of Mat's voice yelling her name from the back door.

"What?" she yelled back.

"I thought you didn't want the dishes to pile up? They're not going to wash themselves." He sounded annoyed

"Keep your shirt on!" she shouted. "I'm coming!" She got to

her feet. "God, that man," she groused. "I just needed to get out of the kitchen for a minute."

"Maybe you should see about getting him to take his shirt off," Deacon joked, getting up out of his chair to stand beside her.

She'd been turning to go but stopped at that comment and stared at him. "Huh?"

He snorted out a laugh and wrapped his arm around her neck, guiding her towards the building. "I'm just saying that maybe what you need is a good pipe cleaning, if you know what I mean." He looked down at her and waggled his eyebrows. "It'll help you relax and get in a good frame of mind."

Josie punched his arm. "Shut up."

Deacon laughed and opened the door, ushering her into the kitchen.

Once they were back inside, Deacon headed to check on Hannah again before going back to the bar. Mat scowled at Josie darkly and she wondered what had crawled up his butt and died. But since she could see he was right about the dishes, she shook it off and got back to work.

17

Mat was in a hell of a mood.

It was surprising, considering he tried to stay on an even keel most of the time.

But watching Josie and Deacon sitting close to each other, hearing them laugh as they walked back to the building after their break, seeing Deacon with his arm slung around her shoulders...

Well, he was in a hell of a mood.

Josie had returned to the dishwasher, and the noise of the machine was drowning out even the pounding country music in the taproom. Mat tried to ignore her and focus on the food orders. Hadn't he decided she'd be nothing but trouble anyway? Hadn't he decided to let it be? She'd be leaving town, regardless. It didn't matter to him in the slightest that she appeared to be a lot more comfortable with Deacon than she was with him.

Nothing would come of it. Deacon was totally committed to Hannah. But Mat wished he knew how Josie felt about the situation.

He frowned down at the burgers sizzling on the grill and wondered why he gave a damn.

Maybe it was because he was sure he'd seen interest in her eyes earlier in the afternoon. Then she'd gotten more distant for some reason.

God, women were confusing.

June came into the kitchen and dumped a bunch of orders on the counter.

"Tell me I can't kill Claude Beecher," she ordered.

"Why?" he asked, glad to be distracted from his thoughts. Claude Beecher was the local used car salesman who'd apparently made the mistake of selling June a real lemon of a car last year. She wasn't exactly the forgiving type, but in this case she had a right to be pissed off. In spite of the warranty she'd purchased, Claude had managed to weasel his way out of paying for any of the many repairs the vehicle had required.

Mat and Deacon had offered to go with Calvin to have a little chat with Claude, but everyone seemed to think that was a bad idea.

Shame.

"Because Hannah wouldn't like it if I killed Claude," June explained. "She already told me she won't post my bail if I fork the asshole." Her grin was sharp. "But I bet Calvin would."

Mat flipped burgers into buns and moved to complete the order he was assembling.

"No, I understand why you can't kill him," he said as he worked. "Killing is bad. I'm just wondering why you're thinking about doing it now."

"Because he's right out there in the taproom with some other fools from the Rotary, daring me to do something about it." She blew out a breath. "I told Jenny she'd better take care of that table, because I can't trust myself."

"Ah." That explained it. "I'm surprised he had the stones to show up here."

June shrugged. "Calvin and I talked to Sam about suing the asshole over the car. Claude probably found out and is trying to get more information. I'll bet Sam's assistant told him we were there. She looked like a sneak to me."

"Wait." Josie came to stand beside him. Mat realized the dishwasher wasn't running, so she must have overheard the conversation. "You went to see Sam? Deacon's brother, Sam?"

He understood her surprise. From what he'd heard, June hated Sam Black because of the way he'd treated Hannah.

"He's an attorney, isn't he?" June shrugged. "I guess he's been okay with Hannah recently. And she's with Deacon now, so I don't have to worry about him sweet talking her again."

Mat hoped she was right.

Josie shook her head. "I don't even know you anymore," she told June. "You're getting, like, mellow."

"Oh, go back to your damned dishes," June snapped. "I'm taking a freaking break. First freaking break I've had in days."

Josie winced. "Do you want me to—?"

"No," June cut her off. "Jenny's got it. I'll be back in a minute, after I freeze my brain." She sighed. "I guess I won't shove a sharp object up Claude Beecher's butt tonight, but I sure want to." She marched over to the coat hooks, grabbed her jacket, and strode out.

"June can be kind of scary," Josie said. Mat tended to agree.

The kitchen door pushed open and Jenny came in, a tray full of empty plates and glasses balanced on one shoulder.

"Man, can those bowlers eat," she said and hoisted the tray to the sink counter. "This will keep you busy, little sis," she said.

"Great." Josie looked less than thrilled as she went back to the dishwasher, taking the warmth of her body with her.

Jenny leaned against the pickup counter, ignoring the orders waiting to be delivered.

"Aren't you due for a break, Mat?" she asked. "We're starting to slow down. You could come out to the taproom and sit for a minute. Josie can take care of things here."

Mat wasn't stupid. He knew when a woman was giving him signals. Jenny's had been subtle, but they'd been there. He'd actually toyed with the idea of getting together with her once or twice. There hadn't been anyone since Gail, but Jenny, with her razor sharp wit, blue eyes, and taut body had definitely appealed. He'd been starting to think about it.

Too bad Josie was the sister who fascinated him now.

"I'm fine here in the kitchen," he told Jenny kindly. He didn't want to hurt her feelings. "Josie and I have things under control."

Jenny straightened and looked from him to her sister at the dishwasher, and back again.

"Okay." She frowned a little.

"It's not like we'd have a chance to talk anyway," he said. The truth was, he probably never would have made a move on Jenny Kline. He certainly wouldn't now, not when her sister was the woman constantly on his mind.

"Okay." Jenny grabbed the completed orders. "Guess I'd better get to work."

Mat sighed as she left and then he went back to the grill. He hoped Jenny wasn't upset.

"You can go out and take a break if you want to," Josie said from behind him. "I can handle things for a few minutes by myself. I'm not that clumsy."

He turned to see her standing next to the dishwasher. Her expression was tight, eyes flaring.

"I don't want to go out there," he said, then hesitated before adding, "I'd rather stay here."

Josie blinked several times as she processed the words. Then he saw her relax a little bit.

"Fine."

She shoved a rack of plates into the dishwasher and it roared back to life.

Mat grabbed another pack of hotdogs from the freezer and got them laid out on the roller cooker, then started a batch of fries.

See? Confusing.

The work ebbed and flowed like it always did in a busy kitchen. June came back from her break, Jenny went on hers, and then Mat took his—although he headed outside instead of to the taproom. It was good to sit down on a plastic chair in the cold, refreshing air after standing next to the heat of the grill.

It was one of the things he loved most about restaurant kitchens. There was pressure and heat and craziness, and then there was the release. And the release was that much sweeter for the craziness that had come before.

He was happy here in Hardy Falls he thought, a little surprised. Even with the damned snow. Who knew?

Table service finally ended around midnight, and all food orders at one, which gave him and Josie a chance to start cleaning up the kitchen. He was getting rid of the grease from the grill—a job he hated—when the kitchen door opened and June poked her head in.

"Can you guys come out for a minute? Albert wants to tell us something."

"What?" Albert might be old, but he had ways of finding out information that would make the CIA proud.

"If I knew that, would I be standing here? Get moving," June ordered, turned, and left.

Mat glanced at Josie, and she shrugged.

"Better go," she said.

They both stripped off their aprons and rubber gloves, and Mat held the kitchen door open so Josie could go into the taproom first. Her body brushed his as she passed, soft and warm. The fact that she smelled a little like grease didn't seem to matter to his libido. Mat tried to stomp it down.

Not now.

He froze when he realized the thought did not, in fact, rule out the possibility, just the timing.

What the hell was he doing?

"Mat!" Deacon shouted from behind the bar. He suddenly realized he'd been standing there like a mannequin for several seconds. Shaking it off, he followed Josie into the taproom.

It looked like the only customers left at the bar were Albert and his three cronies, Harry, Martin, and Joe. Hannah was sitting next to the old men, with Deacon standing on the other side of the bar opposite her. June sat at the far end, and Mat was surprised to see that Jenny was still there. He'd expected her to leave once table service ended.

Jenny caught him looking at her and shrugged. "I was curious."

She was always curious. That was one of the things he liked best about her.

Josie went to sit next to her sister and, wanting a little distance, Mat went behind the bar to stand next to Deacon.

"Okay, Albert," June said. "We're all here. What the hell is so damned important?"

"Was waiting for the place to clear out so we could talk in peace," Albert said. He grinned, showing off his healthy pink gums. "Almost had to send Harry home to his wife."

"I only fell asleep for a minute," the other man muttered. "Shut up."

"Al-bert." Hannah drew out his name.

He waved. "Yeah, yeah. Sorry. Okay, I heard something tonight from the bowling league guys you probably ain't gonna like too much."

Hannah straightened. "What did Pat do now?" she demanded.

"Well," Albert leaned his elbow on the bar, "apparently he told everyone that they can't leave their cars in his parking lot and come over to the Country Time. He told them that as of now, his parking lot is for bowling alley customers only, and everyone else will get towed. He even made a deal with Richie Dunlop for the towing."

Josie frowned. "That's not that bad." She looked around at the rest of them. "Is it?"

"Of course it's bad. It's one more way to screw with Hannah," Jenny said. Josie turned her frown on her sister.

"God, why won't that man leave me alone?" Hannah moaned and put her head down on the bar top. "Why is he doing this?"

June shifted on her seat, looking guilty.

Mat understood, at least partially. He'd heard about how June had dated Pat, how she'd broken up with him, and how he hadn't wanted to take "no" for an answer until she'd basically said it in front of the whole town.

He knew better than most how angry you could get when something like that happened—how that anger could affect your judgment.

Deacon reached over the bar to stroke Hannah's hair.

"It's bad," he told Josie, "because it means the bowlers will either have to move their cars, park in the Country Time lot in the first place, or stay at the bowling alley bar."

"And the Country Time lot is smaller than the bowling alley's," Mat put in, considering it. "We get packed on Friday and Saturday nights sometimes, so it's going to make that worse."

Hannah lifted her head. "It's going to be even more tempting for them to just stay at the bowling alley, especially if our lot is already full and there's not enough parking."

Martin nodded. "Some of those guys are lazy bastards. They won't want to go to the trouble, that's for sure."

"And it's all perfectly legal," Joe put in "Pat has the right to limit the parking in his own lot."

Mat shook his head, impressed in spite of himself. "Who knew Pat was smart enough to think of something like this?"

He shouldn't judge by appearance, but the other man was a total gym rat. He'd kind of assumed all that testosterone had screwed with his brain cells.

"Are you sure Pat thought of it?" Josie asked. Everyone looked at her.

"Who else?" Hannah asked.

Josie shrugged. "Louise?"

"Louise is my friend," Hannah protested.

"Louise used to be your friend," Josie corrected gently. "And now she's going to manage the restaurant of a man who wants to put you out of business." She hesitated. "Louise is smart, you know. This kind of thing sounds more like her. Pat would just want to smash."

Hannah's big eyes filled with tears. "But why? Why would she want to hurt me? What did I do? She's the one who slept with Sam while he was still my boyfriend."

"I don't know." Josie paused again. "I'll have to ask her."

Mat went still. Christ, what was the woman up to now?

"Ask her?" Hannah frowned.

"Sure." Josie clasped her hands on the bar. "I'll just go to the reopening at the bowling alley tomorrow," she announced.

18

___

Josie's declaration was met with a certain lack of enthusiasm.

Mat scowled at her. "Why bother?"

She frowned back. "What do you mean? I said before that I would talk to Louise. I just haven't had a chance because it's been so crazy here. But she'll be at the reopening, so I'll be able to see her there."

"You're wasting your time," he argued. "She works for Pat. She's just going to do whatever he wants her to do."

"Maybe I can get her to see that we should be working together, not trying to drive each other out of business." Josie thought about the notes she'd made the night before while she worked through Hannah's website. "We don't need to compete."

"Try telling that to Pat," Hannah muttered.

Josie shrugged. "I would if he'd listen to me, but I doubt he will." In fact, she was pretty darned sure he wouldn't.

June sipped from a bottle of water and studied her. "Of course we have to compete. We both want the bowlers, don't we?"

"Well, yeah, but the two businesses are different." Josie

leaned forward, excited to be able to share a few of her ideas. "The bowling alley is a family friendly place, or it should be. The Country Time isn't for kids. Those are two different audiences. The bowlers want to come over here and party after leagues, fine. They want to bring their kids to play in the bowling alley arcade and then grab a bite to eat afterward, fine. I'm pretty sure Pat's not going to want a bunch of drunk, rowdy guys shouting at the Phillies at the bar while families are trying to eat at the tables behind them. And we want to focus on the adult customer of legal age, not kids or teenagers with fake IDs." She spread her hands. "Different."

Why couldn't anybody else see this? It was stupidly clear.

"And you think Louise will get that?" June's tone was waspish, but Josie didn't take it personally. She knew the other woman felt bad about the situation with Pat, but it really wasn't her fault.

Josie glanced at Mat who was standing behind the bar, watching her.

"I hope she'll get it," she responded to June. And if she couldn't convince Louise to listen to her, maybe she'd at least be able to get some info on what else they were planning. If Hannah had some warning, she could figure out how to fight back.

"What if Pat gets mad at you?" Hannah was chewing on her thumbnail. "You know how he is."

Pat was a big guy with lots of muscle, and he could be a moron when he got angry, but Josie didn't think he'd hurt her. Not physically, anyway.

"I'll be fine."

June frowned. "He can get nasty."

"You should have some backup," Martin agreed. "Albert, Joe, Harry and I could go with you."

"Then it will be like a gang war!" Josie protested. "Pat knows you're all loyal to Hannah."

"They sure are." Hannah beamed at the old men. They grinned back at her.

"It's 'cause she has the best beer," Joe said affectionately.

"And she lets us watch sports in peace," Harry put in.

"And you can hide out from your wife," Albert added.

They all laughed.

"I'll go with you," Deacon said. "Then Pat won't mess with you."

"Um, didn't I hear through the grapevine that he almost sued Hannah because you were so charming the last time you went in to 'talk' to him?" Josie asked. "And didn't you promise to stay away from him?"

When it had recently come out that Pat had been spreading rumors about Hannah and the Country Time, Deacon had gone to the bowling alley to tell him to stop. Things had deteriorated and Pat had reported Deacon to Josie's mother in her official capacity. He'd also threatened to sue for harassment.

"He won't even know I'm there unless he comes at you," Deacon insisted stubbornly.

"I'd feel better if Deacon went with you," Hannah said.

"Well, I'd feel better if he stayed out of jail, okay?" Josie returned, exasperated.

"Maybe I should go," June said. "Calvin's feeling better. He can come with us."

"What? No!" That would be even worse. If Pat saw June and Calvin together, it would be like waving a red flag at a bull.

"He won't do anything to me," June insisted, reading her mind. "I can handle Pat."

"Not a good idea, girl," Albert said, shaking his balding head at June. "Pat's still mighty angry at you."

"Yeah, he is," Josie said. "And what part of 'I want to talk to Louise' don't you people understand? If you get Pat all worked up, she'll never listen to me."

"I could go," Hannah said.

Josie rolled her eyes so hard they hurt. *Jesus!* "Right. Because seeing you in his place isn't going to make him angry."

"I'll go with you," Mat, who'd been silent as they argued, said suddenly.

She turned to stare at him.

"What?"

"I said, I'll go with you," he repeated, eyes intent on her face.

Jenny shifted on her barstool and looked away.

"No," Josie said at the same time Deacon nodded.

"That's a good idea," he said

"No, it's not." She frowned at Deacon.

"Perfect," June said as if it was a done deal.

"I don't need him to come with me!" Josie shouted, frustrated.

"Pat probably knows you work here," Hannah said to Mat, "but I'd feel better if she wasn't alone."

Mat shrugged. "I'll watch out for her."

"Hello!" Josie pounded the flat of her hand on the top of the bar. They all had the nerve to stare at her as if she was crazy. "I am not going to get in trouble, Pat is not going to mess with me, and I'll be fine all by wittle self. I'm just going to go talk to Louise."

"And I'm going with you," Mat said flatly with no room for argument.

"You're going to piss Pat off even more and ruin the whole thing."

"No, I'm not," he disagreed. "I'm going to go with you, and we'll pretend we're on a date and sit somewhere until you track down Louise. Then I'm going to drink some beer while you talk to her, and after that we'll hold hands and leave, and everyone will think we're going home together and there will be gossip for days."

"Oh, for Christ's..." Josie's protests trailed off when what he'd said sunk in. "Huh?"

Jenny got up and walked behind the bar. She opened the refrigerator and helped herself to a bottle of water.

Mat smiled. "You heard me." He leaned against the back counter, arms crossed over his chest.

What kind of game was he playing?

Flustered, Josie looked around at the others gathered around the bar for a clue as to how she should respond. They were all grinning except Deacon, who was frowning, and Jenny, who wasn't looking at anybody in particular.

Josie turned back to Mat. She just couldn't figure him out. He'd barely said two words to her all night. Now he was watching her in a way that made her feel like a rabbit who'd unexpectedly met a wolf.

And people said women were hard to understand.

Those people being men, of course.

Whatever was going on in the dim recesses of Mat's mind, she could tell there was no point in arguing anymore— assuming she wanted to. She had as much chance of moving the Country Time across the highway as she did of convincing Mat Guerrero not to go to the bowling alley with her tomorrow. He was coming with her, whether she wanted him to or not.

The thought made her shiver.

She dramatically threw up her hands to hide her physical reaction.

"Fine. Yes. Whatever."

Mat nodded in satisfaction and straightened away from the counter. "Let's get going so we can finish the cleanup," he said and headed back to the kitchen.

Josie wondered what she had just agreed to.

She followed him into the kitchen because she wasn't sure what else to do. And it really was sort of her obligation to help, wasn't it?

In the hour that followed, she was more than a little chagrined to find that he really was focused on cleaning. He didn't flirt, didn't explain why he'd suddenly decided to accompany her to the bowling alley, and didn't even talk to her much.

She wasn't sure how she felt about it. Had she been stupid for thinking he might be interested in more than simply watching her back while she was in so-called enemy territory? Probably.

And yet...

And yet there'd been a certain gleam in his dark eyes when he'd looked at her.

Unless she'd imagined it.

Josie wanted to bang her head against a wall. The man was going to make her crazy. Mat Guerrero had to be the king of mixed messages.

When they had finally finished scrubbing everything that needed scrubbing, Mat went to help Deacon close down the taproom, and Hannah came to the kitchen to spring Josie. Tired and a little sore, she started to untie her stained apron, then let out a startled squeak when Hannah grabbed her in a hug so tight it threatened her ability to breathe.

"Thank you," her friend said, rocking her from side to side.

Gasping, Josie grabbed her arms to loosen their hold.

"No problem," she said after sucking in a deep gulp of air.

Hannah reached up and took her face in both hands, pushing her cheeks together.

"I love you," she said.

Josie gurgled and tried to slap her hands away.

Hannah, who even sick with a stomach bug had arms of steel, ignored her, glanced at the kitchen door, and leaned closer, lowering her voice to a whisper.

"Are you sure you know what the hell you're doing?" she whispered.

Josie smacked at the other woman until she relaxed her grip a little.

"Geez, you're strong. I'm going to have bruises. And I'm only going to the bowling alley for Pete's sake."

"Don't be an idiot," Hannah said, gripping her shoulders now. She really was going to be black and blue. "I saw the way you and Mat were looking at each other. The vibes were flying so hard they stung when they hit me."

"Nothing's going on," Josie protested, even though she wasn't sure.

"I think Mat's had a rough time," Hannah said, her expression solemn. "So have you."

"Don't worry, mom," Josie said, reaching out to squeeze her friend's face in turn.

Hannah blew a raspberry.

"You spit on me!"

Hannah tried to get her into a headlock, but she dodged it because she knew the move and the other woman was slower than normal.

"Ladies," Mat said from the doorway. "Don't fall into the fryer."

Josie took advantage of the distraction to grab Hannah and rub noogies on the top of her head.

"Stop it!" Hannah yelped, trying to twist away. "I'm sick, you creep!"

"What's going on?" Deacon asked from the doorway.

Mat looked at him. "I thought we were supposed to be the immature ones?"

Deacon shrugged.

Josie let Hannah go and straightened her polo shirt before brushing back her hair and looking down her nose at the two men.

"I'm leaving, so I'll see you tomorrow," she told them.

"I don't think we'll need too many people tomorrow

because of Pat's thing," Hannah told her, brushing down her own hair. "Besides, Grace and Mary Alice are ready to come back for their regular hours, and Kevin said he's feeling better too, thank goodness. I'm not sure you need to worry about coming in so much anymore."

"Oh." For a moment, Josie felt like she had when she'd been told she was being laid off. It occurred to her that she'd been thinking of herself as part of the Country Time team. But she wasn't, was she?

"I mean, I appreciate everything you've done," Hannah added hastily. "I really, really do. You know I do. But you have other things to worry about, and we're all good now."

"Oh." She did have other things to worry about. Like finding a paying job. "Okay."

The twinge of hurt was stupid. Obviously, she'd been getting too invested and forgotten the reality of her own circumstances, just as her mother had warned she might. Hannah wasn't trying to be mean, and she wasn't throwing her out. This wasn't her job, it wasn't her place, and it wasn't her town—not anymore. She'd be leaving soon to make her own way again.

Somehow the thought made her feel worse.

"Should I pick you up at your house tomorrow?" Mat asked abruptly.

"What?" She blinked at him in surprise, knocked off balance by the change of subject.

"I'm not working tomorrow either, so there's no point in both of us driving. Remember the parking."

She thought she saw...yes, there was a definite gleam in his melting dark eyes, and it wasn't amusement.

Josie swallowed and tried to think. "Um, how about I pick you up instead?" she suggested, desperate to maintain some semblance of control in her life.

He smiled. "Fine."

"Good," she croaked.

"Man," Hannah shook her head. "Talk about vibes."

Josie frowned at her, but Mat just laughed.

They made arrangements for Josie to pick him up at the bookstore around five the next day, and they exchanged phone numbers, which made her stomach jitter a little bit more. She left as soon as she could.

Maybe she should have stayed and tried to talk to him, but frankly she needed sleep. She'd have to be on her best game if she was going to deal with Mat Guerrero.

Jenny had left at some point while they'd been cleaning up the kitchen, so when Josie got home she wasn't surprised to find that, although her sister's pickup was in the driveway, the house was dark. Her mother was on shift, and even Jenny had to be exhausted after the night they'd both put in.

After locking up again, she ran up the stairs to her bedroom, the little lights they always left on at night providing enough illumination so she didn't trip. Once she closed the door of her room behind her, she turned on the lamp on her nightstand, changed into her pajamas, and fell into bed.

Tired as she was, her mind still skittered around like a hamster on a wheel.

How had Jenny taken Mat's offer to accompany Josie to the bowling alley? Was she mad? Unless Josie was mistaken, there'd been signs that Jenny wouldn't have minded more of Mat's attention. Josie herself didn't mind having more of it. She just wished she knew what it meant.

What did he want? Why had he been so withdrawn one minute and obviously interested the next?

Maybe most importantly, what did she want to do about it? Did she want to start something with him, knowing full well that it couldn't go anywhere? Did she want to take a chance on someone she didn't really know that much about? It was one thing to contemplate having fun, sexy times with the man, but now it looked like there was a chance it might actually happen.

A couple hours later, she gave up trying to sleep and rolled out of bed to get her laptop. After she turned it on, she pulled up the website and marketing plan she'd started for Hannah.

This, at least, was something she understood.

Eventually, Josie managed to get some sleep, waking to stare blearily at the clock on the nightstand in the darkened room. She hauled herself out of her blankets and walked over to the window, pulling back the thick curtains, to confirm that it was indeed early afternoon outside, complete with bright late-fall sunshine gleaming on the remains of the snow.

Man, her sleeping habits were going to hell. At this rate, she was going to need retraining before she could take a normal nine-to-five job.

After visiting the bathroom, she explored the house and wasn't too surprised to discover she was alone. Actually, it was a relief not to have to deal with either her mother or her sister.

Only a few hours before she had to leave to pick up Mat at the bookstore.

Then...well, they'd see what happened.

Josie made herself some breakfast and ate it in her room while reviewing the work she'd done the night before. It was good, she decided. Basically ready to show Hannah. Hopefully her stubborn friend would agree to at least some of her ideas.

She glanced at the clock again.

But now it was time to get ready.

She lingered in a long, hot shower, handled grooming tasks that needed to be handled, and after drying and straightening her hair, brushed it until it shone like satin.

Pulling a hank of hair over her nose, she sniffed and was pleased to smell only shampoo, not meat and oil. Just to be sure, though, she smoothed on scented body lotion. If it worked out that she and Mat got close tonight, she didn't want to remind him of a grill.

Josie paused, staring at her naked self in the mirror. She turned this way and that, contemplating her reflection.

Well, if she gave Mat the opportunity to see her naked, she didn't think he'd laugh, anyway. That was something, she supposed.

Just thinking about the possibility of her seeing *him* naked made her shiver.

She spent far too much time on her makeup, and the only thing that finally got her out of the bathroom was knowing it was getting late.

Picking out a suitable bowling-alley-grand-reopening outfit was also an ordeal. In the end, she laid three suitable choices on her bed, closed her eyes, and pointed at one of them. Spritzing on a light perfume, she contemplated the results in the bedroom mirror.

Her eyes were bright and looked bigger with the mascara she hoped she would remember not to smear. Her lips were fuller, thanks to the wonders of lipstick. Her hair hung straight and thick.

"I look good," she assured herself.

Did she look *too* good? She didn't want to seem like she was trying too hard.

She was saved from her own thoughts by the sound of the

front door. It was probably Jenny. Fortunately, a moment later she heard the back door open and close as well, which meant her sister had gone out to her shed studio in the backyard.

Grabbing her purse, Josie took one last glance at the mirror and made a break for it.

As she drove through the soft dusk to the Best Pages bookstore, her heart beat more rapidly than usual, her blood sang in her veins. God, she just wanted to get the night started. Just wanted to see what was going to happen, or not happen.

"You are such an idiot," she muttered.

The storefronts along Main Street glowed in the deepening darkness, but there weren't many cars, so she found parking right in front of the bookstore. Turning off the engine, she hesitated, then grabbed her cell phone and sent him a text that she was there.

She wondered if he'd see it. Some people, like June, didn't pay much attention to their phones. If it had been Deacon, she would have just gone upstairs and gotten him.

But Mat wasn't Deacon, was he?

"Hey."

Josie jumped and nearly slammed her head into the roof of the car when the passenger door opened unexpectedly.

"Jesus Christ!" she gasped when she could catch her breath.

"Sorry, sorry." He was laughing a little as he slid into the car and slammed the door shut behind him.

Hell, what was the frigging point of spending so much time on makeup if the first thing you did when you saw the guy was make a jackass of yourself?

"You startled me," she accused. "What did you do, run down the stairs when I texted?"

"You texted me?" He pulled out his phone and frowned at it. "Oh yeah." Shrugging, he put it away. "I was in the bookstore watching for you."

"Oh." She should have thought of that, but he seemed to have absorbed every drop of oxygen in the car, and all she could think about was the warmth of his big body so close to her.

Mat cocked his head and his too-long hair slid over his forehead.

"You're nervous," he said, sounding surprised.

"I'm not nervous," she snapped, annoyed with herself and him and everything else. "Put on your damned seat belt."

"Why? It's Hardy Falls and we're going, what, three miles?"

"Buckle up. It's the law." She frowned at him until he rolled his eyes and did as she ordered, then watched as he pushed his seat all the way back so his long legs weren't bent at a sharp angle. He grumbled and she couldn't help smiling because he really did look uncomfortable. Her car wasn't tiny, but it wasn't the biggest thing in the whole world either, which made it perfect for the city but a tight fit for a guy like Mat.

"What?" he demanded.

"Nothing."

Frowning, Mat looked directly into her face for the first time. In the car's overhead light, she saw his frown fade and his eyes widen a little as he took in her hair and makeup. His gaze tracked over her face and traced the neckline of the flirty little blouse she was wearing under a leather jacket she'd chosen because it wasn't that cold and she hadn't wanted to be bundled up.

"Right," he said, then fell silent.

It was extremely gratifying.

Feeling much more positive about the situation, Josie started the car, put it in gear, and headed off to Murphy Lanes.

~

Mat still wasn't quite sure how he'd gotten himself into this situation. Why was he here, trapped in a car with Josie Kline, the scent of her wrapping around him until he couldn't think straight?

He shifted in his seat and tightened his hands into fists so he wouldn't reach out and grab her.

She looked fucking amazing. Well, she always looked amazing, but the sight of her now had practically knocked him on his ass. Her eyes were deep wells of shining blue, her mouth full and enticing, her hair a dark satin curtain. And that shirt she was wearing under her jacket dipped down far enough to show the upper slopes of her gorgeous breasts. It made him want to slide it lower so he could see. Touch.

Not a good idea. It hadn't been a good idea a week ago, and it still wasn't. No matter how long she was in town, it remained true that nothing involving this woman would ever be quick or easy.

Too bad he couldn't seem to give a shit anymore. Being around her as much as he had these last few days, seeing her laugh, listening to her bitch—it was all getting under his skin like a persistent itch he couldn't ignore.

He didn't know whether she'd be willing to take things any further with him, but he'd caught sight of a certain expression in her eyes a time or two. And she'd definitely been keyed up at the thought of him accompanying her tonight. It gave him hope that he wasn't the only one who wanted to scratch.

So here he was.

Josie, too, was silent as she drove them through the sleepy little town. When they approached the intersection where the Country Time sat next to Murphy Lanes, she shot him a glance.

"Where do we park?" she asked in her smoky voice.

He frowned out the windshield, glad for something to think about other than his randy libido.

"I don't think we should use up a Country Time parking

space, do you?" he said. "After all, we're bowling alley customers tonight, so we won't get towed."

She flashed him a grin. "My thoughts exactly."

He had to admit that it was a little discouraging to see the packed bowling alley parking lot next to the empty one at the Country Time. Hannah had put out a sign saying people who weren't customers would be towed if they parked in her lot, but he was very much afraid the few cars sitting there were people who had ignored the warnings. Pat's advertising was paying off big-time.

Josie pulled into the bowling alley lot and, after drifting around for a few minutes, managed to squeeze her car into a tiny parking space next to the dumpster.

"How do you expect me to get out?" he asked curiously after she'd turned off the motor. He'd be able to open his door about two inches.

"Carefully." She opened her door into the dumpster. "I think that's Richie Dunlop's truck next to you, so don't worry about dinging it," she added and slid out, slippery as an eel.

"Sure. Easy for you," Mat groused. He was about twice her size. But with some twisting and cursing and, yes, slamming the door into the truck parked next to him, he managed to squeeze out. Fortunately he wasn't wearing his winter gear, or he might have had to cut a hole through the roof to escape.

"When it's time to leave, you can pick me up at the door," he told her as he tried to straighten out his rumpled clothing. "I about lost my masculinity there."

Josie leered. "Can't have that, hot stuff." Then she groaned and slapped her hands over her mouth. Even in the florescent parking lot lights, he could see her blushing. "Lord," she moaned. "Forget I said that."

"Nope." He couldn't have stopped the grin if he'd wanted to. Before he thought better of it, he wrapped an arm around her shoulders and turned her towards Murphy Lanes. "Come on, babe," he said with a leer of his own. "Let's get this over with."

Josie's shoulders stiffened under his arm, but she didn't pull away and he matched his stride to hers as they walked around the bowling alley to the front door.

"It's really busy," Josie whispered, watching more cars pull into the parking lot then meander around looking for spaces they wouldn't find. "I hope they don't park at Hannah's."

"I hope she really does tow the people who do," he agreed.

"Although maybe she should let them use her parking lot. They might go in for a drink when they're leaving."

"Maybe." It was almost like a guerrilla war, he thought, with each side trying to outmaneuver and outsmart the opponent.

There was a line of people waiting to enter the bowling alley through the glass entrance doors, which was also discouraging. Mat guided Josie to the end of it, and saw Richie Dunlop sitting at a table in the entry vestibule. The thin, bearded, somewhat rat-like man was stamping the backs of people's hands as they entered.

"You're kidding," he muttered. "They're stamping hands? You don't even have to freaking pay to get in."

"No, see it's smart," Josie said, grabbing his sleeve as they moved up in line. "Every time he stamps a person, he's stamping that notebook. That way, they'll be able to count later and see how many people were here. And because they're stamping hands, they won't count the same person twice if they go out for some reason and come back."

Mat guessed she was right, although he didn't know how smart it was to trust this task to Richie. Still, it was probably better than counting heads.

"Hand." Richie barked from his seat behind the table when it was their turn. "Come on, come on," he added impatiently. "Don't have all day."

Josie held out her hand.

"Don't you?" she asked sweetly.

Mat bit back a chuckle.

The urge to laugh died when Richie took her hand in his paws and spent far too long stamping the back of it.

"Have fun," he told her. His smile was almost obscene.

Josie lifted her chin and yanked her hand away. "Right." She took a step back.

Mat stuck out his own hand, wishing with everything inside him that he could plant a fist in the other man's face instead.

Beady eyes still on Josie, Richie stamped him sloppily and then put two stamps in his book.

"Who knew you'd grow up to be such a babe, huh Josie?" he said to her. "Looking good."

"I can't say the same for you," she said, then, as if sensing Mat was on the verge of reaching over the table to grab the other man's skinny neck, wrapped her hands around his arm and dragged him into the bowling alley.

"He is such a dick," she said as she pulled him through the crowd. "Hannah and I always used to call him Dickie Dunlop, not Richie."

"If he'd made a move on you, I would have beaten his ass into the ground," Mat told her.

"I know," she soothed, patting his chest.

Hearing her say it, just like that with amusement lacing her voice, dampened his anger. So he flung his arm around her shoulders again and tucked her up against his side. Yeah, it was a territorial move, even possessive, but what the hell. He was tired of playing games where Josie was concerned.

"I wonder if there's somewhere to sit in here," he said, looking around. The place was packed, the arcade was jumping and the bowling lanes, free for the night, were full of people.

"Let's go to the restaurant," Josie suggested, talking into his ear so he could hear her over the people, the music, and the thunder of bowling pins filling the space. "That's where Louise will be."

Her breath against his neck made him want to shiver. That didn't seem like a manly thing to do, so he tightened his hold on her instead.

The bar and restaurant portion of the bowling alley was bigger than he'd thought it would be, and Mat realized Pat had completely redesigned and updated the space. That investment, combined with the fact that the man had pulled it all together in a relatively short amount of time, spoke of a level of commitment he hadn't expected.

"This is really nice," Josie said. "And crowded," she added reluctantly.

The restaurant was separated from the bowling alley section by a rail fence. The bar stretched along one side with tables and booths spread out so people could either watch the action in the alleys or find some privacy, if they preferred. And she was right—it was packed with couples, families, and groups of kids. Several servers spun back and forth through the diners, and two bartenders were grabbing drink orders.

"Everything's half off tonight," Josie said.

"It is?" He looked down at her. "How do you know?"

"It was on the website. I'm sure that's why it's so busy." But she was chewing on her bottom lip and looking worried.

"Let's find a table," he said, and tugged her to a booth that was miraculously empty—probably because the servers hadn't had a chance to clear it, yet. They got to it at the same time as another couple, and everyone stopped and stared at each other.

"Mary Alice?" Josie asked, obviously shocked. "What are you doing here?"

"Oh hi, Josie," Mary Alice said. The woman, normally as open and welcoming as a sunflower, shifted on her feet, her blue eyes sliding to the slender, dark-haired man standing next to her. Mat recognized him as Mary Alice's boyfriend, although they'd never really been introduced. "I didn't know you'd be here."

"Yeah, well, I didn't know you'd be here either," Josie said, crossing her arms and glaring.

"Oh, well, um…" Mary Alice looked at Josie, then at the man again, then wrung her big workman-like hands. "I—"

"Excuse me," a loud female voice said behind them. "But if you're not sitting down, we'd like to get that booth."

Mat turned to see Margo Truelove, owner of the Spun Sugar candy store and head of the town chamber of commerce, standing behind them. She was clinging to the arm of a lanky town councilman with the same assertiveness that her white slacks clung to her robust form.

Margo was apparently wearing pink underwear.

"Sorry, ma'am," he said, pulling out the Texas accent that was almighty useful sometimes. "But we're gonna park here." He nodded towards the bar. "I see a coupla seats over there."

"Oh." Margo blinked at him, blushing as pink as her panties. "Why thank you kindly." Then she twittered and moved off, dragging the councilman after her. The guy looked back at them, his face a little desperate, but Mat only grinned.

"Sorry ma'am?" Josie said dryly. He saw she was watching him with quirked eyebrows. "You're a cowboy now?"

"No, ma'am," he said, tipping an imaginary hat to her. "Just a humble dishwasher."

She rolled her eyes and gestured to the booth. "We might as well all sit down before someone else tries to steal it," she said to Mary Alice.

They settled across from each other, and Josie frowned at Mary Alice again.

"I don't think Hannah knows you're here," she accused. "She would have told me you were coming."

"No, um..." Mary Alice looked around the room as if seeking an answer. The man next to her patted her shoulder.

"It's okay, honey," he said. "I'm Johnny Randolph," he said, holding out his hand to Josie. "I'm Mary Alice's life partner."

Josie blinked at him. "Uh, hi," she said and shook his outstretched hand.

Mat did the same when his hand was offered, and studied the other man. He had developed a definite soft spot for Mary Alice, who was always beaming a slightly crazed smile or scribbling in her little notebook when she should have been waiting on customers. She was also as warm and open as the day was long. Her boyfriend was good-looking and sharp, all cheekbones and dark eyes—attractive in a way that didn't seem like it would belong with Mary Alice's plain, round, good cheer. But seeing them together like this, they...fit.

"My brother, Roy, has a band," Johnny said to Josie.

"I know," she said. "My sister told me that he played at the carnival Hannah had a couple of weeks ago."

"They did real good," Mary Alice said eagerly. "Everybody liked them. And they didn't even drink too much beer or anything until the very end."

"Okay," Josie said, sounding confused.

"That's them there." Johnny nodded to where four men were clustered around the end of the bar. One was tall and skinny, one was short and skinny, one was big with a shaved head and tattoos showing under his black tank top, and the fourth man had probably been a defensive lineman in high school.

"It looks like they're drinking today," Mat observed.

"Yeah," Johnny agreed sadly. "Pat told them he'd cover all their drinks if they worked for free."

"Wait, what?" Josie held up a hand. "They're going to play here today?"

"Oh, but Josie, they have to," Mary Alice said, big eyes growing even wider until white showed all around the blue. "They did so good at the carnival, but they need to get more contacts and stuff, so when Pat came to them and said that this was going to be a really big deal, they had to take the job. They can't just pass up the opportunity. They can't."

"Hmmph." Josie crossed her arms and slouched against the back of the bench.

"And that's why we're here," Johnny said quickly. "When Roy told me they were getting free drinks, I knew we had to keep an eye on them."

"When they drink too much, they sometimes play an extended dance version of 'In-A-Gadda-Da-Vida,' Mary Alice told them urgently. "It's real good, but they love it so much they don't stop. Sometimes you have to pull them off the stage."

You sure the hell did. At the Country Time carnival, Deacon and Hannah had fought about Deacon's father or something, so neither had been paying much attention to the band when the guys had launched into the song. "In-A-Gadda-Da-Vida" was already too goddamned long as far as Mat was concerned, and an extended version was excruciating. The only thing that had stopped the band from continuing forever was the fact that someone, presumably Johnny, had turned off the sound system.

Johnny shrugged. "They don't have much self-control."

"Okay," Josie said reluctantly. "I guess it makes sense that you're here, then."

Mary Alice beamed, as if having Josie's permission made her day.

"Why are you here, Josie?" she asked innocently.

"I wanted to talk to Louise," Josie told her.

"Oh, I don't know her, but Johnny said she was around. Right sweetie?" she asked her boyfriend. Uh, life partner.

"I don't really know her either, but I heard someone say she was working back in the kitchen," Johnny said, smiling fatuously at Mary Alice.

Mat had mixed feelings about that smile. Mary Alice deserved someone smiling at her like that. But seeing it, and knowing nobody was smiling at *him* that way, was a hard punch in the gut.

"I hope I can talk to her because I want to say hi," Mary Alice said. "After all, if she hadn't left the Country Time, I wouldn't have gotten this great job. But she's busy, so I won't bother her."

Since the reason Louise left was because she'd been caught having sex in her car with Sam, Mat was pretty sure it was a good thing she was too busy to talk to Mary Alice. Sometimes Mary Alice didn't pick up on conversation signals all that well.

"I think I should go check on Roy and the guys," Johnny said worriedly. "That's got to be their fourth pitcher of beer."

Mat looked at the band again and saw that they weren't exactly steady on their barstools.

"Might be a good idea," he said.

"They'll start playing in a few minutes. Then they'll be okay." Johnny sounded like he was trying to convince himself.

"Sure."

"The waitress is coming over," Josie said. "Do you guys want anything?"

"No, that's okay," Johnny said, sliding out of the booth with Mary Alice following. "We'll just stay at the bar."

"They don't like it when Johnny watches over them," Mary

Alice said. "But they like all the wedding receptions they've been booking."

Johnny shrugged and smiled sheepishly. "It's habit. All that time on the road keeping track of Roy."

"Remember the night in Pittsburgh when Candy and Animal drank all those tequila shots and talked Roy into a drinking contest?" Mary Alice sighed. "Animal couldn't even sit at the drums that night. And I had to sing backup all by myself *and* play the guitar. But you were still great on lead."

"Yeah." Johnny looked even more worried. "We'll see you later," he said absently to Josie and Mat. Mary Alice waved and let herself be towed over to the bar.

Josie and Mat stared at each other.

"Mary Alice was in a band?" he said.

She shook her head. "I guess there's more to her than meets the eye?" She sounded hesitant.

He opened his mouth to respond but the server, a round woman of indeterminate years with a short cap of brown hair and a big smile, stepped up to the booth and put two menus on the table.

"Sorry it took me so long to get over here," she said cheerfully. "We're packed tonight, so we're all running around like nuts."

"No problem," Josie said, oh so casually. "Pat must be pleased."

The server's smiled broadened. "He sure is. He's worked hard to make this reopening a big deal, so we're all happy everyone showed up. It looks like the whole town!"

"Yeah," Josie said weakly. "Great."

The server chuckled. "Let me get these plates out of your way." Working efficiently, she cleared the table and took the dishes away, then came back and held up her order pad. "Now, my name is Cleo and I'll be taking care of you. Can I get you a drink, or do you need a minute?"

Mat ordered an IPA beer and was surprised when she just jotted it down on her order pad without comment. Pat really had built out his selection if they'd started carrying that brand.

Josie asked for water and pulled one of the menus towards her. "We don't know what we want to eat, yet."

"That's fine, honey. I'll be back with the drinks," Cleo beamed. "We've got a lot of choices now. You're going to have a hard time making up your mind." She winked at them and left.

Josie opened her menu.

"Wow," she said as she frowned at the page. "He's going all out."

Mat opened his menu and that saw she was right. Not only did it offer pizza and burgers, but also appetizers and fancier entrees for the hipster crowd.

"How is he going to be able to support all of this?" he wondered. "I mean, it's a great idea to have choices for the kids," he indicated the "young eaters" portion of the menu, "but he's going to have to keep a hell of a lot of food on hand to be able to have all of this."

"He's not just counting on the bowlers," Josie said darkly. "He wants the college kids, too. He wants everybody."

Cleo came back with their drinks and held up her order pad again. "Decide yet?" she asked kindly. "Don't forget—everything's half price tonight."

Mat ordered a random burger and Josie got a salad. When Cleo smiled and was about to walk away, Josie leaned around Mat to get the server's attention.

"Is Louise in the back?" she asked.

Cleo beamed. "She sure is. Are you a friend of hers?"

"I haven't seen her in years," Josie said, avoiding a direct answer. "Would it be okay if I snuck back to say hello?" She blinked her big baby blues at the older woman.

Cleo looked troubled. "I don't know. It's insane back there." She gestured around at the crowded booths and tables.

"I can only imagine." Josie smiled sweetly. "Will she take a break anytime? I don't want to bother her."

"Well…" Cleo hesitated for another minute. "She's supposed to take a break in about ten minutes. Poor thing's been on her feet all day. I could ask her to come out and see you."

"Perfect!" Josie's smile was beautiful.

Cleo eyed her a little warily, but then someone from another table called and she seemed to decide that she couldn't waste any more time on the conversation.

"I'll tell her," she said as she hustled off.

Josie settled back on the bench and crossed her arms over her chest.

"Perfect," she repeated, looking satisfied.

Mat shook his head and carefully poured some of the beer into the chilled glass and took a sip. Now *this* was perfect.

"Do you think she'll really come out?" he asked, taking another longer sip of the mellow brew.

"I think she's in manager mode," Josie said. "She's working the crowd and she'll be curious."

"Probably she'll look out, see you, and run in the other direction."

Josie shrugged. "If she does, I'll go back to the kitchen, even if Cleo throws herself bodily across my path."

"Determined," he said, smiling a little at the thought of the round Cleo grabbing Josie's ankles to keep her from getting into the kitchen. "She wouldn't stand a chance."

"No, she wouldn't." Smugly, Josie took a drink from the water glass.

Mat turned so he had his arm across the back of the bench seat, looking down into her stubborn expression.

"You really think talking to Louise is going to make a difference? You're not going to be able to force her or Pat to change their minds."

"I know." Josie put the glass on the table, then settled back again. "But she might listen. Or at the very least, maybe I can get a feeling for what she's thinking. I mean, I know I'm not much good at the whole working-in-the-kitchen thing, but I'll do whatever I can to help."

"Really determined," he said, just barely resisting the urge to drop his arm around her shoulders.

"Did you see the drink menu?" she asked. "They have all different kinds of beer now. The college kids will like that. And there are a lot of food choices that will appeal to the townspeople. Even with as insanely busy as it is tonight, they're keeping up with the service."

He shrugged. "I guess."

"And the food's really good, if the smiles are any indication."

"Yeah? So?"

"Look at this place," she said, gesturing to the bowling alley proper where the clatter and crash of bowling balls mixed with the jangle of the arcade games and the rock music pounding over the speakers. "Look at the people. They're having a blast."

He followed her gaze and tilted his head to acknowledge Rob Scanner, Martin's grandson, when he waved. Rob was hanging out with Harry Newman's grandson, also named Harry, who was an officer on the Hardy Falls police force. Mat didn't know if Harry the third was here in an official capacity, but he wasn't wearing a uniform.

Some college kids were clustered around the arcade, and he recognized Austin Grant, the kid who worked for Calvin at the hardware store, standing among them. Families bowled. Kids were running all over the damned place. A couple of older men he recognized as Country Time regulars walked into the restaurant area and took a seat at the bar, just like they usually did at Hannah's place.

He finally understood what Josie was getting at.

"Hannah's in big trouble," he said.

"I think she is." Josie sighed and slumped back, her head resting against his forearm. "She just doesn't have the money to compete with this." She waved around.

"Maybe it won't be like this all the time. Tonight's a special deal." The Country Time crew was a family—rapidly becoming *his* family. He didn't want to think about losing another one.

"Maybe." Josie sounded unsure. She started playing with the napkin wrapped around her silverware, picking at the sticky paper holding everything together, then looked at him, obviously troubled. "If I can talk to Louise, maybe I can get her to see—"

"See what?"

Mat jerked his head around and saw a petite woman with bright red hair standing at the end of their booth. She had brown eyes and an unwelcoming expression.

"Hello, Josie," she said, her voice cold.

Josie smiled, but it was tentative. "Hi, Louise."

21

Josie studied the woman who, once upon a time, had been one of her good friends. Louise's hair was a lot different than she remembered, a brilliant red instead of the soft blond from before. And the other woman looked...sharper somehow. She'd lost some weight, so she was relatively lean, but that wasn't the reason for the new hardness. It was in her eyes and in the tightness around her mouth.

Mat shifted, withdrawing his arm from where it had been resting on the bench behind her. She immediately missed the warmth of his skin.

"I'll just go say hello to some people I know," he said as he slid out of the booth. "Then you two can talk."

Josie smiled at him. "Thanks."

Nodding, he turned and walked away. Both women watched him go.

"Is that Mat Guerrero?" Louise asked.

Josie winced because she'd been unintentionally rude. "Sorry. I should have introduced you."

Louise turned back to her. "As what?"

Josie was confused. "What?"

"As the town slut? The one caught with Hannah's boyfriend?" Louise looked down and wiped her hands on the chef's apron she was wearing over her jeans and T-shirt.

"As my friend," Josie corrected.

"Right." Louise glanced around the room, and Josie saw that there were a number of people staring at them. It suddenly occurred to her how awkward this must be. It had taken guts for Louise to leave the safety of the kitchen to face the crowd. Hell, it had taken guts for her to come back to Hardy Falls in the first place.

"Why don't you sit down," she suggested, gesturing to the bench opposite her.

Louise looked around again, then slid into the booth. But her eyes remained cold.

"I heard you were back in town," she said to Josie, "helping Hannah in the kitchen."

Well, she'd known there would be gossip.

"Trying to." Josie pulled a face. "Not always successfully. I don't know how you do it."

She'd hoped that maybe the attempt at camaraderie would melt some of Louise's reserve, but no such luck. The other woman remained unmoved.

"I do it because I have to. What did you want?"

The abruptness knocked Josie off balance again.

"I just wanted to find out how you're doing."

"And maybe try to get some insider information?"

Josie decided to cut the bullshit because it wasn't working anyway. "Maybe," she admitted, putting her elbows on the table and leaning forward. "Maybe Hannah's wondering what's going on. Maybe I am, too."

"I think it's obvious what's going on." Louise gestured around the room. "We're kicking butt. I'm helping Pat, and I'm doing a hell of a good job."

"It looks like you are." Josie cocked her head. "Why?"

"Pat's been good to me, not that it's any of your business." Louise smiled, but it wasn't pretty. "He's my godfather, you know."

"I know." Josie saw the surprise before the other woman hid it. "Remember, Jenny's my sister," she said, attempting humor.

"Of course," Louise murmured, looking down at the table. "I guess she still knows everything that happens around here. Not many secrets in Hardy Falls."

"No. But even she was surprised to find out you were managing Pat's restaurant. Nobody knew that until a couple of days ago."

Louise shrugged. "We were trying to keep it quiet."

"Hiding?" As soon as the word was out, Josie hid a wince. Antagonizing the woman was not going to win her any points.

Sure enough, when Louise looked up her eyes flashing. "No. Not hiding. I'm through with hiding just because I made one mistake in this godforsaken town. But if people knew I was coming back, it would have been a distraction, and we had a lot to do."

"Gossip would have been one way to get the town to come to the reopening," Josie pointed out cynically.

Louise stared at her through flat, brown eyes. She'd always had such pretty eyes. "Murphy Lanes has to stand on its own. Word got out, but not everybody here tonight came to gawk at me."

"Maybe." Josie looked around at the crowd again. The townspeople had turned out in force. Regardless of why they'd shown up, they all appeared to be enjoying themselves. "It must have been hard to come back," she murmured, forgetting for a second that she and this new, harder version of Louise were not friends.

The other woman's shrug was more a flick of her shoulders, as if she could feel all of the eyes watching her. She probably could.

"It is what it is. After tonight, everyone will know I'm here. I'll deal with it all at once. Then it will be done."

Josie suspected that might be wishful thinking.

Louise started to get up. "Look, if that's all, I have to get back to the kitchen."

"There's something else." Josie stopped her, although she didn't think new-Louise was going to be quite as open to reason as old-Louise would have been.

Louise snorted. "Sure." She settled back down. "I know Hannah put you up to this, so spit it out."

"What makes you think Hannah put me up to anything?"

"You're here. She and Deacon wouldn't have the nerve to show their faces in here again, and June had better never even set foot in the parking lot. Not after what she did to Pat." Louise's eyes snapped.

Josie was taken aback by the sudden fury pouring off the other woman in waves. Her own temper jumped to meet it, because, really? Louise had the nerve to be angry with Hannah and June after what she'd done? What the hell?

"Hey," she said, leaning forward. "Good old Pat is the real problem here, not Hannah or June."

"Bullshit." Louise snorted. "June and Calvin embarrassed Pat in front of the whole town. He loved June and she crapped all over him. Believe me, I know what that feels like. Then Deacon comes in here with all sorts of threats just because Pat had the guts to speak his mind about your precious Hannah."

"First of all, Pat was spreading lies about Hannah that affected her getting a bank loan. Deacon told him to stop. As for June, Pat's the one who pushed the situation by not getting a clue when she tried to break it off with him. If he'd left her alone, they wouldn't have had that smackdown." Josie knew she was snarling and really didn't care. "And who are you to judge, anyway? Like Hannah wasn't humiliated by what you did?"

Louise's face, still round if not as plump, was pale. "If

Hannah had opened her eyes even a little bit, she would have known what was going on. Sam came on to *me,* not the other way around. We'd been seeing each other for a couple of months before we got caught."

Oh, really? Josie was pretty sure Hannah didn't know that part. Her friend seemed to be under the impression that the car incident had been the first time Sam and Louise had hooked up.

"That makes it even worse. You were her friend, and you went behind her back," Josie said quietly. As far as she was concerned, there was no excuse for that.

"Hannah and I were never friends," Louise said with equal softness.

What the hell?

"That is so not true," Josie said, disbelieving

Hannah, Josie, and Louise had all hung out in high school. They had spent nights at each other's houses, gone to the movies, parties, even had a summer vacation together at the shore once. True, Louise had been a year younger, but it had always been the three of them.

And yes, okay, Hannah and Josie hung out the most, but they'd let Louise come along if they were doing anything fun. They'd included her.

And yes, maybe there'd been times when they'd forgotten to include her, but still. They'd almost always tried.

Besides, Hannah had basically created a job for Louise when she'd had to leave college because she couldn't afford to stay. The bar had needed another server, but she'd had to convince her father to let her hire more staff.

Louise remained unconvinced.

"Please. Hannah didn't know I existed unless it was convenient. Sam saw me." She paused. "Or I thought he did. And then when the shit hit the fan, he left me standing there alone and went running right back to Hannah. So you'll forgive me if she's not my favorite person."

Josie gaped at her. "You're blaming Hannah for that? If you're going to blame anyone, blame Sam."

"Oh, trust me. I do." Louise sighed and seemed to deflate a little. "Look. I screwed up. I know it. You can trust me when I tell you that I regret it. But I'm back in Hardy Falls because Pat asked me to help him, and he's giving me a hell of an opportunity to show what I can do. He wants this restaurant to be a success, and I'm going to see that it is." She slid out of the booth and stood next to the table. "Excuse me. I have to go."

She strode off to the kitchen, ignoring the stares and whispers that followed her.

Josie slumped in her seat. "Shit." Obviously Mat had been right. This whole endeavor had been a complete waste of time.

"How'd it go?"

She jumped as Mat slid into the booth opposite her.

"Where'd you come from?"

He frowned. "Uh, the bar? I was watching and saw Louise leave."

She waved it away because it had been a stupid question.

"It went like crap," she said, answering his question. "She didn't even give me a chance to tell her why I was here."

"Want to try again? I'll block Cleo."

"Thanks, but no. She's not going to listen to me or anybody else."

"Not a huge surprise. But I still don't understand why she and Pat are so intent on screwing over Hannah."

"There are a lot of reasons." She shrugged. "Hurt. Jealousy."

Mat's expression was remote as he looked over to where a group of kids played at some new arcade machines. "Emotions are a bitch. They mess everything up."

"Yeah. Why can't people just be logical?"

He looked back at her and smiled. "Because people are messed up, too."

"I guess."

Cleo came with their food, her broad face lacking her earlier good cheer. She put the plates down in front of them before hurrying off without speaking. Josie glumly studied her salad. The food looked great and, if Mat's expression when he took a big bite of his burger was any indication, it tasted the same.

Depressed, she picked up her fork and toyed with the lettuce, wishing idly that she'd gotten a burger, too.

Hannah really was in trouble. If the food had been bad, the service shoddy, or the place dingy, the Country Time might have stood a chance. But the bowling alley's little restaurant sparkled, as if every surface had been scrubbed. The service was prompt and the food was great. Louise always did have a knack for managing and organizing.

"She really hates Hannah," Josie said, feeling even sadder when she thought about it. "I had no idea."

"Hate?" Mat asked through a giant mouthful.

"Well, maybe it's resentment more than hate, but still. I thought we were all friends. Or at least that we were friends before she got involved with Sam. But Louise doesn't see it that way."

He swallowed, then wiped his mouth with the paper napkin. "It's funny how two people can judge the same situation completely differently. Nobody ever really knows another person."

"Louise said she'd been involved with Sam for a couple of months before they got caught," she said.

He went back to his burger and shrugged, a rolling of his broad shoulders. "Not a shock."

"Really?" That distracted her from noticing how well his shirt fit. Shaking her head, she put down her fork. "I still can't believe it. No matter how Louise felt about Hannah, how could she do that to her?"

"Sometimes people aren't who you think they are." He sounded very certain as he wiped his mouth before pushing away his empty plate. "That kind of thing, what happened between Louise and Sam, well, it usually doesn't just pop out of thin air. It builds slowly, and nobody notices until it's too late."

"I suppose." The tone in his voice, the absolute assurance with which he spoke, piqued her curiosity about him again. "Did you—"

She was interrupted by a sharp burst of static echoing through the speakers scattered around the bowling alley. The noise cut through the roar of voices and made her jump about a foot.

"What the hell?" Mat was looking over her shoulder, so she turned, hooking her arm over the back of the bench and sitting sideways on the seat.

The four men Mary Alice and Johnny had left to go shepherd at the bar had moved to a small, makeshift stage set up in a corner of the cavernous lobby. The big bald guy was behind a drum kit, twirling drumsticks and grinning; one of the skinny guys was behind an electronic keyboard; the other was holding a bass guitar looking bored; and the last man was clutching the microphone on a stand, a guitar strapped across his chest. That must be Johnny's brother, Roy.

"Hello, everyone!" he yelled into the mic, his voice echoing over the crash of pins and the noise of the arcade. "Are you ready to party?"

There was some desultory clapping from a few of the people standing nearby, but most of the customers didn't seem to pay much attention.

"We're Roy and the Outlaws!" Roy shouted, "And we're glad to be here!"

"That wasn't their name when they played at Hannah's

carnival a couple of weeks ago," Mat said. "I guess they changed it."

She glanced back at him. "Why?"

He shrugged.

"We're going to be here all night, so get ready to have some fun!" Roy yelled.

"We'll have fun if you shut up!" someone yelled back.

Roy determinedly stuck out his blunt chin.

"All right! I will!" he responded, counted out a beat, and the band launched into its first song.

"'Stayin' Alive'?" Josie wondered aloud. "Really?"

"They sound pretty good," Mat pointed out after a moment. "Roy's falsetto can use some work, but people are already dancing."

He was right. A few of the younger kids had left the arcade and were spinning wildly around the area set up as a dance floor. The college and high school students followed not long after. The older people were a little slower to get out there, but she saw Bernie Housemann doing some kind of a move at the edge of the crowd. Apparently, Roy and the band weren't the only ones who'd been taking advantage of the bar.

"He's going to throw out his back," Mat observed. He was watching Bernie, too, an amused smile curving his lips.

Her hormones stirred with the interest that never exactly went away where he was concerned.

"Want to dance?" she asked. The thought of moving with him was definitely appealing.

He shrugged, ever so casually. "No thanks. I'm fine."

"Oh."

Oops. Well, that was embarrassing. Apparently she hadn't read the signs right, after all.

"Hey." Mat reached across the table and touched her arm. "It's not...I don't..." His eyes slid away, and she thought she saw a tinge of pink under his tanned skin. "I can't dance," he muttered.

Her eyebrows winged up skeptically. "Really?" She jerked a thumb to where the fine folk of Hardy Falls were flopping around on the makeshift dance floor. "Have you seen these people? And you're saying *you* can't dance?" Honestly. He could have come up with a better excuse than that. "If you want to leave, it's fine with me. We can go," she said, trying to sound as if she didn't care one way or the other.

"No, it's..." He shifted restlessly and she began to get a sense of how uncomfortable he was. "I mean I *really* can't dance."

She turned to face him fully.

"Huh. Okay."

He ran his hand through his hair, disturbing the dark strands. "Look. My dad's Mexican, right? Latin rhythm and all?" He threw his arms open. "Nothing."

She folded her arms, feeling an amusement she couldn't let him see. God, it was killing the man to admit that he wasn't good at something.

"Nothing? You're sure?"

"Oh, honey, trust me. I'm sure." He shook his head. "I've tried to learn, believe me."

"Great way to pick up chicks?" she suggested. He flashed her a brief grin.

"It could be." He shrugged. "But not if you damage them in the first five minutes."

"Step on toes?"

He winced. "I actually broke a girl's toe once. I mean, I was wearing boots and she was in sandals, but you know you aren't getting a second date when the first one ends up at the hospital."

Oh, ouch.

"I guess she was pissed off."

He smiled, sprawling back in the seat. "You have no idea. And Gail..." He trailed off and the smile faded.

"Gail?" Josie prodded because she could tell that this was part of his mystery. "I guess whoever she is, she didn't like dancing with you."

"I tried a couple of times because she really liked going out dancing at the clubs. She said I was a gorilla on the dance floor and she was tired of having bruises on her feet the next day, so she'd go clubbing by herself. I told her I'd go and just sit at the bar. She said not to bother."

Josie was pretty sure she wouldn't have liked Gail very much.

"But hey, it sounds like you got a second date with her, at least," she said, trying to lighten the mood.

"Yes." Mat bit off the end of the word and looked away. "Probably would have been better if I hadn't."

No. Josie did not like this Gail person.

"Well, I'm braver than she is and I think you can do at least as well as Bernie." She jerked her thumb to the dance floor again.

Mat snorted out a laugh. "I'm not sure I can move that way."

She looked and saw that Bernie was trying to impress some of the college girls. He did not appear to be succeeding. Was that the "wave" or the "worm"?

"Not moving that way is a good thing," she told him, sliding out of the booth and slinging the strap of her little purse across her body. Standing next to him, she held out her hand. "Come on."

"But—"

"I know what Gail and the others told you," she said. "Who gives a crap about them? We'll just go and have a good time."

He still hesitated.

"I don't want to hurt you."

"I'm fast and I have feet made of cast iron," she assured him, still holding out her hand. Slowly, reluctantly, he took it and let her pull him out of the booth.

They found a corner without many people, and as Roy and his band wailed into "Ain't Too Proud To Beg," Josie took Mat's hands and put them on her hips.

"Just stand there and shuffle your feet sort of side to side," she instructed.

He looked uncertain, but did it. She began swaying with him, adding an extra jerk of the hips and some leg action when it looked like he'd got the rhythm. Then she realized he was focused on her hips instead of his feet.

"Hey." She forked her fingers and pointed them at his eyes, then at her own eyes. "Pay attention."

He grinned. "You're distracting me."

Which might be a good thing because he definitely seemed more relaxed.

Mary Alice and Johnny swung by, both bebopping to the beat. Mary Alice's wide face was sunny with happiness, as always.

"Oh, there you are!" she called. "Aren't Roy and the band doing real great?"

"They are," Josie agreed. Part of her wished the band had sucked because this was just one more success for Pat, but Mary Alice looked so relieved and joyful that she couldn't help smiling at her.

"I hope he doesn't try the guitar riff he showed me this morning," Johnny muttered, then winced when, sure enough, Roy broke into something his guitar couldn't quite handle. "Oh, well."

"They're fine," Josie assured him, as she tried to casually muffle her ear against her shoulder by pretending to scratch it.

Johnny grinned at her—he knew what she was doing. Then he and Mary Alice were gone again.

"She's so happy," Mat said, almost to himself.

"She is. Seeing them together...well, you can see that they love each other."

"Yeah." He seemed to come back to himself and smiled down at her. "No injuries, yet." Just as he said it, she bobbed when she should have weaved and his big foot came down on hers.

Josie managed not to curse but couldn't stop the sharp breath of pain.

"Damn it!" Mat stopped moving. "I told you I sucked at this."

"No!" She grabbed him when he tried to back away. "I'm fine, I'm fine. That was my fault, anyway."

Roy and the band, bless their little hearts, broke into a slow song. "Unchained Melody."

"Come on," she said. "The slow songs are easy. You don't even have to move your feet."

He frowned at her but stopped trying to pull away.

"Come on," she repeated. She slid into him and lifted her arms to wrap them around his neck, notching her body into his. Oh, my Lord, the feel of that man against her. "Dance with me," she instructed, her voice throaty.

The look in his dark eyes wasn't uncertainty, now. It was something hotter, more intense. He swept his gaze over her upturned face and then wrapped his arms around her, settling one hand on her waist and the other on her ass, pulling her even more tightly against him.

"You'd better show me what to do," he said, sounding rough.

She began to move.

22

___

Mat hadn't been kidding when he'd told Josie he couldn't dance. He still remembered the look on Gail's face when she'd taken him to her favorite club, back when they'd first started dating. Her glare of disgust when he'd stepped on her foot for the fourth time would be hard to forget.

But this was different, and he didn't quite know why. When Josie shifted *into* him, with her arms around his neck and her hips tight against his, he started swaying with her. Although, frankly, he wasn't paying the slightest bit of attention to what he was doing. His entire focus was on her body shifting against his, her breath against his neck, the play of muscles along her back, and the roundness of her ass under his hand.

The voices of people and the clanging of machines rumbling under the roar of music all faded. He closed his eyes and dropped his face into her hair, breathing in the floral scent of her shampoo mixed with the earthier tones of her perfume. Or maybe that was just her.

She lightly rubbed her face against his chest and he felt her inhale, as if she was breathing him in, too.

They weren't really doing much more than sliding their

bodies against each other, kind of like slow-motion sex. For the first time, he truly appreciated the appeal of dancing.

Why hadn't it ever been like this before? He'd dated plenty of women, and he'd never felt this way.

He pulled her more tightly against him and moved them into a darker corner of the room. Josie murmured, running her mouth up his neck.

The shiver of response was immediate, and if he'd been thinking, he might have been self-conscious about the way his dick went from zero to sixty in half a second.

Fortunately, he wasn't thinking.

Roy and his group transitioned into another song he recognized: "Faithfully." He moved his hands to pull Josie impossibly closer into the cradle of his thighs. They were barely even swaying now.

"Get a room!"

The voice was loud, unexpected. Josie started and Mat jerked his head up to see Bernie Housemann and Chet Hinkle watching them. Both men were laughing, and Mat wanted to shove the beers they were holding down their throats. It was only because he didn't want to let go of Josie that he managed to stop himself from taking a step towards the men.

Now that some awareness had returned, Mat could see that they had the attention of a number of other people, as well. Some were watching them with obvious amusement, some with bright-eyed interest. Austin Grant pulled away from the girl he was dancing with long enough to give Mat a grin and a thumbs up before wrapping himself around his date again.

Jesus.

"I think we'd better leave," he said to Josie, hearing the gravel in his voice.

She blinked and swallowed before nodding, her face pink in the dim light.

"Might be a good idea," she said, also sounding husky.

Without saying anything else, he grabbed her hand and hauled her after him—past the townspeople, out the bowling alley's glass entry, around the building, and right to her car parked next to the dumpster.

Crackling floodlights didn't alleviate the darkness, and he pushed her up against the end of her car, stroking his hands down her body because he just had to touch her again.

"Oh, hell," she muttered, as she grabbed his hair and yanked his head down to hers. Then she slammed her mouth against his, and he tasted Josie Kline for the very first time.

She kissed him with soft lips and a fierce mouth. No, she feasted on him. So he returned the favor, grabbing her butt and yanking her up onto her toes.

Josie moaned, and he took the opportunity to slide his tongue into her mouth, tasting more of her, encouraging her to taste more of him. Finally, she pulled away a little so that they could draw in a few deep breaths.

"God, Mat." She wrapped her arms around his neck, dug her fingers in his hair, and kissed him again.

Loud, drunken male voices talking nearby finally pulled them back to reality. When she tried to put a little distance between them, he reluctantly let her have some space.

"Go," she gasped for air. "We have to..."

"Go." His breathing wasn't all that steady either. "Keys."

"You drive?" She sucked in another deep breath, which pressed her beautiful breasts more firmly against his chest. He hadn't given her *that* much room. "Where?"

He'd been kidding himself ever since he'd met her. Ever since she'd blown into the Country Time with that blizzard, like his own personal storm.

"My place," he said. Then winced when he remembered where he lived. "No. A hotel."

Josie cupped his face in her hands, rubbing her fingers over his cheekbones.

"Your place is fine."

"I share a bathroom with three other guys."

She winced. "Right. Forgot. Okay, but not too far away."

Mat leaned down and kissed her, losing himself again until somebody laughed nearby. Bernie. He'd recognize that donkey's bray anywhere. No way did he want to deal with the man, now.

"Let's go."

Josie dug around in her purse, pulled out the car keys, and handed them to him, then waited for him to unlock the doors.

"Get moving," she instructed as she climbed into the passenger seat with a lot less difficulty than he'd had getting out of it.

Mat slid behind the wheel, and when Josie immediately shifted on the bench seat to plaster herself up against his side, he kissed her again.

More time passed before he heard the beep of the lock on the truck next to them.

Shaking his head to clear it a little, he started the motor, put the car in reverse, and almost mowed down Richie Dunlop walking up to his pickup.

Mat didn't give a good damn. He peeled away as Richie yelled after them, turned out of the bowling alley parking lot on to the highway and headed to God only knew where. Just someplace private where he could finally have her to himself.

Josie ran her hand down his shirtfront.

"You need to put on a seat belt." He grunted when her wandering hand played with his belt buckle.

"You sure?" Josie sounded coy and cupped his erection where it strained against his jeans.

Mat was not proud of the noise he made.

"Didn't think so." She massaged his length through the material, her hand squeezing and stroking.

"Don't want to..." he drew in a deep breath "...wreck..."

"You won't." He couldn't look at her, but he heard the smile in her voice. She leaned even closer and moved her mouth over his jawline. "You can multitask," she breathed in his ear.

"Jesus Christ." Clutching the steering wheel like a lifeline, he tried to focus on the road while she proceeded to drive him insane. It had been a long time since he'd been touched this way. A *long* time.

He pulled the sedan into the first motel they came across. It wasn't very big, just one building with two floors of rooms overlooking the parking lot, but the freak snowstorm a couple of days ago had scared off most of the sightseers, so it looked pretty empty.

Mat parked with a screech of brakes, shut off the engine, and turned to Josie. He grabbed her and plundered her mouth, showing her without words how desperate she'd made him.

"God." Finally, he had to let her go so he could breathe. "Stay...here..." he panted.

She was slumped against the seat, her eyes dark in the ambient light of the parking lot.

"'Kay," she wheezed.

He got out of the car while he still could, untucking his shirt to try and cover the obvious bulge in his pants. Dear God, he was as hard as a teenager.

Moving quickly, he walked into the office. The kid at the front desk took one look at him and smiled slyly. Any other time that would have annoyed him, but at the moment all that mattered was the fact that once Mat signed the register and handed over his credit card, he got a room key card.

Back in the car, he couldn't even glance at Josie because if he did, he knew there was a good chance they'd never even make it to the room he'd just paid for. So he focused on not burning rubber as he pulled away from the office, although the engine did roar when he stomped his foot down on the gas.

Somehow he found the right door with the right number

on the first floor at the far end of the building. Somehow he parked. Somehow he got out, waited for Josie to do the same, locked the car doors, and took her hand. Somehow he didn't kiss her before he led her into the room. Somehow he remembered to shut the door behind them, pull the drapes, and turn on the lights. He had a brief impression of two double beds and an air of relative cleanliness. Then, he turned to stare at the woman who was suddenly the only thing he could think about.

She was standing near the closest bed, staring back at him. Her eyes were huge and luminous, her soft mouth a little swollen, and her face a pink from whisker burn. If he had anything to say about it, she was going to be chafed in some other places, too, before the night was over.

He took a step towards her and then stopped because he couldn't quite read her expression. A little dazed but maybe uncertain, as well?

Shit.

"You want this, right?" he growled because he didn't want to assume anything. "You're sure?"

Please God, say "yes."

There was a moment of hesitation—just long enough to make his heart stop—and then she smiled. He could see her whole body soften, like stone melting, and she relaxed. It was only then that he realized how tense she'd been.

"I'm sure," she said, then threw her little purse on the nightstand and came over to him to wrap her arms around his neck.

"Thank Christ." He took her mouth in another kiss. It started out as demanding as the others had been, both of them wrestling for control, both of them hungry. But somewhere along the way it changed. Became more about exploration. Teasing nips, tempting tongues, breathless gasps.

Mat let his hands roam down her body, cupping that excellent ass again before reaching around and up to knead her breast.

Josie pulled away to sigh, her own hands busily unfastening his shirt, running over his chest, rubbing his nipples. She pulled away.

"We didn't stop at a drugstore," she pointed out, breathless. "I don't... Do you—?"

"We're covered," he assured her, then groaned when he remembered he hadn't exactly been active in this area lately. "Well, for one time."

Josie smiled up at him, her eyes dark and deep in the light from the bedside lamps.

"Let's make it count," she whispered.

He pulled her close again, and this time ran his hand under her blouse, so silky and sexy. But not as silky and sexy as her skin. He moved up to her breasts, teasing them through her bra before reaching around to unfasten it so he'd have some room to play.

Josie gasped, leaning back when he plucked her nipples, wordlessly encouraging him to go further. He complied, sliding his mouth up and down the length of her neck, over her cheek, finding her mouth again, and sinking in. She clutched at his hair, pulling him closer.

He needed her on that damned bed five minutes ago.

Still eating at her mouth, he lifted her. She wrapped her long legs around him, chewing on his earlobe as he half carried, half fell over to the nearest bed and practically threw her onto it. She bounced and giggled when she hit the mattress. The laugh turned to a moan when he came down on top of her.

"Mat..."

He backed away a little bit, so he could look at her. Then, carefully, he removed her blouse and dropped it onto the floor, slipped off the bra—pretty and pink—and tossed it down, as well.

The bra was not nearly as pretty as what it had covered.

Ravenous, he bent his head and ran his mouth over her

breasts, first one, then the other, until she was squirming against him and yanking at his hair. When he finally took her nipple in his mouth, sucking and chewing, she gasped and cursed at him.

"Naked…" Josie panted. "You…now…"

What a great idea.

Mat pushed away from her and yanked off his shirt. Then he stood and shucked off the jeans she'd already loosened, along with his briefs, socks, and shoes. He grabbed his wallet, got the all-important condom, and put it on the nightstand before turning back to her.

She was lying there looking like a debauched angel, naked from the waist up, rumpled from the waist down. When she grinned at him, he felt his heart stutter, just a little bit.

"Looking good, hot stuff," she said, waggling her eyebrows at him. She held out her arms to him. "Come here."

Putting a knee on the bed, he watched her gaze fix on the hardness of his shaft jutting out in front of him. She licked her lips, staring. "Get over here."

Mat found himself chuckling as he dropped down on the bed beside her, then quickly sobered when she rolled onto her side and took his length in her small, soft hands. She tugged them up and down, and swirled her fingers around the tip.

"Jesus." He drew in a deep breath as she bent her head and lapped at him. Reluctantly, he tugged on her hair until she stopped. "I only have one condom," he warned. "I'm not wasting it."

Josie's eyes were hooded and hot when she looked up at him. "Have you been tested?" she asked throatily.

He nodded. "Sure. But you shouldn't take any chances."

She smiled at him softly. "I trust you." And she bent her head again, swallowing around him.

Mat felt every muscle in his body go rigid as she worked him, his hand gripping her thigh as he tried to keep control. He felt the scratch of denim under his fingers and suddenly realized she was still wearing jeans. Getting her undressed suddenly seemed imperative. He needed her naked *now*. He needed to be inside her *now*.

Pulling away from her just about killed him, and he almost came right on the spot when she pouted and licked her full lips. Breathing through his teeth, he practically ripped the rest of her clothes off her body and threw them haphazardly around the room.

Josie laughed, but he didn't care. Sliding his hand up her thighs, he dipped his fingers into the core of her, feeling the heat and the liquid pooling. She arched up against his hand, cooing a little with excitement. He loved the noises she made.

Mat grabbed for the condom, ripping the packaging and rolling it over his engorged length with hands that shook a little.

It had been a *very* long time.

He positioned himself at her entrance and pushed in slowly, managing to hold himself back with an effort. When he was fully seated inside her, she wrapped her legs around his hips, dug her heels into his butt, and pulled him down to her so that she fully encircled him.

"Ride 'em, cowboy," she breathed and surprised a laugh out of him.

Mat started moving. Back and forth, faster and faster, until he was slinging his hips against hers. The sound of their flesh meeting was loud in the quiet room.

Josie's head was flung back, her hands scrabbling at his shoulders as if she was trying to find something to hold onto, urging him to go even faster. He felt the tension building inside her and desperately tried to hold on, wanting them to go over together.

"God, Mat!" she groaned.

Finally—*finally*—just when he thought he couldn't last a

second longer, when his rhythm was ragged as his body reached for fulfillment, Josie spasmed around him, her fingers digging into his shoulders like claws.

The waves of her body milking him was the last straw. With a shout of pleasure, he let go of his restraint and poured himself into her.

Moments passed in silence. Then the tension, along with everything else inside him, drained and Mat collapsed, rolling so he wouldn't crush her.

"Holy cow," Josie murmured, panting in his ear.

"Yeah."

After another moment, he forced himself to sit up and deal with the condom, hobbling over to the bathroom to clean up before stumbling back to her. He lay back on the bed by her side and curled around her, pulling her against him, and cupping her breast possessively.

The casual comfort of the situation gave him pause, and some of the utter relaxation he'd felt ebbed away.

Josie must have sensed a change because she ran her hand up and down his arm.

"Second thoughts?" she asked.

"No." Not really. "You?"

"No." She continued to stroke his arm, and he felt interest stirring again. Too bad he couldn't do anything about it at the moment. "You do realize we're going to play the lead in the gossip mill tomorrow, right?" she asked.

He hadn't really thought about it, but she was right, of course. The locals of Hardy Falls did love their gossip.

"It doesn't matter," he said. After all the talk he'd had thrown his way in Texas, this would be nothing.

Josie turned her head to look at him over her shoulder, her dark hair a tousled cloud against the cheap motel pillowcase.

"Really?"

Bending his head, he kissed her cheek tenderly.

"Really."

Josie turned away again, her body relaxing a little in his arms.

"Good." She was quiet for a long time, then licked her lips. "Was this a one-night stand, Mat?"

He'd been watching her tongue, but the question got his attention.

"Do you want it to be?" He didn't know how he'd feel if she said "yes."

Josie shook her head. "No."

Mat let out the breath he didn't realize he'd been holding. "Then it's not."

She was quiet for a long moment. "You know I'm going to have to find a job soon."

"In the city?" he asked carefully.

Jose shrugged. "Somewhere."

But probably not here.

"I just, you know, thought I should mention it," she said. Her body was tense again, braced against his.

Gently, he turned her in his arms until they were facing each other, naked on top of the comforter, legs tangled.

"It's okay," he said, pulling her head down onto his chest, carding his fingers through her tangled hair. "But maybe we can have something until you leave."

She nuzzled her face against his chest.

"Yes," she said. "We will."

23

Josie looked over at Mat as he drove them down the highway to the Country Time the next afternoon.

What had she done?

Well, she'd had some pretty terrific sex, so she'd done that.

In fact, after he'd recovered, Mat had gotten up and gone to a 24-hour convenience store for more condoms. So she'd had pretty terrific sex several times last night. They'd both had a lot of pent-up demand.

Although she couldn't quite figure out why Mat's demand had been so pent up. Sexy bastard that he was, there had to be plenty of women willing to help him out with that particular problem.

Shifting in the seat because she was a little sore from all of the un-penting, she considered his profile.

"What are you looking at?" he asked, his mouth quirking into a smile.

Giving in to the impulse, she leaned over and kissed the edge of that mouth, lingering as the taste of his skin exploded across her tongue.

"You," she said softly.

"Don't start," he warned, moving his hands to grip the steering wheel in a way that made her smile. It was so obvious that he wanted to be gripping her instead. "We're almost at the Country Time."

"Oh. Right." Josie flopped back in her seat. "I don't know what we're going to tell Hannah about Pat's reopening."

"Not to mention yours," he said.

"Shut up!" She slapped his arm but found herself grinning.

Her reopening had been...grand.

After the excesses of the night had calmed, they'd slept until well into the afternoon, curled together like puppies, then woken each other with slow and sleepy kisses before heading to the shower. Once they'd inhaled the muffins and coffee Mat had run out to get, Josie had texted Hannah to see when she'd be at the Country Time.

Now, the terse response read. *Get over here.*

When she'd relayed the message to Mat, he'd sighed. "Hannah's gonna be pissed."

More than pissed, she was going to be scared, Josie thought as she watched the trees on the side of the road slide past the window. And maybe she should be. Pat was putting a lot of effort and money into the restaurant, and with Louise there to hold him back from some of his more jackasserdly behaviors, it might actually be a success.

"I wish I could have changed my clothes," she said, knowing the state of her clothing was going to cause comment. Her jeans were okay, but her blouse looked like it had been tied up in a knot for a week.

"Want me to take you home first?" Mat asked, quirking his eyebrows at her.

"No. I just want to get this done." Besides, when Mat had been out getting the condoms, she'd sent her mother a text to tell her she wouldn't be home that night. The reply, a cryptic *I see*, had her wincing.

Probably not a good idea to head back to the house with Mat.

Mat turned off the highway into the Country Time parking lot and drove around the building.

"Looks like Hannah's not the only one here," he commented. "That's June's car. And Mary Alice's, I think."

"Great." Josie sighed.

Mat parked, and after they both got out of the car, he walked over to her and tossed her the keys.

"A pleasure to drive your machine," he said soberly, then grinned. "Was it good for you, too?"

She punched him in the stomach.

He didn't even pretend to flinch, just slung his arm around her shoulders.

"Come on. Let's get this over with."

Josie wrapped her arm around his waist, tucking her hand familiarly into the back pocket of his jeans. She tried not to get overheated by the feel of his butt flexing when he walked, but she ended up digging her fingers into the taut flesh under the denim.

"Stop it," he growled. She laughed, liking the fact that she had the power to bother him, too.

They walked together to the back door and he opened it for her, rolling his eyes when he realized it wasn't locked.

Josie shrugged and started to step into the kitchen, but she couldn't help reaching up and kissing him on the mouth as she went to move past him.

"Stop that," June's voice snapped her back to awareness just as the kiss had started to deepen. "Screw after you tell us whether you knocked some sense into Louise."

Spinning around, Josie saw June standing next to the grill, wearing big rubber gloves and holding a scouring pad in one hand. Her other hand was fisted on her hip.

"Sorry we're late," Mat said, the sound of laughter in his

voice. He gently pushed Josie the rest of the way into the kitchen, then closed the door as he followed her.

June smirked. "I know what you two have been doing, and I even know where you've been doing it."

Josie scowled at her. "You don't know everything."

"Really?" June threw down the scouring pad and pulled off her gloves. "The kid that was working the overnight shift at the Starlight Motel last night is a buddy of Austin's. He recognized Mat and told Austin he was sure he was there with a woman. Austin told Calvin when he went into work today that he figured it was Josie because you two were hanging all over each other at the bowling alley. Calvin called to tell me." She smirked again. "Word travels fast."

Josie glowered. "It sure the hell does."

June cackled. "Come on. We've been waiting."

She led the way through the swinging kitchen door to the taproom. Deacon was standing behind the bar, leaning on the top, a mug of coffee at his elbow. Hannah was sitting across from him, Mary Alice next to her.

"Here they are," June called, heading to the big coffee pot behind the bar. "Both of them. Funny, huh?"

"June," Mat protested mildly, following her to the coffee.

Josie looked at Hannah and saw that her friend was scrutinizing her.

"You look rested," Hannah said demurely.

She was pretty sure she looked ravished, but she really couldn't find it in herself to regret the fact.

"I feel terrific," she said and sat on the stool next to Hannah, then grinned at Mat when he handed her a mug of coffee. "Thanks, sex machine," she cooed.

"God," he said and took a long drink from his own mug.

There was a pause as everyone else in the room stared at them.

"Okay, then," Hannah said. "So that happened."

Josie crossed her legs and sipped perfectly prepared coffee. "Obviously," she said, knowing it sounded smug. Well, she felt smug. Her dry spell had been well and truly broken. Every inch of her body felt well...tended.

"I'm so happy," Mary Alice said, beaming as she leaned forward to see around Hannah. "Johnny and I saw you guys dancing to Roy's band, and Johnny said to me, 'Those two are an item,' and I said 'I hope so,' and then Roy started on 'Faithfully,' and that's our song, so we didn't talk anymore, and when I looked again you were gone."

"Did Roy play 'Unchained Melody'?" Hannah asked, sounding a little nostalgic. "That's Deacon's and my song."

Hey! Josie thought. *That's Mat's and my song!*

Wait—they had a song?

"It sure is." Deacon reached over the bar to stroke Hannah's arm. "I still remember Roy's band playing it at the Wounded Sparrow."

They shared a look that was not entirely fit for company.

"Oh, Roy plays 'Unchained Melody' real good," Mary Alice said. "He was playing it when Johnny and I first noticed Mat and Josie dancing together." Her face grew troubled as she looked at Hannah. "Are you sure you're not angry at me because Roy and his band played at Pat's event? I didn't know how to tell you, and then I got sick, and then I thought maybe I *shouldn't* tell you, but then last night I realized you'd hear about it anyway and I needed to tell you because I didn't want you to think I was lying to you or keeping anything from you, because I wasn't."

"Mary Alice." Hannah put a hand on the other woman's arm, stemming the flood of words. "I already told you ten times. We're fine."

"Are you sure?" Mary Alice blinked her big eyes.

"Positive."

Deacon frowned at Mat. "You and Josie...got together after dancing to Roy and the Bounty Hunters?"

"They're not the Bounty Hunters anymore," Mat told him. "I think they're called Roy and the Outlaws now."

"They're still trying to find themselves," Mary Alice said. "But I think another band has that name, so they'll have to change again."

"Whatever." Deacon was still considering Mat. "You danced," he said, then turned to Josie. "And you aren't limping."

Josie couldn't tell how Mat felt about the little dig because he was busy doctoring his coffee.

"He's *fine*," she assured them all and gave Mat an exaggerated eyebrow waggle.

Deacon rolled his eyes. "Roy must be freaking Cupid," he muttered.

"He really does good when they play at wedding receptions," Mary Alice told them.

"You know there are going to be rumors all over town today about you two," Hannah pointed out to Josie. "If Mary Alice noticed you, um, dancing, you can bet other people did, too."

"Oh, lots of people were looking at them," Mary Alice said eagerly. "I heard Pat saying that he should charge them for the floor show."

Josie felt herself blush. *Well, geez.* They hadn't been *that* bad.

Hannah smiled at her sympathetically. "You'd better get ready," she warned. "You know what people are like in this town. They'll want to see what they can find out."

"I guess," Josie groused and took a sip of her coffee.

"Will you all just shut up about this?" June asked as she settled on the barstool on the other side of Mary Alice. "I don't give a damn about Roy and his band or Mat and Josie hooking up. They can have sex on a table in the taproom for all I care."

"That would be uncomfortable," Mat said.

June glared at him. "I want to know what the hell happened at that freaking reopening, and I want to know it now. Don't make me pull it out of you."

Hannah sighed. "Frankly, I kind of hope people do come in to check you out," she admitted. "We could use the business. Last night was dead. I even sent June home early because we didn't need table service."

"You tried to send me home early," June corrected.

"Well, if you wanted to stay and clean the bathrooms, that's your problem." Hannah didn't even glance at June; she just watched Josie with big hazel eyes. "So, what did you think?" she asked, obviously trying to sound as if it didn't matter, when anyone could see she was holding her breath.

Oh, boy.

24

Josie glanced at Mat who'd settled across from her with his forearms on the bar. He shrugged.

"You'd better tell her," he said.

Hannah's eyes widened.

"It was good?" she asked in horror. "That's what June said Calvin said Austin said, but—"

"It was really good," Josie told her apologetically, shifting so she faced her more fully.

"Everyone seemed to be having fun," Mary Alice put in, not exactly helpfully. "The food at the restaurant was wonderful, and Johnny said they had a lot of fancy beers."

All of the color drained from Hannah's face. "They have a lot of beers?" she whispered.

Josie reached out and grabbed her friend's hands where they were clenched on her lap.

"Look, I'm not going to lie. Mary Alice is right, but I honestly think they might be overreaching with the restaurant and bar."

Hannah's hands clawed into hers. "How?" she squeaked desperately.

Josie considered. She wanted to reassure her friend, but she didn't want to lie to her.

"Well, they have a number of IPA beers, which will appeal to the hipster and college crowd, but won't do much for the bowlers. And they won't have them on tap like you do. Their menu had a lot of different entrees, but I'm not sure that keeping all those items will be cost effective. The bowlers are just going to want plain beer and burgers or pizza. It looks like they're trying to be all things to all people."

"But the food was real good," Mary Alice put in, then ducked when June slapped her on the back of her head. "Sorry."

"No, no." Hannah shook her head back and forth. "No. I need to know. And it was..." she drew in a deep breath "...really crowded? It looked crowded. The parking lot was full."

Josie winced. "It was packed."

"It was also a special event, and Pat had advertised the hell out of it," Mat reminded them. "Plus everything was half price. I figure he's going to have to pay for all of these upgrades, so things are bound to get more expensive.

Hannah turned to him, her expression a little wild. "You're right, aren't you? He's going to have to raise the prices. And he doesn't have the kitchen or the staff to handle that kind of operation for long, does he?"

"The bartender said he'd hired a bunch of people," Mary Alice corrected her. "And the kitchen looked busy. We could see it from where we were sitting—when people went in and out."

June slapped her on the back of her head again.

"Sorry," Mary Alice apologized.

"It's okay." Hannah did not sound okay. "I have to know, don't I? I have to know. It's always better to know. And now I know. And I have to. Know."

Deacon quickly came around the bar and stood behind her. He pulled her back against him and massaged her shoulders.

"Baby, it's going to be okay," he soothed. "You'll see. It will be fine."

Hannah let go of Josie's hands and swiveled on the barstool to curl into his chest.

"I can't compete," she whispered. "Not with that kind of money."

June shifted. "I can go try and talk to Pat," she offered. "He started pushing you because of me. I'll tell him to knock it off."

"I'm pretty sure that will just make things worse," Deacon said. "He's pissed off at you, and anything you do is just going to fan the flames." He shrugged, one big hand rubbing up and down Hannah's back. "I think he's using you as an excuse, but he's never liked the Country Time stealing his restaurant business. As soon as George ran off with the money, he saw an opportunity. Something like this was bound to happen."

June relaxed a little bit.

"Oh, but Josie talked to Louise," Mary Alice said, looking at Josie with her round eyes. "What did she say? Did you talk her into being nice?"

Josie winced again because here was another topic she hadn't wanted to discuss. But it had to be said, right?

"Not exactly," she admitted.

Hannah straightened away from Deacon. "Were you able to tell her your ideas about them being a fun center and all that?" Her eyes were somewhat frantic, as if she was a drowning woman clutching at a rapidly deflating life preserver.

"Not exactly," Josie repeated, rubbing the back of her neck as she glanced at Mat again. He hadn't said much, but the way he was standing near her and watching her let her know that he had her back.

"Louise is still mad at you," she admitted. Hannah might as well know the truth.

Hannah sat bolt upright. "*She's* still mad at *me*? What the hell?"

"Yeah, I don't get it, either," Josie admitted. "But she said you never knew she existed unless it was convenient. Pat's been really supportive of her, so she's loyal to him."

"She had sex with my boyfriend!" Hannah yelled. "While he *was* my boyfriend! In her car! In my parking lot! I mean, yes, it worked out for the best, but still!"

"I know, I know," Josie held out her hands, palms out, feeling like she was facing a wild animal. "I'm not saying I understand it. I'm just telling you that she's not willing to listen to me because I'm your friend."

"But she's my friend, too!" Hannah wailed. "Or, she was," she amended more quietly.

Josie did not tell her that Louise had said they were never friends. That was unnecessary and wouldn't help anything.

"Maybe Sam can talk to her," Mary Alice suggested.

Everyone looked at her, and her round eyes grew rounder.

"I mean, he was talking to her last night," she said quickly, "so maybe he can, again."

Josie frowned because this was new. "Sam was there last night? I didn't see him." She looked at Mat. "Did you?"

"No." He shook his head.

"Oh, it was after you two left," Mary Alice said, eager to be helpful. "Johnny and I were walking to our car, and we saw Sam and Louise standing outside. They didn't see us."

June frowned. "Might be worth a shot. If they're still talking, maybe he can get her to see some sense."

Mary Alice's expression grew troubled. "Well, I heard her yell at him and say that he was an asshole before she went back into the kitchen."

June sighed. "Or not."

"But he didn't leave," Mary Alice insisted. "He went in after her, and she didn't push him back out the door, so she must have listened to him."

Deacon smiled at the server. "I don't think we can count on that," he said kindly.

Hannah slumped. "He probably just made things worse. That's what Sam does best." She curled into Deacon's chest again. "What am I going to do?" she whispered. "If everyone starts going to Murphy Lanes, if the bowlers stay over there... I'm going to lose everything." She started to cry, and Deacon wrapped her up in his arms.

"Don't give up, Hannah," he murmured. "It hasn't happened yet, and we'll just have to make sure it doesn't."

"How?" she demanded.

Deacon looked helpless.

"We'll do the best we can."

"I always do the best I can," Hannah sobbed. "It's just not good enough!"

June looked down at the wooden bar top, her mouth tight.

Mary Alice blinked rapidly, her eyes wet with tears.

Josie thought it might be time to share her ideas. She wasn't sure if they were worth anything, but Hannah looked like she was going to start sucking her thumb any minute. This couldn't continue. Hannah had to pull herself together, or she might as well save the time and money and close the doors now.

"Listen to me," she said to her friend. "You are not going to just sit here and lose everything. This isn't dependent on Pat. He hasn't beaten you. This is on you, and you are going to put up one hell of a good fight." She tried to inject as much authority into her voice as possible. The client's perception of, and excitement for, a project always mattered the most.

Hannah glared at her. "Yeah, I'm pretty sure you don't know what you're talking about. There are only so many customers to go around, and if Pat grabs them all, there won't be any left for me." She sniffled.

"I do know what I'm talking about, and Pat doesn't have to

take them all," Josie insisted. "I keep telling you—you two are catering to two different audiences, or you should be."

"Bowlers are the same audience, and they're like my whole business." Hannah scowled at her.

"That's what you have to change. This place does not have to be 'bowlers only.' It's not written into the freaking charter. You need to look at what you're doing and change how you think about it. You need to reimagine your business."

"Reimagine my business?" Hannah rubbed the back of her hand under her nose. "What the hell are you talking about?"

"It's a bar," June put in, throwing open her arms. "No imagination necessary."

"Well, it's a bar, but what makes it different?" Josie tried to think of how to explain what she was trying to say. "You need to think about why people like to come here, what you can offer them, the kind of place it is."

"We had to do that when we wrote the business plan," Deacon said. "The mission statement."

Josie pointed at him. "Exactly. Except the mission statement doesn't go far enough. It's easy to say, 'This is a bar.' You need to go further and ask, 'What's the brand?' 'What's the spin?'"

Hannah frowned. "A brand? I don't have a brand, and I don't like spin."

"It's just..." Josie drew her hands through her hair in frustration "...you have to give people a reason to be excited to come here."

"They should know that already," June said stubbornly, crossing her arms over her chest and jutting out her chin.

Thanks, June.

"Yeah, well they don't. They don't always know, or they forget, or they're freaking passing through and don't even know the Country Time exists." Josie struggled to hide her frustration and failed. She knew what she was talking about, damn it! She took a deep breath and tried to calm herself down.

"Look," she said. "You've been coasting along for decades because the bowling alley restaurant and bar has always sucked. But now it doesn't." She watched Hannah's eyes grow big and was sorry for being so blunt, but her friend needed to know the truth. "The food was good, there were a lot of different kinds of beer, and the service was first rate, especially considering the crowd."

Hannah's eyes widened even more.

"But not everyone will want to go to the bowling alley, or they won't want to stay there after their leagues," she added hastily.

"If it's easier to stay..." Deacon said, looking worried.

Josie nodded. "Right. So you have to give them a reason to leave. And you have to attract the people who want what you have to offer. So why should people come here? You have to tell them. And you have to remind them why it's fun to come here."

"Advertising?" Hannah wrinkled her nose. "I don't like advertising."

Josie sighed. "That's pretty obvious, considering you don't do any. Advertising's not always a bad thing, you know. Not if it helps people realize you exist."

"I don't think we can pay for advertising," Deacon said.

"I'm not talking about that, anyway. There's a ton of work to do before you go there."

"Like?" Hannah demanded.

Amateurs. Honestly.

"First," Josie said patiently, "you have to decide how you're going to present your business. What makes it different? Why should people check you out instead of Pat? Why should the college kids and tourists come here instead there? What's your brand?"

Hannah was sitting straight now, not leaning on Deacon. Her shoulders were back and her face was stormy. That was good. Well, except for the fact that the storms were directed straight at Josie.

"How about I don't have a brand?" she challenged, arms crossed defiantly. "How about that? How about I just do what I do and don't worry about that stupid marketing bullshit? Huh?"

Josie felt her own hackles rise. "Marketing is not bullshit. It's important."

Hannah snorted. "Really? I don't think so. Marketing is just lying to people to talk them into buying stuff they don't really want or need."

Well, ouch. Working in marketing was only Josie's career, that's all.

"Hannah," Deacon said, rubbing his hand over her shoulder.

Mat had tensed, June appeared ready to explode, but surprisingly, before Josie could reply, Mary Alice reached over and touched Hannah's arm.

"But Josie is right, Hannah," she said. Some of the usual vacancy had left her expression, and her big blue eyes were focused for once. "Pat is changing, but he's also out there telling people about it and telling them why they should come in and check him out. You're not."

"But they should know!" Hannah wailed, throwing her hands wide. "Why don't they know? We've been here for a hundred years. They've been coming here! They should know!"

"Because things change," Josie said gently. Mary Alice's interruption had given her a chance to rein in her anger. "Things change and people change and businesses change and you need to change."

Hannah slumped. "I hate change."

"And you've had to do a lot of it," Josie said sympathetically. "But that's just the way it goes."

"You have to flow like water in a stream," Mary Alice said. She blinked when they all stared at her. "What?"

Deacon shook his head and turned back to Josie.

"What do you think we need to do first?" he asked.

Okay. Josie felt like she was putting on an old, comfortable shirt. True, in her last job she'd been more of a worker bee, but when she'd worked on the teams handling smaller accounts she'd been a lot more involved with the clients.

"First, you need to think about your business. And I mean, really think about it. What do you give people that Pat doesn't?"

"Maybe we should have another meeting to talk about it," June said. She looked suitably chastened. "With everyone. Kevin and Grace. Calvin."

"You just want Calvin here," Josie teased a little, hoping they were friends again. She hated when June was mad at her.

To her relief, the older woman grinned. "Damned right."

Josie smiled back.

"And Johnny," Mary Alice said.

"And Johnny," Hannah agreed. "And everybody," she said, looking around at them all, then back at Josie. "Thanks," she said quietly before launching herself at her for a big hug.

"Awwww," Mary Alice cooed. "That's so nice."

25

Josie exchanged her rumpled blouse for a Country Time polo shirt and manned the dishwasher again that night. Mat took charge of the grill, so Hannah could spend time doing other things. He seemed happy to be cooking, although Josie couldn't imagine why. She was still traumatized from the time she'd been alone in the kitchen.

She liked being with him while he worked, though—watching him move, helping him prepare sandwiches and sides. At some point they had developed a rhythm, so the work fell into a routine fairly quickly.

Josie grinned at the dishwasher, as she pushed in a tray of dirty dishes. She was pretty sure she knew *exactly* when that rhythm had developed.

"Don't smile at an appliance like that," Mat reproved, coming up behind her to kiss her exposed neck underneath the ponytail.

"Okay, I'll only smile at your appliance, big boy," she promised, and he laughed before moving to the fryer.

In the hours that followed, Josie spent a lot more time waiting for something to do than she had on previous nights.

But at least there *were* dirty dishes to wash and sandwiches to prepare. That meant that there had to be a few customers out in the taproom, anyway.

"Not as busy as normal but better than last night," June reported, as she stacked completed orders on a tray to take out to the taproom. "But if Margo Truelove doesn't stop flapping her jaws about the bowling alley thing, I'm going to cram her teeth down her throat."

"Yeah, don't do that," Josie cautioned.

June shrugged and left.

"Do you think it will actually help if Hannah rebrands this place and does some advertising?" Mat asked. He flipped a few burgers, then got a basket of fries out of the oil when the alarm went off.

"I don't know," Josie admitted. "I hope so." She chewed her lip while pulling clean dishes out of the dishwasher. "Pat sure has a lot more money than she does."

Mat came over to her and, holding his hands out so that he wouldn't get grease on her, kissed her cheek, then slid his mouth over to hers and sank in for a long, hot kiss.

"Money isn't everything," he said when he let her go.

"Okay," she gasped.

He grinned and went back to the grill.

Josie had some trouble focusing on much of anything after that, so she let herself get swept up in the routine of the work. If there were no dishes to wash, she helped Mat. She could tell he liked bossing her around, so she made sure to argue with him every now and then.

Finally the food service ended, and they switched to cleaning.

"Why do I have to scrub the counter tops?" Josie complained as she worked. "You're the one who made them dirty."

"Because you have to do what I say," he answered, leering suggestively. "Kitchen wench."

She stopped scrubbing to frown at him.

"You're getting a swelled head."

Mat sidled up to her, kissed her, and then slowly stripped off one of the rubber gloves she was wearing. His eyes were dark, his mouth soft and sensual. He brought her hand to his lips and kissed it, giving her palm a sharp little nip that made her catch her breath.

Josie stared at him, captured by his expression—the need, the desire.

He licked her palm to soothe the small hurt, then drew her hand down his body to the front of his jeans.

"My big head is not the part swelling," he murmured, as he placed her hand over his growing erection, surprising a laugh out of her. She cupped him, testing his length through the material and found that he was, God, swelling quite nicely. Suddenly desperate, she stood on her toes and captured his tempting mouth for a kiss of her own, flexing her fingers at the same time.

"Stop," he choked, breaking from the kiss and pulling away from her hand with obvious reluctance.

She leaned forward to kiss his collarbone where his skin was exposed by his Country Time polo shirt, humming because he tasted so sweaty and good.

"Josie, no," he panted and pushed her away more forcefully. "We still have to work for another hour."

"Yeah, I'm pretty sure you two had better leave before you have sex on the floor." Hannah's voice was dry as dust behind them.

Josie jumped and turned to see her friend lounging against the doorjamb.

"Hi," she said, then had to clear her throat when her voice cracked. "Uh, hi. We were just cleaning."

"Cleaning. Is that what you call it, now?" Hannah pushed herself away from the door. "Take off. I've got this."

"Don't have to tell me twice." Working quickly, Mat stripped off his gloves and apron, throwing them in the direction of the appropriate bins without coming anywhere close to hitting them. Turning Josie around, he pulled off her apron while she got rid of the remaining glove, then grabbed her hand and towed her toward the door. They hesitated only long enough to get their things.

"Meeting tomorrow," Hannah told them, as they shrugged into their coats. "Around two. Bring ideas."

Josie waved acknowledgment and thanks, then found herself being unceremoniously yanked out of the building. They ran to where her car was parked, and Josie found herself pushed up against the side of the vehicle, being kissed within an inch of her life.

Oh, yes please. She grabbed fistfuls of his hair to pull him further down, so she could make her own demands.

Mat leaned back, sucked in some air, and unlocked the car doors because somehow he'd ended up with her keys again. He opened the passenger door and maneuvered Josie between it and the body of the car before his mouth went back to devouring hers.

"God!" she gasped when he broke the kiss to run teeth and tongue down the length of her neck, while those big, skilled hands cupped her breasts. Desperate to feel his weight on her, she tugged at him until she was lying across the front seat of the car, his thigh between hers, his hands running up under her polo shirt, hers scrabbling at his back. She was starved for him.

The sharp blast of a horn abruptly jerked them back to reality, as an SUV rumbled to a stop beside them. Panting, Josie pushed herself up on her elbows while Mat, also breathing heavily, turned to look over his shoulder.

The utility vehicle engine idled and the driver got out.

"I've already had to cite one couple for public indecency in this parking lot," Josie's mother said. "I'd rather not have to do it again."

Oh, God.

The heat of desire froze instantly, and Josie shoved Mat away so she could hastily pull down her shirt and scramble to her feet.

"Mom?" she squeaked, shaking her head to get her brain back in the game. "What are you doing here?"

Jackie Kline leaned against the SUV, arms and legs crossed. The poor lighting behind the Country Time put her face in shadow, so Josie couldn't see her expression. That was probably a good thing.

"When my youngest daughter goes off the grid, I figure I'd better try and find her," Jackie said with a deceptive calm.

"Oh." Josie winced. "I told you where I was," she protested weakly.

"You told me you wouldn't be home last night," her mother corrected. "And my officer, Harry, was at the bowling alley. So I could guess who you were probably with. But I expected you to show up eventually, or at least reply to my text."

"You texted me?"

"Yes. When you still weren't home, and it was time for me to go on shift."

Oh, man. She must have missed the text notification sound on her phone. She just hadn't thought to check it recently.

"Sorry," she said to her mother. "I guess you were worried."

"You think?" Jackie asked sarcastically.

Crap.

"I was here," Josie said, gesturing. "Working in the kitchen."

"Yes. When I didn't hear from you, I called Hannah. She told me you were at the Country Time."

Crap, crap, crap.

"We're sorry, Chief," Mat said. In contrast to his rumpled clothes and hair, his tone was formal. He shrugged. "It's new."

Her mother considered Mat and then looked back to Josie. She felt herself blushing fiercely.

"I know how it is," Jackie said at last. "I know what it's like to get...caught up. Just, maybe, let me know everything's okay once in a while."

"I will." Josie felt horrible that she'd worried her mother.

Jackie sighed and took off her hat to run a hand through her short cap of hair before clamping it down on her head again. "Look," she said to Josie. "I know you're an adult. I know you were alone in the city. I know it was far more likely you'd run into trouble in New York than here in Hardy Falls. I knew you were with Mat, so you were likely fine. But now I'm expecting you to be home, so I get concerned if you just disappear and don't answer your phone. Okay?"

Josie nodded quickly. "Okay. I'm sorry, Mom," she added.

"No, no. I'm probably being overprotective." Jackie sighed again. "Humor me, all right?"

"I'm—"

"I assume you're using protection?" Jackie demanded of Mat.

"Oh, God." Josie was beyond embarrassed, but Mat just nodded.

"We're safe," he assured her.

"Good." Jackie opened the driver's door and moved to get back into the SUV. "And for God's sake, no sex in cars. I mean it. I don't want to have to issue another citation."

"No problem," Mat said, and Josie wanted to punch him for the smile she could hear in his voice. "Not comfortable anyway."

"Humpf," her mother snorted and settled behind the wheel before slamming the door shut. She rolled down the window and stuck her head out. "I assume you won't be home tonight, but I suggest you at least stop and get some clean clothes. And call me later."

"Sure," Josie said weakly. Her mother smiled, rolled up the window, backed out, and drove off.

"Well, that was interesting," Mat said.

"Oh, my God," Josie moaned. She sank down onto the passenger seat and dropped her head into her hands. "Oh. My. God."

"Guess that broke the mood."

Josie raised her head to stare at him. "My mother almost caught us having sex in my car. What do you think?"

"The key word is 'almost.'" He crouched in front of her. "What now?"

She frowned at him. "What do you mean, 'what now'?"

"I mean," he leaned forward to kiss her softly, "now that we're not, uh, caught up, do you want to drop me off at my place? You can go back home and we'll say last night was great, but we'll see what happens later? Or do you want me to take you back to your house, you can get some things, and we'll head to our friendly motel?"

Josie stared at him.

"What do you want to do?" she hedged.

"I asked you first. But, for the record, I'm all for the motel. Like I said last night, I don't want this to be a one-night stand." He leaned forward and kissed her again.

When he pulled back, she looked into his face and trailed her hand over his cheek, feeling the hair roughened skin under her palm.

The smart thing would be to make a break now.

But she didn't want to be smart.

"We'll have to split the bill. Motels can get expensive," she murmured.

"Who cares?" His kiss was not soft this time. It was deep and wicked, and it left her gasping and clutching at him when he finally lifted his head. Dimly, she realized that his hands were supporting her and he pulled her into the cradle of his body so she could feel the evidence of his arousal, hard and throbbing against her.

"I love your ass," he said, nibbling on her earlobe. "And your legs. I especially love them wrapped around me."

"God." She tried to get as close to him as she could. "I don't need clothes. I won't be wearing clothes tonight. Let's just get to the motel. I'll get everything in the morning."

He kissed her, then pushed her away. "Sounds good to me."

Josie scrambled into the passenger seat and slammed the door shut behind her while Mat ran around to the driver's side. He pulled her over to him and kissed her again before starting the engine. She saw that he was grinning.

"What are you laughing about?" she demanded.

He turned to her and the grin widened. "I don't think I've been this anxious since I was sixteen." Putting the car in gear, he backed out of the space, then shifted to "drive" so quickly that gravel spat out from under the tires. "In fact, I don't think I was like this when I *was* sixteen."

She grinned back at him, slid over, and tried to grab him.

"No." He tilted his hips away. "Keep your hands to yourself, you sex fiend."

She drew in a deep breath. "Drive fast."

They went back to the motel they'd used the night before, and Mat told her that the same desk clerk was on duty.

"Kid asked me if I wanted to book ahead for the week," he said as he drove the car away from the office. "Asshole."

"What did you say?" she asked, curling her fingers into her palms so she wouldn't reach over and pet his biceps flexing enticingly as he steered.

He shot her a grin. "I said 'yes.'"

"I really will help pay for it," she said, feeling guilty because so far he'd taken care of everything. "I've got some money."

Mat reached over and massaged her thigh. "It's fine," he assured her.

Maybe she should have argued, but Josie had other things on her mind. They pulled up in front of the first-floor motel room, and Mat tugged her out of the car and inside the door. They fell on each other, any tentativeness long gone. Now Josie knew for certain what he could do for her. And what she could do for him.

Hmmm...it would be fun to do things to him.

Pushing him away a little bit, she dropped to her knees in front of him and looked up.

Mat drew in a sharp breath, his eyes half-closed, burning with lust. She could tell that this position pushed a few of his buttons, and she couldn't have been more delighted. Especially since it pushed a few of hers, as well.

She sat up on her knees and reached for his belt, eagerly pulling it from the loops and throwing it across the room, then pulled down the zipper of his jeans. Slowly, she slid them and his briefs down his long, thick legs.

His legs weren't the only things long and thick, and she couldn't help licking her lips as his erection bounced free, already weeping with his desire.

Desire for her.

"Josie," he muttered. More of a moan, really, and that delighted her, too.

She grabbed him and ran her tongue up his length, hearing his muffled curse. When she looked up, she realized it had been muffled because he was wrestling his way out of his shirt. He threw it on the floor and stood basically naked, chest moving up and down rapidly as he breathed.

She loved his chest—the swirls of dark hair over tanned skin and hard muscle.

"Don't be a tease," he told her roughly. "If you're going to hold me that way, do something about it."

"What do you want me to do?" she asked, shocked by the deep throaty sound of her own voice.

"What do you think?" He wrapped a hand around the back of her head and urged her closer. She went eagerly, swallowing him down.

Mat's hands flexed in her hair, and she forgot about everything except bringing him as much pleasure as he brought her. Forgot about everything except driving him insane. Liquid pooled deep inside her as her own desire mounted.

When he was groaning and moving his hips in a way that told her he was about to lose all control, he pulled her off him, lifted her to her feet, and kissed the hell out of her. Within moments, she found herself naked and tossed on the bed, much as she had been the night before. He quickly put on the condom. She was pleased to see his hands shaking.

That was good because she was shaking, too.

Mat came down on top of her, and she wrapped herself around him as he slid into her, already moving before he got all the way in. He bit her shoulder, lapped her nipples, and slung his hips into her, totally out of control.

She scratched and bit him in turn, as she strained toward the height she knew she could reach with him.

For a few seconds—minutes—hours—she rode the knife's edge of sensation, the point before the precipice. Then it broke, she broke, it all broke, and she went flying off into space as Mat shouted and went with her.

26

Josie was barely awake when Mat finished cleaning up in the bathroom and persuaded her to roll over on her side so he could pull down the comforter. He climbed under it with her, and she fell asleep wrapped up in his arms.

When she woke again, she was alone in bed. The sun was shining in through the motel room curtains, and the shower was thundering in the bathroom.

As she listened, it turned off. A moment later, Mat strode naked into the room.

"Morning, sunshine," he said when he saw she was awake, coming over and giving her a quick kiss that tasted like toothpaste. "You don't have to get up, yet. It's pretty early."

Much to her disappointment, he backed away and, not bothering with underwear, got his jeans off the floor and pulled them on.

"Careful," she yawned, as he carefully tucked himself away before zipping up. "I still have some uses for that."

He winked at her and slipped into his shirt, then stepped into his running shoes without socks. "Seriously. Stay in bed.

We don't have to check out, and I'll put the 'do not disturb' sign on the door."

"Where are you going?"

He grimaced and picked up his briefs and socks, then stuffed them in his pocket. "I forgot that I promised Ms. Gregory I'd clean out the gutters on the bookstore building. She sent me a text an hour ago. She's less than pleased. I need clean clothes, anyway." He grinned. "And some more supplies."

"Oh." Reality intruded on her afterglow. "I should go home," she said, struggling to a sitting position. "I need clothes, too. And I want to get my notes together before we see Hannah this afternoon."

He wasn't listening, his attention completely focused on her naked breasts. She snapped her fingers in his face.

"Up here," she said, pointing to her eyes.

"That ship has sailed, honey," he said, reaching out to tweak her nipple. "And you either have to cover these up or help me get naked again."

She was tempted—boy, was she tempted—but she did have to be a reasonable adult sometimes. Besides, if Ms. Gregory was expecting him, she'd just keep hounding him until he showed up.

"Later," she promised, moving his hand away from her breast.

"Are you sure?" he asked.

For a minute she was confused, then she realized he was asking if she was sure that she wanted to spend another night with him.

"Absolutely."

He nodded, obviously pleased with her response.

"Then just drop me off at the bookstore before you head home."

She raised her eyebrows at him, as she got out of bed.

"Really? You're going to let me drive?"

Now he was admiring her naked butt. Basically, her naked everything.

"You can drive any time you want to, baby."

Hmmm...she'd keep that in mind for tonight.

Grinning, Josie sauntered into the bathroom. Maybe she swayed that butt he liked so much a little more than was strictly necessary.

After she took a quick shower and dressed in her now extremely rumpled clothes, they left the motel. It was nice, Josie thought as she maneuvered her car through the Hardy Falls mid-morning traffic, to have him sitting next to her, his arm on the back of the seat and his fingers playing with her hair.

She pulled up next to a hydrant in front of the bookstore, and he gave her a long, lingering kiss.

"I'll see you later," he murmured before kissing her again.

"Mmmm...you will," she answered, chasing his mouth when he would have pulled back.

"Stop it." He was laughing as he avoided her. "If you think your mom was mad about the whole parking lot thing, wait until she catches us having sex in your car on Main Street."

Well, he did have a point. She pouted, wishing she could say 'the hell with everything' and follow him up to his room.

Still laughing, he opened his door and slid out of the car with flattering reluctance, then leaned back in to look at her. "Tonight." It was a promise.

Josie drew in a deep breath, all playfulness suddenly gone.

"Tonight," she agreed.

Mat grinned at her, slammed the door shut, and sauntered towards the bookstore.

Josie watched him go. So did two other women he passed on the sidewalk. One even turned around to admire him, until her friend laughed and pulled her sleeve.

Mine, Josie thought, almost snarling at the pair. *That fine ass is mine.*

For now.

The thought was a little sobering. She put the car back in gear and pulled away from the curb, heading home.

When she got to the familiar house and pulled into the driveway, Josie was glad that she didn't see Jenny's pickup. She suspected her sister would be less than pleased with recent developments. Her mother's police SUV was also missing, and that was a relief, too.

She let herself in and ran up the stairs to the sanctuary of her old bedroom, wincing when she saw the neat stack of folded clothes on her bed, obviously out of the laundry. Her mother must have washed them.

Well, she'd make it up to her. She'd do all the chores for a week.

Next week.

Josie sank down on the bed and twisted the knotted decorative thread on the bedspread, frowning at her tennis shoes.

Maybe she should just call Mat and tell him that she couldn't be with him anymore. That would probably be for the best. Then she wouldn't have to worry about her family's reactions.

Except...

Except she didn't want to stop seeing him. This thing with Mat might be new, and most likely short-term, but it still somehow felt like it was...special. More than a casual fling. Much more than she'd expected. She didn't want to disrupt everyone, but she didn't want to throw away the chance to see what happened, either.

Was that selfish? Maybe.

Probably.

And yet...

Trying not to feel guilty, she packed her duffel bag with

some things she'd need. Because it was still early, she decided to distract herself by reviewing the work she'd done for the Country Time, so it would be fresh in her mind for the meeting. At least Hannah was willing to talk about making changes, because she really did need to make them.

Josie considered the draft of the web page she'd roughed out and decided it wasn't perfect, but it would do for now. She could tweak things after they'd all talked, assuming Hannah wanted her to keep going.

And assuming she had the time, she reminded herself. She really did need to get serious about looking for another job. It was fine to take a break, but her mother was right. She couldn't afford to get derailed.

Positioning the pointer over the directory folder where she kept all of her job search links and documents, she hesitated, then powered down the laptop instead.

"Later," she assured herself.

Besides, she had to think about it. Hannah wasn't the only one who had to consider her branding. Josie was going to have to come up with a brand for herself. Or at least a way to sell her skills. You couldn't throw a rock in Manhattan without hitting a graphic designer—at least not in the section of town where all the ad agencies were located. She'd have to find a way to stand out.

Did she want to work in Manhattan again?

"Do I have a choice?" she muttered and stuffed the laptop into her duffel bag.

Gathering her things, she unlocked her bedroom door, and peered out into the hallway then, moving quickly, jogged down the stairs and out to her car. She drew in a deep sigh of relief when she made it without running into either her sister or her mother.

She'd call or text her mom to let her know that she wouldn't be back for at least a few days. And she'd have to make it clear that she was going to make it up to her. She'd make it up to Jenny, too. She'd make it up to both of them.

Starting the car, she pulled out of the driveway and headed back to the Country Time.

When she turned into the parking lot and drove around behind the building, her heart beat a little faster at the sight of Mat's truck sitting next to Deacon's SUV and June's car. Anticipation, she assured herself. Nothing more.

She parked and got out, then waited as another car pulled in beside her. A few seconds later, Grace emerged from the driver's seat.

"Hi, Josie!" the girl called.

"Hi, Gracie!" she responded.

"Do you know what this is about?" Grace asked, walking over to her. The cornrows in her hair were neat, and her beautiful mocha skin gleamed in the afternoon sun.

"Do you swim in moisturizer?" Josie asked without thinking.

Grace blinked her big golden brown eyes, then grinned.

"Makeup is a wonderful thing."

Josie doubted that any amount of makeup could make her look as good as the girl, but she let it go.

"We're just going to be talking about the business," she said, going around the car to get her laptop.

Grace studied her. "Why do you have a duffel bag with you? Your mama kick you out?"

Josie cursed herself. Why hadn't she thought to carry the laptop separately? "Um, laundry," she said weakly.

Grace crossed her arms and kicked out a hip. "Uh-huh. Sure. You know I hear things. For example, I heard that you and Mat were all over each other at the bowling alley thing."

"We were dancing." Trying to distract the girl, Josie headed to the building. It didn't work. Grace trotted after her.

"Right. Then Drew, he works out at the motel on the highway, said that Mat came in and got a room, then came back the next night and booked for a week."

Crap.

"Uh..." Josie didn't know why she was embarrassed. It wasn't like everybody in town didn't already seem to know she and Mat had been together. As June had said, word traveled fast. It's just that now they'd know it would be for a week.

Grace punched her in the arm. "Way to go, girl. That man is *fine.*"

The back door opened before Josie could respond, and the fine man in question peered out.

"Are you two coming in?" Mat asked politely, eyes gleaming. "We could hear you talking."

Crap.

"Sure." Giggling, Grace went into the kitchen. But when Josie tried to move past him, Mat grabbed her arm.

"Uh-uh. Not so fast there, sugar."

Before she could avoid him, assuming she would have wanted to, he bent his head and kissed the hell out of her right there in front of Grace and God and everyone.

"Wow," Grace breathed when he lifted his head.

Mat chuckled, probably because Josie was wearing, she was sure, a dazed expression. He kissed the tip of her nose before letting her go.

"If you two are going to keep that up, this meeting's going to take forever," Hannah observed. Shaking herself, Josie looked around Mat to see her standing at one of the prep counters. Kevin was at the grill, a bright smile on his round face.

"Like you and Deacon aren't pawing each other every spare moment," she said, pushing Mat aside so she could step into the kitchen and close the door.

Hannah's smirk turned wicked. "Damned straight."

The door from the taproom opened, and Deacon poked his

head in. "What are you guys doing? We only have an hour before we need to get this place ready."

Hannah, still grinning, held up a bowl of pretzels, walked over to him, and kissed him softly on the mouth.

"So stern," she cooed.

It was a little disgusting. Josie hoped she didn't sound that way when she was talking to Mat.

But she was afraid she was starting to.

Grace left them to head into the taproom. Kevin, Hannah, and Deacon followed. Mat held Josie back.

"We weren't finished," he said and kissed her again.

A moment later, the kitchen door opened, and this time Kevin poked his head in.

"June says to get a move on because we are getting old out here," he reported, dark eyes glittering with amusement. "There is time to kiss later, no?"

"Yes." Josie gave Mat an apologetic glance, then clutched her laptop to her chest and went with Kevin into the other room.

27

In the taproom, Josie saw Deacon was standing behind the bar, drinking from his habitual mug of coffee. How the man managed to sleep with all of the caffeine he ingested was beyond her. On the other hand, she thought, as Hannah went up to him and casually ran her hand over his back, maybe he didn't care if he slept.

"Hi, Josie," Calvin called from a seat at the end of the bar. June was curved into his body, leaning into the arm he had draped around her waist. Grace was sitting next to them, and Kevin had positioned himself to stand like a mountain nearby.

Mat had followed her from the kitchen and went behind the bar to grab a coffee mug from the stack.

"Want some?" he asked her.

"Hell, yes."

Grinning, he got another mug and moved towards the big coffee maker just as the kitchen door swung open again to emit a breathless Mary Alice and her boyfriend, Johnny.

"Oh, hi everyone!" Mary Alice beamed her slightly crazed smile. "Sorry we're late. We were...busy." She blushed bright red and looked at Johnny with an expression of adoration. He smiled at her and pulled her closer to his side.

"I understand you're talking about the business today," he said in his smooth tenor voice, as he seated Mary Alice next to Grace and then took the stool beside her.

"Er, yes." Josie sincerely wished she could clear her mind of the image of Mary Alice and Johnny getting...busy. "And we'd better get to it, or there won't be much time before we have to open."

We have to open.

This wasn't her place.

She glanced at Mat.

He wasn't her man, either.

She really had to remember that.

"So talk." Hannah scowled at Josie. "Yesterday, you said I had to 'reimagine' the business. How?"

Showtime.

"Okay." Josie opened her laptop on the bar. "Like I said yesterday, you can't keep doing what you've always done," she said to Hannah while she logged in. "The world is different, even here in Hardy Falls."

"So?" Hannah snapped.

"Soooo," Josie said patiently, "you have to adjust."

"Adjust what?" June demanded. "That's the part I don't get. We're a bar. We're open to anybody who wants to drink. End of story."

"And we've been in business for over a hundred years," Hannah put in, sounding a little defensive. "We must be doing something right."

"Of course you are," Josie tried to sound soothing instead of frustrated. She called on all of her experience working with nervous clients. *Patience... patience...* "But you can't hold on to the vision of what the Country Time has been. You have to look at things a little differently and not depend so heavily on the bowlers. And that means you have to decide what your brand is and get out there with it."

"We have a brand," Hannah snarled. "We offer beer and raucous good times."

"Easy there." Deacon patted her arm before looking at Josie. "You said we need to let people know why they want to come here instead of going to the bowling alley or any other place in town. How do we do that?"

"Right." Josie focused on the problem. "Look, your web presence is pathetic. You don't even have a Facebook page, for God's sake. And your website." She shuddered. "Where in the world did that come from?"

Hannah looked a little shamefaced. "Billy set it up for me for free. I never had time to deal with it. It was the only thing he ever did to help out."

"Yeah, well, he didn't do you any favors." Since Billy was the former dishwasher who'd run away to join a carnival, it wasn't a huge surprise. "You don't even have the freaking menu listed. Or the kinds of beer you have on tap. Or much of anything else. Heck, you don't even own a domain name!" Her voice rose as she went through the list.

"What I'm using is free!" Hannah pointed out.

"Yeah, and anyone doing an Internet search is going to see that."

Josie and Hannah glared at each other.

"Ladies," Calvin soothed. "We can argue about domain names later." Josie jumped a little when he spoke; he'd been so quiet that she'd kind of forgotten he was there. When she looked at him, she saw that he was watching her intently, eyes sharp. June, sitting with her hand on his thigh, was watching her, too. In fact, everyone gathered around the bar was watching her. She squirmed a little and reminded herself that she really did know what she was doing.

"Gosh, you should have told me you needed a website,

Hannah," Grace said. "I know tons of people who could have set one up better than Billy." Her pert nose wrinkled with disdain.

"Well, who cares anyway?" Hannah pouted.

"You should care!" Josie yelled at her, losing the patience she was trying to hold. "How the hell do you think people are going to find you?"

"I told you! They already know about me!" Hannah yelled back.

"Bowlers know about you! Locals know about you! But the tourists don't know about you. People outside this one-horse town don't know about you."

"I think that's a one-stoplight town," Calvin said mildly. "We have more than one horse."

Josie threw her hands up, then drew in a deep breath and slowly let it out. She had to get herself under control.

"Look. Pat's restaurant is great. That's going to steal some of your business. Not all of it, but some of it. You. Have. To. Change." She leaned across the bar as she said the last words very slowly and deliberately.

Hannah's pout deepened.

"I don't want to. I just want everything to go back to the way it was."

"I know, honey." And she did understand. But Hannah didn't need sympathy right now. She needed a kick in the pants, or she was going to lose everything. "But you need a plan, or it will be bad."

Hannah sighed and cuddled into Deacon for a hug. Then she walked around the bar and sat next to Josie.

"Okay." She took a deep breath. "Talk to me."

"All right." Josie relaxed a little and pulled up her notes on the laptop. "First, what is it that makes this place special?"

Hannah looked a little lost. "Raucous good times?" she said meekly. It was a question.

"Sort of." Why couldn't anybody see this? "This is a friendly neighborhood hangout. Not a dive, but a place where the locals come to drink and talk. No kids. No loud bowling alley disturbing them. No arcade."

Hannah straightened in her seat. "Right."

"If you want to go out for a drink on an inexpensive date, if you want to watch the Phillies lose, if you want to hang out with your buds, this is the place to come. Not the bowling alley. The bowling alley is where you go with your kids when you want a family night out. It's where teenagers can hang out, or college students can blow off some steam. The bowling alley is 'Chuck E. Cheese's.' You're 'Cheers.' You're where people go to get away from kids. The place where tourists can come to get some local flavor without wrecking their budget. A really nice place halfway between a diner and a country club or the Fallside Restaurant."

Hannah was frowning again, but it was a thoughtful frown. Josie breathed in a little sigh of relief. Her friend was finally starting to listen.

"Aren't we those things now?" she asked.

"Mostly," Josie agreed. "You just have to make a few tweaks. And more people need to know about you. Word of mouth is great, but we have to expand that word. So first, you need a better Internet presence. We have to update your," she swallowed, "web page. I roughed one out. It's just a draft." She pulled it up on the laptop and turned it so that they could all see.

"That looks pretty nice," Hannah agreed reluctantly. "I like this," she pointed at the little logo Josie had designed. It was just a "C" and a "T" interconnected in a font that she felt read as both "rustic" and "neighborly." Finding that damned font had taken a long time.

"It looks good," Deacon said, leaning over so he could see the screen better. "Static web page?" he asked.

"For now. But it would be good if Hannah started a blog or had some other way of interacting with people online."

"A blog?" Hannah tugged at her hair. "When the hell do I have time to write a freaking blog?"

She was going to have to find time to do something, Josie thought, but she didn't want to go there now.

"When the website is finalized, you should use that as the basis for the rest of your social media platform."

Hannah looked horrified. "What social media platform?"

"Yeah, that's what I thought when I tried to find one," Josie shot back. "Don't you think Pat is doing this?"

"No," June countered. "Pat wouldn't know how to do this."

"Well, guess again." She pulled up the bowling alley website with all of its integrated video clips and links to various other platforms. She showed them how smoothly you could navigate the page, how much information there was on offerings, and, finally the blog Louise had apparently started a couple of weeks ago. The latest entry—one that hadn't been there the last time she'd looked—was all about the grand reopening. There were lots of high-definition photos and even a little video clip. She clicked on links to show the accompanying posts on Facebook, Instagram, and Twitter, as well as all of the comments they'd garnered.

That shut them up.

"They have three thousand followers on Facebook," she said into the silence. "You don't even have a Facebook page."

Hannah opened her mouth then shut it again.

"You have to get out there," Josie repeated before turning back to her proposed website. "This is just a rough draft, so we need to personalize it. Make it say 'neighborhood hangout.' Replace the stock photos," she pointed at them, "with *your* photos. *Your* customers. *Your* town."

"I know where we can get tons of high-quality photos that

will work," Calvin said and nudged June in the side. She glared at him.

"Honey, you can't keep hiding," he said cryptically.

"Yes, I can."

"What?" Josie asked, looking between them.

June's scowl deepened. "I maybe take pictures," she said.

"Oh, I remember!" Mary Alice said, beaming. "I showed you how to use that editing program. Your photos were wonderful! They would help a lot."

"I forgot," Hannah said. "Mary Alice is right, they're terrific."

June relaxed a little, but she still seemed embarrassed.

"Yeah, well, I don't know about that. But you can use them if they'll help."

Josie hoped to holy hell that they would be worth using. She did not want to be the one to tell June they couldn't use whatever photos she'd taken.

Calvin wrapped his arm around June's shoulders and turned to Josie.

"So other than getting all of the online stuff setup, what else were you thinking?" he asked.

Josie frowned and pulled up her notes, glancing through them quickly.

"You need to expand the menu," she said to Hannah. "What you have is good, but you need some other options."

"Like what?" June challenged. "We're not going to be serving four course meals here."

"No, I was thinking that you could expand what you already have. So, not just beef hamburgers but also buffalo, turkey, venison, maybe even ostrich. You can grill a portobello mushroom cap and treat it like a beef patty for a vegetarian option. Offer a few more choices in toppings or sauces. Maybe come up with a signature Country Time burger to feature on the website. Sweet potato fries. A vegetarian wrap or two. Actual salads—the green leafy kind, not just the ones with mayonnaise."

"An ostrich burger?" Hannah frowned. "Really?"

"You're not going to sell many to the regulars, but the college kids will love it. And they'll also love the vegetarian options." Josie took a breath. "And I think you need to start opening for lunch."

Hannah gaped at her. "Lunch?"

"Lunch. You're missing the traffic from the factory guys or townspeople out on their lunch breaks. And if you have a good menu, they'll want to come check you out. That's why I think you should also add in some soups. Have one or two soups a week. Make a big vat and store it. Offer a soup and sandwich lunch special."

"I can make a gumbo that will set people on fire," Kevin chuckled. "My wife and kids, they love it when I am with them." The smile left his face, and he looked uncharacteristically sad.

"Oh, Kevin!" Mary Alice jumped off her barstool and flew to him, then wrapped him in a hug. "They'll be able to be here soon."

The big man shifted his shoulders and smiled again, patting Mary Alice on the back with one huge hand. "Thank you, my friend. But in the meantime, I can make my gumbo for the boss lady, no?"

"If you're interested, I've got a hell of a good chili recipe from my grandmama," Mat offered. "Won't be a problem to put it together, and it can be stored, too."

Hannah pulled her hands through her hair again. "More ingredients. More people to cook and prep. More hours and probably more staff. More equipment."

"I know. I know it's a lot to take on." And the money was going to be a big problem. "But it will all pay off in the end."

She hoped. "If you want this to be a neighborhood hangout, you want people to come in and, well, hang out."

"They do that now," Hannah said, her chin set. Josie wanted to punch that stubborn jaw, but Deacon would probably beat her up.

"We want them to do it more," she said, striving to cling to patience. "So you have to give them a reason beyond the food and beer."

"And raucous good times," Mat added.

"Actually, we need to bump that up," Josie corrected him. "We want the good times to be more raucous than a bunch of bowlers sitting around talking about their scores, but not so raucous that my mother gets called out here on a regular basis. What do you think about a pool table?"

Hannah gestured around the taproom. "Where?"

"Good point." Josie frowned. "So how about darts back in the corner?"

"There are dart leagues," Calvin said. "We could see if there are any around here. Just make sure the targets are aimed away from the rest of the room," he added.

Josie beamed at him. Calvin really was very smart.

"Plus, I think you should have a live band with dancing at least once a month," she said. "Maybe every weekend or every other weekend."

"Again," Hannah flailed her arms, "where?"

Josie took yet another deep breath. "You're going to have to make room." Honest to God, her friend was stubborn. And scared. Hannah dug her heels in when she got scared. "Look. You want this to be a destination. Someplace people choose to go, not just a place people end up because they don't have another option. Because now they *have* another option," Josie said, as she cast a sidelong glance in the direction of Murphy Lanes.

Hannah stuck out her bottom lip.

"So maybe they come for the beer, to get away from the kids, or to hear some live music sometimes," Josie slogged on.

"Oh, I know Roy and his band would love to play here again," Mary Alice enthused, rushing back to the silent Johnny and putting her large hands on his thin shoulders. "Right, Johnny?"

He nodded and carefully sipped the coffee someone had gotten him. "But they'd need to be paid," he cautioned. "If Roy wants to keep living in the basement, he's going to have to start paying some rent or at least cover his own food."

Mary Alice's face looked troubled. "Oh, but—"

"And Animal's mom said she wasn't going to keep making payments on his motorcycle, so he needs to come up with some cash," Johnny continued. He smiled up at Mary Alice and patted her hand. "Think about it, honey. They get paid for the weddings they do. They can't give away their time on the weekends when they could be earning money."

Hannah's face dropped. "I don't have any money," she said. "And even if we find George, I won't get my money back."

No, she wouldn't.

Now came the really tricky part. Feeling a bit like a bar-owner whisperer, Josie faced Hannah. She took her friend's shoulders in her hands.

"You are going to have to find money," she said. "You need investors."

"I don't want investors," Hannah said, repeating the argument Josie had heard before. "Investors mean responsibility, and I have too much responsibility as it is."

"I've already told you that I want to invest," Deacon said. "You made me a partner, but you never let me contribute any cash. I've got some money."

"Johnny and I would invest," Mary Alice said. "We want to."

"So do I," Calvin put in.

"I could invest," Mat said and shrugged. "Ms. Gregory's rent is cheap."

"You've heard all of this before," Josie said, looking right into Hannah's eyes. "You know there are other people who will invest, too. Albert, Harry, Martin, and Joe, for four of them. And there are others."

"I could have another carnival," Hannah said desperately. "That brought in some money. We could have a snow carnival. Or a Thanksgiving carnival. Thanksgiving is only two weeks away. Maybe a Christmas fair."

Josie shook her and then had to force herself to stop shaking.

"Hannah," she said. "Get real. Do you want to keep this business or not?"

Hannah pulled away from her grip and got up to walk to the double entry doors. She looked out through the antique leaded glass.

"Decision time, babe," Deacon said, his bright blue eyes filled with love and empathy. "What do you really want?"

Hannah turned to face them but didn't say anything.

"Sometimes you have to do things you don't like," Mat said. It sounded like he was talking from experience. "And sometimes it's a little risky."

"Whatever you decide is okay with me," June said. Then she shrugged. "But I think if you don't want to change anything, or if you're too scared to rip off the bandage and do it, you might as well just close and save yourself the trouble."

Josie blinked at June in surprise. She scowled back at her.

"What? I don't have common sense? Even I can see that we can't keep things going the way they are." Her expression hardened. "Pat is stealing the business, so if we want to keep it, we have to fight. But you need money to do that. I ain't got money, but my honeybee here has some, and I've got my own set of skills."

"You sure do, sugar," Calvin cooed and bussed a kiss down her neck. She slapped the side of his head.

"My counselor told me to find another job," Grace said, "but I like it here. I hope we stay open."

"I also wish to keep this job," Kevin put in. "But this is not about me. You must do what you think is best, boss lady." He shrugged his massive shoulders. "We do not often like to change, and we do not often like to take chances or risks. But sometimes we must."

Kevin knew this all too well.

"If you decide to take on investors, have Sam draw up the paperwork for you," Calvin said. "You want it to be legal."

"I can run the investment pool," Mary Alice put in. "Well, actually Johnny will have to be the broker of record, since he's the financial planner. But we can get it all set up and invested correctly. Right now, you'll just need most things in a money market fund anyway, until you get the business turned around. But I can set up the books to track who invests what and the rates of return on their deposits." She blinked when they all stared at her. "What?"

Josie shook her head to clear it. "Think about it," she said to Hannah.

"I don't think I need to," Hannah said. Her voice was quiet, and her eyes were wide and terrified. "We'll do it."

"Do what?" Josie asked, confused.

"All of it." Hannah sucked in a deep breath. "The investors. The menu. The lunch service. The website. The freaking blogs and social media. The reimagining."

"Really?" Josie's voice squeaked, surprised and maybe a little afraid of what she'd started.

Hannah swallowed hard. "Yes. You're right. If I don't change, I might as well close. And I don't want to close. I don't want to run away."

Deacon went over to her and took her face in his hands.

"Sure?" he asked.

Hannah nodded. "Sure."

He hugged her.

Josie looked at Mat and found him watching her. She thought she saw a gleam in his dark eyes.

"Way to go," he said.

She hoped to hell he was right.

28

J osie kept fairly busy the rest of the night, running the dishwasher and helping Kevin when he needed it which, unfortunately, wasn't often. Mat was at the bar because Deacon had decided that since everyone was there, he and Hannah would take a rare night off together.

Hannah had protested loudly, but he'd ignored her. After a phone call an hour later to check up on things, nobody heard from either of them again that night. Josie suspected Deacon had found a way to keep his woman occupied.

Even though the noise and activity of the kitchen was less than it had been before the bowling alley restaurant had opened, it still distracted her enough that it wasn't until later, when she and Mat were back at the motel after dropping off his truck at the bookstore, that the full reality of what she'd done hit her.

Josie lay on the bed, waiting for Mat to finish in the shower and panicked.

Dear God.

What had she talked Hannah into? Why had Hannah listened to her? She didn't know what she was doing. She should have just left it alone and found another way to help. Who was she to tell her best friend in the whole world that she needed to put other people's money at risk? That she should go into debt?

Oh, man, Hannah was going to be in so much debt. If the business failed...

Logically, Josie knew Hannah needed to make changes. But now that she'd accepted the plan, the risks seemed terrifying. It had been a hell of a lot easier to sit in a cubicle in a Manhattan high rise, coming up with plans that involved seemingly limitless money and clients she didn't know on a personal level. She didn't love those people.

Overwhelmed and frantic, Josie grabbed her laptop and waited impatiently for it to boot up. She opened the draft of the website she'd been working on.

Was this good enough? Did it say what needed to be said? Was it something that would help people seek out Hannah and the Country Time?

"Hey, do you want—"

She jerked her head up and stared wildly at Mat, who was standing in the bathroom door, lean hips wrapped in a towel, broad chest glistening with stray drops of water. For once she didn't appreciate the sight.

When he saw her expression, he immediately moved over to the bed and smoothed his hand down her back,

"Jesus, what's wrong?"

"I'm freaking out," she admitted, trying not to hyperventilate.

He frowned. "Why?"

Josie laughed, and even she knew the sound was more than slightly unhinged. "Why? Why? Why do you think?"

Mat considered her for a moment, then he gently tugged at the laptop.

"No!" She tried to clutch at the computer. "I need that. I need to—"

"You don't need to do anything right now."

"No, I really do," she insisted, scrambling up on her knees so that she could pull the laptop away from him. "I need to think...I need to plan..."

"And you'll do all of that. Tomorrow."

"But—"

He managed to wrestle the computer away from her death grip.

"You're tired," he said, avoiding her attempts to grab it back. "Probably exhausted. You need to sleep."

"Sleep? I can't sleep," she argued. But even as she said the words, she had to bite back a yawn that threatened to crack her jaw.

"Right. You'll be able to think better in the morning." He shut down the laptop and took it to the dresser on the other side of the room. "Sleep now. Marketing plan later."

He was probably right that she would be more clearheaded after some rest, but it was so hard to let go. "I thought we were going to—"

Mat grinned at her as he walked back to the bed, and this time she was able to better absorb the view of him draped only in a cheap motel towel.

"Oh, don't worry. I'm sure something will...come up later."

"But—"

He pretended he hadn't heard her and instead encouraged her to stand. Then he stripped her of every stitch of clothing until she stood naked in front of him. Josie thought that maybe something had, uh, come up, so she reached for him, but he just pulled back the bedding and urged her to lie down, moving her with his strong, competent hands. He pulled the comforter up to her chin with almost maternal care.

Or like a man taking care of something precious.

After he checked the door to reassure himself that it was locked, he turned off the lights, dropped his towel, and climbed into bed with her, her back to his front. His body was warm, and he smelled fresh from his shower. She felt herself relax, as his arms came around her. She hoped she didn't smell like fryer oil, but she suddenly was much too tired to care.

"What did I do, Mat?" she asked sleepily.

"About what?"

"Hannah. I gave her all of these ideas. I told her she needed investors. I talked her into it. All that debt. All that responsibility."

"If Hannah doesn't change things, she's going to lose the business. We both know that. You said it yourself."

"Yes, but..." Her eyes opened, as her mind started racing again. "Who am I to tell her what to do? I can't even run my own life. Who am I to tell her how to run hers?"

"You're helping Hannah. You're showing her that she needs to do things differently, and you're right."

"But—"

"Hannah needs you. Not only to give her some hard truths, but to help her figure out how to be competitive. To help her see how she can think about her business differently. You see it, but she doesn't. Now she's starting to."

Josie twisted around to face him, trying to see him in the shadowed darkness of the room. "Really?"

"Yes, really." He kissed her, tugging on her bottom lip before raising his head again. "I don't know why you think you don't know what you're doing, because based on what I saw back at the Country Time, you've got it locked down. What you came up with is great. Hannah's been coasting along, and she can't anymore. You're just trying to help her find the right way to paddle before she gets washed away in the flood."

"What if she still goes under?"

"Look at it this way. If she doesn't try something, she'll go under, anyway. If she tries the things you're suggesting, maybe she's got a chance."

"Maybe."

He ran his mouth from her cheek to her ear before raising his head.

"I don't know why you put yourself down, but you have to stop it. Just because you can't handle the kitchen or wait tables—"

"Hey!"

"—doesn't mean anything. Those aren't your things. What you showed us today? Those are. Those are your things. So, maybe Hannah's not the only one who needs to do some reimagining, because baby, you're way more than you think you are."

Well, how was she supposed to respond to that, except to roll over on top of him and kiss him until they were both breathless, laughing, and tangled in the bedding?

And something had definitely come up.

Afterward, they both drifted off, but the morning sun filtering through the motel drapes woke Josie only a few hours later. She got up to use the bathroom, then sat on the bed watching Mat sleep. He looked so much more peaceful with those wary dark eyes closed. Younger, without the creases of time on his face.

Way more than you think you are.

Was that true?

She had always liked envisioning the way companies could present themselves. Not big companies but little ones like the Country Time. She'd always enjoyed looking at what they were doing and loved trying to find ways to help them.

But you didn't have many chances to do that sort of thing in a big Manhattan ad agency, especially not if you were someone low on the proverbial ladder. You did the best you could with what you were given to work on, but you never had the chance to see the whole picture.

With the client she'd been working on when she was laid off, Don had stolen every idea she'd brought up. And he'd never let her know if her suggestions had made any difference whatsoever.

Maybe she could start her own business.

The thought popped into her head, and Josie chewed on her lip.

It had occurred to her before that she might be happier on her own, but it had never seemed practical to leave a company where she had, she believed, security. Now the company was out of her life and she was beginning again. Could she take this opportunity to point in a whole different direction? If she did a good job with the Country Time, could it be the start of a portfolio to entice other clients?

Her own business.

Could she do that? Could she make it work?

Did she want to?

Mat blinked up at her and pulled her from her thoughts.

"Your brain is so busy, it woke me up," he complained.

"Sorry." She got back under the covers and cuddled against him, breathing in his scent.

"It's too freaking early. Go back to sleep," he yawned.

"Okay."

But she lay awake for a while longer, thinking about possibilities and whether or not she wanted to try to make them happen in Hardy Falls.

And whether Mat would want to be part of them.

Every day it was getting harder to think about leaving. Every day it was getting harder not to wish for more.

So much for a lighthearted fling.

29

After a good night's sleep followed by some even better morning sex, Mat was feeling pretty damned great. The buzz dimmed a little when Josie got out of bed and headed for the shower, saying that she wanted to go home to see her mother and work on Hannah's stuff. When he protested, she insisted he was too big of a distraction and promised that she'd stop in at the Country Time later. Then she kissed him so sweetly that he would have agreed to anything.

He got her to drop him off at the bookstore on her way through town so he could get his truck and take care of a few things before work. She gave him a brilliant smile when he got out at the curb, and he stood watching her little car drive away before he realized what he was doing and went inside.

The room he'd called home for the last couple of weeks looked even smaller and darker than usual, so he opened the curtains to let the sun flood the space. Then he stood, just staring down at Main Street.

If things kept going with Josie, maybe he should think about renting an apartment. It would be cheaper than a motel, and would definitely have more room.

Aggravated with himself, he went to his dresser and pulled out more underwear. Why was he even considering an apartment? It's not like the thing with Josie was going to last. She'd be heading back to Manhattan soon, and he'd be here. Maybe they could try a long distance relationship, but they never worked.

His cell phone rang and, grateful for the distraction, he pulled it out of his pocket to look at the caller ID.

Guerrero, D.

His mother.

She'd left more messages over the last couple of days, but he hadn't called her back. The fact that she kept calling was something of a surprise. He'd expected her to give up by now.

The buzzing ring stopped, then started again.

He was tempted to send her call straight to voicemail and turn off his phone, but he knew that he was being a freaking coward. He couldn't avoid her forever. Might as well get it over with.

Clicking to answer, he put the phone up to his ear. "Hello?"

"So, you finally decided to answer, huh?"

"Hello, Mama." He sat on the big bed and settled back against the headboard, closing his eyes. Dorothy Guerrero was pissed off—he could hear it in her voice. His mother's ancestors might have come straight from Germany, but being married to Antonio Guerrero for forty years had melted away whatever icy reserve she might have inherited. He didn't think she had inherited a whole heck of a lot of it in the first place. She'd always been the one they'd had to watch out for when they did something wrong, not his father.

"I don't appreciate you ignoring us, Mateo," she continued, her voice hard. "What if we needed to get in touch with you? What if we had an emergency?"

"Is this an emergency?"

"No, but it might have been."

"Look, Mama," he said, even though he knew trying to be reasonable was probably a waste of time. "Letty and Maria didn't try to call me, and neither did Papa. I didn't even get emails from anyone, so I knew it wasn't a family emergency. "

"I'm only calling because the person who wants to talk to you can't get through."

Fuck. Shit. Damn.

"So this is about Gail." He knew it.

"Yes. Listen to me, Mateo," his mother said. "That poor girl has been to the house several times. She said she can't get through on your phone, and she begged me to call you."

He sighed deeply. "I told you before I left that I didn't want to talk to her."

"I know that's what you said, but the sweet thing is willing to forgive you for walking away from her on the day of the wedding. The day of, Mateo! She lost so much money on the dress and flowers, and she had to return all of the presents."

"She should have kept them."

"Well, she couldn't, could she?" his mother spat. "Now you listen to me, Mateo Guerrero. You have a second chance to get back the best thing that ever happened to you. She says she loves you, forgives you, and wants you back. Even though her mother and I were humiliated by what you did, I know that you're not a bad man. I know that you love Gail." Her voice softened. "I don't know why you did it, Mateo, but you hurt that girl. For whatever reason, she wants you back. You need to think about it before you ruin your life. You need to come home to her."

Mat closed his eyes. What the hell kind of game was Gail playing now? Why was she running to his mother? And what kind of bullshit was this about wanting him back?

"Mama," he said, feeling every one of his thirty-five years, "I'm not going back to Gail. I'll never go back to her."

His mother was silent for a long moment.

"I don't think I know you anymore," she said, and hung up.

Mat clicked off his phone and threw it on the nightstand, then rubbed his face with both hands. The sadness and disappointment in his mother's voice ripped at him. He wished to hell that he could tell his family the truth about why he'd walked away, but Gail had pleaded with him not to.

And he'd done what she'd wanted. He'd let the blame for ending the wedding fall on his shoulders. Hell, he'd even let her keep the damned engagement ring. Gail had gotten sympathy and support from her family *and* his. He'd lost a lot of friends, and his family had basically kicked him out of their lives. The expression on their faces the last time he'd seen them...

He got up, paced over to the big window again, and stared blindly out at the street.

His mother hadn't even asked him how he was, where he was, or what he was doing.

Suddenly, the anger and resentment that he normally kept tamped down roared to life. He went back to the bed and picked up his phone. He'd deleted Gail's contact information a long time ago, and he'd blocked her on his phone, but he found an old text in the phone's trash folder and called the number. She answered on the second ring.

"Mat!"

"What are you trying to prove?" he demanded. "Leave my family out of this."

"Please listen to me." Gail's voice, sweet and light, flowed over the phone, and for a moment he felt like he'd been slapped just by the sound of it. "Please."

"Why the hell are you going to my mother? Haven't you done enough to fuck up my life?"

"I know, I know." He could hear her crying on the other

end, so she must be somewhere private. "I'm sorry," she sobbed. "I'm so sorry."

He sighed deeply, his body slumping, as he sat on the bed.

"I know," he said, because he did. She was sorry about the whole mess. Just not sorry enough to tell everyone the truth.

"I never meant to hurt you, Mat," she said. "Never. I really was going to go through with the wedding and be a good wife to you."

"What about Alicia?"

"She understood." Gail's voice caught. "That was going to be our last time."

"Right." The fact that their last time had happened only a few hours before Gail was supposed to marry another person hadn't seemed to be much of a consideration. "You can actually marry Alicia now, you know. Even have a family."

"Not here." She was hiccupping. Her round face would be pale, her eyes glistening with tears. Gail did the whole crying thing pretty well. "The school district wouldn't keep us. And my church..."

Mat sighed again. "Gail," he said, "what the hell do you want from me? Why are you bugging my mother with this shit about wanting to get back together with me? We both know you don't want that."

"Oh, but Mat, please listen." She sounded urgent now. "There have been rumors going around the school. Somebody saw Alicia and me out one day, and the parents are talking. One mother already moved her child out of my class."

"That's too bad," he said, feeling no emotion.

"We've been trying to make people think she's comforting me."

He bet she was.

"But it's been a long time since you left, and people don't believe it anymore." She drew in a breath. "I thought you could come back, and we could start seeing each other again, and then go through with the marriage like we planned."

"Are you fucking kidding me?"

"No, no!" Gail sounded desperate. "Don't hang up, please. Listen. I know you don't want me to be your wife anymore, but I wouldn't have to be. We'll just let people think that for a while, and then I'll get a divorce or something. But it won't be your fault at all. I'll make it good with your family and my family, I swear I will. It will all be the same as it was, Mat. It will all be the same. It will be good, please."

Josie's face came into his mind. Her body. The sweet passion she showed him every time he touched her.

"No," he said.

"Mat, please! Think about it! I love you. I love you so much. And I'll make it good for you. I promise."

"No," he repeated and clicked off the phone.

It rang a few seconds later, so he turned it off completely and sat back on the bed.

Why would she think he would consider it? Why would she think there was a chance?

She thought that he still loved her, and she was afraid. But even if he still had feelings for her, even if he'd been willing to go along with her crazy scheme, he'd never be able to trust her again. She'd hidden everything she was and played him for a fool.

He thought of Josie laughing, scowling, and arguing. He didn't think that woman could hide a damned thing—her face would give everything away.

But, as Gail had just reminded him, what he thought wasn't always the truth.

30

After dropping Mat off at the bookstore, Josie headed home. She found her mother sitting at the kitchen table with a sandwich and a glass of water.

"Hi, Mom," she said, walking over to give her a kiss on the cheek. "I'm glad I got to see you before you left for work."

"I'm off today, thank goodness. Getting a late start since Jenny's working and wasn't making noise to wake me up." Jackie reached up to cup Josie's face in her hand. "And how are you doing, baby girl? I haven't seen much of you lately."

Josie knew she was blushing.

"You know why I haven't been here," she muttered, sitting down opposite her mom. "I told you that I would be with Mat this week."

"Hmmm." Jackie studied her. "And what happens after this week?"

"I don't know." Josie played with the scratches that had decorated the table top for as long as she could remember. "I hope I can see him while I'm here. I guess we'll work something out." Assuming Mat was willing. She thought he would be. Her face heated again.

"Right." Her mother took a bite of her sandwich and considered her as she chewed. "You actually believe that."

"What's that mean?" Josie demanded.

"Honey, you might have been living far away in the big city, but I still know my girl." Jackie smiled. "You're involved with him."

Josie shifted on her seat. "Well, of course I'm involved with him. You know I've been with him."

"Beyond that." Jackie set down her sandwich. "You're falling for him, kiddo."

"What? No. I'm not falling for him!" Josie was appalled.

"Of course you are. Hard and fast. It must be a family trait."

"It's just sex!"

"That's not the way you're wired, Josie," her mother said kindly.

"Yes I am!"

"Oh, please. I haven't seen you in days, and when I talk to you I can practically hear the little hearts in your voice."

"Well, I guess I'm infatuated with him, but that's all it is, Mom." She could feel the desperation fluttering in her throat. "I mean, he's a really great guy, but there's nothing more." No, she couldn't be falling for Mat. Couldn't be getting in so deep this soon. That wasn't the way this thing was supposed to go.

Her mother studied her. "Okay," she said at last, although it was obvious she didn't believe it.

"How's Jenny?" Josie asked, trying to change the subject.

Jackie considered her a moment more, then shrugged and went back to her sandwich. "She's fine," she said after a swallowing.

"Is she mad at me? Um, I think she liked Mat, too." Josie winced because just saying it that way made her feel like she was back in high school.

Her mother smiled. "Maybe a little."

"Oh, gosh, Mom, I didn't mean to—"

"Jenny had a rough time with that so-called artist of hers, so when Mat showed up, someone new in town, and he was nice to her, I think she developed a crush on him." Jackie pushed back her empty plate and wiped her mouth. "It didn't go anywhere."

"I don't want to her hurt her."

"I know, honey. But you're going to need to talk to her sooner or later."

Josie looked down at the table. "I will." Sometime.

"Good." Jackie patted her hand. "Now. I'm not going to interfere with you the way my mother did with me, but I am going to remind you again that you need to find a job."

"I know. I'm going to start looking." She'd just been a little busy.

"Right." Jackie appeared skeptical. "You know how long it takes to get through the interview process."

"Maybe there are other options." Like starting her own business here in Hardy Falls.

"What does that mean?" her mother asked, as bright-eyed as a bird.

"Nothing. Forget it." It was probably a stupid idea, anyway. Josie clapped her hands together and forced a smile. "Okay, I've been a slacker. Is there anything I can do to help out around here?"

Jackie was silent a long moment before returning the smile. "How about the laundry?"

"On it." Josie got up and headed out. She could feel her mother watching her leave the room.

As she gathered dirty clothes, separated them into loads, and put the first load in the washer, she tried to control her panic. Was her mother right? Was she falling for Mat?

No. She couldn't be. She'd gone into this thing with her eyes wide open, knowing that it wasn't going to be long term. Even if she pursued the silly idea of being a freelancer here in

Hardy Falls, what she had with Mat probably wouldn't last. They'd gone to bed because they'd both had the urge—and they'd wanted to have some fun. That was all. They had chemistry, and they'd wanted to explore that chemistry. End of story.

Her mother had just misinterpreted a healthy and enthusiastic fling. After this week was over, chances were good they wouldn't be seeing as much of each other, anyway. She couldn't expect Mat to keep renting motel rooms, and she sure couldn't afford to do it.

It was probably a good thing.

The thought made her sad.

In between loads, she sat at the kitchen table and worked on her laptop, trying to focus on Hannah's problems instead of her love life.

If she left town—when she left town—she was going to have to talk to Hannah about maintaining all of this work. Maybe that would be a service she could offer, if she started her own business here? She could provide some kind of maintenance package, including updating social media. It could have different tiers and...

"Looks good," her mother said, as she swung by and peeked at the draft of a new menu design. "Ostrich burger? Really?"

"It's just a thought." Josie glanced at the clock and winced when she saw the time. "I'm sorry, Mom, but I have to go. I need to talk to Hannah before she opens. I want to run a few things by her."

"Okay." Jackie smiled. "And you won't be home tonight."

Josie cleared her throat. "Um, no."

"Well, I'm glad we got to spend a little time together today."

"I'll be home, Mom. I promise."

"I know, honey." When Josie got to her feet, her mother wrapped her up in a huge hug. "I'll see you later."

Josie clung for a moment, then gathered up her things and

headed out to the Country Time. Mat was probably already there.

She couldn't control the thrill that went zinging through her system, but she refused to dwell on it.

However, when she pulled into the Country Time's parking lot a few minutes later, she was surprised not to see that his truck. Oh, well. Maybe he'd gotten delayed. It wasn't opening time yet, anyway.

The kitchen was empty when she walked in the back door, so she pushed through to the taproom. She found Deacon standing alone at the bar cleaning shot glasses.

"Hey," he called when he saw her.

"Hi. Where is everybody?"

"We were almost out of rolls, so Hannah went to get some," he told her. "She's been a little distracted, so she didn't notice the supply was low. June has the night off, so Grace will be in later."

"Oh." Josie settled on a stool at the bar. "Is Mat here?" she asked casually.

Deacon grinned knowingly. "No. He's not due in yet."

"Oh. Okay." She tried not to be disappointed. She'd see him soon enough. "I wanted to talk to Hannah about a few things," she said, as she watched Deacon work. "You didn't say much yesterday. What do you think she should do about the business?"

He shook his head and put the clean glass on the stack before picking up another one.

"Doesn't matter. I want her to do what she thinks is best."

"Come on," Josie wheedled. "You have to have an opinion."

Deacon stared around the taproom, as he absently polished the little glass.

"This is a good place." He glanced at her. "This is a good town. Hannah belongs here."

"So do you."

He shook his head and turned away. "She won't marry me," he said abruptly.

"What?" Josie was honestly shocked. "What the hell?"

Deacon smiled a little at that. "I've asked. More than once. But she said she doesn't want to saddle me with her financial problems."

"God! How stupid is she?" If her friend had been there, Josie would have smacked her.

Deacon's smile broadened. "Pretty damned stupid."

Josie got up and walked behind the bar to give him a huge hug. "I'd marry you in a heartbeat," she assured him.

He wrapped his arms around her and pulled her into his chest.

"Don't say it if you don't mean it," he laughed. "I'm feeling kind of vulnerable."

That made her hug him even tighter. She knew the soft and chubby shy kid living inside this impressive man. Other people might not see his insecurities, but she knew.

Pulling back, she looked up at him.

"Do you remember when I taught you how to dance?" she asked.

"Yeah. And then you went with me to the fall formal, so I wouldn't have to go stag."

"So neither of us had to go stag," she corrected. "Hannah was dating Sam."

Deacon tilted his head as he studied her. "How come we never ended up together?" he asked.

Good question, but she knew the answer.

"Hannah," she said simply.

"Hannah." His eyes held hers. "Do I need to apologize for that?"

Once she'd dreamed of having this conversation, but that had been long, long ago.

"I had a crush on you back in high school, you know," she

admitted, thinking of her sister and Mat. Her mother was right —she needed to talk to Jenny. She understood how it felt to be on the outside looking in.

His eyebrows winged up. "Me?"

"If I'd known how you would turn out, I would have tracked you down, Deacon Black. So if that Hannah doesn't get her ass in gear, you come see me, okay?"

She was kidding, when there'd been a time she might not have been. Not entirely. His grin told her he understood, and he kissed her on the cheek.

"Well, isn't this nice," Mat said from behind her.

Josie dropped her arms and turned around, happy he was there. She sobered instantly when she saw he was standing at the kitchen door, arms crossed, face expressionless, except for the wild fire blazing in his dark eyes.

"Mat?" she said, taking a step toward him.

"Oh, no please. Don't let me interrupt."

Puzzled, Josie looked back at Deacon.

"What's wrong with you?" he asked Mat, frowning.

"You really can't figure it out?" Mat sneered.

"No, because I don't know what's going on," Deacon said slowly. Josie could tell that he was trying hard to remain calm.

"You don't? How about a man who's supposed to be committed to a woman making out with someone else when her back is turned?" Mat glanced at Josie. "How about a woman who's trying to poach her friend's man."

Josie's jaw dropped in utter shock. "What?"

"Wait. Are you accusing me of cheating on Hannah with Josie?" Deacon demanded, equally offended.

"Hannah's a sweet girl, and she doesn't deserve for you to treat her this way. Either of you." Mat's voice was flat. After that one look at Josie, he'd kept his entire focus on Deacon. "If you can't be man enough for her, then you need to step away."

"Hey!" Deacon's chest expanded with outrage. Mat ignored him.

"And you," he said, finally turning to Josie. She almost wished that he hadn't. The expressionless mask was gone, and the disgust she saw in its place had her stomach roiling. "I thought maybe, just maybe, we were starting something. Guess I was wrong, huh? Were you just waiting for a chance to make a move on Deacon?"

"A move? What move?" She was totally at a loss. "We were just goofing around! What in the serious hell, Mat?"

His lip curled. "Right. 'Goofing around'. God, I even saw the signs, and I ignored them. Again. I am such an idiot. You know what? I'm out of here."

Turning on his heel, he slammed through the kitchen door. A moment later, they heard the back door open and close.

Frozen, Josie and Deacon stared at each other.

"What the fuck?" Deacon asked.

Josie shook her head, stunned. What was that? Where had that come from?

He'd looked at her as if she was something filthy. She wrapped her arms around herself.

Hannah came in from the kitchen, a paper grocery bag in her arms.

"Mat almost ran me down when I turned into the parking lot," she said. "What's wrong?"

Deacon went to her and kissed her before taking the bag and putting it on the bar.

"Mat thinks he saw something he didn't," he said, then shrugged helplessly. "I guess."

"He didn't even talk to us," Josie whispered, trying to understand what had just happened. "He just assumed."

Hannah was obviously confused, but she went to Josie to give her a hug. Josie pulled back, shock giving way to anger. She welcomed it. Embraced it.

Oh, *hell* no. There was no way he was going to basically call her a slut and get away with it.

"I'm going to find him, and I'm going to rip him a new asshole," she growled through her teeth.

Hannah nodded her approval.

"I'll help you dig the grave for the body," she said.

Josie kissed her on the cheek. Now here was a real friend. Hannah didn't even know what had been said, but she was on her side.

"I just want to beat the shit out of him," Deacon said, and Josie realized how angry he was.

"Me first." Because she was damned well going to get some kind of an explanation. Or payback. Or both.

Deacon looked at her for a moment, then nodded abruptly.

"Kick him in the balls, honey," he called after her, as she marched out of the building.

She intended to.

31

Josie's wave of anger carried her first to the motel, but Mat wasn't in the room they'd so recently shared. Riding on fury, she drove across town to the bookstore, parked, and strode around the side of the building to the tenant entrance. Without giving herself a chance to think, she shoved it open and jogged upstairs to the second floor.

She knew which room Mat was renting because she'd visited Deacon once or twice when he'd lived there, so she marched to his door and knocked.

Nothing.

She knocked again, pounding this time.

"What?"

His voice was sharp and abrupt.

"Let me in," she ordered.

"Go away, Josie."

No. No way. She deserved a goddamned explanation. The way he'd looked at her... It had been horrible.

Trying the knob, she found it unlocked—which was a bit of a surprise. She pushed into the room, slamming the door shut behind her.

Mat was standing at the window, staring down at the street. His only reaction to her unexpected intrusion was to glance back at her for a moment before returning to his contemplation of the scenery. That made her even more furious.

"What the hell, Mat?" she demanded "What the hell was that all about? You think I'm having a thing with Deacon? Seriously? Or was this just your way of breaking up with me?" She snorted, even though her heart felt heavy and painful in her chest. "You could have just told me you were sick of paying for the motel room. No need to go all dramatic."

He didn't turn around.

"Seeing you with Deacon showed me a different side of things, that's all."

"For God's…" She clenched her fists on her hips. "What the fuck is your problem?"

"My problem?" He finally faced her. "My problem was walking into the Country Time and finding the woman I'm currently sleeping with trying to start something with her best friend's boyfriend. That's my problem."

Josie threw her hands wide. "We were just talking!" she yelled, so frustrated she wanted to scream. "There was nothing going on!"

Mat's mouth tightened.

"I know what I heard," he said more quietly.

"I don't even know what that was." Josie drew in a deep breath and willed the tears away. She would never forgive herself if she started crying now. "And whatever it was, you never considered that you might be wrong, did you?"

His dark eyes latched onto her face. "Are you honestly going to deny that you were hugging Deacon? That he kissed you? Please. I'm stupid, but I'm not that stupid."

"He kissed me on the *cheek*. It was *nothing*.We were *talking*."

"With your arms wrapped around each other."

"He was upset. I'm his friend. I was trying to help." She

swallowed. "Even if you think I'd go behind your back, do you honestly think I would hurt Hannah like that? Is that what you think of me?"

Mat stared at her for a long moment, then he walked over to the bed and sat down. He rubbed his hands hard over his face before letting them drop. "You love Deacon," he said. "I could see it."

"I do, but not the way you mean. Well, not now," she amended, because she wasn't going to lie to him. "Back when we were kids, I might have felt a little differently. But not for years. It's always been Hannah for him, so it never went anywhere. It never would have gone anywhere. It never will go anywhere. We are friends. End of story."

Mat was silent for a long time.

"I don't know if I can believe you," he said finally.

She flinched because that felt like he'd just stabbed her.

"Okay." She swallowed hard and the anger ebbed away, leaving only sadness and exhaustion behind. So, just like that, just that suddenly, it was over. If he couldn't trust her, then there wasn't anything for her here. "Okay," she repeated as she walked to the door. "I'll, uh, just get out of your way then."

"Wait," he said as she was reaching for the doorknob.

She hesitated, then turned to face him.

He didn't look at her, just ran his hands through his hair.

"I heard you say that Deacon should come see you anytime," he said. "And that you were sorry you waited too long to track him down."

"I was just kidding around because he was feeling bummed."

"And that you taught him to dance." He looked up abruptly, and Josie's breath caught when she saw the spark of hurt in his eyes. She took a cautious step toward him.

"We were kids."

"I thought it was something special with us, but you'd already done it with Deacon."

She stopped. "You're jealous about something that happened over ten years ago?" she asked in disbelief.

He laughed without much humor. "What do you think?"

"That you should trust me."

"Trust is...difficult for me," he admitted.

"Yeah, no shit."

He laughed again, and it was more natural this time.

There weren't any chairs in the small room, so Josie sat next to Mat on the bed, careful not to touch him. She intertwined her fingers in her lap.

For a moment, they were both quiet.

"Do you really think I could hurt Hannah that way?" she asked finally. "That I could hurt you? Do you really think I'm such a liar?" Because if he did...

"No." He sighed and the weariness was deep in his voice. "No."

Something released inside her, but she didn't move any closer to him.

"Then why did you say those things? You looked at me like you...hated me."

He shook his head.

"You jumped to conclusions," she pressed. "Why?"

He didn't say anything for several long minutes. Then he sighed again.

"Gail."

Josie nodded her head. It wasn't really a surprise.

"She hurt you," she said.

"Yes."

"She humiliated you, and it was about more than just dancing."

He snorted out a laugh.

"Oh, yeah. A whole fuckton more."

She glanced at him and saw that he was staring at the floor. "I think you need to tell me about her."

"I don't want to," he said honestly.

But she couldn't let it go again, not now. Maybe he had a right to privacy, but he'd painted her with the same brush as this other woman. She deserved to know why.

"You have to." She turned to face him fully, her bent knee on the bed and her other foot on the floor. "You judged me without listening to me because of something she did. I don't know if we're still going to have a relationship, but I have a right to know about her." She swallowed. "The things you said, the way you looked at me...hurt. I have a right to know," she repeated.

Mat glanced at her, his dark eyes hooded. He shoved to his feet and began to pace restlessly around the small room.

"I don't like talking about it," he said.

Josie didn't answer. She just watched him.

It was breaking her heart to see him so obviously upset—breaking her heart that they might be finished—but she'd been telling the truth. The things he'd said, and the fact that he couldn't seem to trust her, hurt. Even if he'd only been lashing out and was overreacting, it still hurt.

Mat stopped in front of the window and stared down at Main Street, again. He was quiet for so long that she thought he wasn't going to say anything. Her wounded heart bled a little bit more.

Come on, she thought. *Don't let it end like this.*

Still not looking at her, he sighed.

"When I finally left the army, I moved home to where my family lived. Galveston." He turned his back to the wall. "I couldn't stay with them. I guess they meant well, but I just couldn't stay there. So, I got a job on one of the offshore oil rigs out in the Gulf of Mexico."

"That's where you met Deacon."

"I'd been there a while when he came on board, so I was his supervisor." He smiled a little. "Got to make him run for his living." He shrugged. "We hit it off, anyway."

"What about Gail?" she prodded to keep him on track.

Mat rubbed a hand on the back of his neck. He was staring down at the floor again, his expression remote. "You get time off when you work on the rigs. It depends, but usually you're out there for a couple of weeks at a time, then you go home for a while. So, I had a little apartment in Galveston. It felt weird not working. On the rigs, you're 'on' basically twenty-four/seven, just like in the army. So on shore, I'd spend time out at the bars, just drinking and talking to people. Or I'd go to the clubs to try to pick up women."

She couldn't imagine he had much of a problem in that department.

"Dance clubs?"

He smiled again. "Well, I didn't actually dance. Mostly just sat and drank. Sometimes Deacon was with me, sometimes not. It depended on whether or not he'd found a friend of his own."

She wasn't exactly sure she wanted to hear about Mat and Deacon out on the prowl, but that didn't matter.

"And you met Gail," she said, trying to keep him going.

Mat nodded. "I met Gail. She was dancing, and so pretty it made my heart hurt. Blonde hair, blue eyes, smile as big as Texas, body like a supermodel."

Yeah, she really wasn't sure she wanted to hear this.

"She came over to talk me because her mama knows my mama really well. We clicked right away." He paused. "Or I thought we did. I took her home with me and that was that."

Okay, she definitely didn't want to hear this. Ruthlessly, she tamped down her jealousy and kept her mouth shut.

"Turned out she's was an elementary school teacher, out of college a few years. She worked with disabled and academically challenged kids."

Oh, great. So the perfect Gail with the sunny smile and the body of a supermodel also had a noble career. As opposed to Josie, who designed spam and junk mail for a living.

"When I told my mother what was going on, she was absolutely thrilled. Soon, I gave up my apartment and moved into Gail's house. No sense in paying rent if I'm never there, right?"

"She was good with you being gone?" Josie asked through clenched teeth.

"Yeah. She was real good with it. So much so, she started complaining when I was home. She said she just wanted to have fun with her friends without worrying about me being bored. She liked dancing a lot, and I didn't, so I guess I was okay with it. But we started having fights because I didn't know why she wouldn't just go dancing when I was away and then stay with me when I was home. She said that she had the right to live her own life."

Uh-oh.

"I mean sure, we fought, but I was happy she didn't bitch about my job all the time like some of the other guys' girlfriends and wives did. And she did take care of everything when I was gone. All of the responsibility fell on her, so I didn't think I should make too big a deal about it." He turned to look out the window again. "She said she loved me."

"Something happened," Josie ventured.

"I thought we were good. I thought I knew her friends. I knew that she knew mine. Our families were over the moon. I bought her a ring and asked her marry me. She said 'yes.'"

"But..." Josie said because that obviously wasn't the end of the story.

"We were getting married in her parents' church. I was supposed to stay out of the house that morning because it was bad luck to see the bride, but I had forgotten the poem I was going to read at the reception."

He stopped and Josie kept silent, willing him to go on.

"I'd written her a poem. It was bad, but I thought she'd get a kick out of it. She was supposed to be getting a manicure with her maid of honor, so I thought I'd run home and get it."

Uh-oh.

Josie had a bad feeling she knew where this was going.

Mat shot her a look over his shoulder. "It was such a cliché. I let myself into the house and headed for our bedroom. The door was open. Moans and the sounds of a creaky bed." He shook his head. "Just like a bad movie."

"Who was he?" Josie asked, her voice thick. "One of your friends?"

Mat turned to face her. "She. Another woman. I walked in the bedroom, ready to rip the guy's head off, and found Gail in bed with the counselor at the elementary school where she works. Alicia Evans. Her maid of honor. I walked in and there they were, naked, sweaty, and obviously desperate for each other. Desperate in ways Gail never was for me."

"Did they see you?"

"They looked up, saw me, and scrambled to get under the sheets. Gail's wedding dress was thrown into the corner." He paused. "I still remember how it looked, all rumpled up next to a chair like it was a piece of garbage."

"What did you do?"

He shrugged and looked at her again. "I left. It was obvious, even to me, that she'd been lying to me all along. I don't really remember what I was thinking, to tell you the truth. I was almost at the door when Gail caught up with me. She was buck naked and crying. She begged me to marry her, to go through with the wedding. She said I could do whatever I wanted to do. I could divorce her in a year if I wanted, but please, please just marry her."

Josie watched him close his eyes, and she knew he was reliving that moment.

"But you didn't," she said gently, as she got up to go to him.

No matter what was happening between them, she couldn't stand to see him like this.

"I couldn't," he corrected.

Of course he couldn't. Josie wrapped her arms around his waist and snuggled herself up into his body. He stiffened at first, but then held on. In fact, he held her so tightly she wasn't sure she'd be able to breathe.

"She begged me," he repeated into her hair. "And when she knew she wasn't going to talk me into going through with it, she begged me not to tell anyone why. She and Alicia could be fired if anyone on the school board found out they were lovers—that they'd been lovers for years. At the very least, it would cause gossip and scandal. Her family would kick her out."

Josie buried her face into his chest. "So you called off the wedding and took the blame."

"Yes."

"And your parents were upset."

"Mama was livid. I called everything off three hours before the ceremony, and she was humiliated in front of all of her friends. My father, sisters, and the rest of the family disowned me. They won't even talk to me."

"But you never told them why you did it."

"No." He took a deep breath. "I worked out my contract on the rig and left Texas. And now I just found out that Gail's been after my mother to get me to contact her. I have her blocked, so she couldn't call me."

Well, that explained a few things.

"Do you know what she wants?"

"I finally talked to my mother this afternoon, and then I talked to Gail." He shrugged. "She and Alicia were caught out together, and people are starting to gossip. Parents are getting upset. It was bound to happen sooner or later. You can't have a connection like that and expect to keep it hidden."

"What does she want you to do about it?"

He shrugged again. "Marry her."

Incredulous, she jerked away and stared up at him. "The hell you say? Is she a moron?"

Mat's eyes, which had been flat and lifeless when she'd first come into the room, twinkled a little. "No, just scared and desperate."

"Why in the world would she think you'd be willing to help her out like that?"

"I don't know. Because I helped her before? Because she doesn't know what else to do?"

"How about pulling on her big girl panties and dealing with it?"

"That's probably not going to happen," he told her, and she could feel him relaxing under her hands. "Poor Alicia."

"Fuck Alicia."

"No thanks."

"Fuck Alicia and fuck Gail and fuck you, too, for even thinking I could be like her." Angry again, Josie tried to shove him away, but he held on and wouldn't let her move. "You hurt me, you bastard. You judged me and hurt me, and it was for nothing—for no reason at all! It was because this bitch can't grow up and admit who she is, so she's trying to use you. And you think I'm just like her." She could hardly see him through the repressed tears.

"No, I don't. I really don't." He pulled her closer. "It's just... seeing you right after talking to her...seeing you laughing with Deacon again, like you've done before...and he kissed you."

"Jesus! He kissed me on the cheek!"

"It looked like more from where I was standing. I just went off."

"Deacon is my friend, and if you can't handle that—"

"Josie." He kissed her with fierce desperation. "I never meant to hurt you," he said, lifting his mouth just far enough so he could speak. "I just...seeing you...I was already feeling like an idiot, and—"

"You are an idiot," she told him and reached up to pull him back down. "Now shut up." She kissed him.

His mouth covered hers, ravaged hers. Then he lifted her up in his arms and carried her back to the bed.

Josie found herself clinging to his shoulders, desperate to get closer to him, and desperate to feel him on her, in her, with her. He pulled back a scant inch.

"Okay?" he asked, voice like gravel.

It took her longer than it should have to realize that he was asking if it was okay if he made love to her.

She stared into his face. Deep in his hot eyes, hidden behind his passion-flushed features, she saw the need.

He needed her.

For now.

"Yes," she breathed and pulled him back down.

Maybe she was being stupid. Who knew what might happen the next time something shook him? But at the moment, it didn't seem to matter.

He got her naked, even though he remained fully clothed. It was erotic to feel the scratch of denim across her skin, to know that she was on display for him as he feasted on her body. With all of the things they'd done to and for each other, Mat had never been like this before. His entire being seemed focused on her, intent on her reactions and responses. Even the slightest shiver would bring him back to that spot to repeat the caress, the lick, the bite, until she thought she was going crazy.

She tried to roll on top of him, but he held her in place and lifted his head from where he'd been tormenting her nipple.

"My turn now," he wheezed. "Yours later." He ran his hand up her leg, in between her thighs, and speared her with his fingers.

Josie arched off the bed and, mindless with need, let him have his way with her.

And he did. Fingers. Mouth. He opened his jeans with shaking hands and drove into her. Then they were both bucking, straining towards each other, and towards completion. Finally, the waves of sweet relief ripped cries out of both of them, and they held onto the knife's edge of satisfaction for long moments before collapsing back into the rumpled covers.

Once their breathing had returned to normal, Mat got up and dealt with the condom. He crawled into bed beside her and hauled her up against his chest.

"I'm sorry," he murmured. "I'm sorry I didn't listen to you. I'm sorry I jumped to conclusions. It's just that I thought I had something with Gail, and it turned out to be total bullshit. I guess I don't trust myself."

Josie knew that for a guy like Mat, trust was everything. But she still wasn't sure where it left her.

32

They drowsed for a little while, then Josie felt Mat shift on the bed and sit up.

"Where are you going?" she murmured sleepily.

"I have to work," he reminded her. "I'd better get changed and cleaned up, but you can stay here if you want to."

"No." Her jaw stretched in a yawn as she struggled to sit. "I'll go with you. Maybe I'll be able to help."

By the time they pulled themselves together and Mat drove them back to the Country Time in her car, it was almost five o'clock but the parking lot was practically empty. That was disheartening, especially when Josie looked at the bowling alley and saw all the cars over there.

"Damnit," she muttered. This was a league night. Unless the bowlers had disobeyed Pat's rule about moving their cars, not many of them had left Murphy Lanes.

"It's early yet," Mat said, reading her mind. "Most of the leagues don't finish until later."

"I guess."

Mat parked her car next to Calvin's big, red truck, then turned off the engine. Josie got out, but he made no move to follow her. Surprised, she opened the door again and leaned down. He was glaring at the steering wheel as if it had offended him.

"Are you coming in?" she asked politely.

His frown deepened. "If I go in, I'll have to talk to Deacon and Hannah."

Ah.

"Does Deacon know about you and Gail?" she asked.

He shrugged.

"Maybe you should tell him?" she suggested.

He shrugged again.

Josie sighed. *Honestly.*

"It might help him understand."

"He'll just think I'm a moron."

"You told me," she pointed out. "And I don't think you're a moron. At least not as far as Gail is concerned."

"You're different," he grumbled.

Hiding her smile, Josie straightened. "Suit yourself. I'll tell Hannah to bring the dishes out here, and you can lick them clean."

Thinking about "Mat" and "lick" in the same sentence was enough to give her the vapors, so she shut the car door and headed for the building.

A moment later, she heard the car door slam, and then Mat was beside her. He draped his arm around her shoulders.

"Fuck it," he said.

They went into the kitchen and stopped short when Hannah turned from the grill, a spatula in one hand. She studied both of them without expression.

"About time you showed up," she said to Mat, her normally warm voice sounding very cool.

Josie ducked out from under his arm.

"Mat needs to talk to Deacon," she told her friend.

Mat sighed, but he didn't argue.

"He's at the bar, like normal," Hannah told him. "But if he's willing to talk to you, get June to watch it and go somewhere else."

"Thanks." Mat smiled at Josie and left.

Hannah turned her stare on Josie. "You two seem pretty chummy after what happened," she pointed out.

Josie wasn't entirely sure what to say. "We talked and he apologized."

"That simple?" Hannah sounded skeptical.

Josie shrugged again. "He had reasons for acting the way he did, but he believed me when I told him that he had misunderstood."

"Right."

They were interrupted when Mat and Deacon came into the kitchen. Mat waited while Deacon kissed Hannah and shrugged into his coat, then the two men headed outside. Hannah stared after them with a worried expression, but the fryer timer went off and she turned to take care of it.

"Can I help?" Josie asked.

"Maybe later." Hannah looked at her over her shoulder. "Calvin's at the bar. He was asking for you. I think he wants to talk to you."

"Oh. Okay."

That was a little strange, but she liked talking to Calvin. With one last glance at the back door—she really wanted to peek out to see if the men were talking or punching—she headed out to the taproom.

Sadly, it was mostly empty. There were a few people scattered around the bar, and a group of college kids were clustered at a table, but that was all.

Well, it was early.

Depressed, she settled next to Calvin at the bar.

"Hey," she greeted him.

Calvin eyed her speculatively, and she had to remind

herself that she didn't have a "recently got laid" sign plastered on her forehead.

"Hi," he said. "Are you okay?"

She frowned. "Yes. Why?"

"Because we heard that you and Mat had a fight," June said with her customary abruptness, as she came back behind the bar opposite them. "And we heard he said some things that weren't so nice."

Crap.

"It's okay," Josie said hastily. "There were reasons, and we talked it all out. We're good. He's apologizing to Deacon now." Or they were beating each other up in the parking lot.

June snorted and went to get a drink for a patron.

"It's not very busy," she said to Calvin, trying to change the subject.

"No. But it's still early."

That was going to be their mantra.

"Everyone's at the bowling alley," June snapped as she walked back to them. She looked at Calvin. "I need to go talk to Pat. I could make him see—"

Calvin grabbed her arm, as if he was worried she'd fly off to go do that right away. Knowing June, it was a possibility.

"We talked about this," he said with enviable patience. "You know it will only do more harm than good. Pat's not going to listen to you."

June frowned at him, then pulled away and grabbed a beer glass. "I guess." She filled the glass with beer from a tap and went to give it to a customer.

Calvin smiled. "She just wants to do something. Not being able to make it better is killing her."

"There's really not much she can do."

"I know that, and you know that, and even she knows that, but..." He shrugged.

"Yeah."

"At least Hannah is going to make some of the changes you suggested," Calvin said, obviously trying to be positive. "They were good."

"You think?" She didn't want to sound needy, but it was nice to get some feedback.

"Yes. I do."

"Some of the changes I suggested are pretty big."

His smile was sharp. "If you're going to fight, then fight big."

"And if you fail?" Josie asked, her insecurity roaring back with a vengeance.

Calvin's smile turned kind, and he patted her shoulder.

"Then you fail. But at least you tried. That's better than laying down and waiting for everyone to walk all over you. At least you're in the ring swinging."

June stood across from them again. "Did you ask her?" she said to Calvin.

"Oh, yeah. Hannah said you wanted to talk to me." Josie tried to sound confident, but she didn't think she'd succeeded. Calvin burst out laughing at whatever expression she had on her face.

"Well, I'm not going to ask you for your first born child or a million dollars," he teased. "I just wanted to talk to you about a business proposition."

Josie's eyes widened, which made him laugh again.

"Christ, kid. I'm offering you a job."

"A job?" Her voice squeaked, damn it. "Me?"

"Well he sure ain't offering it to me," June said. "We already have an...arrangement." She leaned over the bar and kissed Calvin on his lean cheek.

He smiled at her with so much love that Josie felt like an intruder. But when he turned back to her, he was all business.

"There's a big-box home improvement store a few miles out of town," he said.

"I know. They opened a year or two ago." Hardy Falls might

be small, but the area was growing. The chain stores were starting to move in.

Calvin nodded, frowning a little. "Yeah. We can't compete with the prices, so we compete with excellent customer service and a willingness to work with different contractors or do special orders."

"That's smart." She started mentally running through some possible hooks. He'd want to emphasize the home town aspect. Highlight the knowledgeable staff and willingness to go the extra mile...*Everything you need, right next door*...something like that.

"We're going to offer handyman services through a company my father is starting," Calvin continued. "A lot of the people around here are older, and they need help fixing up their houses."

"That's a good idea." She remembered her mother telling her about an elderly woman who'd called the police because she'd heard rustling noises. When Harry had gone out to investigate, he'd discovered that she had a mouse infestation. He'd done what he could, but the police couldn't take time to make repairs to keep out mice. Not even in Hardy Falls.

Of course, her mom said Harry had gone back to the lady's house when he was off duty to help her out, but still.

"People need someplace to call," she said slowly, thinking it through. "One stop shopping. You sell them the parts, and your father installs them, or whatever."

He nodded. "Exactly. We don't want Hardy Hardware just to be the local hardware store. We want it to be the first place people think of when they're fixing up their houses or making repairs. We want them to come to us for what they need, for advice, to be hooked up with a handyman or one of the local contractors. We want to be the hub."

"Sounds like a lot of work," Josie cautioned, even though she agreed with the idea.

"We need to offer something the big-box stores can't, and that's personal service. We know who you are, and we care who you are. That's what's going to keep the business going."

Albert Cromwell and Harry Newman, grandfather of Officer Harry Newman, walked in. June went over to take their orders, as the old men settled at the bar. It didn't surprise Josie that Officer Harry had gone to help the lady with the mouse problem. His grandfather would have done the same.

"I think you have some good ideas. What do you want me to do?" she asked Calvin.

"I want to hire you to help me get the word out. Yes, I could go to an ad agency in Scranton or Allentown or wherever, but you know the area and you know the people. I liked what you said to Hannah, the ideas you had for her. And more than that, I liked that you could see the possibilities when Hannah couldn't. I want you to look at my store and see them."

Josie's stomach twisted. Could she really do that?

"I'm not sure I—"

"I'm sure," he interrupted her. "We need a better website, social media, all of it. We're out there, but I'm not sure we're implementing it properly."

"Well, yes, but I'm a graphic designer. I don't know about where you should advertise or anything."

"I have some ideas, and you're already going to be looking into all of that for Hannah, right? Also, I need something *to* advertise. I need the ad copy and graphics, the Internet presence, and some help with the branding. I need to reimagine my store, just like Hannah has to reimagine the Country Time."

Josie's thoughts were racing. She could see the hardware store and the changes Calvin was talking about. He had an idea of his audience. She just needed to find the right way to target that audience.

"I'll have to think about it," she said.

Calvin nodded. "And think about your charges, too." He

smiled a little. "Depending on what they are, maybe we could go with more of a cafeteria plan."

Josie chewed her lip. "Send me an email with what you want to do in order of priority, and I'll look at it."

Calvin put his hand on her shoulder. "Thanks."

"You know I'm going to need to look for a job," she cautioned him. "If I find something, this would have to be a moonlighting gig."

"I understand." He squeezed her shoulder and slid off the barstool. "But you might want to think about changing your mind."

"What do you mean?"

"There are a lot of small businesses in this town, and we're under a lot of pressure. Used to be there wasn't a fast food restaurant within twenty miles, now there are five out on the highway—anything you could want to eat. I hear the new mall in Friendsville is already drawing away business from the downtown. Ms. Gregory said bookstore sales are down, and she's blaming the Internet and free shipping. We're all going to need help to keep going."

"You mean start something here?" Hearing him echo exactly what she'd been considering was making Josie's heart beat fast with fear and excitement.

"I know it's a big decision, but think about it. I'm pretty sure you'd find plenty of willing clients." Calvin looked around the taproom at the golden wood and the splashes of color from the lanterns over the tables. "Everything changes." He smiled back down at her, his eyes crinkling at the corners. "All of us have to change, too." He flicked her nose with his finger. "Maybe even you."

Josie watched him walk away, absently admiring his easy, confident stride. He stopped opposite June and pulled her over the bar for a deep kiss before dropping her back to her feet and sauntering out through the kitchen door. June looked slightly dazed, and Josie admired that, too. She bet it wasn't easy to knock June off her feet.

"He's been thinking ever since he heard what you said to Hannah," June said, as she grabbed a bottle of water and took a long drink. "The man's got ideas."

"He does." They sounded like good ideas, too. "Calvin's really smart, isn't he?"

June beamed at her, looking as proud as if she'd just said, "Calvin cured cancer."

"He is," she said. "And he's determined to keep the hardware store going."

"Then smart is good."

Could she do this? Could she actually make enough money freelancing to make it possible for her to stay in Hardy Falls?

Was that what she wanted?

Josie pushed off her barstool and waved at Albert and Harry. "I'm going to go talk to Hannah. One problem at a time."

June cackled. "Never been my experience that things come at you single file."

"Ain't it the truth?" In her life, problems arrived in clumps.

When she went into the kitchen, Kevin was standing behind the grill. She greeted the big man who grinned at her cheerfully.

"Where's the boss?"

"Office," he said as he sashayed over to the hotdog roller.

Josie headed to the office before he could put her to work, pausing briefly at the back door to listen. Nothing. Maybe the boys were actually talking.

She found Hannah seated behind her desk, frowning at a sheaf of papers. When Josie knocked on the doorjamb and stepped into the tiny room, that frown was transferred to her.

"What are you doing, now?" Josie asked.

"Reading," Hannah replied.

"Reading what?"

"Papers Sam dropped off for the investor pool. I cannot properly express the depth of hatred I feel for legal jargon. Not to mention the fact that Sam being around makes Deacon jumpy." She put the paperwork aside and studied Josie. "How are you? Really?"

"Okay. Really." Josie settled into the visitor's chair across the desk from her friend. "Mat and I are fine. It was just a misunderstanding."

"Deacon told me what Mat said." Hannah's frown deepened. "Are you sure—"

"I'm sure." Josie broke in. "There are reasons why he overreacted. And I'm not going to tell you what they are," she said, interpreting Hannah's look. "I think he's talking to Deacon, and Deacon can tell you. But he told me in private."

Hannah's frown morphed into a scowl. "We don't keep secrets," she reminded Josie. "Remember?"

"It's not mine to tell." Josie thought about what she could say. "He's been through a lot, and seeing Deacon kiss me, well, he thought it was more than it was."

Hannah's scowl was black.

"Deacon kissed you?"

"You said he told you what happened."

"He left out that part."

"Don't worry." Josie reached over the desk to rub her friend's hand. "Deacon just kissed me on the cheek, Hannah. It was absolutely nothing. Mat was behind me so it must have looked different to him."

"Oh. Okay." Hannah relaxed. "Well, I'm glad I don't have to fire Mat. He's one of the best workers I've ever had here. I don't have to fire him, right?"

"Absolutely not."

Hannah studied her for another minute, then nodded. "Okay. But you'll tell me if that changes?"

"I sure will," Josie confirmed. "So what's going on with the investor pool?"

"Beats me. I don't even know what the hell I'm reading." Hannah drew her hands through her hair. "All of this stuff just bounces off my brain." She slapped her forehead.

Josie got up and pulled her chair around the desk. "Let's both look at it."

A few minutes later, she had to agree. The words were bouncing off her brain, too, but it looked like everything was spelled out. In great detail.

"I think it's okay," she said to Hannah.

"I guess." Hannah dropped her head onto the desk. "So much responsibility, Josie."

"I know." Josie ran her hand down Hannah's back. "Maybe we can figure out another way."

"No." Hannah raised her head. "You were right. If I don't make some changes, I might as well close. It was pitiful here last night, and tonight's even worse. I know part of that is because the bowling alley thing is new, so people want to check it out. But some of them will never come back."

"No," Josie agreed. It was true. There would be people who would take the other choice.

"I need to change things and I need money. So," she drew in a deep breath and let it out, "Investor pool."

"I'll contribute," Josie said.

"No you will not," Hannah smacked at her shoulder. "Not until you have a new job."

Josie thought about Calvin's offer. "I have a freelance gig here in Hardy Falls."

"Yeah? Who?"

"Calvin wants me to come up with a plan for the hardware store to help him compete."

"Oh, so that's what he wanted." Hannah nodded. "Calvin's always on top of things."

Josie smirked. "Especially June."

The both groaned. Then they both laughed, and they only laughed harder when June poked her head in to see what was going on.

June walked away muttering to herself.

33

Josie was relieved there were no signs of bruises or broken bones or anything when Deacon came into the office a few minutes later. She assumed he and Mat hadn't punched each other at least.

Deacon must have guessed her thoughts because he smiled at her.

"Everything's fine," he assured her, then looked at Hannah. "I'm going back to the bar. Mat's at the dishwasher."

"I can work the dishwasher if you need Mat to do something else," Josie volunteered.

"No you can't." Hannah frowned at her. "You have to design things that will keep me in business and make me lots of money."

"But there's no pressure."

"Of course not."

Deacon laughed at them and left.

"I'm glad the menfolk didn't beat each other up," Hannah said once he was gone.

Josie looked at her in surprise. "You were afraid that would happen, too?"

Hannah shrugged. "Deacon was really, really upset." She paused. "I think he was hurt. Mat is his friend."

"I hope they're okay now." Josie pushed to her feet and pulled the visitor chair back around the desk to its original position. "I'd better go check on the other one."

Hannah sighed. "Men."

Josie nodded in agreement. "Can't live with them, can't shoot them."

She left as Hannah laughed.

She went through the taproom and was pleased to see people in bowling shirts scattered around the space. In the kitchen, Kevin was making pasta salad a lot more competently than she ever had. Waving at him in greeting, she headed over to Mat at the dishwasher, and waited while he shoved a tray of dirty plates into the machine and hit the button that sent everything rumbling. He noticed her standing beside him, grinned, and bent to kiss her quickly.

"You seem a lot more relaxed," she observed when he raised his head.

"Hmmm. I'm taking a break," Mat yelled to Kevin.

The other man rolled his eyes but smiled broadly. "Always the dishwashers are slackers."

Mat stripped off his rubber gloves and gave Kevin the finger, which just made him laugh. Then he grabbed their coats and towed Josie outside.

It was chilly, so she was grateful when he slung her jacket around her shoulders as soon as they got to the little employee rest area with the plastic Adirondack chairs.

"I just didn't want to talk in the kitchen," Mat said, shrugging into his parka. "And I figured you'd ask questions because you're nosy."

She shoved her arms into the sleeves of her jacket and managed to elbow him in the gut. It made him grunt a little, but she suspected he was just patronizing her.

"So?" she demanded. "How did it go?"

Mat focused on zipping up his coat. "I told him."

"And?" God, it was like pulling teeth.

He shrugged. "What could he say except, 'you poor bastard'? He'd only met Gail once or twice, so he didn't really know her. He was just pissed that I hadn't told him before now."

"But you two are good, right?"

"We're good."

"You apologized?"

"Yes." The way he bit off the word made her smile. It killed him to have to apologize to Deacon. "Were you talking to Hannah?" he asked in a blatant attempt to change the subject.

Josie hid another grin but decided to let it go.

"I talked to Calvin first." She wasn't quite sure why she was bringing up Calvin's offer, except that she wanted to see what Mat thought about it. "He asked me to do some work for him. Design a webpage, social media presence, those kinds of things."

He frowned. "Really?"

"Calvin is trying to start up some new services to make sure the local people go to him instead of the bigger home improvement stores."

"Smart."

"It is." She hesitated, then pressed on. "He said there are other local businesses that could probably use help, too. Like a marketing consultant or something. Someone who already knows the area and the challenges. He thinks I fit the bill."

Mat studied her for a moment.

"Are you saying you want to start your own business? Here in Hardy Falls?"

"Maybe." She wished she could read his expression, but she couldn't see his face very well in the crackling parking lot lights. "It might be a good opportunity."

"An opportunity to be a marketing consultant?" He sounded skeptical.

"More than just that. I'd actually already been thinking about it, even before I talked to Calvin. I could do what I did in the city, what I'm doing for Hannah. Design for marketing. Advertising and branding. Websites and social media. Help businesses get out there where people can find them." She frowned as she mulled it over. "Yes, I did mostly graphic design in my last job, but when I worked on teams for smaller clients, I was much more hands-on. What I don't know, I can learn. I'll have the work I do for Calvin and Hannah to build up a portfolio and create word of mouth." She talked faster, getting more excited as she put her ideas into words. "All of the small businesses around here are fighting to survive, and I can help them. I can even work on events for the town council. I could come up with a menu of services, and offer things that are recurring, like site maintenance, as well as the one-offs. It would be like a...a landscaper who also offers lawn service." She paused to draw in a deep breath. "What do you think?"

He was watching her, his face inscrutable in the dim light. "It doesn't matter what I think."

Josie blinked at his flat tone.

"Well, of course it matters. Why else would I be telling you all this?"

In fact, she was quite desperate to know exactly what he thought about the possibility of her staying in town.

"Ever since you came here, you've been focused on getting back to New York City. In case you haven't noticed, this isn't it."

"I've been focused on getting back to the city because that's where my contacts are. I know people there. And there are a ton of ad agencies there."

"None of that has changed."

"No," she admitted slowly. "This would be something new. A new challenge. A new beginning." *With you.*

Mat didn't say anything for several long moments, and her stomach began to churn.

It occurred to her, a little belatedly, that she might be making a huge mistake. After all, just that afternoon Mat had flat out told her he didn't know if he could trust her. Yes, he'd apologized. Yes, he'd seemed to regret saying the words. But what if that apology hadn't meant as much as she'd assumed? What if she was the one jumping to conclusions this time? She thought his confession about Gail, the whole baring-of-his-soul thing back in his room, had meant something important, that it was a turning point for them. What if she'd totally misread the situation?

Josie swallowed. Suddenly she was standing on the edge of a precipice, and she hadn't even known it was there.

"Do you think this is a good idea?" she asked carefully, needing his answer but not sure she wanted it.

"This isn't about me," he said finally. "I want you to do what's best for you. And if that means going back to New York, that's what you should do."

Josie wrapped her arms around her middle. Why couldn't he give her some idea of how he felt? Any clue about whether or not he'd be happy if she stayed?

"Do you want me here or not?" she asked bluntly.

Mat stared into her face, his eyes dark and glittering.

"If you decide that's what you want to do," he said.

Nothing. He was giving her nothing.

She turned and walked away from him, moving over to the scrub trees lining the edge of the parking lot.

"Josie? What's wrong?"

When she didn't answer, he followed her. At least he had enough sense not to try and touch her.

Maybe he'd been counting on her leaving, and now she was screwing up his plans. After all, when they'd started this thing between them, it had been with the understanding that it would be short-term. What if he wasn't telling her how he felt because he didn't feel anything?

"So, you don't care what I decide to do," she said, turning to face him.

"No." He shook his head when she flinched. "I mean, I only want you to stay in Hardy Falls if that's what you really want to do. I don't want you to regret it."

"I appreciate that. I do. But it would still be nice to know how you feel." She watched the trees sway in a sudden chilly breeze.

"If you decide to stay here because of...me...us...and then you regret it..."

"We would talk about it like grown-ups." She drew in a deep breath to try and remain calm as her temper bubbled. "God, Mat, I'm not a third grader. I *can* communicate."

He ran a hand through his too-long hair. "I've lived inside a lie before. I've lived with someone hiding how she really felt. I don't think I could handle doing it again."

Ah. There she was. Gail.

Still.

Always.

Mat might not really think Josie would have an affair with Deacon, but he wasn't sure that she would be honest with him. He didn't trust himself enough to know that he could trust her.

"Everything in this world isn't about Gail," she snapped before she could stop herself.

"I never said it was."

"Oh, please!"

He ran a hand through his hair again. "Look, she never wanted to be married to me, but she let herself get talked into it because that's what other people expected. Then she started to regret it and hate me. I don't want that to happen with you."

"And I'm not some scared girl who can't tell the truth. If I think I've made a mistake, I will freaking tell you, and we will deal with it." Her voice rising with frustration, Josie threw her hands up and waved them around. "For Christ's sake, Mat! If I have to change jobs again, it's not the end of the flipping world. I will just find another job and we will talk, and if we still want to be together, we will work it out. I'm not asking you for permission here. You telling me how you feel about me staying in town just lets me know whether or not I have another reason to take the risk!" *And lets me know that you care at least a little bit.*

Mat crossed his arms and glared at her.

"Why are you overreacting? I'm just trying to say that I'll respect your decision, whatever it is."

"No! You're afraid to tell me how you feel because you don't want to show any emotion!" she shouted at him, angry and hurting.

His hands dropped.

"What the hell? I tell you how I feel all the time!" he shouted back.

"Bullshit! You tell me you want me, but you don't show me anything else."

"Yeah? You don't show me anything else either."

"Well, I'm trying to now, aren't I? And I can't even get you to tell me that you want me to stay!"

"Maybe I don't want you to stay!" he shot back.

Josie sucked in a sharp breath. That one hurt. *Sucker punch.* The temper drained and all she felt was empty.

Wow. He couldn't get much clearer than that, could he? Even Josie could pick up that signal.

"At least you're being honest," she said, grateful that her voice still worked.

"Josie—" He took a step towards her but she retreated, so he stopped.

"No. If that's the way you feel, I need to know, right?" She tried to smile at him, but didn't think she pulled it off. So she'd been stupid and thought there was more between them than there apparently was. So she'd thought that they might have a future together. That it was at least a possibility. Now she knew. "Okay. Geez, I guess I was just getting in too deep, wasn't I? Sorry about that. Totally my bad."

"Wait—"

She held up a hand and he stopped again.

"I'm not saying I won't start up the business here in town, but it's good to know where we stand. See? That's all I wanted. That's all you had to say."

"Jesus! I'm not saying that's how I feel! I don't even know why I said it!"

She needed to get away. She couldn't think when he was standing so close that she could feel the warmth from his body. "Give me my car keys."

"What?" He sounded absolutely frazzled. Too bad.

"Give me my car keys. You're going to have to get a ride from Deacon after work."

"Josie—"

"No." She cut him off because she really couldn't talk to him anymore. "I need to think. I need to get my head together." *I need to get away from you.* "I'll get my stuff out of the motel room and head to Mom's."

"That's not what I—"

"Keys."

Slowly, reluctantly, he pulled her keys out of his jeans pocket and handed them over.

"Thanks. I don't think we should see each other for a while, at least not the way we have been. All right?"

"Josie—"

"I need time to get my head screwed on again." She shrugged. "I guess I was on a different page. Hope I didn't make you feel uncomfortable. I'll, uh, I'm sure I'll see you around." Then she made a break for it, practically running into the Country Time for her purse. She told Hannah she was leaving, and before her friend could ask too many questions, hurried back out to her car.

She'd wondered if he would try to stop her, but he was still standing at the edge of the parking lot when she climbed into her car. He was probably glad she wasn't pressing him anymore.

See? Stupid.

Revving the engine, she spun gravel and drove away.

First she stopped at the motel and gathered her things, amazed at how much had accumulated over such a short period of time. It was almost like she'd been nesting and hadn't even realized it.

She left the keycard on a table and took one last glance around the room to make sure she hadn't forgotten anything. The sharp pain of looking at the space they'd been sharing almost kneecapped her.

No. Not now.

She left quickly, fully intending to go directly to her mother's house and barricading herself in her bedroom. Instead, she found herself driving down one of the back roads that wound around Hardy Falls Lake.

The lake lay peaceful in the darkness, glistening in the meager moonlight. Even through the closed car windows, she could hear the thunder of falling water growing louder as she drove, and came around a curve in the road to face the small bank of waterfalls that gave the town of Hardy Falls its name. On the shore opposite her, the Fallside Restaurant perched on its craggy outcropping, shining under a blanket of fairy lights that reflected like sparkles in the waterfall spray.

The park surrounding the lake closed at sunset, so there were barriers across the picnic area parking lots. Josie pulled over to the side of the road and turned off the car's engine. For a moment she just sat, staring at the waterfalls lit with the lights of fairies, and watched the breeze rattle trees in the reflected glow. The snow had brought down most of the leaves, but a few still clung to their branches, waiting to drop. Waiting for the right moment.

Mat had been right about one thing—she'd never expected to stay. Never wanted to stay. Never wanted to end up back in the complicated web of small-town life.

But in the city, all she'd done was work. She'd lived in Manhattan for a lot of the time she'd been working there, and she'd rarely explored any of it.

On the other hand, Mat was also right about the reasons for going back. She knew people there and she'd already gotten emails from recruiters asking for her resume. It was just that Manhattan didn't seem to be her place anymore.

Everyone changes.

Mat was hung up on Gail. Well, to be fair, it was probably more accurate to say he was hung up on the consequences of Gail. Josie didn't think he still cared for the other woman, but maybe she was reading him completely wrong once again.

It didn't matter, anyway. She had made plenty of mistakes in her life, but she refused to be with someone who didn't really want her around. Someone who saw another woman when he looked at her. If a guy was going to get angry at her, it should at least be because *Josie* had done something wrong.

She stared out at the dark lake and wondered, as she had in Mat's rented room over the bookstore, where that left her.

Not with him.

Mat had said that she was more than she thought she was, and that helping Hannah with her website and marketing was really her thing. When she'd tried to explain her idea for the business she was imagining to him, she'd seen how it could be. She'd gotten excited about her work for the first time in years.

The problem was, she couldn't see any of it without Mat.

The sudden understanding blew through her like the wind in the trees.

"Oh, God."

Somewhere along the way, she'd fallen in love with Mateo Guerrero.

When had it happened? *How* had it happened?

"Shit," she muttered. Why did her mother have to be right about this, too?

She was so totally screwed.

34

S till not quite sure what the hell had happened, Mat watched Josie get into her car and drive away. He wanted to stop her, follow her, yell at her that of course he wanted her to stay.

But he kept himself from going after her. That would defeat the point of the whole thing. Besides, she was right. They both needed a break to calm down.

Except he was afraid she meant the break to be permanent.

Confused and angry, aching in a way that made him even angrier, he headed back to the kitchen. He slammed the back door so hard that Kevin turned to him with eyebrows lifted in surprise.

"Dis probably have something to do with Josie," the big man observed.

Mat snarled at him and went into the taproom where he found Deacon pulling some beer for customers.

"You'll need to give me a ride home," he said shortly.

Deacon glanced at him.

"I figured. Hannah told me Josie was gone."

Once again, there was no friendliness in the other man's

face. Mat nodded abruptly and headed back to the dishwasher, glad for the pile of dirty dishes he saw next to it.

The rest of the night passed slowly, and he bitterly regretted all of the business they'd lost to the bowling alley. If he'd been busy, maybe he wouldn't have had time to think.

Where had things gone so wrong? He'd only been trying to respect Josie's freaking decision, give her space to choose what she wanted to do. Didn't women want freaking space to make up their own minds?

So he didn't want her staying in town just because it was what *he* wanted her to do. Was that so wrong? He was going out of his fucking way not to pressure her. Was that a crime? He wanted her to be sure because he didn't want her to be miserable. Did that make him a monster?

And he wasn't still hung up on Gail, damn it. God, he should have known it would be a huge mistake to tell Josie about Gail.

Then he remembered the expression on Josie's face when he'd spewed that bullshit about not wanting her to stay in town, and his insides clenched.

Why had he said something stupid like that? It wasn't true. Far from it. She'd pushed him into a corner, and he'd lashed out without thinking. He *always* thought before he spoke, unless he was talking to Josie Kline. Why did he constantly screw up around her?

As he waited for something to do, he found himself staring at his cell phone. More times than he could count, his finger hovered over Josie's speed dial. Then he'd realize what he was doing and jam it back in his pocket.

No. He'd talk to her in a day or two when she was more rational.

He wasn't sure why that thought made him more tense.

All things considered, he wasn't surprised when Deacon

came into the kitchen and told him, with a distinct chill in his voice, that Hannah was springing them early.

Growling with frustration, Mat turned on his heel, grabbed his coat, and walked out, leaving Deacon to follow him.

The other man was silent as they drove back to the bookstore, not speaking until after he'd pulled into a parking spot.

"I don't know what's going on with you and Josie," he said, "but you need to fix it."

"Don't you think I want to?" Mat snapped.

"I have no idea. Just do it."

Shaking his head, Mat climbed out of the SUV. Deacon sped away.

Rather than going up to his room, he got into his pickup and drove out to the motel. When he opened the door to the room they'd been using, it became all too evident that Josie had been serious when she'd said she was going to get her things and go to her mom's. There was no trace of her left in the space they'd shared.

The realization slammed through him that somehow, even after everything, he'd still thought she might be there, waiting to fight it out with him.

The fact that she wasn't, that she really was gone, dowsed the rest of the anger that had been simmering since they'd argued. He spotted her keycard on the table next to the door and touched it before slipping it into his pocket.

Maybe he should go to her. Talk to her.

But what could he say? How could he fix this?

What did he want to say?

No, it was better to wait. Calm down first, then try to explain.

"You tell me you want me, but you don't show me anything else."

"Yeah? You don't show me anything else either."

"Well, I'm trying to now, aren't I? And I can't even get you to tell me that you want me to stay!"

"Maybe I don't want you to stay!"

Sighing, he started to pack up his things.

Later, back in his room over the bookstore, Mat found himself standing next to his rumpled bed, breathing in Josie's scent clinging to the sheets and remembering her standing in the middle of the room, yelling at him because he'd thought she was having an affair with Deacon. In that case, yes, he could admit he'd judged her based on the way Gail had acted. But he had just talked to his ex-fiancée, so the memory of her betrayal was fresh in his mind. Otherwise, he wouldn't have jumped to conclusions.

Right?

Desperately needing air, he dropped his things haphazardly and walked over to the window, shoving it open to let in the crisp, Hardy Falls November night. The weather forecasters said that it was warmer than usual, but Mat still thought it was pretty damn cold. When the wind blew around him he shivered, but he didn't close the window.

Was Josie right to say that he was making everything about Gail?

No, he assured himself, leaning against the casement and staring out into the darkness. Josie had overreacted, probably because of what he'd told her earlier in the day. Their conversation about whether he thought she should stay in Hardy Falls had nothing to do with his ex. How could it? Mat only wanted Josie to make up her own mind without worrying about his feelings.

Of course, now she might be under the impression that he didn't have *any* feelings for her.

He ran his hand through his hair.

No feelings? God, what a joke. He had so many feelings he didn't know what to do with them all. He just knew they terrified him. Fucking scared him to death. What if he was honest with her, and he was wrong again?

Like he'd been with Gail.

But Josie wasn't Gail.

The stray thought made him freeze as much as the chilly wind blowing in through the window.

Josie wasn't Gail. Of course she wasn't.

Mind racing, he clenched his fists on the windowsill and stared into the face of the breeze whipping the draperies and bringing the hint of rain into the room.

Josie cared about him. She had to. He could see it. That was why she'd been pressing him to find out if he wanted her to stay. That was why she'd looked so devastated when he'd been a freaking cowardly asshole and told her that he didn't.

What if he told her how he really felt and she stayed? What if she was miserable?

"If I have to change jobs again, it's not the end of the flipping world. I will just find another job, and we will talk, and if we still want to be together, we will work it out."

The situation wasn't the same as it had been in Texas. The woman wasn't the same. Nothing was the same. Even he wasn't the same.

"You telling me how you feel about me staying in town just lets me know whether or not I have another reason to take the risk!"

. . .

He suddenly knew that she'd been telling the truth. He was not responsible for her decision. All he could do was participate in it. If he didn't open his mouth and tell her how he felt, she'd never know. Then she might not leave town, but she would definitely leave him.

She'd already left him.

And he wanted her back.

His heart was pounding as hard as it had in the desert when he'd been facing an unseen enemy.

He was standing at a doorway. All he had to do was walk through. Take a chance.

Because she was the one.

Gail never had been. Even though it seemed like she should have been perfect for him. Maybe he'd loved her in a way, but there'd always been something missing—on both sides.

When he'd caught her with Alicia, the pain had probably been as much about pride as it had been about love. If it had been Josie, well…He drew in a deep breath.

He wouldn't have just walked out, that was for damned sure.

He was in love with Josie Kline. He loved her big, generous, loyal heart, and her feisty attitude, and her beautiful, open face.

And she thought he didn't want her.

"Christ." He had totally fucked up everything.

He wanted to call her right then, or better yet, head over to her mother's house and demand to see her. Fortunately, he still had enough sense rattling around in his head to realize neither were good ideas. What he wanted to say had to be done in person, not over the phone, and he sincerely doubted that Chief Kline would appreciate him showing up at her house at three o'clock in the morning.

But when he forced himself to go to bed, he lay sleepless, staring at the ceiling, remembering how Josie had given herself to him so sweetly right here just a few hours ago. He was such an idiot not to have seen it before, not to have known. Casual? There was nothing casual about this.

Turning onto his side, he buried his face in the pillow she'd used and breathed in her lingering scent. God, he missed the hell out of her. Josie was essential, and he needed to tell her so. Then she'd just have to forgive him. End of story.

35

Josie watched the morning sun streaming through her bedroom curtains, throwing patterns around the room. She'd lain in bed staring at the ceiling for most of the night trying to forget about Mat and, when that failed, focusing on coming up with a plan of what to do next.

One thing she had decided was that she didn't want to go back to Manhattan. It was too big, too impersonal. Since she'd been in Hardy Falls, she'd realized how much she'd missed the town while she'd been away, missed the way everyone cared about their neighbors and got all up in each other's business.

When—if—she left, she wanted to find someplace where she could be part of a community, again. Maybe she would head down towards Philadelphia. Not the city itself, necessarily, but the surrounding suburbs. Even if she ended up working in a more populated area, there were lots of smaller towns within commuting distance that might be able to give her what she was looking for. She could talk to Calvin. He'd worked in Philly for years and would be able to help her make connections. And her brother Jordan lived in one of the swankier areas close to the city, too. She could probably convince him to let her stay in his condo's spare bedroom short term. That would be a smart alternative. Logical.

Except...

She couldn't quite shake the notion of setting up her own business here in Hardy Falls—of making a fresh start in her home town and helping the people she'd known her whole life. This idea was the first time she'd been excited about work in, well, forever. And she knew that she wouldn't get a better chance at a new beginning. After all, she had a home base, savings, severance, and unemployment. All of which should buy her time to get established and see what could happen. If she needed more money to pay her bills, she could work part time at the ski slopes over the winter, or at the casino in Mount Pocono. She could run a dishwasher now. She had skills.

Of course if she stayed in town, she was bound to see Mat. That was the real problem, wasn't it? It would be much, much easier to run away.

But what would it say about her if she gave up everything she wanted and left simply because she'd made a mistake?

Mat didn't own the freaking town. If anything, she had more right to be here than he did. They hadn't done anything wrong, anyway. There was no reason for her to scurry off with her tail between her legs. They'd had an affair, just as they'd said they would. It was her own fault that she'd fallen into the trap of thinking it was something more. Of wanting more.

There was a soft knock on her door.

"Josie? Are you awake?"

Jenny. Great. She'd managed to avoid both her sister and her mother when she'd slunk home the night before, and had kind of hoped she'd be able to get her act together a little bit before she had to face either of them.

"Josie?"

"I'm awake. Come on in."

The bedroom door pushed open and Jenny poked her head inside, smiling faintly.

"I brought you coffee."

"Thank God." There was a lot to be said for a sister who knew you that well.

She sat up and grabbed the steaming mug, and somehow managed to drink half without bothering to breathe.

"Perfect," she sighed when she came up for air.

"I thought you'd need it." Jenny tilted her head, considering her. "You look tired. Did you get any sleep?"

"Sure," Josie said evasively. Maybe a few minutes here and there.

"Hannah said that you were pretty upset."

Josie stared at her. "When did you talk to Hannah?"

"Last night. She called me because she couldn't get through on your cell and wanted to make sure you'd made it home."

Frowning, Josie grabbed her cell phone from the nightstand and winced when she saw the screen was dark.

"I forgot to charge it."

"I was going to check on you, but Mom said you'd come in so quietly that she didn't think you wanted to be bothered."

So much for her family not noticing her.

"Hannah said you and Mat had a fight," Jenny said.

Josie was going to have to have a little chat with Hannah about her blabbermouth. She took another sip of the coffee, afraid of what she would see if she looked at her sister.

"We did," she admitted because why the hell not? Apparently everyone knew, anyway.

Jenny came and sat beside her on the bed, then threw an arm around her shoulders and hugged her close for a moment.

"I'm sorry." Surprisingly, she sounded like she meant it. Josie risked a glance and saw only sadness and empathy on Jenny's face.

"I hate that it hurt you when we, um, got together," she said in a rush of honesty. "It just kind of happened."

Jenny looked away.

"He seemed like a great guy, and he was gorgeous and flirted with me before you came home. I thought..." she let the words trail off as she met Josie's eyes with a forced smile. "Then I saw you two together that day at the Country Time, and knew I was wasting my time."

"Jenny—"

"I guess I was jealous." Jenny sighed and drew back a little bit, curling her blue-streaked hair around her ears before looking down at her hands and picking at some paint dried on her knuckles. "It's just that he seemed to see me, and that was nice. You know? You and Jordan always have your acts together. I'm the total screwup of the family. It was nice when a good guy seemed to notice me."

Josie gaped at her. "What? You're not a screwup!"

Jenny laughed without much humor. "Yeah? I beg to differ. And I'm pretty sure Mom would agree. So, when Mat clicked with you, I thought Jesus, is she going to get him too? Is she going to get everything?"

That shocked Josie enough to make her lean forward and grab her sister's arm.

"God, Jenny! Do you still feel that way?"

Jenny smiled the forced smile again. "Not really." Then she shrugged. "Maybe a little. But that's on me."

"I have no idea why Mat and I clicked. You're the awesome one. I'm afraid of everything and I always do exactly what I'm told."

"I'm the one wasting my life."

"The hell you are!" Josie was getting more upset by the second listening to her creative, talented sister talk like this.

"Stefan thought so."

"That loser? I can't believe you care what he said."

"Mom feels the same way."

"She does not!"

"Oh, she's been pretty clear," Jenny said.

"Well, then she's wrong." Josie would have to ask her mother about it later. "You are doing exactly what you want to do, and you're not letting anyone stop you. I know I asked you whether it was worth it." She felt pretty bad about that now. "But I'm jealous of what you can do. I don't think you're wasting your time. If anything, I'm the one who's screwing up."

Jenny looked at her through her fall of hair. "You have a college education and a career."

"I'm the one who got laid off from a job I hated because I was too scared to leave it first. I'm the one who was working almost twenty-four/seven because my dick of a supervisor was trying to push me out and wanted to steal my ideas."

"You hated your job?" Jenny turned to face her fully. "I always thought you liked it."

Josie drew in a deep breath.

"I lied," she admitted. She'd hated that job for years, even before she'd started working for Don.

"Then why did you stay?"

"Student loans. Did you know they never go away?"

"Oh." Jenny seemed startled, as if she'd never considered that aspect of the situation before. "Man, that sucks. What are you going to do now?"

"Well, I have an idea," Josie said slowly. "It may be stupid, though."

"Really?" Jenny actually looked interested. "What?"

"I was thinking of staying in Hardy Falls and starting my own business." Josie explained what she had in mind. When she'd finished, Jenny frowned thoughtfully.

"You know, I can see that," she said after a moment. "I can see you doing that. You'd be good at it. You know a lot about the small businesses around here, and I'm sure Mom has contacts. Even Missy might be interested in talking to you."

"Really?"

"She's been thinking about a website. She probably won't want to do much else, but who knows?"

Josie felt the "zing" again—the breathless hope that her idea might work. But...

"It's pretty risky." For a whole lot of reasons.

Jenny shrugged. "Everything worthwhile is."

"And, uh, Mat's here," Josie pointed out.

"You just had a fight. I'm sure when you talk—"

"No." Josie sucked in air. "I think Mat and I might be done." Just saying it made her ache.

"Are you sure?" There was only sympathy in Jenny's face as she pulled her in for another hug. "I'm sorry."

"So, it's going to be hard if I stay. Because he's here and I'll have to see him."

"It will be," Jenny acknowledged. "But you'll deal with it. You always do."

"I think..." Josie swallowed hard and started again. "I think I might be, sort of, in love. With him."

"Oh, honey." Jenny wrapped her up in her arms.

They sat like that for a while, but broke apart when the doorbell rang.

"What the—?" Jenny frowned at the alarm clock on Josie's dresser. "Who's that?"

Josie straightened and reached for a tissue to blow her nose.

"Missy?" she suggested.

"Not yet." Jenny got to her feet as the doorbell rang again. It was followed by pounding on the door. "Jesus. I'd better go see."

"Be careful."

Jenny left the room and Josie climbed out of bed and pulled on some clothes, in case she had to go to her sister's rescue.

Through the open bedroom door, she could hear voices, but they were too far away to make out. Then she heard Jenny's quick footsteps on the stairs, and her sister slid into her room. To Josie's surprise, she closed the door behind her.

"Who was that?" she asked, even more alarmed when she saw Jenny's expression. "God, it wasn't Stefan, was it?"

"What? No." Jenny shook her head. "It's not my man—"

"You shouldn't call him your man—"

"—it's yours."

"—and he's hardly a man at all if he..." Josie let her words trail off and she blinked. "What?"

"It's Mat. He looks like absolute hell, and he wants to talk to you."

"What?" Josie squeaked.

"You heard me." Jenny grabbed her shoulders and pushed her towards the hallway. "Now, go brush your teeth and comb your hair, and then go see what he wants."

"But—"

"And tell him you'll be staying in town."

"But—"

Jenny grabbed her shoulders. "You need to face him sometime. Are you a mouse, or are you a woman?"

"Eeek?"

Jenny shook her gently. "I know better than that. Look, he's here and he definitely wants to talk to you. So talk." She drew in a deep breath and let it out slowly. "You never know what might happen."

"I don't know. What if he's just here to make sure I'm leaving?"

"Then he's stupid. But what if he's here to make sure you don't?"

Josie gulped and stared at her.

"Take a chance."

Take a chance.

She caught a glimpse of her reflection in the mirror and grimaced. There was no way in hell that she was going to see the man when she looked like this.

"I need ten minutes," she told her sister.

Jenny smiled. "Good."

Mat had waited as long as he'd been able, which meant that he was at Josie's mother's house at eight o'clock in the morning. As he rang the doorbell, he hoped that Chief Kline hadn't been on the overnight shift. If she was overtired, she might answer the door locked and loaded. Still, he couldn't find it in him to care too much. He just wanted to talk to Josie.

There was no answer, and he started to worry that she'd already left town, even though her car and Jenny's truck were both in the driveway. He rang the bell again. Maybe it wasn't working? He pounded on the door.

"Jesus. Hold on."

That was Jenny's voice. He waited impatiently as the locks turned and the door opened as far as it could with the security chain still on.

"Jenny." He tried to sound civilized but didn't think he'd succeeded. "Is Josie here?"

"Mat?" The blue eye staring at him through the crack widened. "What the—?"

"I need to talk to her, Jenny," he said. "Please."

She considered him for another moment, then the door closed in his face. He started to pound on it again, but heard the chain rattling, and then it opened. Jenny stood barring the entrance with her arms crossed, glaring at him.

"You hurt her."

"God, I know." Feeling like hell, he ran a hand through his

hair. He hadn't slept at all, just watched the clock. "I need to talk to her," he repeated. "Explain. Apologize."

"I'm not sure I believe you."

"You're not the one who has to," he shot back, his temper fraying. "I have to see her."

For a moment it looked like Jenny wasn't going to move, but then she finally took a few steps back and gestured for him to come into the house. He was glad because otherwise he would have had to pick her up and move her out of the way.

"Wait there," she said, pointing to a small living room. "I'll see what she says."

Mat nodded and went to where she'd indicated.

Jenny ran up the stairs. Which meant Josie was here.

The thought settled him but not enough for him to relax. Instead, he stood in front of a big picture window and stared at the quiet neighborhood street, listening to footsteps and some muffled voices overhead.

"She needs to take a shower," Jenny called. "You're going to have to wait."

"Fine." He wasn't going anywhere.

There was a roar of water, and he knew it was the shower upstairs. Unhelpfully, his mind immediately displayed memories of what Josie looked like all sleek and wet and naked with her arms reaching out for him. What she felt like as he slipped into her.

Enough of that, he told himself. All he needed was to have to face her with a massive boner. That would make a great impression. It was bad enough that he hadn't thought of taking a shower himself. Or shaving. Or changing his clothes for that matter.

The water turned off. After more long minutes, he finally heard footsteps and turned to see Josie standing on the stairs, staring at him.

"Josie."

The speeches he'd prepared, every thought in his head, fled now that she was actually there. All he could do was appreciate how she looked with her hair damp and shiny, her face glowing from the warmth of the water, and her blue eyes big and wary. He moved closer until he could smell her soap, shampoo, and her clean skin, and he just wanted to pull her up to his body and kiss her. But he didn't because he knew she wouldn't want that.

"Mat." Her voice was cool, and he couldn't read her expression as she descended the rest of the stairs. "What are you doing here?"

Mat drew in a deep breath because here was that doorway, waiting for him to walk through. If he told her how he felt, she'd be able to hurt him worse than Gail ever had. Worse than anyone.

He froze, his tongue thick in his mouth, his palms sweating.

Josie cocked her head. "Did you just come over to make sure I was leaving?"

It was the pain in her voice that broke his paralysis. He could see the evidence of a sleepless night around her eyes and mouth.

He wasn't the only one who was vulnerable. He'd hurt her. And he had to fix it.

"When you were asking me whether or not I wanted you to stay in town, you were really asking me how I felt about you, weren't you?"

She looked away. "I think you were pretty clear."

"No." He took a step towards her but stopped when she backed away. "I was a coward. You needed an answer and I was terrified, so I just lashed out and said some shit I didn't mean."

She looked at him again.

"What does that mean?"

"I want you to stay in Hardy Falls," he said. "With me," he added for clarity.

She didn't say anything, but seemed skeptical so he pressed on. He was in it now, so he might as well go balls to the wall.

"I told myself I didn't want to pressure you, but that was a lie, too," he said, determinedly slogging through the words. "I wanted to pressure you. I wanted to beg you to stay and give us a chance. But it's also true that I only want you to stay in town if it's what you want to do, and not because it's something *I* want you to do."

"Because that's what happened with Gail," Josie said quietly.

"Maybe." He floundered a little before getting himself back in gear. "Yes. What happened with her... unmanned me, I guess you could say."

"Mat—"

He plowed on, needing to get it all out. "It wasn't the fact that she was closeted that killed me. It was the fact that I hadn't seen it. Gail had been going behind my back the whole time I'd known her, and I was totally oblivious. It wouldn't have made a difference if she'd been with a man. I didn't know. She was using me, and I didn't know."

Just saying it made him wither a little inside, but he had to come clean.

"It made me second-guess everything and back away from everyone. But you're not Gail. You won't treat me the way she did. And now you think I don't want you, and nothing could be further from the truth." He took another step towards her, and this time she didn't move. "God, Josie. Don't you know that I want you? Can't you tell? I've never wanted anyone the way I want you."

It sliced him when the skeptical expression remained in her eyes.

"And what if I've decided to go back to the city? Or maybe move down towards Philadelphia?"

"Then I'll go with you."

He hadn't thought of it before, but of course he would go with her.

"And what if I don't want you to go with me?"

That one made him bleed a little, but he squared his shoulders because she deserved to get her punches in.

"I'll just follow you." He smiled slightly. "I'll get Jenny or Hannah to tell me where you are, and I'll hang around you until I'm so annoying that you take pity on me and talk to me again."

Her eyes were huge. "For God's sake, why would you do all of that?"

And here we are.

Mat drew in another breath and took the step.

"Because I love you."

Her jaw dropped open in absolute astonishment.

"I was stupid and I was scared, but I love you, Josie," he said. He let the truth of the words flow through him. "I'm hoping you can put up with the fact that I talk out of my ass sometimes, and that you can forgive me for being a total douchebag who was afraid to be a man."

He realized she was crying and tensed, his stomach tight because tears couldn't be good, could they? But then he saw she was smiling, too. What the—?

"You love me," she choked out.

His mouth was so dry he could only nod.

"Mat!" She flung herself at him, and he was so relieved that he almost collapsed to the floor. Wrapping her up in his arms, he tried to absorb her into his skin and kissed her until she pulled back.

"I love you, too," she said.

Mat let that wash over him, let it make him feel powerful instead of vulnerable, and kissed her again.

He found himself being tugged upstairs into what he figured was Josie's bedroom. She closed the door behind them and locked it, isolating them from the world. Then she pulled him down onto her bed.

Their lovemaking seemed new, almost reverential, with each of them touching and kissing as if they'd never seen each other before. He took his time exploring her body. Each portion of skin he exposed was a treasure he needed to worship, until they were both gasping and urgent. When he was finally inside her, she moaned his name, clutching at him with all her strength.

Afterward, they lay spooned together with his front to her back. He absently stroked her sleek breast, weighing it in his palm, loving the feel of her.

"You're more than you think you are, Mat," Josie said quietly into the silence.

He stilled his hand. "What are you talking about?"

She squirmed around until she faced him, her legs intertwined with his.

"You think you're a loser because you didn't know there was something going on with Gail, but you're wrong. You're not a loser. Gail grabbed onto you because she was scared and you are strong. She knew you'd protect her. And you did."

He snorted.

"You did! Look at what happened. You basically lost your family because you've stood by your word and kept her secret. You are a wonderful man, Mateo Guerrero. And you're so much more."

He had to kiss her then.

"I hope you like Hardy Falls," she whispered when he pulled back so they could breathe again. "Because I'm going to try to make my business idea work."

"You were going to stay even though I was being an ass?"

"I would have just kept out of your way."

"I hope you won't do that now."

"No." She grinned at him as if she was his own personal

sunbeam. "Now I'm going to be in your way as much as possible."

"Good."

Mat realized he didn't give a damn about Gail or Alicia or his parents or anything. They really didn't matter.

His life was his own. His life was with Josie.

It felt pretty damned right.

EPILOGUE

The day before Thanksgiving, Josie was sitting at the Country Time's old wooden bar alongside most of the staff. They were waiting for Hannah to finish whatever she was doing and tell them why she'd asked them all to come in for a meeting. At the moment, she was in her office and they were entertaining themselves by watching Mary Alice decorate the big glass mirror behind the bar with Christmas-themed plastic, static clings.

Josie grinned at Mat, who was getting them both coffee from the big pot that was perpetually simmering in the corner. They needed the caffeine. It had been a very active night.

Her grin morphed into a smirk at the memory. He turned, caught the look, and winked at her.

So far, so good, she thought with satisfaction. Mat had moved out of the room over the bookstore and into an apartment because, as he said, they needed privacy and he couldn't afford to keep renting motel rooms. Ms. Gregory had let him out of his lease because the apartment he moved into was hers, too. The woman was a shark.

The important thing, as far as Josie was concerned, was that now they could spend as much time together as they wanted. Realistically, they'd probably start getting on each other's nerves at some point, but at the moment she regretted every second she spent away from him.

The thought made her feel soft inside, as she watched him move around behind the bar.

He hadn't heard a peep from his family since he'd talked to Gail. It made her sad because she knew that it hurt him, even though he'd never admit it. She wanted to fly to Galveston and insist that the Guerrero family get their heads out of their collective asses. At the very least, she wanted Mat to tell them the truth. He'd smiled when she'd made the demand and said that it didn't matter.

Stubborn man.

Honorable man.

So, she had decided that they would make their own community and had invited everyone they cared about over to their new apartment for Thanksgiving dinner.

Their apartment.

It was probably too soon to think that way, but it was how she felt.

Her mother had actually taken most of Thanksgiving day off, so she and Jenny could come and celebrate after they visited Josie's uncle's family in the next town. Josie had begged off due to hostess duties. Hannah and Deacon were coming, as were Mary Alice and Johnny. June and Calvin would be there after they visited his parents, assuming his mother didn't freak. Grace would stop by at some point. Even Kevin, who had been uncharacteristically melancholy the past few days, was coming.

Barring an emergency, they'd all be together. Well, except for her brother, Jordan, who'd apparently decided it was more important to party with some clients than come home to see his family. Talk about being an asshole. He'd made her mom really sad with that phone call.

Josie shook off the thought because it was Jordan's loss, and there wasn't much she could do about it. Instead, she focused on picturing Mat spending all day cooking in his own little kitchen instead of at the Country Time. He'd have the time of his life.

"Shouldn't we be decorating with turkeys instead of Santas?" Grace asked. She was sitting next to Josie, her elbow resting on the bar and her chin in her hand. "It just makes Christmas seem so rushed."

"The store didn't have any turkey clings," Mary Alice said practically, as she carefully positioned a sparkling green reindeer next to a neon yellow sleigh. "They didn't have any Thanksgiving things at all. Except pumpkins."

"I don't see why we need goddamned clings in the first place," June grumbled. She was sitting at the other end of the bar looking even more annoyed than usual. "Those look like someone puked Christmas-shaped jelly."

"We're being festive," Mary Alice told her firmly.

"Great."

Mat laughed and carried two mugs of coffee over to Josie. He handed her one and then settled on the barstool beside her. She took a sip and realized it had been doctored exactly the way she liked it, so of course she had to give him a kiss to thank him.

He responded, as he always did, and she enjoyed the taste of coffee on his tongue.

Yup. She was pretty gosh darned pleased with the man.

Their coupledom was apparently getting to be old hat for the rest of the Country Time crew, because everyone ignored them. Soon an argument broke out about whether or not they should put up a Christmas tree right after Thanksgiving.

Deacon, his arms folded and his eyes anxiously trained on Mary Alice as she teetered on a chair to reach an upper corner of the mirror, expressed concern about having a full sized tree in one corner of the taproom.

"People can get kind of rowdy sometimes," he pointed out. "Don't you think they'll throw ornaments or knock it down? Especially if we're going to have a band and dancing pretty soon?"

Hannah had talked to Johnny's brother, Roy, and he'd been pretty enthusiastic about becoming regular entertainment. But he had sheepishly admitted that Johnny was right. He couldn't keep working for free, so he wouldn't be able to start until they had working capital.

"We'll put the tree somewhere safe," Mary Alice said. Deacon took a quick step forward when she tried to climb off the chair and almost fell on her ass. "We need a tree. A tree is homey. And lights. Lots of little fairy lights, like at Fallside."

"As long as you do not try to put anything in my kitchen," Kevin told her. "No lights. No tree. None of those green branches everyone likes." He was standing near the kitchen door, solid as a rock, with his big arms crossed over his chest.

"Oh, but Kevin," Mary Alice turned too quickly, and Deacon had to steady her again. "We need the whole place to be pretty so we can all get in the spirit and be a friendly neighborhood hangout, just like Josie said we're going to be."

Mary Alice had embraced the branding.

The big man shrugged. "I just know that the health inspector wants a kitchen to be a kitchen, no? And everyone will frown if parts of those green branches get in the food."

Well, he had a point there.

Mat poked Josie in her arm to get her attention. "What did that Milhouse guy want?" he demanded. "You said you were going to tell me before the meeting."

She couldn't control a smug smile as she recalled the conversation she'd just had with Chester A. Milhouse, founder and still majority owner of Milhouse Advertising, the firm where she used to work.

Trying to control her unseemly glee, she kissed him again.

Eventually he pulled back and poked her in the side this time. "Tell me."

"Now you understand that some of this is just me reading between the lines, so I might be making assumptions." Mr. Milhouse had been extremely circumspect, but she was positive she'd heard frustration in his ancient warble. Josie settled against the bar. "You know how I told you about Don pushing me out of my job after stealing my ideas?"

Mat stiffened. "Yes," he said shortly.

"Easy there, big guy. This is good. It sounds like he had been moving up the corporate ladder thanks to an affair with his boss. And he was trying to pull the same shit with Heather that he pulled with me. Going behind her back. Being the hero with the big client, etcetera, etcetera."

No surprise there.

"Heather went to Mr. Milhouse when she realized what was happening, but he ignored her. Boys club and all that. He tried to play it off like he hadn't really known what was going on, but I'm not sure I believe that. He might be old, but he knows everything that goes on in that place."

"Anyway, it turns out that Heather was right to be concerned. They had a big meeting with the client a week ago, and two days later the CEO laid her off. Mr. Milhouse said they were under the impression she hadn't been adding much to the process, and that she'd been holding her team back. Which left Don in charge of everything."

"Uh-oh." Mat thought about it, then grinned. "Donnie's going to crash and burn, isn't he?"

Josie flew her hand in the air, then plowed it into the bar top and made an exploding noise.

"Oh yeah. Heather was smarter than anyone gave her credit

for, including me. She'd already been in talks with a rival agency. Not only did they hire her the day after she was laid off, but three of the top graphic designers gave their notice to follow her."

"Nice. What now?"

"Well, if Don really was as brilliant as everyone seemed to think, he'd be able to build a new team to implement what they have planned for the client. But..."

"He's not," Mat said with definite satisfaction.

"He sure isn't."

"So why did Milhouse call you?"

"He asked me to come back. Better position, higher salary."

"I wondered if that was it," he said. It made her very happy that there wasn't the slightest twinge of worry in his voice.

He shouldn't worry. They were together. If her path took her out of town, she knew he'd go with her. And she'd already told him that if he decided to leave, she'd be right there beside him. After all, once her business was up and running, she could do it from anywhere.

There was no way in hell she was losing this man. At least not without a fight of epic proportions.

"Interestingly enough, Don apparently just happened to mention that some of the ideas they'd presented to the client had originated with me. He said that Heather had insisted he lay me off, but he didn't want to do it because I'd been a valuable team member."

"What an ass." Mat frowned. "Why is he giving up credit all of a sudden?"

Josie had wondered the same thing, and she couldn't control her wide smile.

"I think it's because the reality of his situation is finally starting to dawn on him. He is absolutely panicking."

Mat answered her grin with one of his own. "Couldn't happen to a nicer guy."

"Exactly."

"What did you say to Mr. Milhouse?" he asked curiously.

"I said, 'No thank you, sir.'"

"Good." Mat nodded. "You're already busy."

She was. She'd overhauled Hannah's website and created her social media profiles, and now she was in the process of finalizing the new advertisements she was going to put in the Scranton and Stroudsburg papers, as well as in Ms. Gregory's online newspaper. Then there was all the work she was doing for Calvin's store.

"I do still need to make money while I'm building my port-folio and customer base," she pointed out. "If they ask me to freelance remotely, I might consider it."

"Okay, but don't forget you need to budget in some time for me," he warned.

As if she'd ever forget that.

She batted her eyes at him. "Don't worry, hot stuff. You're top of the list."

Another argument was going on around them. This one was about Christmas music. Mary Alice wanted them to switch to a station that was playing Christmas music twenty-four/seven. Deacon said that he might have to stab out his eardrums by the middle of December if they did that.

"Some of that crap is fine," he argued. "We can go one hundred percent right before the holiday, but for five weeks? No thank you. It's bad enough they've been playing it in the grocery stores since October."

"But Deacon, it's *country* Christmas music," Mary Alice insisted.

Oh, dear God.

Kevin grinned at Mat.

"Do not worry, my friend," he said. "We will not be able to hear that much in the kitchen."

Hannah had been so happy with Mat's efforts in the

kitchen that he was now working as the other chef, helping Kevin when he was here, and running the kitchen himself when he wasn't. He also stood in as the backup bartender when Deacon was off. Hannah helped in the kitchen, as well, but the new arrangement freed her up to take care of the million and one other things that needed doing. They were going to have to hire a dishwasher, but hopefully Hannah was going to tell them that she was changing up a few things, anyway.

Hannah's office door opened and she strode down the hall carrying a bunch of papers.

"Tell Mary Alice that we're not playing Christmas music twenty-four/seven between now and Christmas," Deacon instructed her.

"Why not?" Hannah went up to him and kissed him on the mouth.

He scowled at her.

"Because if we do, I'm going to come in when you're not here and break the speakers," June told them.

Mary Alice pouted. "Oh, June."

"We'll talk about it later," Hannah said, frowning at the clings on the mirror. Some of them did look a little lumpy, Josie thought. And one of the reindeer looked more like a kangaroo. But the colors were very festive, if toxic.

"Good job, Mary Alice," Hannah said, sounding unsure.

Mary Alice beamed.

Hannah shook her head and put the stack of papers down on the bar.

"Okay, so thanks for coming in. I wanted to let you all know what's going on before we're off celebrating tomorrow," she said.

"Good idea, seeing as how it's our job and all," June told her.

Mary Alice walked around the bar to sit next to Grace. "Did

you open the money market account at the bank like we talked about, Hannah?"

"Deacon and I did that this morning." Hannah ran her hands through her hair. . "So, um, Sam drew up the appropriate paperwork."

"Where's Sam?" Grace asked guilelessly. "Is he coming to the meeting, too?"

"No, I—" Hannah broke off when the kitchen door opened and Sam strode into the room, as if he'd been waiting to make an entrance. He stopped when he saw them all staring at him.

"What?"

"Why are you here?" Hannah demanded.

"You told me you were having a meeting, so I figured I'd show up in case you had any legal questions." He smiled at Grace but, since Josie was on one side of her and Mary Alice was on the other, he moved to sit further down the bar. "Can I get some coffee?" he asked Deacon. "Or a beer?"

Deacon bent down, pulled a water bottle out of the little fridge under the bar, and tossed it to his brother.

Sam huffed out a breath. "Fine." He twisted off the cap and took a long swallow. "So, what did I miss?"

"Mostly Mary Alice decorating for Christmas," June told him.

He glanced at the big mirror. "Ah."

"I was just getting ready to tell them that the investor fund is ready to go." Hannah obviously had decided it wasn't worth a fight to get him to leave, so she turned her attention back to the rest of her audience. "Like I was saying, we have a contract for people if they decide they want to invest. It says what we're promising and all—"

"And provisions in case it doesn't work out," Sam put in, lifting a finger.

Hannah winced. "Yeah. And that. So, uh, I guess you can tell people now."

There was a definite lack of enthusiasm in Hannah's voice, but Josie could understand that. On the other hand, she was glad her friend was finally taking this step. She desperately needed capital.

"I'd tell my father but, well, you know." Deacon shrugged. Apparently Hannah had a major falling out with Dr. Black, Deacon and Sam's father, before Josie moved back home. He wasn't likely to invest, which was too bad since the guy was loaded.

"Calvin's in, and I told Ms. Gregory," June said. "She's interested, but she'll want to grill you first."

"My dad said he'd like to invest," Grace put in. "And Austin said he'd talk to his father about it. I'll tell the rest of the kids."

"I'll call Johnny and let him know," Mary Alice beamed. "I can't believe we'll be part owners of the Country Time!"

"No, I'm still the owner," Hannah corrected firmly. "I'll keep the investors informed, but they won't have a say in how the business is run."

"This is Hannah's business," Sam cautioned Mary Alice. "You're not buying stock, just lending her money for a certain rate of return."

"Oh, sure." Mary Alice smiled. "That's what I meant."

Hannah looked a little worried but shook her head.

"Josie came up with a lot of good ideas. Some of them will take money, so we can't do them right away. But we're going to try to change things up as much as possible to go for the whole 'friendly neighborhood hangout' vibe." She pulled papers off the pile and handed them out. "I want to add a few items to the menu as soon as we can, so we'll have to come up with new recipes and ingredients, and that kind of thing."

Kevin smiled, holding the paper in his big fist as if it was a baby bird. "I will show you how to make my special gumbo. It is a family secret, no? And I will show you how to make it spicy enough to make people shoot flames from their mouths." He laughed his big, rolling laugh.

"Thanks." Hannah grinned back at him. "I was thinking we'd add a few new things to see how it goes. Once we know, we can add some more."

"I'll update the menu on the website," Josie assured Hannah as she jotted some notes. With these changes, Hannah's brand new domain would be up and running by the end of the day. The Facebook and Twitter pages were already live, and she was trying to think of how they could use Pinterest or Instagram. Maybe she could use June's photos there, too.

Which reminded her...

"June," she said, looking around Grace to the other end of the bar. "I wanted to tell you how great your photos are. I'm really impressed."

To her amusement, June actually blushed and shifted a little on her seat.

"I guess they're okay."

"I was thinking of hanging some art by local artists to kind of tie us more to the community," Hannah put in. "Jenny's going to give us a painting or two to display, and she knows a lot of other people. But I was wondering if you'd let me hang a few of your photos, too?"

June actually squirmed.

"I guess. Sure. What do I care?"

Except Josie had a feeling that she cared a lot.

"Oh! If we have an open mic poetry reading, I could read some of my poems!" Mary Alice exclaimed.

"We'll see," Hannah said weakly. "Um, I guess that's all for now. We have a lot more ideas, but I have to wait until I have more money for some of them."

Deacon massaged the back of Hannah's neck. "We'll just do the best we can, honey."

Hannah sighed and then squared her shoulders. "We need

to move forward. The carnival we had a few weeks ago saved our butts for the short term, but this is just the beginning." She shot a smile at Josie. "We're reimagining ourselves."

"A new beginning," Mat murmured into Josie's ear. "For all of us."

Reaching up, she slid her fingers through his silky dark hair and pulled his head down for a soft kiss.

"It will be awesome," she assured him.

And it would.

She could see it.

THE END

Turn the page to read the an excerpt from

Expecting Love
Welcome to Hardy Falls, Book 4

EXPECTING LOVE
WELCOME TO HARDY FALLS, BOOK 4

Sometimes love gives you more than you bargained for

Although Hannah Frederickson spends a heck of a lot of time worrying about her business, owning the Country Time Bar and Grill gave her a family of friends and led her to Deacon Black. The man of her dreams hiding in plain sight.

Now life suddenly promises to get even better and offers Hannah more than she ever imagined. If only Deacon could see it the same way.

June Esperanza found a home she did not expect when she moved to Hardy Falls. And, years later, she got a second chance at love with Calvin Hardy, the only man who ever mattered.

June should be deliriously happy, not dealing with a challenge that terrifies her. And Calvin needs to back off and let her come to terms with it all in her own way.

As Christmas approaches, two couples just starting out face a new adventure with a mixture of hope and fear, love and joy. Find out if they can withstand the challenge in this heartfelt, romantic novella.

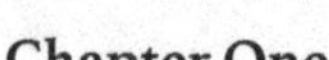

Chapter One

Hannah Frederickson stared at the cheerful Christmas-themed static clings decorating the mirror on the wall behind the bar at her tavern, the Country Time Bar and Grill, and tried not to let another wave of nausea swamp her. The queasiness had been coming and going for a few days now, which hardly seemed fair considering she'd gotten pummeled a month ago by the nasty stomach bug that had swept through town. She'd assumed she'd finally kicked it, but it looked like the damn thing was back again.

"Typical," she muttered as she went to grab a can of ginger ale from a little refrigerator under the bar. Just her luck that everyone else would get better except her.

She did *not* have time for this, damn it. She had to keep the Country Time alive, had to find a way to re-invent the hundred and fifty-year-old business, and had to bring back the customers stolen by the renovated bar at the bowling alley next door. Easier said than done since her accountant, and uncle, George, had embezzled all of her money a few months ago, and the bank had declined her request for a loan. Which meant that on top of the rest, she had to start a freaking investor fund, too. Not to mention planning for New Year's Eve and the Christmas party she'd just decided they had to have.

No, she didn't have time to be sick. She couldn't keep things alive if she felt half-dead.

It was strange, though. When she'd had the bug before, it had knocked her flat. This time the nausea seemed to come in waves. And she felt strange. Different, somehow.

As she tentatively sipped the soda, the kitchen door swung open, and her friend, Josie Kline, strode into the taproom. She was frowning down at her tablet computer, and Hannah sincerely hoped she hadn't brought her yet another potential advertisement for approval.

Josie, a graphic designer, among other things, was trying to start her own business in town and had taken it upon herself to haul Hannah and the Country Time kicking and screaming into the twenty-first century. That was the only reason Hannah suddenly found herself the proud owner of a domain name, a website, and social media accounts all over the damned place.

She'd never worried about that crap before. After all, how was she supposed to manage social media and a website when there was barely enough time in the day to manage the business they were supposed to promote?

As far as she was concerned, Josie was just going to have to handle all of that, and thank God the other woman was planning on sticking around now. Her friend had fallen head over heels in love with Mateo Guerrero, one of the Country Time's chefs / bartenders / dishwashers. Mat was ridiculously overqualified for any of those positions, of course, but he seemed happy to be there. Honestly, Hannah didn't know what she'd do without him.

So Mat and Josie could never leave. That was all there was to it.

"Don't tell me you want me to make more decisions," Hannah whined.

Josie looked up and transferred her frown from the tablet to Hannah. "You're pale," she said disapprovingly.

"I feel pale," Hannah admitted.

"Well, then sit down, for heaven's sake."

Probably a good idea. She got a glass of ice and put it and the little can of soda on the bar, then went around to slump onto one of the barstools.

She couldn't believe how wonderful it felt to get off her feet. She was beat, and it was only noon. That did not bode well, considering neither Mat nor Kevin, the other chef, were working tonight, and she had planned on taking care of the kitchen by herself.

"You should have stayed home," Josie said, sitting next to her.

The other woman was practically glowing with happiness despite her current look of concern. It was very nice to see. Hannah smiled at her, then shook her head.

"Couldn't. Too much to do."

"There's always too much to do."

"But Christmas is coming soon, and I have to plan the party."

"You know, if you'd wanted to have a Christmas party, maybe you should have thought about it a little earlier than today," Josie suggested equably.

"I know, I know." Hannah ran her hands through her hair, feeling alarmingly weepy. "But Pat is having a Christmas party, so we have to have one too."

Pat Murphy, the owner of Murphy Lanes bowling alley, was doing everything in his power to steal her best customers—the bowling league members and the students from nearby Pocono University. His latest effort was a blow-out Christmas party complete with free games, half-priced food, and surprise gifts from Santa.

Hannah had been focusing her efforts on New Year's Eve— always a high point for the bar—but she'd woken up in a panic that morning with the realization they couldn't just let Pat walk away with the other major holiday. They had to try to attract *some* of the business. So she'd come in early, massaged the accounts for money, and managed to line up a band—Roy and the Outlaws—mostly because Roy was basically the brother-in-law of Mary Alice, one of her waitresses, and Pat had already booked another, rival, band.

When she'd spoken to Roy, he'd sounded determined. They were both fighting for survival.

"Pat's really upped his game," Josie interrupted her thoughts. "He and Louise are doing a good job on the new restaurant," she added, not very helpfully.

"Shut up." Hannah's stomach clenched, because Pat, and Louise, his niece, really were kicking her butt.

Josie shook her head, her sleek dark hair shifting on her shoulders. "It doesn't matter. You and Deacon are going to pull this place through, and Pat and Louise can suck it."

"Yeah," Hannah said and smiled at the mere mention of Deacon Black, her best friend, lover, and partner. Who knew she'd find the love of her life working right under her nose as her main bartender?

God, she loved Deacon, loved him from the top of his brutally short brown hair to the bottom of his big feet, usually clad in running shoes. She especially loved his huge, warm, incredible heart

"If you're going to pull this Christmas thing off on such short notice, we need to get the word out," Josie said. "And ad buys are a lot more expensive at this time of year."

"I don't need ads," Hannah grumbled.

"Yes, you do. I know you think it's fine for Grace and her friends at the sorority to put up hand-made signs all over the place like they did for the carnival you had at the beginning of October, but we need to do a little bit more than that."

Hannah pouted. "The hand-made signs worked," she argued even though she knew she was being a stubborn ass. Grace, another one of her waitresses, was a student at the university and she and her sorority sisters had done a good job pimping the hell out of the carnival they'd held to raise money.

"They did," Josie agreed. "And the fact that you had a giant roller coaster set up in a field right next to the highway didn't hurt either. But this time, unless you plan on Santa and his eight tiny reindeer landing a sleigh in your parking lot on a sparkly rainbow, you're going to need a little more exposure."

"I guess," Hannah muttered and twisted the soda can on the old wooden bar top. "What do you think we should do?"

Josie looked relieved, and Hannah felt guilty because she really was making her friend jump through hoops.

"We need to put out some ads," Josie said, pulling her tablet closer to her and tapping out a few commands. "We can get *The Hardy Falls Gazette,* of course." The internet newspaper run by Mathilda Gregory, the local librarian, was the only news source specific to Hardy Falls. "And it sounds like we might still be able to get into one or two of the regional newspapers, although you won't get a great rate."

Hannah swallowed, her nausea rising again at the mere thought of the cost. "Okay."

Josie smiled at her. "And we'll have Grace and her friends post signs on the campus. I called the university, but they won't let me put an ad up on their student news site since you're a bar."

Hannah swallowed again. "Okay. What do you need from me?"

"Well, some clues about this Christmas party would be nice," Josie said dryly. "I know you booked Roy and his band, but what else were you planning? Half-priced drinks? Food? Raucous good times?"

"I don't know." Hannah was horrified to find she was almost in tears. "I don't have the slightest idea! I just know we can't let Pat steal all of our business." Her stomach suddenly roiled sharply. "Oh, God!"

Launching herself off the barstool, she bolted for the ladies' room and emptied the pitiful contents of her stomach into the nearest commode.

Panting, she settled back on her heels and waited until she was sure that everything was willing to stay in the appropriate place. Then she crawled back to her feet, flushed the toilet, and stumbled out the stall door, coming up short when she saw Josie standing at the sinks waiting for her.

"I would have come in and held back your hair, but you hate that."

She did. Some things were meant to be private.

Her friend held out the glass of ginger ale, and Hannah took it gratefully, rinsing out her mouth and spitting into the sink. She didn't want to take the chance of swallowing anything yet, but she thought this might have been the big volcano for today.

"Come on," Josie said and, with one arm around Hannah's waist, led her to her office as if she was her patient, which, admittedly, wasn't far from the truth.

Josie settled her in the desk chair, then straightened and looked worried.

"This happens every day?"

Hannah closed her eyes. "For the last couple of days."

"You should go to the doctor."

"It's just strange. When I had the stomach flu before, I couldn't even move. This time it's off and on. And I'm so tired. All I want to do is sleep."

"Uh huh." Josie sat in the visitor's chair on the other side of the desk. "Um, Hannah? Have you ever thought that you might be," she shrugged, "pregnant?"

"What?" Hannah's eyes flew open. "No. Of course I'm not pregnant."

"You're on the pill?"

"Well, not right now, but my gynecologist told me it was probably going to take months, maybe years, for me to get pregnant. Because of the endometriosis and all." She'd been battling that since puberty. "And Deacon and I want to have kids, of course we do, so we thought I should come off the pill to give my body a chance to adjust."

Josie frowned. "So Deacon's using a condom?"

Hannah blushed. "Well, no," she admitted. "But it's too soon." Her doctor had been confident it would take a while, and she'd encouraged them to begin trying as soon as possible. Hannah remembered that conversation very well. It had been difficult to hear that she might never be able to have Deacon's child.

But now...

She stared at Josie with a combination of awe, happiness, and dawning terror. "It hasn't been that long since I came off the pill," she whispered.

Josie shrugged. "It only takes once to get the job done."

Well, it had certainly been more than once.

"Oh, my God." Hannah burst into tears.

"Hey, hey, hey." Josie ran around the desk to her and hugged her. "Hannah. Come on now."

"I'm so happy!" Hannah said, clinging to her friend. "A baby, Josie! A baby with Deacon." Her head spun with the emotions coursing through her. Happiness. Giddiness. Fear. Doubt.

"Oh, my God," she pulled away and looked at Josie. "I might be a mother."

Josie's big blue eyes filled with tears. "You need to take a pregnancy test," she warned. "We can't just assume."

"I'll go out and get one now."

"And if it's positive, you need to make an appointment with the doctor."

"As soon as I'm done peeing on the stick."

"And you have to tell Deacon."

"Oh, my gosh!" She could feel her whole face lighting up at the thought of telling Deacon he was a daddy. She beamed at Josie. "He had to run some errands, so I'll tell him as soon as he gets back." She giggled almost hysterically. "I don't want to call him and make him crash the car."

"Take the test before you tell him," Josie warned.

"Oh, yeah." She should probably be sure before she sprung it on the man. "I'll go get it right now."

"I'll get it." Josie put a hand on her shoulder to hold her down. "Maybe I'll head over towards East Stroudsburg."

"Oh, but—"

Josie held up a finger. "Hannah, you don't want to be using Walsh Pharmacy for this little purchase. News would be around town before Deacon gets back."

Hannah winced. "Oh. Right." Hardy Falls could win a gold medal for gossip in the next Olympics.

Josie frowned thoughtfully. "Neither of you will be fit to work tonight, so I'll ask Mat to come in. Then you guys can have some alone time."

Hannah straightened, the business owner taking over for a moment. "Mat's already worked six days straight because Kevin was off."

"He won't mind." Josie grinned. "I'll stay to keep him company, and he'll be able to boss me around in the kitchen. He likes that. Is June working tonight, too?"

June Esperanza's primary role at the Country Time might be the head server, but she'd been working there since Hannah had been thirteen. June could handle any job in the place without breaking a sweat.

Hannah nodded helplessly, not able to stand up to the energy of Hurricane Josie.

"Good. We'll take care of the Country Time, and you and Deacon can talk."

"Okay."

Josie went to the door, then turned back, her smile as wide as the sun and just as bright.

"Hannah. You might be pregnant."

"Oh, my God." Hannah breathed.

Josie sniffed and went out.

Hannah sat for a long time with her hands on her belly, trying to imagine the little life that could be in there.

Now she was afraid to take the test, because what if they were wrong? What if she really did just have the stomach flu?

She'd be devastated. So would Deacon.

"I think you're in there," she said to the tiny bundle of cells she hoped was currently dividing at a rapid clip. "I think you're my baby, but we'll just make sure, okay?"

She rubbed her hands on her stomach. It was odd that it still felt the same. Still relatively, although not completely, flat. Still the same tightness of her jeans. Still the same looseness of skin, because she'd never been a hard body. And yet, suddenly, everything might change.

"Everything could be different now," she whispered.

If they were right, and the test came back positive, there were still risks—big ones. Lots of mothers lost lots of babies in the first trimester, and those were mothers without her health issues. Anything could happen.

Her breathing stuttered, and her heart started galloping wildly in her chest.

She couldn't protect this child growing inside her. She couldn't do anything to make sure it would be all right. That it would be born without problems. That it would live a long and healthy life. She couldn't make sure everything would be okay.

God, she was having a nervous breakdown, and she wasn't even sure she was pregnant yet.

Josie was right, and she should probably wait, but she needed Deacon desperately. She needed him to hold her while they faced this thing together.

Grabbing her cell phone from her jeans pocket, she speed-dialed his number.

"Hi, beautiful," he said after the first ring.

"Hi." She sucked in a breath so she wouldn't burst into tears again and scare the poor man. "So, um, where are you?"

"Just leaving the grocery store. Are you okay? Still sick? You sound strange."

"No, I'm fine, it's just..." she hesitated. "Can you come back?"

"I'll be there in a flash," he promised, the concern in his voice intensifying.

"Good." She disconnected and leaned her head against the back of the chair.

A baby.

Wow.

Expecting Love

ALSO BY BETSY HORVATH

ABOUT THE AUTHOR

Betsy Horvath was raised on a steady diet of old MGM musicals, Nancy Drew, and Harlequin romances, so nobody should have been shocked to discover that one day she would be writing romance novels of her own. Especially not once became clear that, when given the opportunity, she could sing the entire soundtrack from the *Sound of Music*, regardless of whether or not anyone asked her to (nobody ever did), and that the only books she ever wanted to read were the ones with happy endings (which made things interesting in college).

Let's face it, Betsy is a hopeless romantic. But she's good with it.

www.BetsyHorvath.com
betsyhorvath@betsyhorvath.com